IN THE APPROACHES

Also by Nicola Barker

Love Your Enemies
Reversed Forecast
Small Holdings
Heading Inland
Wide Open
Five Miles from Outer Hope
Behindlings
Clear
Darkmans
Burley Cross Postbox Theft
The Yips

IN THE
APPROACHES

NICOLA BARKER

FOURTH ESTATE · London

Fourth Estate
An imprint of HarperCollins*Publishers*
77–85 Fulham Palace Road,
Hammersmith, London W6 8JB
www.4thestate.co.uk

First published in Great Britain by Fourth Estate in 2014

1

A catalogue record for this book is
available from the British Library

ISBN HB 978-0-00-758370-6
ISBN TPB 978-0-00-758374-4

Printed and bound in Great Britain by
Clays Ltd, St Ives plc

MIX
Paper from
responsible sources
FSC
www.fsc.org   FSC C007454

For my dear friend, Claire Clifton;
Hastings' favourite Floridian

1

Miss Carla Hahn

'Well I suppose as we must all seem very dull and *pedestrian* to such a bold and cosmopolitan gentleman as the likes of our Mr Franklin B. Huff!' Mrs Barrow ruminates, borderline resentful, as I hand over a crisp, ten pound note and she shoves it – unacknowledged – into the pocket of her pristine housecoat. 'What with all his escapades amongst them hordes of filthy *banditos* and drug-smugglers and what-not in the dusty prairies of Mexicano.'
'Mr Franklin *D*. Huff,' I correct her.

'He was only telling me the other day as how he keeps a collection of shrunken heads,' she continues, eyes widening. 'Stores 'em in an old suitcase, he does. No word of a lie, Carla! Thinks as they're historical artlifacts!' she snorts. 'I says, "Wouldn't those be the actual heads of real-life dead folk, Mr Huff? Isn't that a sort of sacrelig?" But he just lowers his book and peers at me over his spectacles, all lofty-like. "It's the *culture* there, Mrs Barrow. They have a different way of going about things. Everything's fast and loose. Life is cheap."

'"The men are men and the women are glad of it!" I jokes, but he just returns to his reading, face sour as a slapped arse. So I says, "It must all seem very dull and *pedestrian* here in Pett Level to a chap such as yourself, Mr Huff, what with all your adventurings amongst them buckaroos and rancheros and the shrunken heads and what-not ..." and he says, "I can't pretend I'm not finding it a little flat, Mrs Barrow, a tad wispy and windswept and *prarochial* for my tastes, perhaps."'

As Mrs Barrow finishes speaking we both gaze up from the bus-stop, in unison, towards the large, concrete block of the old Look Out which crowns the top end of Toot Rock. It is here that Mr Franklin D. Huff is currently sitting, in glorious isolation, fully suited and booted, intermittently gusted by the sea wind, partaking of a picnic lunch.

'They say as he "went native" out amongst all them strumpets and gunsels,' Mrs Barrow murmurs, squinting, ominously, into the eternally drab yet still pitifully hopeful early autumn light, 'but I find that hard to believe, Carla, when I sees him of a morning, sitting on the balcony in his socks and his braces, smoking his pipe like one of those right and proper gentlemen straight off the cover of an old sewing pattern.'

'*Who* says that, exactly?' I ask, frowning.

'I beg yours?'

'*Who* says he—?'

'Them Sullivan boys down at the New Beach Club for one,' Mrs Barrow interrupts. 'Seems as he's got his-self temporary membership,' she snorts, 'by hook or by crook ...'

She gives me a significant look. 'Glory O'Dowd says as how he drank up their whole stock of gin in the first week after Mrs Huff left. On the second week he comes out in hives. Both cheeks was covered!' She chuckles. 'I thought, That's the gin, that is! Mother's Ruin! But I kept it *schtum* as your old dad would say.'

She taps her lips with a thick, brown, heavily calloused finger.

'You mentioned that he'd broken the dining table,' I interject, 'and a chair in the living room?'

Mrs Barrow promptly removes the finger. 'I've never known a man so accident-prone!' she gasps. 'This morning I heard a yell as I was hanging out the washing. I rushes round there, Carla, and Mr Huff – as God is my witness – is lying flat on his face in the middle of the allotment, his head in the last of the season's cabbages. Turns out as he tripped in a badger hole! Sprained his wrist! I says, "Did you put out them monkey nuts for the badgers last night, Mr Huff? You know them's the rules at Mulberry Cottage. Miss Hahn is very particular on the monkey nuts being put out. She has herself an arrangement with them badgers, Mr Huff, and they don't likes it one bit if gets itself broke."'

She shakes her head, forlornly. 'I mean there was holes dug all over the lawn, Carla! The leeks was all pulled up! It was chaos – pure chaos! But he just cusses and rolls about, belly-aching like a big girl! I mean imagine a man such as that surviving in the tundra, Carla, where there's no laws and no pavements and no manners and no taps? Doesn't bear thinking of!'

'The dining table ...' I persist.

'Later on I see as he's thrown some old soup tins, a fly paper and a broken milk bottle into the flower bed by the little girl's shrine,' she adds, scowling. 'I thought, Well that's as why you ended up arse-over-tit, Mr Huff! Shrunken heads or no! You don't need to be messing around with forces beyond your ken, my friend. The tundra's *your* business, Mr Huff, but we has our *own* ways of going about things up here on Toot Rock. Wispy and *prarochial*, indeed! Ignore 'em at your peril, sir!'

She shakes her head, scowling.

'I suppose I should have a quick word with him,' I murmur, registering the hungry grumble of the Rye bus on the Fairlight Road as Mrs Barrow takes out a scarf and ties it around her head, forming a small knot under the chin and pulling the two ends tight with such a jerk that one might almost imagine the cosmopolitan Mr Huff's head compressed between them.

'I won't pretend as I'm not prone to having the odd grumble about the quality of the furniture in Mulberry,' she confides. 'I know as it has *historical* value, Carla, and all the rest of it' – she raises a jaundiced brow – 'but it's just a pile of old driftwood and matchsticks for the most part. Even so, how one middle-aged man on his lonesome-ownsome can cause so much mess and mayhem is quite beyond me, I swear!'

She reaches out her hand towards the oncoming bus and it slows to a gradual halt with a blood-curdlingly cacophonous squeal of brakes, as if each of her calloused fingers has summoned a banshee from between its wheels.

'All as I can say is: I hope his poor wife paid you the full deposit – in cold hard *cash* – before she upped and ran off!' Mrs Barrow barks over the engine noise, then clambers on board. I pass over her old shopping trolley. It has a tricky wheel on the right-hand side which is sometimes given to seizing up. She grabs it, gives the offending wheel a practised kick, then disappears into the bus with a sharp – and suitably conclusive – bantam-like cluck.

2

Mr Franklin D. Huff

In the end it was Carla Hahn who approached me. I knew the only way to draw her in – the *only* way – would be to ignore her completely. It had taken six weeks, in total. I was sitting on top of the gun emplacement eating a stale, unbuttered roll and a jar of pickled walnuts. She was slightly out of breath after cycling up. I'd seen her from atop my airy lookout talking to Mrs Barrow at the request bus-stop on the Sea Road. Mrs Barrow – like so many of the permanent residents on Toot Rock, not to mention those of Pett Level in the flatlands below (although the weekenders, I confess, are of a different complexion altogether) – appears to hail from an indeterminate epoch. She seems to have no presentiment whatsoever that she's living in a modern age: the 1980s for heaven's sake!

This morning, as she skivvied, we had an extraordinary discussion about the Home Computing Revolution. She'd gleaned via the elusive Mr Barrow's tabloid rag (Mr Barrow is Toot Rock's very own smooth-skinned McCavity; he may only ever be apprehended as an absence) that something called the 'Apple Mackintosh' was, as of this very day, to be made available, for money, in shops, to the general public. She was unable to comprehend how or why this much heralded object would be in any way better or more useful than a standard typewriter: 'And they only ever as write out *bills* to torment us poor working folk with those!' she muttered. I silently held up my book. 'It's all the same to me,' she grumbled. 'Words is words is words is words.'

'Well, thank goodness Trollope and De Quincey weren't of your blinkered mind-set, Mrs Barrow!' I quipped, then went on to laboriously explain the demarcation between mechanical, electronic, analogue and digital technologies – even drawing a little diagram on the inside back cover of my jotter. I cogently summarized Claude Shannon's *Mathematical Theory of Communication* and Moore's Law in what I hoped were layman's terms. I said, 'This is the Third Industrial Revolution, Mrs Barrow. You are witness to the genesis of a new era: the Information Age – the paperless office, the revolutionary concept of information sharing. This is bigger than people walking on the moon,' I said. 'One day our entire lives – everything, literally *everything*: transport, personal hygiene, sex – will be digitized.'

As Mrs Barrow brushed out and then re-set the fire I explained how I'd been posted as a foreign correspondent to California during the late 1960s and how it'd been – by a lucky coincidence – the fertile breeding ground, the *hub*, of all these extraordinary, nay *game-changing* hypotheses. I told her how the scientists had discovered a way of sending letters to each other via computer: digital letters! Mrs Barrow paid great heed as she flitted about the cottage – a spry grey squirrel in pleated skirt and pop socks – with her bucket, her broom and her mop. Then, once I'd completed my lecture, she placed her hands on her hips, laboriously cleared her throat and said, 'I remember as when they invented the ballpoint pen, Mr Huff. Everyone making a big old fuss about it, they was. Now it's just something and nothing. I'm as happy to be using a *pencil* myself! Nobody cares about the ballpoint pen no more, Mr Huff. This'll be the same. A flush in the pan. You mark my words.'

★   ★   ★

'Those walnuts have been in the cupboard for at least five Christmases, Mr Huff!' Miss Hahn yells up at me, throwing down her bike into the long grass. I've seen her throw it down before. Many times. Toss it down, without a care. I find it difficult to marry this apparent recklessness with her complete fastidiousness in regard to every detail connected to Mulberry Cottage. The *lists*! The *rules*! The special requirements! I also observed the pointed way she used my surname. Of course we made the booking for the cottage under Lara's maiden name: Ashe. I'm no fool. We'd never have got it for the full eight weeks otherwise.

'They have sentimental value?' I ask (somewhat facetiously, I confess).
'Sorry?'
'The walnuts?'

'Mrs Barrow tells me there's a problem with the dining table,' she says, swiping her short, unkempt, sun-bleached blonde hair impatiently behind her ear. I can instantly tell that she cuts it herself. She's that kind of a woman. No make-up bar a light smear of Vaseline on the lips and the angular bone of either cheek. Dressed in a pair of men's baggy, canvas trousers (rolled over at the waist and belted with what looks like a length of old rope) and a drab, linen blouse in grey or brown – or both, or neither – un-ironed but worn and worn into a flat shine, buttoned right up to the neck. Scuffed plimsolls on her feet, no socks. She has broad shoulders and is tanned. She is built like a swimmer. I see the German in her, and I see the Soviet.
Around the nose – the chin. Poor thing.

'It collapsed,' I say, screwing the lid back on to the walnuts. 'I'd placed the television on top of it to try and improve the reception. It caved under the weight. The middle flap seems to've been constructed out of plywood. That or the woodworm's got the better of it. Either way, the table is irretrievably damaged, although – on a positive note – the picture on the TV's been much clearer ever since.'

'Your wife left,' she says, her eyes – the colour of a mean bruise, edged in octopus ink – slitting, infinitesimally.

'The second week.' I nod, studiedly indifferent. 'Mrs Barrow mentioned it? One of the other neighbours, perchance?'

Of course nothing ever happens in this ludicrous place without the neighbours mentioning it! A fool might imagine it to be the kind of wonderful location where a person might be rendered invisible – somewhere an artist or a criminal or a film star might flee in order to cultivate a precious, fragile sense of anonymity; a place where you might melt into the fringes, the margins, the nothingness; a place of privacy – insularity – isolation – retreat. But Toot Rock is not like that. Oh not at all! Not a whit of it.

'She ran over a cat,' Carla Hahn says, inspecting my tie with a small frown, her hand lifting, unconsciously, to her own very slightly frayed collar.

Her hands are the colour of boiled gammon! Extraordinary! Raw-looking. I quite pity her those awful hands.

'Yes. The tail,' I confirm, 'in broad daylight. The cat was immensely fat. She was reversing at high speed, drunk as a skunk.'

'The tail' – she nods, slightly baleful, now – 'was later amputated, and at some considerable cost to the owner, I'm told.'

'You heard all about it, then?' I smile, sarcastically.

'He's my father's cat.' She shrugs.

'Oh. Mrs Barrow didn't mention that,' I murmur, somewhat perturbed by this sudden, quite unexpected, turning of the tables.

'I think you'll probably discover, on further acquaintance, that Mrs Barrow generally prides herself on leaving out the most important detail in any story. In fact you could almost say it's her speciality.' She smiles. Good, straight teeth. But the eyes

... *Tsk!* Watch out for those eyes! Dead as a dodo's! Deader still! A predator's eyes (the dodo, to its eternal credit, was a humble vegetarian). These are a carnivore's eyes. These are the eyes of a pterodactyl, a tyrannosaurus rex.

'He was your father's cat ...' I ruminate, trying to work out the wider implications of this unwelcome detail, somewhat on the hoof, I'll admit. 'And I suppose that horrendously fat dog I see you dragging up and down the beach every morning and evening is your father's dog?'

'Strictly speaking, he was my late mother's cat,' she explains (ignoring the dog comment). 'He's called Rolfie. He's forty-one years of age.'

'The average life expectancy of a cat is fifteen,' I say, incredulous.

'Yes. I know.' She nods, solemnly. 'Rolfie is an incredibly old cat.'

'So Rolfie has lived almost *three* times longer than the average cat?' I persist, then promptly calculate: 'The equivalent age – in a person – would be two hundred and ten.'

'Yes,' she confirms, patently unshaken by the comparison. I just can't let this one go. 'Doesn't that strike you as a little ... uh ... improbable?' I wonder.

'Yes' – she nods again – 'highly improbable. It's perfectly amazing. A miracle of nature. And then your wife drove straight into him. Drunk. In broad daylight. At high speed.'

'Oh. Well, I apologize for that,' I mutter.

'My father *was* rather traumatized,' she idly adds, gazing dreamily at the clouds scudding across the sky above my head.

'In all my born days,' I muse, 'I've never heard of a cat living to forty-one years of age. He must be the oldest cat in the world. The oldest cat in the known universe.'

'You have a ladybird on your fringe,' she murmurs, squinting slightly. 'In fact you have two. Yes. Two. They appear to be … to be copulating.'

'You have very red hands,' I respond, swiping at my fringe.

'I'm allergic to disinfectant.'

'Then why don't you wear rubber gloves?' I demand.

'And latex,' she adds.

In truth I'm not entirely certain if there *are* two ladybirds on my fringe. This worries me. I've had no previous intimations that Miss Hahn might turn out to be an unreliable witness. Quite the opposite. A little mouse. I was told. A *lamb*. Wouldn't say boo to a goose. I was told. Damn. *Damn*. A propensity towards lying could prove catastrophic to my plans.

'Anything else?' I wonder.

'Sorry?'

Her eyes are back with the clouds again. She seems to find great solace in the clouds, much as I do myself.

'Allergies?'

'Uh, nickel,' she confirms, 'and arrogance.' She smiles. 'You?'

'Bullshitters.'

'Oh, me too.' She nods, most emphatically.

I can see now that this isn't going to be all plain sailing. A short silence follows, punctuated by the cries of several gulls and the shrill whistle of a farmer in a nearby field, directing his sheepdog from the comfort of his tractor cab.

'I'll need to pop around to the cottage and have a look at that table,' she eventually murmurs; 'perhaps you might provide me with a convenient time to come over when you know for certain that you'll be out?'

I'm still fiddling with my fringe.

'The ladybirds have gone,' she adds. 'They flew away home.'

'I may need to get back to you on timings,' I say, with a measure of diffidence.

'Fine.' She shrugs. 'Well you have my number, Mr Huff.'

'Yes I do, Miss Hahn.'

She turns and picks up her bike. She suddenly seems very annoyed, but why exactly I am not entirely sure.

'You seem rather annoyed,' I say.

'Don't be ridiculous!' she exclaims, piqued. 'Do enjoy the rest of your afternoon.'

And off she stalks, red hands and all.

What a curious woman she is! So brusque. A suggestion – a mere shadow – of the Germanic in her accent. Unkempt. Chaotic. Not unclean, just …

Unattractive. Well, not unattractive. But boyish. Uncouth. And untrustworthy, too – possibly. Yes. And tragically repressed! Poor little thing! A hysterical virgin. Ha! Obviously. *Obviously*. Could tell that from a mile off.

3

Miss Carla Hahn

Shimmy is outraged by Mr Huff's behaviour – so irked, in fact, that I almost regret telling him about it. I am soaking his gnarled old feet in a plastic bowl (the iced water scented with sage and lavender oil), while heating up some minestrone soup for a late lunch.

'Zis Mr Huff has insulted us all!' he exclaims, in typically exaggerated fashion (all shrugs, waving arms and eye rolls). 'First ze careless assault by his drunken wife on poor Rolfie, zen zat monstrous "letter of apology" – a veb of deceit from start to finish; the *shiksa* vas driving at high speed you say?' I nod. 'Yes, apparently.'

'Mrs Barrow tells me she always stinks of raw spirit!' he declaims.

'In her defence,' I interject, 'Mrs Barrow often confuses the smell of perfume with—'

'Ha! Mrs Barrow iz nobody's fool, Carla!'

'And on the one, brief occasion that I actually met Mrs Ashe – Mrs *Huff* as we now know her – I did notice that she applied her perfume rather liberally. She was a quiet woman, very polished, well-groomed, *sophisticated* …'

'Und now he haz insulted us all, *en masse*!' Shimmy throws up his hands with such violence that the water in the bowl containing his feet starts to slosh.

'Mind your feet!' I say.

'He *questions* za age of Rolfie? *Oi!* If he questions za age of Rolfie zen he questions ze integrity of your *Mame*! If he

questions ze integrity of your *Mame*, he questions *my* integrity, und *yours* too, *meine* Carla!'
'He simply said that—'
'He's calling all of us liars! *Feh! Fardrai zich deyn kop!* Pass me his letter again, *bubbellah!*'
I pass Shimmy Mr Huff's letter. It reads:

Mr Shimmy,
Mrs Barrow informs me that the cat which my wife Lara knocked into yesterday was yours. We are so very sorry. In Lara's defence, the light was poor. She reversed from the driveway in Mulberry Cottage (where we are currently residing) and out on to the road with considerable care and was horrified when she realized that your cat had failed to get out of the way. It had been lying in deep shadow. It is a very heavy cat, and not, I imagine, especially nimble, although it did run off at some speed after the incident took place. The tail appeared kinked, but Mrs Barrow assures me that the tail has always looked like that.
    I do hope the cat is all right. I am not a great fan of cats – of domestic pets in general – but I would never dream of hurting one in any way, shape or form.
Yours, in sympathy,
Franklin D. Huff

'*See* zat?' Shimmy points at the letter, accusingly. 'Za *shmendrick* doesn't even *like* cats.'
I take the letter back. Mr Huff has strange handwriting. Tiny. Very neat and joined up. Huge loops on the l's and d's. Even on the odd t. I immediately sense that this is the handwriting of an immensely inconsiderate man. A fussy but careless man, prone to self-aggrandizement. Of course I have no expertise in handwriting analysis. This is all just going on pure instinct.
    'He really is an awful man,' I say.

'*Oi!* A *piste kayleh*! A *nishtikeit*! Arrogant! Insincere! Cold-hearted! Hates animals! Hates Pett Level – our home! Our *retreat*! Hates *life itself, bubbellah*!' Shimmy throws up his hands again.

'An immensely vain man,' I agree, 'with the most horribly condescending manner. The very *thought* of him crashing around in beautiful Mulberry ...' I shudder.

'You're sure ve can't evict him? I mean ze assault on poor Rolfie? You say he's refusing to feed ze badgers? *Genug iz genug!*'

I nod.

'Ve must seek recompense, *Mizinke*!' Shimmy murmurs. 'Vengeance!'

'What do you suggest?' I wonder, slightly uneasy.

Shimmy shrugs, pondering. 'If ve didn't own za property zen a small pebble through ze bathroom window. *Dos iz alts!* Maybe ve remove ze bulb in za porch. Hide his bin. *Farshtaist?*'

'Let's not stoop to his level,' I counsel, 'let's just ignore him, *Tatteh*, and hope to God he'll go away. Let's just be dignified and aloof and ludicrously polite.'

'If you vant to beat a dog you find a stick!' Shimmy objects.

'He's lower than a dog,' I grouch, 'he's beneath contempt. Who cares if he finds us "wispy" and "parochial"?! We're a fair, decent, right-thinking, *unpretentious* people in Pett Level, *Tatteh*, and that's what really counts.'

'A nice, little potato in hiz exhaust, *hah*?!' Shimmy volunteers.

Forty minutes later and I am walking Rogue on the beach (or – strictly speaking – dragging him along behind me like a giant and mutinous, heavily lactating sow) when who should I see striding towards me, at improbable speed (head down, hands thrust deep into his jacket pockets) but the man of the moment: Mr Franklin D. Huff! I observe that his footwear is completely unsuitable: black, patent-leather dress shoes clumsily kicking up giant arcs of sand and shingle! I pity him his unsuitable footwear! I do. No, *no, really* I do.

I stand and await his approach (while Rogue laboriously masticates a piece of sea kale), hoping that he has settled on a date for my maintenance trip. But instead of stopping when he draws abreast of me, he just storms straight on past! No acknowledgement of any kind! None! Not even so much as a cursory nod!

I turn, rather astonished, and call after him – 'Have you worked out a time yet, Mr Huff? For the maintenance works?' – and am shocked when he spins around on his name as if stung, stares at me, in complete amazement, then down at the dog, then back up at me again, his lean face contorting wildly, points an accusing finger at us both and virtually yells, 'What on earth are you *thinking*, Miss Hahn? To feed a dog to that monstrous size? Whatever possessed you? It's an act of the most extreme cruelty! An obscenity! A crime against nature! It's a travesty, don't you see? Call that *care*?! Call that *love*?! Shame on you, Miss Hahn! Shame on you for not knowing any better! Shame on you, Miss Hahn! And shame on your idiotic father!'

Then off he storms.

I can only … I can't …

Deep breath. *Deep* breath. Count backwards, slowly, from twenty to one.

Deep breath. That's better. Good. That's …

AAAARRRRGHHH! It's virtually impossible for me to describe the violent effect Mr Huff's insulting words have on me! How dare he? How *dare* he?! The initial confusion followed by the shock, followed by the embarrassment, followed by the outrage … That this man, that this … this … that this awful, *arrogant* … *URGH!* I'm just … I am just … I am shaking from head to toe. I am slightly dizzy. I blink. Everything blurs. I blink again. I feel this … this *heat* in my belly, in my chest. I open my mouth and I simply … I *pant*! I pant like a wounded beast! And then I feel something burning on my cheeks. Tears! He has made me cry! Mr Huff has made me cry! And I am so angry that Mr Huff has made me cry that I pant even harder. And my stomach is hurting. It's *hurting*. (I am hit! I am stung!)

I turn and head back in the direction from which I came. Everything is misty. I sense my feet pounding across the sand. Rogue is dragging along behind me. Several figures enter my peripheral vision but they are nothing, merely fleshy shadows. One of them speaks. It is Georgie Hulton who is digging up lugworms. I can't answer. I just keep on walking. After about thirty or so paces I stop, with a gasp, drawn up short by the macabre sight of a small, dead sand shark, its belly split open, its guts writhing with tiny, pupating maggots. I stare at it for several minutes, and only the clarity of its predicament – the horror of its outline, the exquisite brightness of its intestines – restores me to anything remotely akin to a semblance of normality.

Damn him! Damn Mr Huff! I hate him! I *hate* Mr Huff! I hate him! I hate him! I *hate* him!

4

Mr Franklin D. Huff

Kimberly Couzens is dead. Kimberly – *my* Kimberly – dead! Lara just rang. There was a garbled message when I got back to the cottage. 'I'm sorry, Franklin, but Kimberly is dead. She died. Something to do with a tooth. It was very quick. I just spoke with her mother. She died on Saturday. Four, five days ago. The funeral's on Friday. I'm really sorry. I know you might find that hard to believe after … well. Yes. No need to go back over it all again, eh? I just want you to know that I'm *very* sorry, Franklin. Honestly. I'm … Okay. Bye.'

I listened to the message three times ('Something to do with a tooth?!') and then rapidly calculated back. I *spoke* to Kimberly five days ago and she was absolutely fine. Vital. Exuberant. Laughing. Mocking. *Alive.* So how on earth is this possible? How can she be dead? *How?* After everything she survived? And why do I feel so … so empty, so *flat*? Not angry. Not raging. Not tearful. Not …
It almost seems – disappointing. A let-down. Laughable.

Kimberly – snuffed out. Defunct. *Dead.* She hopped the twig. She popped her clogs. Stupid, hopeful, brave, indefatigable Kimberly. Dead. *Dead.*

Oh God, what the hell to do now? The funeral's on Friday, but I'm broke! Can't even afford the plane fare. The stupid travel agent – the bastard airline won't … 'What?! Not even on *compassionate* grounds?' I yelled.

Oh God. She's dead. Where to go? How to …? I'm only *here* because of Kimberly. I'm here *for* her. As a favour.

Because of her dotty mother. We'd been agonizing about Trudy's declining health for months – upwards of a year, in fact. She'd been growing increasingly confused, woolly, *dithery* – and Kim simply couldn't cope. I mean Trudy was meant to be *Kim's* buffer – her back-stop, her support (a rich irony!). Bottom line was, Trudy needed to go into sheltered accommodation.

But how the heck to afford it? After much heart-searching and arguing and sulking (in equal measure, on both our parts) Kimberly Fed-Exed me the only remaining thing of any value she possessed: the negatives of those infernal photos – the 'picture diary' of Bran Cleary, Kalinda Allaway and their daughter, Orla, 'in hiding', that infamous late summer of 1972.

I was given a brief to sell them to the highest bidder, and had agreed a good price for her – with a fair amount of wrangling – but then Kimberly underwent a sudden (not untypical) change of heart, damn her (*Damn* Kimberly! Damn her! Poor Kimberly. *Dead* Kimberly). She'd found out something unpalatable about the purchaser and had developed a whole host of last-minute 'scruples'. We didn't discuss the details. It was obviously a painful subject for us both. But we rose above – same as we always do. Same as we always did – Kim and me. Kim and I. We two. *Us.*

The Catholic Church was interested, obviously, but Kimberly wouldn't countenance the idea, just on the off-chance … Well, I suppose she thought they might simply get swallowed up (her gorgeous images) – subsumed – in a maelstrom of clerical bureaucracy. It was illogical. But that's Kim for you. Or that *was* Kim, before …

'Something to do with a *tooth*?'

It was stupid. And time-consuming. And expensive. I complained about the cost (human, financial). 'I have an import/export business to run in Monterrey,' I grumbled, 'and a tower of translation work to be done.' The truth was that the photos had already disappeared – to all intents and purposes – by dint of being stuck in an old trunk at the end of Kim's bed for the past twelve years. But that was okay, apparently. That was different. Kim wasn't their jailer, she insisted, but a broody hen perched lightly atop. This handful of fragile spools was Kimberly's creative and emotional legacy. She never said it, because it didn't need saying. It was the unsayable. But I knew.

She was highly conflicted over the whole thing. We both were. In the end she persuaded me to go to a publisher with them, to flog them (for less money) in the guise of a book, but the publisher offering the best price (and it was a good price, a great price) still wanted text – *con*text. Who might be expected to provide that? Kim herself? No. She couldn't – wouldn't – trust herself. 'I was way too close to the whole thing,' she insisted, 'and I'm "the bad guy", remember? The scapegoat?'

'Well maybe you should try and see this as an opportunity,' I valiantly suggested, 'a chance to *alter* those popular misconceptions ...'

'But are they?' she murmured. 'Misconceptions, I mean?'

I couldn't answer. I really wish now that I had – in retrospect – just with ... I don't know ... the benefit of hindsight. But I couldn't. I just couldn't bring myself to respond. Call it mean-spiritedness. Call it pride. Call it whatever you damn well like. You're probably right.

'I was blind-sided by it all,' she sighed, 'I was bowled over ... seduced. And above and beyond that, I really don't want the whole "tragic" angle to eclipse ... well ... "the work".'

In a toss-up – a fair gamble – Kimberly would always – *always* – have opted for death over pity. Poor Kimberly. So defiant. So flawed. So proud. So ...

Scared? Was it fear that kept them quiet?

Superstition?

Loyalty?

What was it? What was the indelible hold Bran Cleary had over them all: strange, little Orla, crazy Kalinda, the countless others? Witchcraft? Voodoo? Charm? *Art?!*

'Okay, Kim,' (yet another international call at completely the wrong time of day. Kim isn't – wasn't – ever happy unless a conversation was charged at peak rates. It was her last great extravagance. 'Keeps you on your toes, Frankie-boy,' she'd laugh, 'keeps you sharp!') 'so who else, then? Eh?' I demanded. 'Who else can be trusted? Any suggestions, Oh Wise One?'

'I do have somebody in mind,' Kim confided, and then, with typical unreasonableness – balls-out, that was my Kim – suggested Franklin D. Huff. Yes. *Me.* Franklin D., no less: currently occupying the not-especially-coveted role of Jilted Lover. Betrayed Friend. Fall-Guy. Stooge.

There were weeks of heated negotiations. 'You seriously feel you can trust me with this?' I was astonished – touched – horrified! Trust me? I could barely trust myself! Wasn't I the *last* person to be trusted? The most angry? The most cynical? The most dark? The most wounded? 'That's precisely *why*, Franklin,' she'd chuckled (I always loved her laugh), 'and because – when push comes to shove – you're a born professional.'

This was not a commission I was eager to accept. Quite the opposite. This was the story I'd been running away from – at high speed – for twelve, long years. Several others (some reputable, others less so) had been pitilessly tossed against the jagged rocks of this sorry tale and left horribly becalmed. There were just way too many angles. The narrative was dangerously overloaded. How to gain access? There was the mysterious death of Bran Cleary while on remand, for starters, after a bomb (the second bomb he'd been 'unwittingly' connected with) planted – or being stored? Transported? – in the boot of his car went off. All the dodgy political stuff. There was the curious disappearance of crazy Kalinda, aka

'Lonely' Allaway, his wife (the fame-hungry vengeful Australian shepherdess). And Orla? Poor, sweet Orla Nor Cleary – their daughter? The tiny-armed girl visionary? Where even to *start* with that particular hornets' nest?

'Simply go back to Mulberry,' Kim sighed (with typical clarity), making it sound like the simplest undertaking in the whole world, 'and just inhale the atmosphere. You missed out the first time around. Aren't you intrigued to have a little snoop about? Apparently they've kept the cottage exactly as it was – like a kind of shrine. They do short- and medium-term rentals. They're very picky about tenants, though, so keep your head down. Be discreet. Why not invite Lara along for the ride? Build some bridges. Make it into a little holiday! I'll cover all expenses from the advance. Try and reach out to the people who were there – on the periphery, in the background. Knit. Walk. Relax. *Breathe.* It doesn't have to be the final word or anything, just a … I don't know … a cut and paste job – a kind of *collage*, a human *collage*.'

'But none of them will talk!' I argued.
'Several of them already have,' she corrected me. And she was perfectly right. Several had.

Of course what I didn't tell Kimberly was that we actually needed way more than that. To raise any kind of worthwhile sum on the photos I'd had to make a series of strategic promises to the publisher – moral compromises, of sorts – which Kimberly (as yet) had no inkling of. They wanted to smash the whole Bran Cleary cover-up wide open. They wanted a hatchet job on Kalinda. And Orla? That all-too-familiar 'victim of circumstance' *schtick* writ large: the ever-popular 'vulnerable minor led astray by the wicked Catholic machinations of Father Hugh Tierney' angle.

Why did they want these things, exactly? Oh … They wanted them because, well, I'd promised them. I'd offered them all up on a platter. Kim'd thank me for it in the long term, I was certain. Once I'd exonerated her – and, by extension, myself – once the royalties started rolling in. She said it herself: I was a consummate professional (a professional *what*, though?! Cuckold? Fool? Dupe?).

Let's face it – this was the story dear, old Kimberly (dead Kimberly) was too close to tell: the awful truth. Although how to gain access to it, first-hand? Kim was right: several people *had* spoken out publicly, yes, but only the small players – the bit parts – and never candidly. Father Tierney had become a Benedictine monk and entered a monastery. He was virtually a non-starter. Father Paul Lynch (of Rye, now retired) had proven curiously gnomic and diffident. Seems they'd all contracted the disease Kim herself had fallen prey to.

Although Carla Hahn, Kim had confided, was definitely the one to watch out for. She'd been the family's nanny and cleaner during their time in Pett Level and had later inherited the house. 'She was very quiet, rarely spoke. I don't know why, but I always thought of her as "the other camera". She had this strangely unsettling *watchful* quality about her. Engaged but unengaged. Hardly uttered a word to me the whole week I was there. Smiled a lot. A strange girl, very tight – tender – with the child, training to be a nurse.'
Carla was the key, Kim maintained, the 'inside-outsider'.

So I came. I waited. I made connections with the other witnesses. Lara left; there'd always been … well … fault-lines. I drank heavily for a few weeks. Just the atmosphere of this place – the *house*. This awful feeling of … the simplicity, the roaring quiet, the certainty. An unbearable *itchiness*. In my head. In my *soul*. As if the place, the sea, the furniture, the entire house were all slowly rejecting me. Developing a gradual intolerance. I know it sounds …
Or was that just …?

Then the phone call – the garbled message. Kimberly Couzens was dead. *Dead!* Something to do with a botched tooth extraction. Kimberly Couzens was dead.

I left the cottage in my suit and dress shoes. I was empty, *flat* (remember?) and I was paradoxically Day-Glo; blank and cynical, yet strobing with emotion. *Urgh!* I was neither. I was both. I was confused. I was walking away from my feelings and I was running straight into them. It wasn't … I wasn't … I … I dunno.

I staggered down on to the beach. I just put one foot in front of the other. I tried not to think. I tried desperately to process the news. I could, but I couldn't.

Of course we had never been formally divorced, Kim and I. It was one of the many things Lara couldn't forgive me for. Yes, I *petitioned* for divorce: 23rd December 1972. She was still in Ireland. In hospital. The date is singed into my brain with a cattle iron – the day of the Managua earthquake. Even my hurt, my outrage at Kim's devastating betrayal couldn't be allowed to take centre stage, couldn't bask, bleeding, in the limelight. Nope. God went and killed 2,000 people, in one stroke, and I – by necessity – was left feeling petty and pitiful.

It was tough. I was wounded (*I* was wounded! What a joke!). But her burns were so bad that I couldn't follow through with it. We were a team. Above and beyond everything else, Kim and I were a team. I was the ears, she was the eyes. Funny to think of it that way now. The ears stopped working a long time ago. They waxed up. They froze. They ceased functioning. Why? I have so many reasons, each one so tiny and humble and insignificant; each one merely an ant – or a black, darting termite – but collected together? An infestation. A great hill. An immovable mountain.

And the eyes? After the 'accident', they thought they could save at least one of them – on the right-hand side. It was her camera eye, her all-seeing eye. She had such high hopes for it. She was such a fighter. But full vision never returned. And she was melted, poor Kim, like a candle.

We moved her into a granny flat in Toronto. Her mother, Trudy (the actual granny), lived upstairs. And everything cost. From that moment onward, everything was calibrated – rage, hurt, resignation, paranoia, claustrophobia, frustration, resentment – through a shiny curtain of dollars and cents. I opened my import/export business in Monterrey, Mexico. We struggled along, me here, her there. How else to manage it?

Did I forgive her? No. Did I stop loving her? No. Could I let go? No. And Bran Cleary? My dear friend Bran (whose injuries had totalled a slightly sprained wrist, some bruising and a broken nose because – ever the gentleman – he had *opened the car door for her* – for *my wife!*). Did I forgive him? No. Did I stop loving him? No. Could I let go? Yes. *Yes. Yes.*

I let go. I moved on. I never wanted to feel that way again. People have often asked me my professional opinion (although what profession I belong to now I struggle to decipher – laughing stock? Entrepreneur? Crook? Social worker?). Did Bran deserve what happened to him? Was it all just bad luck? A conspiracy? Was it revenge? Murder? Something beyond that – the (God forbid!) 'supernatural'?

No more questions! I just didn't want to speculate. I didn't want to engage. I didn't want to let it all in again. And yet here I was, immersed in the whole mess right up to my chin, resenting every moment, *hating* every moment. Wishing I was dead. Why did she ask me? Why did I agree to it? And now Kim. Poor Kim. Brave Kim. Un-Kim.

Call that … call that *fair*?!

5

Miss Carla Hahn

The eternally fragrant, sweet-natured and well-meaning Alys Jane Drury is absolutely appalled by what I have done (how might I have imagined it could be otherwise?).

'Whatever possessed you, Carla?' she demands. 'He's such a nice man! So very interesting. Debonair. Handsome. All those lovely curls! And so incredibly *polite*. I just don't understand how …'

She is silent for a moment. I hold my breath and press the receiver even tighter into my ear.

'It's so out of character!' she finally declares. 'Did Shimmy put you up to it?'

'No,' I insist (perhaps a split-second too quickly), 'it was all my idea. I mean Shimmy wasn't happy – after the incident with Rolfie, obviously …'

'But you said Mr Huff had already apologized for that.'

'Yes. He had. Well, in a manner of speaking. The letter was very arrogant. And a complete tissue of lies about the exact circumstances of—'

'To protect everyone's feelings, perhaps?' she interrupts.

I ignore this. 'He actually went so far – in the letter – as to admit to not even *liking* cats.'

'*I* don't like cats,' Alys snorts. 'Well, not especially,' she qualifies.

'But that's because you love birds, Alys!' I insist.

'Franklin – Mr Huff – likes birds,' she counters. 'He made a huge fuss of the parrot when he visited. Teobaldo even allowed him to stroke his chest. And Teobaldo *hates* people. He won't even let *me* do that. We spent ages talking about the birds of Me-hico. He collects feathers – exotic feathers. For the shrunken heads. But he never kills anything. He's very strong on conservation. Very respectful of the environment which I thought was just lovely.'

'Shrunken …?' I echo weakly, half-remembering something along the same lines that Mrs Barrow had said.

'Didn't he tell you? He has a business which manufactures shrunken heads. The kind you get in Peru. He makes them in Me-hico and exports them. They're incredibly beautiful. He showed me a sales pamphlet. I mean disgusting but beautiful. Hand-stitched. Extraordinary. Some sell for thousands of dollars. People collect them. He makes them with carved animal bones and skins. He has a small team of ex-gangsters and addicts in Monterrey working for him. The whole enterprise is run like a kind of *social* programme …'

I think it would be fair to say that Mrs Alys Jane Drury (widow) has been thoroughly won over by Mr Frankin D. Huff (con-artist). The woman is besotted.

'Rather odd, don't you think,' I muse, 'that Mr Huff should come here with the express intention of finding out things about *you*, and then should end up talking endlessly all about *himself*?' I pause, meaningfully. 'Did it ever dawn on you that maybe …?'

'It might all be just a ruse?' Alys promptly fills in for me, sharp as a tack. 'A "technique"? To beguile me? Uh, yes. It did occur to me, as a matter of fact.'

'Oh,' I say, deflated, 'well, good.'

'It may interest you to know that several times in the course of our labyrinthine discussions he actually encouraged me to hold things back. He'd say, "Let's not trespass any further into that, Alys. I can see how you're struggling. Save it. *Preserve* it. Some things need to remain truly inviolate …"'

'Are you serious?!'

28

After even only the briefest of acquaintances with Mr Huff, I find it difficult to imagine him readily employing the phrase 'truly inviolate'.

'Absolutely,' Alys insists.

'And then what?' I ask.

'How d'you mean?'

'Well *did* you change the subject?'

'Uh ...' Alys ponders this for a moment. 'Sometimes. Yes.'

I roll my eyes and start to walk over towards the window, but am prevented from doing so by the tangled phone cord. I grimace and start the laborious task of unwinding it.

'Well, for what it's worth, he was still *incredibly* rude about Rogue's weight,' I mutter (smarting at the mere memory), 'unforgivably rude.'

'Rogue *is* horrendously overweight, Carla,' Alys sighs, 'Rolfie too, for that matter. Your father systematically overfeeds them. It's awful – strange – *cruel*. You're always moaning on about it yourself ...'

She has me there, admittedly.

'In Shimmy's defence,' she blithely continues, 'it's probably the expression of some profound, deep-seated emotional conflict or trauma, possibly relating to the persecution of the Jews.'

'He *is* fat,' I murmur, slightly shame-faced now, 'but to be so ... so forthright about it, and so mean, so horribly judgemental—'

'Mr Huff has been resident in Pett Level for almost six weeks now,' Alys interrupts, 'and in that entire time has hardly breathed so much as a *word* to you, Carla. Perhaps you might be feeling a little ... I don't know ... sidelined? Ignored? *Piqued?*'

'That's ridiculous!' I exclaim, horrified. 'I never had any intention of speaking to the man! I've been actively avoiding him. Why else did I hire Mrs Barrow to clean the cottage? To act as a go-between? I was actually *glad* he didn't approach me – relieved.'

'Sorry ...' Alys interjects, 'there's interference on the line.'

'I said I was *glad* he didn't approach me,' I repeat, louder, briefly desisting from my frenzied untangling.

'Right. Okay. So that's why you approached *him* this afternoon ...' she wryly observes.

'I didn't!' I squeak. 'He's staying in the cottage, *my* cottage, and by all accounts he's gradually dismantling it, piece by piece. His wife ran over *Mame*'s cat, for heaven's sake! What other option did I have? He lied about his true identity on the lease. They signed in under Ashe ...'

'Yes, yes. And of course you just naturally presumed ...?' I can hear the infuriating smile in Alys's voice, and behind it (like the alternating layers of blue-grey wash in the lowering sky of a fine watercolour painting) a parrot muttering, 'Baldo! Baldo! Baldo! Baldo!' culminating with a deafening, 'WAH!'

'Presumed what?' I demand, wincing (although I know exactly what she's about to say).

'That he wanted to talk to *you*. That he's obsessed by *you* – stalking *you*. That *you* would naturally be the "crucial witness". The main focus. The hidden key to it all! You've been actively looking forward to rejecting his advances, but he hasn't actually made any. He's been the perfect gentleman! Face it, Carla, you're more obsessed than he is!'

'I didn't presume anything ...' I grumble, wounded. Once again – as a distraction – I start untangling the line. 'Although it was perfectly reasonable to assume that after he'd approached pretty much everyone even remotely connected to the Cleary visit ... I mean he tracked down the *milk*man, Alys! Old Billy Peck who was always deaf as a post. He tracked *him* down. And the woman who ran the mobile library – I don't even remember her name!'

'Meredith Brown. So perhaps he got what he needed from other sources?' Alys suggests brightly.

'Yes. *Yes.* Maybe he did.' I sullenly play along.

'I mean it's not anything too in-depth that he's after, just a series of captions for this little book of photographs. By Kimberly Couzens. That Canadian woman. The photographer. You know – the one who was with Mr Cleary when …'

'Well hopefully he's satisfied with what he's got,' I concur, moving a couple of feet closer to the window (as a consequence of my untangling), 'and now he'll clear off and leave us all in peace.'

'Hopefully,' she echoes (perhaps not entirely convinced).

'Is it raining in Hove?' I wonder.

'It was earlier. Fairlight?'

'Tipping it down.'

I gaze out at the rain.

'Are you thinking of heading back?' Alys wonders, after a brief silence.

'Sorry?'

'To the cottage. To sort it all out.'

'No!' I snort, then, 'Yes. I am, actually. But he'll probably be home again by now.'

'You should go anyway, and if he *is* there, apologize. Make it heartfelt. It was an awful thing to do, Carla. He'll think you're completely unbalanced!'

I grimace.

'And after I told him – at such unbearable length – about what a dear little lamb you are!' she murmurs, softening.

I promptly *baaaa* (it's automatic, semi-ironic, perfectly sincere). I have always – *always* – been Alys's dear, little lamb.

'Exactly!' She chuckles. 'But don't just hang around in Fairlight pointlessly over-analysing everything like you normally do. Each second counts. Your honour is at stake here – and that of the entire community, by default,' she adds.

Great. No pressure then. I solemnly inspect the rivulets of water trickling drably – incessantly, *wetly* – down the windowpane. Of course she is right. Alys invariably is. I *will* go. I was angry. I was wrong. I have behaved like a maniac. I am at a moral disadvantage. It simply won't do.

I draw a deep breath and steel myself, preparing to say my goodbyes, but am momentarily distracted by an unexpected rumble – very low, like a long, metal snake of conjoined supermarket trolleys being pushed, some distance away, across a wide expanse of tarmac. Oh God, I recognize that sound! My skin instantly starts to prickle its automatic response (Quick! *Run*, Carla, *run!*). Seconds later (and I haven't even shifted by so much as a centimetre) – *pouf!* – my garden shed evaporates.

6

Teobaldo

Baldo! Baldo! Baldo! Baldo! WAH!
WAH!
'Sun' near 'cage'! Yay! 'Sun' near 'cage'! Look at 'sun'! *Joy!*
Blink! Look at 'sun'! Near 'cage'. Happy. Happy 'sun'. *Rock,
rock, rock.* Happy!

Hup! Whassat? Eh? Ooogh! Ooogh! *Oooooogh …!* Urgh! Big
poo! Aaah. *Aaaah!* Good.

Where'd it go?
Eh?
Twizzle head.
Eh?
Where'd poo go?
Ah!
Look! *Look!*
'Seed bowl'!
Yay!
Baldo crap in 'seed bowl'! Baldo crap in 'seed bowl'!
Yay!

'Sun' near 'cage'. Happy! Happy 'sun'! Crap all done.
Aaaah! Happy moment. Happy moment. Crap done. In bowl.

Now what?
Wanna fly! Wanna fly! Wanna fly!
Nest. Where's nest? Why no nest? Wanna nest. Baldo find
'twig'. Baldo find 'straw'. Baldo find soft, soft, soft … Wanna
fly! No. No. No fly. No nest. Sad. Sad moment. Sad Baldo.

Whassat?!

Itch! Urgh! Itch! *Itch!* *ITCH!!!* Gotta ... gotta ... Oooh! Yeah. Yeah ...

Scratch, scratch, scratch. Feather, feather, feather! *Look!* Soft feather down like grey snow! Good! Good for nest. Oh. No. No nest.

Poor Baldo.

Hmmn.

  'Room'.

'Cage'. 'Chair'. 'Lamp'. 'Dresser'. 'Ceiling'. No sky! 'Ceiling'. No sky! Dead sky. Gone sky. Can't ... can't ...! No sky! Wanna fly.

Sad moment.

  Whassat? *'Sun'*! Baldo, look! See 'sun'!

Getting closer!

Joy!

Baldo! Baldo! Baldo! Baldo!

Hmmn.

Egg.

Why no egg?

Why no nest?

Bounce! Bounce! Bounce! Bounce!

Baldo! Baldo! Baldo! Baldo! Wah! *Wah!* WAH!

  Oh ... Uh-oh ... Here she comes, here she comes. Jailer! Bitch! Here she comes! Bow, deep bow. Respectful. Deep bow. Baldo, Baldo, Baldo, Baldo ...

Away she goes again! Gone. *Gone!* Lonely Baldo. Ruffle feathers. Where's the ...?

'Mirror'! Ring the 'bell'! Look in 'mirror'!

WAH!

  Look! Look! Whosat? Whosat? Spirit parrot! Whosat? Eye! Evil! Beak! Sharp! Dead parrot! Ghost parrot! Whosat?

WAH!

Ruuuun!

Wanna fly! Wanna fly! Wanna fly!

Escape!

Huh?

Whassat?! Roar! Waterfall! Thunder! It's the screaming monster! YAAARGH! She's back! Bitch is back! She's got the metal monster! Horrible! Horrible! Waterfall! Storm! Thunder! Death! Terrible roar! Angry monster! Hungry monster! Under 'chair'! Under 'little table'! Bitch is riding the metal monster! Under 'cage'! ... *WAH!*

Wanna fly! Wanna fly! Wanna fly!

Can't! *Can't!*

Rock, rock, rock, rock. Fear! Fear! Fear!

Where?

Where?!

Run down the 'perch'! Jump into the 'bowl'! Throw out the food. Sod off! Go! Scram! Take that! Take that! Hah! *WAH!*

Yay!

Sudden quiet! Brave Baldo! Clever Baldo! Dead monster! *Preen!*

'Teobaldo! **** **! *** Teobaldo! ******!'

['*Teobaldo! Stop it! Bad Teobaldo! Enough!*']

Yes! That's me! Teobaldo! That's me! Happy! Happy! Dead monster! Hah! Here she comes.

Urgh. Finger. Urgh! Kill the finger! Eat the finger! Urgh!

Come on! Head tip. Watch finger! Waggle finger!

Come on! Come *on!*

Bitch.

WAH!

'*Teobaldo!* ***** ****** ** **** ****! ***** ***! *** ***! **** ******** ** **********!'

['*Teobaldo! You've messed in your food! Silly boy! Bad boy! Stop throwing it everywhere!*']

Baldo a girl. La la! Baldo a girl. La la! Baldo a girl, you bitch jailer fool.

Where's Baldo's egg? Eh? Bitch?

Where's Baldo's mate? *Eh?*

Where's Baldo's nest?

Just. Let. Baldo. *Go!*

Wanna fly! Wanna fly! Wanna fly!

Rock, rock, rock, rock.

No fly.

  'Cage'.

'Cage'.

What Baldo do so bad? Eh?

  'Ceiling'. 'Cage'. Dead wings. Can't ... Can't ... Trapped. Panic in bones. Dead wings.

Itch! *Itch!* Ruffle feathers. Scratch!

Breuuugh!

That's better!

Breuuugh!

That's better!

  Baldo! Baldo! Baldo! Baldo!

Uh-oh! Here she comes again!

'**** **** Teobaldo! **** ********** *******! ***** ***** **** *** *****, eh?

'Pretty boy! ***** ***** **** *** *****? Eh? ** ** *** ******? Eh? **** *** **** *** ******? **** ** ****** * **** ** *** *** ****** ** *** ******* ** ******** **** **** ** ** *** *****. Eh? Pretty boy!'

[*'Stop that, Teobaldo! Stop scratching yourself! What's wrong with you today, eh?*
'Pretty boy! What's wrong with you today? Eh? Is it the hoover? Eh? Don't you like the hoover? Well I'm afraid I have to use the hoover if you persist in throwing your food on to the floor. Eh? Pretty boy!']

Baldo! Baldo! Baldo! Baldo!
Pretty boy! Pretty boy! Pretty boy!
But Baldo a girl!
La!
Baldo a girl!
Ta-dah!
Pretty boy!
Preen!
Eh? *Eh?!* Where 'sun' go?
Huh?
Where 'sun'?
Where'd it go?
WAH!

7

Mr Franklin D. Huff

I don't know why I imagined I'd make it all the way around to
Hastings before the tide came in. It was an ambitious scheme,
at best – not so much even a scheme as a blithe notion, a
vague 'urge', a complete spur-of-the-moment thing – and I
was (quite frankly) unsuitably shod. It's a challenging walk,
much of it demanding – with the tide coming in, out of sheer
necessity – a measure of energetic clambering and even
leaping from large rock to large rock.

An ambitious scheme, as I've said. A foolish scheme. And
then, when I finally made it back (forty-eight hours later!
Barely still in possession of life and limb) … On my eventual
return … The conquering hero (ha, ha, ha) …
Urgh! How else can I describe the vileness I encountered? Just
… just … just plain … *urgh!*

Yes. *Yes.* So it *was* a rather silly plan, in retrospect.
Irresponsible. I am currently in possession of the Tide Tables
for Dungeness, Rye Bay and Hastings (courtesy of our Ms
Hahn, no less; part of the cottage's Welcome Pack). Pett
Level doesn't actually have its own Table (too small,
insignificant) – it falls 'in the approaches' of Rye Bay and
Hastings, but even so, it still doesn't demand much basic
common sense to puzzle the tides out. I didn't tarry to make
this calculation, though, just grabbed my keys and my wallet
(no. Not the keys, just the wallet) and blithely set off. It was a
silly scheme. It would be fair to say that I sincerely regret it,
now. I do. I really do. I regret the leaving, but gracious me!

The return! When I finally dragged my way back home (no
bus fare! That endless trudge from Hastings over hard road
and soggy field!) ... On my eventual ...

I see it clear as day in my mind's eye: that lone dustbin
perched – somewhat improbably – atop the Look Out (visible
from quite some distance off). A warning shot across my
bows. An omen. But I just gazed at it, quite innocently, idly
pondering the logistics of it all. How on earth did that ...? I
mean it's a difficult enough scramble up there without ...

I was just way too frazzled to register that this was *my* bin,
that this was *my* issue ...

Perhaps I was actually heading for the New Beach Club
(that previous afternoon but one) although the NBC is
actually in the opposite direction to Hastings, so possibly not.
Or, better still, to The Smuggler (which is *en route*), for a stiff
drink or three. I don't precisely recall. Although I was
dangerously short of cash. Yes. Only had enough for a
Schweppes bitter lemon or a Coke. Perhaps I was just ...

What was I doing?
Letting off steam?
Getting some much-needed air?
Thinking things through on the hoof?
Walking it out?
All of the above?

I don't really know why I left (it's honestly just a blur now
– a pointless irrelevance), but then to return to ... I mean to
come back to the cottage (my *base*, my *home*, my ... my *lair*),
stagger into the bedroom – exhausted, depleted – and find ...
Urgh!

The bin was definitely a warning. Then the porch light
wouldn't work. The bulb was missing. Then ...
Urgh. Urgh. Urgh!

It now occurs to me that perhaps I hadn't taken the news
of Kimberly's passing quite so well as I'd initially thought.
How I loathe that word: 'passing'! It smacks of the

clairvoyant: the velvet curtain, the spotlight, the odour of a cheap cigar. It's a verb that tiptoes gingerly around the ineffable absolutes of mortality: the stiffness, the coldness, the imminent putrescence. The ineluctable *gone*-ness.

'Passing'. It's an end without an end – an end without a beginning, even. A cowardly avoidance.

But how else to … to get through all those unbearable sentences – those endless, stewing thoughts – each one punctuated by the thudding, hammer-blow of 'dead'? That savage, nail-in-the-coffin word. I used it – I *had* used it – countless times in the first short while after hearing the news (that garbled phone message), but its regular use – all that relentless thud-thud-thudding – had begun to bump and bruise my *very core*. The body was inside the coffin! Bang, bang, bang! The lid was sealed! Bang, bang, bang! But still the word kept on providing new nails, and of course they needed to be applied (demanded it), to be neatly and dispassionately embedded. But where? The wall? The door? My heart? My head? My soul? *No!* No, I had to get rid of that word. I had to eliminate it. It had suddenly become too real, too meaningful. How even to approach it now without … without feeling the urge to emit a terrible, wolf-like howl? Without jabbering? Without flailing around? Falling to my knees and tearing at my clothes? Without an all-out collapse, in other words? Surely it's better to just … just use something else, something less definitive, something that evades … that compresses … that *curtails* the connected emotion. A band-aid word. Yes. A slightly vague, pointless, polite, peripheral word. To cleverly create a separate universe in language and then quietly retreat into it, to hide, like a cringing ninny, from … from …

From Kimberly's passing?

Yes.

Kimberly has passed … Oh, look! There she goes! Hear the whistle? Kimberly! She's a heavy-goods train thundering through the station of life (no timetabled stop) and then into the glorious bleakness – the billowing clouds of dry ice – beyond. Only the truly adventurous – the demented hobo, the illegal, the felon – would consider running after her and hitching a ride. Those trains are heavily guarded, I've heard. No. Better just wait a little longer on the welcoming, well-lit platform and flick through the local paper (great article about piles. Wonderful small ads. Nothing really amounting to 'news', as such) then head over to the kiosk for a hot cup of coffee (avoid the tea. The tea's dreadful, like warm iron filings. It's been stewing for days inside a giant rusty urn).

Just stand back (always respectful, mind) and let that old, heavy-goods train rumble on through …
Rumble.
Rrrrrrumble?
Gracious me! A sudden outbreak of goose-bumps on my forearm. How odd!
Uh …
No.

No. Let's not talk of death, eh? Death sticks between the teeth like a pesky piece of sweetcorn husk. Sweetcorn's way too ambitious a vegetable for a man in my state. I need mashed potato softened with milk. Or mushy peas. Or a lightly seasoned dollop of glowing swede, shining with butter. Or porridge. I need porridge! I need custard! A soft-boiled egg!
I'm too delicate!
Coddle me!
Uh …
No.

It wasn't a great scheme, in other words. I wasn't genned up on the Tide Times. I just headed out – flew out.
Perhaps I was more upset than I thought. Everything felt very sharp – the light, the sound of the gulls, the *waves* – the damn Channel so unapologetic, so vital, so unbearably bloody *there*;

the texture of the pebbles on the beach, the individual grains of sand ... Everything sharp. Everything cruel. And then ... What happened?

I'm struggling to ... uh ...

Ten paces after I saw Miss Hahn and her ridiculous dog – that awful, fat dog; a barely perambulating canine offence, a cruel joke – I suddenly stopped short and thought, God. Did I actually just *say* that? Did I actually just speak those words from here ... up here ... from this mouth? The exchange – *was* there an exchange, though? – fell across the beach in front of me like a shadow in bright sun. I moved, it moved. Good heavens! Did I actually just ...? No. Surely not! So I promptly strode on. Had to get through it. Simple as that. Fight or flight. Fight *and* flight. Pure instinct. Couldn't think. Didn't want to. Continued walking.

It's possible the plan hadn't even been fully hatched at that stage – the epic hike. It was barely in incubation. I was just ... still can't quite remember what I ... I think it was just ... just getting away from that word. The relentless hammer-blow of that word.

'Good afternoon, Ms Hahn! The renovations? Uh ... not now, dear. I'm ... uh ... My wife just died. We weren't really married ... well we were, but in title alone. We lived on separate continents. But I still reserve the right to be *intensely* pissed off – alternately numbed, bewildered, *shattered*, even – by the news. All right, Miss Hahn? Okay with that, are we? Is that *acceptable* to you, Miss Hahn? It is? It *is*? Good! Great! Toodle-oo!'

I just ... I just ... I wanted to blurt it out! Yes! I wanted to castigate, to blame – worse still, to *share*. I felt this sudden, overwhelming urge to unload! To unburden, to spill out my guts to that awful Miss Hahn with her ... her frayed collar, her fat dog, her man's trousers and her Soviet-style nose. But why *her*? Why then? Why there? *Eh?!*

Happenstance. Pure happenstance! A fluke. She could've been anyone! That's why. And worse still, I'm sure I even found myself thinking: eyes on the prize, Franklin! This could actually prove useful – playing the sympathy card! I did! I swear! But then I suddenly realized (hammer-blow – *bang!*) that without Kimberly there *was* no meaning – no book (and no Advance! *Bang, bang!* Double whammy!). And I also realized that I couldn't play the card if I didn't accept the feeling. And I didn't accept it. No! I just didn't. So I stopped myself. I tried to find a suitable cover for my confusion. My mind was racing (but there was no race, no track, just miles and miles of empty *air*) and I found myself blurting out … Uh … What? Did I say that the dog was fat? Yes. *Yes.* I think I did, actually. But then the dog *is* fat. Big deal! I merely stated a known fact! No harm done there, then.

And so I calmly walked on. And a while later it started to rain. And I can remember the pebbles and the rocks all shiny in the wet. And my shoes – dress shoes – splattered with mud. And I remember how high the cliffs were. So high. So improbably high … *Woo! Woo-hoo!* (I'm spinning around, gazing upwards, woo-hooing, like a jackass) … Oh look – *there* … See that black bird, just circling above? Is it a raven? A chough? Do they even *have* choughs in this part of the British Isles? Or ravens for that matter? Uh … No. Possibly not. What's that …? (Stops spinning, staggers slightly.) What's that extraordinary … uh …?

And then … And then – *Wham! Bam! Alakazam!* – forty-eight hours had passed me by, in what felt like the merest of breaths, and I was waking up in the cells with the mother of all hangovers, a tin bucket by the bed, splayed across a creepy, squeaky, rubber-coated mattress, no bed-linen, no blanket, not so much as a pillow – a humble *pillow* – to rest my pounding head upon.

Oh. And there was a baby rabbit tucked away snugly inside my vest. My suit was still wet. The pockets were full of leaves.

White ash? Eucalyptus? After approximately five minutes a young constable brought me some sweet tea and said that they were releasing me without charge but I needed to provide them with some details of my identity. I had no idea at this stage that I was missing an entire day. A day had been stolen! But by whom?! My wallet (a matter of secondary importance; it was empty, remember?) was also gone. Apparently I'd been apprehended by a passing member of the local foot patrol – in riotous mood (me, not the copper) – drinking on the beach the previous morning with a couple of reprobate old fisher-folk. I'd tried to break into a church: St Thomas of Canterbury and the English Martyrs (in St Leonards) which contains exquisite painted murals (stencils, but still lovely) by Nathaniel Westlake, no less. Amazing. Yes – *yes*! I *had* broken in (I have no memory of this) and I'd confessed a pile of hysterical mumbo-jumbo, in Spanish, to the priest, then knelt and prayed with him (we'd conversed freely – he was born and raised in Alicante), then jumped up and ran off. I'd tried to make a sled out of a bakery pallet and had careered down the Old London Road on it (I was relatively successful, in other words), ending up in a large bush of pampas grass (slightly cut lip – evidence of white fluff in hair). I had stolen and eaten half a loaf. I was wearing lipstick (yes!). Orange lipstick. In giant circles around my eyes. Three cigarettes had been stubbed out on the top of my hand. My right hand. And the rabbit? A dwarf breed. Quite rare. Of indeterminate age, it transpires. Nobody knew where it had come from, only that I'd been finding great solace in it. The officer had kindly fed it a carrot.

It was a white rabbit with pink eyes. I walked all the way home with it held in a makeshift sling fashioned out of my jacket. Even now I find it incredible to think that I would have walked all that way with it. I am no fan of small mammals. I have given it a temporary berth in the bath. In the bath the enamel turns its white fur a yellower hue. Strange how the act of comparison can suddenly transform one clearly defined object into something else altogether. Life has a nasty habit of doing that.

I noticed that there was a tiny hole in the bathroom window. Later on I found an even tinier stone in the toilet bowl.

But that was not all I found. Oh no. The bin, the missing bulb, the hole in the window (all serious, in their own way, admittedly) were as nothing by comparison (that rabbit in the bath phenomenon, remember?) with the thing I found in my bedroom. I say 'thing', but it was more than a mere 'thing', it was a performance, a staging, an extravaganza. It was a complete one-act drama. I hate to oversell it, but ... come with me. Enter the room. Push open the door and then grimacingly recoil. There is a smell ... Not even a smell, a stink, a vile, ungodly odour. Something so foul, so rank, that mere words – simple, uncomplicated *language* – cannot do justice to its offensiveness. A slap in the face. A *physical* reaction. A *gut* reaction. A violent recoil. An existential shudder. A withering of the soul. A shrinking. A boring at the nostril. A tearing at the throat.

But where? From whence doth this rancid odour hail, pray tell? (I've fallen into Olde English in a pathetic attempt to try and encompass how *primordial* this smell is, how primitive, how base, how ... how *medieval* – and how fearful I am, how confused, how repulsed; but still pretending, nevertheless, to be bold, pretending to be jocular; call to mind, if you must, a cheery fifteenth-century soldier – a Man of Fortune – or, better still, a palsied whore or cocky jester.) I search the room, a shirt over my face. My forehead is instantly dripping with sweat. My hand is a claw. I am a zombie. My body is panicking. It's instinctive. The smell is so ... so *engulfing*.

Eventually I settle on my suitcase, my empty suitcase (old leather, a gift from my maternal grandfather when I went up to Cambridge). It lies under the bed. I drag it out by its handle. I am so full of dread. Hands shaking. Palms wet. I steady myself. My heart is pounding. One, two, three – Come *on*, Franklin! Grow some *balls*, man! – I throw open the lid.

NNNAAAAARRRRGGHHHH!

So much worse – so, *so* much worse – than I could possibly have anticipated! Several hundred huge, buzzing bluebottles swarm out of the case and into my face. It is as though the devil himself (I'm an atheist, but bear with me) has been compressed in that small space. And now he is free. And he is angry. The *sound*! The intensity of that roar! The violence of those wings! The sense of un … un … unexpurgated *filth*! And remaining? In the case? The putrefying corpse of a dead shark. A dead *sand* shark, no less.

Urgh!

Urgh!

I vomited – instantly, spontaneously – on to my own, damp lap.

The sheer indignity!

Words cannot do justice. No. *No*. Sometimes, even justice – even *justice* – cannot do justice.

8

Miss Carla Hahn

I am trapped (a pathetically bleating shrew dangling from a savage hawk's bloodied talon) in the midst of a polite exchange with the indomitable Bridget 'Biddy' West, who is manning the Post Office counter in the Fairlight General Store (Biddy: 'So how many metres of garden did you say you have left, now, Carla?' Me: 'Uh … Eight? Nine? I'm not very metric. Eleven or twelve good strides from the back door.' Biddy: 'The shed was quite some distance away from the property, then?' Me: 'There's an old extension out back. A sun room that Tilda – the owner, Tilda Gower – closed in with a little pine-wood sauna. It's … The bungalow is basically just a series of tiny extensions, one next to the … uh … to the … uh … other.' Biddy: 'So you've told Matilda about the landfall?').

At this (let's call it the second 'uh …' moment) I am horrified to espy the giant bulk of Clifford Bickerton (previously observed, minutes earlier, driving his van – at considerable speed – towards Hastings on the Fairlight Road) blocking all the light from the windows in the door.

Bugger, bugger, *bugger*! I was certain I'd got away with it this time! I'd been so careful, so stealthy (had even jumped behind a buddleia to be 100 per cent sure)! Has he been – *is* he – following me again? Why oh why didn't I just answer his calls and have done with it? Why didn't I just speak to him directly when he came to the bungalow the other afternoon, in person, to offer help? Oh bugger, bugger, *bugger*.

The bell cheerfully tinkles as the door is pushed open and Clifford squeezes himself inside like some huge, red otter gently violating a disused vole hole. Whenever Clifford Bickerton enters any environment constructed for standard human habitation an atmosphere far more appropriate to a Grimm's fairy tale is promptly established. He is big, powerful, tall, auburn-haired and bushy-bearded with hands like pitchforks and feet like hams. He has been uniquely fashioned for the barn and for the field.

'So you've told Matilda about the landfall?' Biddy repeats, ignoring the placid and unassuming Clifford completely.

'Uh ...' I am thrown into confusion, 'Yes. No. That's ... that's actually why I'm sending this letter.'

I point towards the letter which I am currently buying stamps for as Clifford smacks his head into the light fitment and quietly curses.

'You couldn't ring her?'

Biddy continues to ignore Clifford.

'No. She's still travelling.'

'The Great Wall?'

I nod. 'She has an itinerary. Her next official pit-stop is somewhere called Huanghua. But she's been delayed by an infected mosquito bite on her heel. Every few months I receive a letter ...'

Clifford is currently inspecting the rack of cellophane and Sellotape. He picks up a packet of Blu-Tack. He seems deeply engrossed in the writing on the back.

'Is that her name in Chinese, then?' Biddy wonders, indicating the top line of the address.

'No. I think it says something like ... uh ... "to the crazy, European lady traveller who is walking the Great Wall. I humbly ask that you – the wall guard at Huanghua – please keep this letter for her until she arrives, when she will reward you generously for your kindness. A thousand blessings ..." All very flowery and Chinese. I don't know, exactly ...

50

something like that, anyway. She sends me her next contact address enclosed in each letter so I can just cut it out and glue it on to an envelope.'

'Oh.' Biddy nods.

'It's all fairly hit and miss,' I continue (suddenly compelled – through guilt and embarrassment – to blather on, inanely). 'The wall's over five thousand miles long. Although Tilda seems to think it's even longer than that. In her last postcard she said she'd recently met someone – a Chinese historian or a geographer – who told her that the wall originally spanned over fifteen thousand miles ...'

'I simply don't understand why Matilda bothered buying that bungalow in the first place if she never had any plans to live in it,' Biddy sighs, taking the letter from me and dropping it on to the scales.

'No.'

Clifford has now moved on to the rack of birthday cards. 'Although I suppose it gives you a roof over your poor head,' she kindly concedes, 'so you can rent out your little cottage in Pett and don't need to be getting under the feet of your dear old dad.'

'Yes.' I nod (concerned that she might be confusing my reassuringly tough head or my utterly incorrigible father with someone else's head – someone else's dad – far more deserving than mine).

'Have you ever actually *lived* in the cottage since you inherited it?' she wonders.

'Uh. No, *no*. I've always been committed to—'

'Someone's birthday?' Biddy raises her voice to finally acknowledge Clifford.

Clifford is inspecting a card very closely. He is so engrossed that he doesn't seem to hear her.

'SOMEONE'S *BIRTHDAY*, RUSTY?' Biddy bellows.

Clifford's entire body jolts with surprise. He drops the card
then bends down to pick it up, inadvertently bumping into a
wicker basket containing bags of kindling.

'Mine,' he says, then, 'Sorry,' (to the basket).

'Yours?' Biddy scowls.

Clifford clumsily retrieves the card.

'The day before yesterday.' Clifford nods.

(Oh God! The day of the landslip! I have forgotten Clifford's
birthday again, *dammit!*) 'It's visible from space,' he adds, as a
somewhat lacklustre afterthought, 'the Great Wall.'

'Happy birthday for ... for ...' I start to murmur, agonized.

'Are you planning on getting *yourself* a card, Rusty?' Biddy
wonders, with a supercilious smirk.

'Uh ... no.'

Clifford puts the card back down on to the rack.

'Thank you,' he mutters.

'Because you're two days late!' Biddy delivers her ringing
punch-line with considerable pizzazz.

'I was actually just after some ... uh ... matches.' Clifford
grabs a pile of kindling and then moves over towards the
'shop' section of the store. There he grabs a packet of Tuc
biscuits and proceeds to the counter which is currently vacant
because Biddy is in the P.O.

Biddy snorts, amused, then checks the weight of my letter
on her scales and inspects her list of foreign postal prices.
'I'd be scared stiff to go to bed at night,' she murmurs, neatly
tearing a small selection of stamps from their sheets, 'I mean
you can never be sure. A bit of heavy rain and the clay just ...
it just slips. And there goes your home! Off a cliff! A *high*
cliff! Into the sea! Everything you own – everything you've
worked for – all gone! *Kaput!*'

'And an airmail sticker, please,' I remind her.

'Poor Dr and Mrs Bassett lost the best part of their front
kitchen. She said they found the cat in a cupboard almost
half-dead with fear.'

'They were up most of the night calling for it.' I nod.

'For the life of me I don't know why the council doesn't do more to enforce the demolition order,' she tuts.

'Tilda's place is still perfectly livable,' I interrupt, 'and the Bassetts haven't actually occupied the front kitchen since the last big drop …'

'You're all nutty as fruitcakes!' Biddy mutters, pushing over the stamps and the sticker. 'That's two pounds and seventy pence please, Carla.'

I pass her the money, then quickly affix the stamps.

'Well I suppose we should all just be grateful that nobody was actually hurt on this occasion,' she concedes, generously.

'Yes. We should. We are. Thanks.'

'Although it's only a question of time if you ask me,' Biddy persists. 'There's no point fighting against nature, Carla. I say that as someone who spent much of their childhood in India – Bangladesh as it now is. The Indians respect Mother Nature. Don't have any other choice. They know, first-hand, what she's capable of.'

She hands me my change.

'I'm sure that's very true,' I concede, limply (and I am, too).

Without prior warning, Biddy's disapproving radar suddenly shifts focus and is now centred on the hapless Clifford.

'Enjoying that, are we, Rusty?' she demands, scowling. Clifford has idly picked up a copy of the local paper from the shop counter and is blankly perusing the front page. He quickly throws it down with a stuttered, 'Nnn … n … no!' (Biddy, who was once the headmistress of our local primary school, traumatized several generations of small children with her searching questions, her piercing looks and her perpetual air of slight disapproval until a stubborn hip injury put an end to her reign of terror in 1978 or thereabouts.)

I turn for the door, muttering my thanks, but Biddy stops me in my tracks.

'Shall I put that in the post-bag?' she asks, reaching out for the letter. I hand it over, somewhat regretfully (it never feels like you've actually *sent* a letter until it's been shoved into the hungry mouth of a bright, red postbox. Oh well).

I thank Biddy again and start for the exit. I am actually through the door (jingle-jingle!) and halfway across the little car park before Clifford finally catches up with me, as he inevitably must.

'I left my stuff on the counter,' he pants. He is still holding the Tuc biscuits.

'You've still got the Tuc biscuits,' I observe.

'Damn.'

Clifford inspects the Tuc biscuits, foiled.

'You'd better go back in,' I caution him, 'or Biddy will eat you alive.'

'Yes.' He nods, not moving.

I am about to go on to apologize for not responding to his calls (and his visit etc.) when I can't help but notice the new jumper he's wearing, partially hidden under his scruffy, khaki work coat. It's a pure horror: a fashionable Pringle; pale yellow in the main, the front a vile knitted patchwork of interconnected pink, white and mauve diamonds.

I instinctively wince. 'Birthday present?' I ask.

'Alice.' He nods. 'She was so pleased with it – cost her almost a week's wages. I just didn't have the ...'

'Does it fit properly?'

I push back the frayed sleeve of his work coat and pull away, worriedly, at the cuff. There's not so much as a millimetre of give.

'It's a bit snug,' he concedes.

'Isn't that interfering with your circulation?' I wonder.

'I have no feeling in my hands,' he confirms.

'Can you actually get it off?'

'Nope,' he sighs. 'It'll tear when I do. So I'm just keeping it on for as long as I possibly can.'

'I did that with a sticking plaster once after a polio injection at school,' I fondly reminisce, 'and I developed blood poisoning.'

'I remember.' He nods.

'How high can you lift your arms?'

With considerable difficulty he lifts them to a 65-degree angle. 'There are two tiny holes at the armpit and the elbow,' he explains, 'which have allowed a certain amount of flexibility.'

'You need to get it off, quick,' I warn him. 'Isn't it difficult to breathe?'

'I feel entombed' – he nods – 'like an Egyptian mummy. Although it's fine,' he rallies, 'so long as I don't over-exert myself.'

'But what if you get a call out for the lifeboat?' I demand.

He shrugs.

'There are little marks on the side of your neck,' I observe, with increasing concern, 'little welts. It's like ...' I shudder. 'It's like an expensive, lambswool python has swallowed you up, whole.'

'I tried to get it off this morning,' he confesses, 'but I couldn't do it by myself. I knew if I asked Mum or Dad or Bill it'd get straight back to Alice in a flash. They all think it's bloody hilarious.'

'Gracious me!' I stare at the welts on his neck, somewhat daunted (almost as if they aren't friction burns at all, but tender little love bites). 'You must really care for her,' I reason, jolted, 'to put yourself through all this discomfort just for the sake of not ... for the sake of ... for a *jumper*. And such a – I mean I hope you don't mind my saying so – but such a ... a ...'

I don't have the heart to say it out loud.

'Yes.' He looks suitably crestfallen at the notion. 'We've been engaged for eight years now. I suppose I must probably feel something.'

(Clifford and Alice, a local milkmaid, were engaged after she proposed to him, in 1976, a leap year, and he was just too kind to say no. At least that was always *his* version of events. Alice plays the scene quite differently, by all accounts.) I nod. Now it's *my* turn to look crestfallen. I decide to take it on the chin, though, and promptly rally. I draw a steadying breath and strengthen my resolve. I know that the worst thing I could possibly do under these particular circumstances would be to offer Clifford any form of assistance.

No. I shan't. I shall not. I will not – must not, *definitely* not – offer Clifford Bickerton any kind of help. I must never help Clifford Bickerton, and I must never *receive* help from Clifford Bickerton.

Oh, but the urge to offer help is so ... so natural, so instinctive, so spontaneous, so ... so ...
No. *No!* No help, Carla. No offers of help! None.

'Go and pay for the biscuits,' I promptly tell him, 'then pop around to the bungalow. I can't possibly leave you like this. I have a pair of shears ... Uh ...' I pause, scowling. 'At least I did have a pair of shears ...'

'In the shed?' he asks, almost tender (I suppose men *will* feel emotional about outbuildings).
I nod. 'I *do* have some kitchen scissors, though,' I persist.

His face lights up. It *lights* up. Every pore and auburn whisker is suffused with joy.
No! *No*, Carla! *Bad* Carla! Mustn't. Offer. Help.
Will. Not.
I. Must. Not.
No. Help.
None!

Ten minutes later and he is kneeling on the worn kitchen lino and I am brandishing the scissors in front of him.
'Sure you're all right with this?'
'Yup. Do it.' He braces himself.

I kneel down beside him and gently slide the bottom blade of the scissors under the right-hand side of the jumper's collar.

'Stay very still,' I instruct him, leaning in closer. It is difficult to find the correct angle and draw the blades together without resting my lower arm and wrist against his leonine neck and cheek. Ah, and there's that all too familiar 'Clifford smell' of candle wax, sleeping puppies and engine grease! A lovely smell. The smell of industry and loyalty and good intent.

'Your Tikhomirov study of the birches is on the floor,' Clifford quietly observes.

'Uh … Sorry?' I re-focus.

'Your painting of the birch trees …' he repeats.

'Oh. Yes. Of course. It fell down. During the landslip. It was the only casualty inside the house. The bottom of the frame snapped.'

'I remember the day you bought that.' He smiles tenderly at the memory.

'Yes.'

I adjust my arm, frowning, and start to cut. The jumper curls away beneath my hand on both sides like two obliging slithers of apple peel. The trusty old vest below has – to its eternal credit – somehow managed to stay intact.

'I'll fix it if you like,' Clifford volunteers, 'the frame.'

'It's fine,' I insist, 'I can do it myself. Some strong glue …'

'Oh. Okay.' He is slightly hurt yet resigned.

'I still love it. I still love birch trees,' I muse. '*Berezka*. Beautiful *Berezka*. I don't know why, they just make me feel so … so …'

'Russian,' he murmurs.

I start.

'I really like all your new propaganda posters …' He inspects the busy walls, thoughtfully, his eyes pausing on an early 'Liberated Women Build up Socialism!' poster which features a wholesome Russian peasant girl brandishing a pistol. Next to it the 'Think About Those Who Are Starving!' poster in blue and black with a loaf, cup, bowl and ominous, pointing hand.

'I've been using them as a cheap way of covering up all the stains on the old wallpaper,' I explain, 'although they're way too good for a kitchen, really—'

'I see your collection of Russian lacquered boxes has increased a fair bit since I last visited,' he interrupts, flexing his chest as the scissors finally break through the jumper's waistline. 'And the Soviet china figurines ...' He tips his head towards the old dresser. 'Is that a new Lomonosov Chow?'

'Uh ...Yes. I found it wrapped up in a big box of Uzbek fabrics. In an antique shop near Hythe ... D'you think you might manage to pull it off manually from here?'

Clifford tries to yank the jumper from his shoulder but his arms are still stiff and he has no luck.
'Shall I cut down the back?'
He nods and shuffles around, obligingly.
'Has Shimmy been to visit you here lately?' he wonders.
'Shimmy?' I pause, briefly, before answering. 'Uh. No. Not of late. He's still not especially mobile. That problem with his feet.'

Clifford turns his head to peer towards the blades as I insert them, pressing gently into the nape of his neck.
'Why d'you ask?' I wonder, slightly anxious. He doesn't respond so I recommence cutting again.

'I've been doing some work for a man in Bexhill who's trying to get shot of a collection of Soviet army surplus stuff – a gas mask, a transistor radio, a canteen and a vodka flask, some military badges ...'
'Sounds interesting.' I continue to cut.
'He showed me a little, wooden sewing kit – a travelling kit – in the shape of a minaret. And a group of Kiddush cups – the sterling silver ones. Not a complete set. I think he had five in total. In fact ...'

58

'I can see how this might've been expensive,' I muse, smoothly running the scissors – and my hand – down the back of the jumper, 'it's very soft.'

'Soft but lethal,' Clifford affirms.

'And very bright. Luminous, almost.'

'A statement piece.' Clifford smiles, wanly.

'Is that how Alice described it?' I wonder, chuckling.

'Uh …' he frowns, obviously not wanting to appear disloyal.

The scissors cut the waistband and I pull back with a measure of satisfaction (like a smug Lady Mayor on cutting the ribbon at a local fete): 'The Pringle is vanquished!' I grin, throwing down the scissors and grabbing the jumper firmly at the top of his arm in order to yank it off. 'Clifford Bickerton is finally liberated from the scourge of lambswool!'

I pull, but the jumper hardly gives. Instead I yank Clifford towards me and we both nearly topple sideways. He tips but steadies himself, his weight supported on his arm which is now planted, firmly, between my knees. I stop myself from falling by simply holding on. His bicep is like a giant squash. So hard. He doesn't automatically straighten himself.

'Don't let go,' he murmurs, into my hair. I am close to his ear. I long to press the cool outline of it against the skin of my forehead. It's a random urge. Silly. But Clifford has such nice ears. Good ears. Familiar ears.

'I've been reading that Ivan Yefremov novel you bought me for Christmas,' I say, turning my head away, releasing my grip, delighting – thrilling, even – at my considerable powers of self-control, 'the sci-fi thing. *Andromeda*. It's very good.'

'That was three Christmases ago,' he answers, thickly.

'Pardon?'

'It's from three Christmases ago.'

'Oh. Well it's very good,' I repeat.

He suddenly straightens himself and clambers heavily to his feet. He walks to the window and peers out.

'What did the surveyor say?' he murmurs, coolly assessing the damage.

I stand up myself. 'Tiered gardens are all the vogue, apparently.' I try to make light of it.

'That bad?'

'No. *No*,' I lie.

'You've still got the sauna,' he observes. 'That sauna is indestructible.'

I grab the scissors from the floor and walk over. 'Although I haven't seen a single bird on the feeders since it happened.'

'Strange. You wouldn't think they'd be that bothered.'

'They have wings.' I nod.

I take a hold of his arm, lift it and gently insert the bottom blade under the cuff. As I start to cut something terrible occurs to me.

'Hang on a second … the landslip – wasn't that your birthday? You came around here on your birthday? Then you ended up searching for a lost cat half the night?'

(The Bassetts had informed me of these small details the morning after. It had been Clifford who'd bravely ventured into the front kitchen – just as dawn was breaking – at the pathetic sound of mewing.)

Clifford doesn't volunteer anything further.

'How'd you find out?' I wonder.

'The coastguard.'

'Ah.'

'They were thinking of sending out a boat, so I drove over to check things out.'

I nod. At last his first arm is free. He flexes it, gratefully. I commence work on the second.

'Georgie Hulton said he saw you in tears on the beach the other day. You were out walking Rogue. He said you'd just been talking to your tenant – a Mr Huff.'

'What a ridiculous name!' I mutter, cheeks reddening. 'Mr Huff! I'll huff and I'll puff …'

'Was he bothering you?' Clifford demands.

'Don't be ridiculous,' I snort, 'it was windy. I got sand in my eyes, that's all.'

'Georgie said he called out to you but ...'

'I mustn't have heard him.' I shrug.

Clifford says nothing and the second arm is soon freed. I step back, grinning. Clifford stands there in his vest. All plain and uncomplicated in his vest. I am so pleased, so relieved, to see that awful jumper finally gone, to see him back to his giant, scruffy but utterly pristine self. Pure now and unadulterated. I bend down and start scooping up the abandoned segments of jumper and suddenly, for no reason I can think of, I feel like ... like tearing at those expensive bits of luminous wool, throwing them down, cursing them, jumping on them. Instead I quickly carry them over to the bin (these dangerous and provocative pieces of knitwear) and am about to lift the lid and toss them in when Clifford appears behind me, pulling on his old khaki jacket and asks if he might possibly hold on to them, as a keepsake. 'Of course,' I say, 'sorry. Of course you can. Of course you must.' I pass them over. He is saying something about being late for a job. I nod. I say something about I don't know what exactly. He almost bumps his head into a reproduction ceiling beam. I walk ahead of him to the door. I am saying inconsequential things, about the farm, about his mother. Then he is gone.

I stand in the tiny hallway for a moment, still holding the scissors, scowling. Then I walk through to the kitchen again. My thoughts keep returning to Shimmy, what he'd said about Shimmy. 'Has Shimmy visited the bungalow lately?' Strange. Why'd he say that? Why'd he ask that?

I cast my eyes around the room, frustratedly, irritably. It is then that I see an alien, little object on the edge of the counter-top. *What ...?* I frown and draw closer. It is a tiny, wooden, Russian minaret, a humble thing, home-made, daubed in worn white and ochre and black. I pick it up, fascinated, and twist the small, stiff bulb which eventually comes loose to reveal – hidden within – a little selection of slightly rusty needles, pins and a small roll of faded threads.

Oh my goodness!

How utterly adorable!

Clifford Bickerton.

Clifford bloody Bickerton!

'Never. Offer. Help. Carla. Hahn,' I murmur.

9

Mr Franklin D. Huff

I don't know why, but I have the distinct feeling that Mrs
Barrow knows more than she's letting on. When she arrived
for work this morning (pristine gingham housecoat, Dr Scholl
wooden sandals combined with thick tan tights, brown nylon
A-line skirt, trusty emu-feather duster held incongruously aloft
like the proud baton of a Marching Band leader) the whole
cottage was still shrill with the hyperactive buzz of bluebottles.

I had found some brief respite, overnight, in the small,
spare room (the 'box' room as I casually refer to it) which
seemed like the only place in the whole cottage not utterly
overtaken (doused, *eclipsed*) by the rank odour of rotten fish.
The flies were everywhere – *everywhere* – yet this was also the
only place in the entire cottage that they didn't seem to feel
especially drawn to. Not a single fly came in to pester me as I
fitfully slumbered (or if they did, I had no inkling of it),
although the door had – somewhat stupidly – been left ajar for
the best part of the night after a lumbering visit to the
bathroom.

I showed Mrs Barrow the damage (almost with a small
measure of pride – a secret hankering for approval: Mrs
Barrow! Observe my suffering – my confusion – my
persecution!).

'The bin has been dumped on top of the Look Out.' I
pointed.

'The bulb on the front porch is gone … Presumed stolen.

'A tiny pebble has been thrown through the bathroom window
...' (Of course I didn't take her in there, the rabbit being
hidden, temporarily, under an upturned washing-up bowl.)

And finally ... the *Pièce de Résistance*! I led her out on to the
little back porch (the postage-stamp-sized – and badly fenced
– scrap of garden to the fore; a lovely mess of blue and
mauve: wild asters, bugloss, scabious and sea holly; cusping a
sheer, thirty-foot drop to ground level, but still hemmed in
from the beach proper by yet more dampness: some swampy
common ground, the thin end of the not-so-Grand Military
Canal, the road beyond and, of course, the sea wall) where
the big fish is currently *in situ* on the old bench (which I
broke the back slat of two days ago while removing a boot).
She pinches her nose.

'It was hidden in my suitcase under the bed,' I explain.

She thinks for a short while. 'You're sure as you didn't put
it in there yourself, Mr Huff,' she wonders, 'and then forget?'
I am – quite frankly – incensed by this question.

'What earthly reason d'you imagine I might have had for
doing that?' I demand.

She shrugs.

'This is a *shark*, Mrs Barrow! How exactly do you expect I
might go about acquiring a *shark* in these Godforsaken
environs?'

'Oh I think you'll find as they're very common in these
parts, Mr Huff,' Mrs Barrow insists. 'When Mr Barrow
worked out on the fishing boats we would eat sand shark very
regular. Once or twice a week. I'd have thought a
cosmopolitan gentleman such as yourself, Mr Huff, might be
quite *partial* to the odd plate of good quality shark meat.'
I stare at her, astonished.

'A nice bowl of shark fin soup,' she persists. 'Surely them
Mexicanos are all wild for shark fin soup.'

'Shark's fin soup is a Chinese delicacy, Mrs Barrow,' I stiffly
inform her.

'Shark is very edible, Mr Huff,' Mrs Barrow doggedly continues, wafting her hand gently in front of her face, 'although the mistake you made here, Mr Huff, was to leave the internal organs in place. Always be sure and gut a shark on the beach. Mr Barrow is oft wont to say that.' She smirks. 'Then the gulls'll kindly do the rest of the work for you.'

'I think you misunderstand me, Mrs Barrow ...' I start off.
'Or they makes a fine bait,' she continues, 'if you can only bear the stink, mind.'
She winces.
'I have never eaten shark, Mrs Barrow, nor have I ever *considered* eating shark,' I maintain.
'Well if the urge ever takes you again, Mr Huff, might I suggest as you soak the gutted fish flesh in milk or bicarbonate,' she volunteers. 'The worst of that honk is the ammonia, see ...?'
Again? If the urge ever takes me *again*?!

'Like I say,' I repeat, quite sharply, now, 'I have never eaten shark and I have never—'
'Well you can eats it in all manner of ways, Mr Huff!' she promptly eulogizes. 'Tastes just like mackerel, it does. You can have it fresh, frozen, dried. The liver is specially prized for its oil. A person can even make leather goods from the hide if they so feels the urge.'

'My point is—'
'I just deep fries it in a nice, light batter, Mr Huff. Better still, after soaking the steak in milk, dip it in beaten egg, then a thin layer of flour, then pop it in a hot, oiled pan ...'

'While this is all very educational, Mrs Barrow ...'
'Or make yourself a plain stew, Mr Huff, with chopped carrots, onions, leeks, parsnips, potato ...'
'... I fail to see how ...'
'... nice tin of plum tomatoes ...'
'... this has any relevance with regard to ...'
'Salt. Pepper. Basic stock. Bay leaf ...'

'… the rotting carcass of a shark suddenly appearing …'
'Celery. Did I forget celery?'
'… as if by magic …'
'Be sure to only throw in the diced fish at the last minute. Big handful of chopped parsley to serve …'
'… or … or *voodoo* …'
'Then hey presto, there you have it: sand shark stew, Mr Huff!'
'Gumbo,' I interject (broken).

'Pardon me, Mr Huff?' Mrs Barrow looks a tad offended.
'Gumbo,' I repeat.
'You can call it mumbo gumbo if you likes, Mr Huff' – Mrs Barrow is still more offended – 'but a regular-sized sand shark such as this one here will provide a good hearty family meal, and without breaking the bank, neither.'

'No, *no*, gumbo, Mrs Barrow! *G*umbo: an American fish and meat dish. A stew.'
'Oh.' Mrs Barrow doesn't look convinced.
'Although gumbo has plenty of garlic. And it's generally accompanied by a handful of rice.'

Mrs Barrow's eyes widen in horror. 'I'm afraid as Mr Barrow won't *tolerate* garlic, Mr Huff! Makes him belch something rotten, it does! Nor rice, neither, except in puddings of course, and even then he generally prefers some sago. He don't have no stomach for all that foreign muck, Mr Huff. A plain English stew is perfectly all right by him, thank you very much.'

Mrs Barrow rocks back on her wooden soles, arms crossed. 'Garlic is the mainstay of South American cuisine,' I stolidly maintain, 'and it actually has many impressive anti-bacterial qualities …' I suddenly find myself listing them, almost as if the list itself will somehow validate the feelings of hurt and distress I'm currently experiencing as a direct result of my perceived ill-treatment by the vindictive, bin-stealing, fish-hiding, garlic-hating people of the Great British Isle: 'It's good for wounds, Mrs Barrow, ulcers, colds, bladder problems ...'

Mrs Barrow starts at the mention of bladder problems. 'I'll as thank you to please refrain yourself from trespassing into areas of such a deeply *intimate* complexion, Mr Huff!' she exclaims, turns on her heel and heads back inside, affronted. I remain on the balcony for a second, momentarily nonplussed, then turn and follow. She disappears into various rooms and can be heard banging the wide open windows shut.

'D'you think it's a good idea to be closing all the windows, Mrs Barrow?' I call through. 'Isn't it better to give the flies every opportunity to disperse?'
Mrs Barrow stomps back into the kitchen-diner, shaking her duster around. She marches into the sitting room, still wafting, and slams the window shut in there, too.

'Mrs Barrow?' I follow her into the room.
'Mrs Barrow? D'you not think it might be better if we ...?'
As I irritably address her I am slightly bemused to observe a series of skittish, disparate bluebottles suddenly unify and cohere (like a swarm of wild bees, or pre-roost starlings) on to an expanse of the whitewashed chimney breast behind Mrs Barrow's shoulder, then doubly bemused – nay, astonished – to see them forming into a coherent shape. A large ... a large ... *what*? Uh ... An ... an X? Yes ... an ... uh ... Then they busily adjust, and the X ... well, it *tips* ... it tips on to its side and what were formerly the two 'horizontal' lines are fractionally reduced to produce ... How fleeting is this moment? I blink. Nope. *Nope.* Still there ... *still* there ...
A kind of *cross* shape! An actual cross! Large as life! On the chimney breast! A big, black, buzzing cross!

The hairs on the back of my neck promptly stand on end. Mrs Barrow is speaking.
'There was none of 'em in the little room,' she ruminates, 'did you happen to see that, Mr Huff?'

She turns and double-checks that the window is properly shut. I merely gape. I am inarticulate. Does she even notice the deafening cross of flies – right there – immediately to her left? I lift my arm and start to point vaguely as the cross shifts again; a diagonal line forms between the top of the vertical line and the further reaches of the horizontal line to the left and a … *yes* … it's now a four. A perfect four. A *four*!

Mrs Barrow finally satisfies herself that the window is properly closed, spins back around swishing her duster (like a hoity-toity priest on Palm Sunday condescending to scatter holy water on to the unwashed masses), disperses the flies, quite unthinkingly, then pushes past me and disappears once again into the back section of the cottage. Three seconds of silence, before:

'*Euceelyptus!*' she bellows, victorious.

'Sorry?'

I start to follow her. She is standing on the threshold to the small, box room.

'In the little girl's room!' She points with her duster.

'Euceelyptus! That's *her* smell. Well I never!'

Mrs Barrow seems delighted. I push past her and step inside the room, sniffing.

Eucalyptus! She's right. I have no idea why I didn't notice it before! It's stringent. *Clean.* And very powerful.

'Well Carla's as told me on many an occasion how she can't abide the smell. She's allergic! Disinfectant, see? She always says as the whole place is full of the scent of it. The little girl's smell! Orla's smell. Although they was as thick as thieves when that poor child was still alive – if you could *call* it a life, as such,' she cavils, 'and it was no different then, neither. Not as I'd know, mind. I was off in Dymchurch that entire summer nursing my sister-in-law – God bless her soul – who was down with the dropsy. Terrible it was – for a while. We all thought as she'd miss the birth of her first grandchild. She was quite frantic about it as I recall. Then she suddenly got herself better. Died one year later of a heart attack. But it was very quick. Blessedly so, Mr Huff.'

Mrs Barrow crosses herself and heads back to the kitchen. 'Euceelyptus!' she chortles. 'Flies can't abide the smell of it! Wait till I tells Carla about this!'

I remain in the room – inhaling suspiciously – and am soon drawn to my suit jacket which is slung over the back of a small, rickety whitewashed chair by the bed. I check the pockets (pure instinct) and draw out several handfuls of leaves – eucalyptus leaves. *Eucalyptus* leaves! Remember? From my little Hastings misadventure?

'Mrs Barrow?' I yell through, but am interrupted by a scream. Mrs Barrow has finally discovered the little rabbit in the bath.

'It's a rabbit, Mrs Barrow!' I yell. 'Just a rabbit – a dwarf variety.'

Mrs Barrow comes storming back through. 'We has a strict no-pets policy, Mr Huff!' she chastises me, hands on hips. 'It's right there in the contract: large print! Miss Hahn could happily evict you for less!'

'It's not mine!' I insist. 'I found it!'

'Whereabouts?' she demands.

'In … in … in …in my vest,' I respond (but not all that convincingly).

'It's been doing all its jobbies and what-not in the *bath*, Mr Huff!' Mrs Barrow is not remotely mollified. Then, 'In your *vest*?!' she echoes, a few seconds later.

'Yes. In amongst my vests,' I modify. 'Inside the small chest of drawers. I'm planning to phone the local constabulary,' I say, 'to investigate.'

'You think it's a matter of sufficient import to be bothering the police with?' she asks, taken aback.

'Why not, Mrs Barrow?' I demand. 'This was breaking and entering! Trespass! It's not just a small matter of a couple of kids having a little bit of harmless fun at my expense. The bin alone – yes, fair enough. But *this*? It's far more … more focused, more *personal* than that. These are the actions of a man or a woman with a serious grudge; these are acts of pure spite – *considered* acts, Mrs Barrow, and I naturally feel duty-bound to treat them as such.'

'Trespass?! But you left all them doors unlocked, Mr Huff!' Mrs Barrow interjects.

'How'd you know that?' I demand.

'Lucky guess.' She shrugs. 'You always as leaves 'em open, Mr Huff. Old habits dies hard. I imagine that's as what comes of living loose among all them free-and-easy types in the slums.'

'An act of … of *vengeance*,' I persist, refusing to be waylaid.

'To put a rabbit in your vests, Mr Huff?' she scoffs.

'No. No! Not that so much as …' I start to correct her, then, on second thoughts, 'Yes! Yes! The rabbit! To move the bin and steal the bulb and … and the fish and the rabbit. Yes. Exactly.' I nod.

Mrs Barrow considers all this for a few moments, which prompts me, in turn (I mean what's to be considered?) to raise the stakes a little. 'I don't want to say anything that might alarm you unnecessarily,' I murmur, 'but I think it only fair to warn you that during my time working as an investigative journalist in South America I had a measure of involvement with …' – I lower my voice a fraction – 'with operatives from the higher echelons of the CIA – the *highest* echelons, in fact. This was a long time ago – '68 – and they were by no means my finest hours, Mrs Barrow; I was sacked, ignominiously; disgraced – I can't stand here and pretend otherwise – but there are still … there are *wounds*, festering wounds …'

'You think as the CIA went and put a rabbit in your vests, Mr Huff?' Mrs Barrow is naturally sceptical at the prospect.

'Not literally, Mrs Barrow, no.' I shake my head. 'All I'm saying is that I'm highly practised at reading signals –

70

understanding gestures – I'm *au fait* with the subtle language
of revenge – of tit-for-tat – at a very basic, very primitive
level. In Mexican gang culture the concept of *retribucion* is at
the very heart of how—'

'Now you look here, Mr Huff,' Mrs Barrow interrupts,
plainly startled, 'I has a great deal of sympathy with your
predicament, don't nobody ever dare tell me otherwise …'
I humbly nod, gratified.

'I got two eyes in my head, Mr Huff, and I can plainly see as
how *upset* you is, like as if you saw a ghost, almost, Mr Huff
…' – she inspects my grief-strewn visage with some attention
– 'but all's I need you to understand is that poor Miss Hahn –
Carla – don't need the burden of your problems with the CIA
weighing down on her shoulders right now. That girl is
burdened enough already: what with the rental problems
because of all the cranks what comes here and takes the right
royal mickey out of her decent nature, her crazy dad with his
bad feet and his fat dog, not to mention the awful landslip
which swallowed up her shed – full of all her tools and such –
not two days since up there in Fairlight …'

I start.

'Sorry? A—'

'I don't know as if you realize, Mr Huff,' she continues, 'how
precious this little cottage is to poor Carla. Mulberry might
not look much to folks such as you and I, Mr Huff, but to
poor Carla …' She frowns. 'It'd be no exaggeration to say as
it was her life, her … her *world*, her … her very *soul*, Mr
Huff.'

'Well we can't have rotten fish and … and broken windows
and stolen bins and deeply distressed residents impinging on
our poor, dear Miss Hahn's fastidious *soul*, Mrs Barrow, can
we?' I blithely respond (yes, *yes*, there *is* an element of
facetiousness). 'Perish the thought!'

'Rabbits, Mr Huff!' Mrs Barrow maintains. 'Don't you forget
them rabbits, neither!'

71

'Just so, Mrs Barrow.'(I am finally now beginning to understand Miss Hahn's former contention that Mrs Barrow is generally wont to find the least important detail in any course of events to be the most significant. In this instance the actual offence of these recent developments to myself – my dignity – as opposed to Miss Hahn's *perceived* offence at second-hand.) 'Which is exactly why I am determined to alert the relevant—'

'Although now I comes to *think* about it, Mr Huff,' Mrs Barrow reasons, 'this is as likely to be an attack on poor Miss Hahn as it is on you! All the crackpots what comes to this place, you know, such as yourself. All those difficult cases, the religious maniacs and the Irish and the gypsies and the swindlers. And as if that's not bad enough, there was always the problems with her mother when poor Carla was growing up; her being a German and what-not, a foreigner, very bossy, always sticking her oar in, working for the council and taking pleasure – active pleasure it seemed like – in tearing down people's beach huts and little homes on the marshes over yonder, though she paid for it in the end, I suppose. Went totally doolally with dementia, poor soul. Not to mention her father being such a difficult, work-shy Jew. I mean piano-tuning isn't a way to make a proper living, Mr Huff. It's dreadful! Even *carneys* got more self-respect! Who cares if the piano is a little bit off key, anyways? You can still bang out a good old tune on it ... Yes' – she nods – 'I do think as it's our duty as to protect her from these curious developments, Mr Huff. In fact ...'

She wanders off, wafting the duster. 'I should telephone Rusty. *He'll* know what to do. Rusty Bickerton always has Miss Hahn's best interests at heart, Mr Huff. Forget the constabulary. They're as good as idiots in these parts anyways. Rusty'll set things straight and we won't need to bother dear Carla with none of it. I think that's the best course. I really does.'

'But Mrs Barrow ...'

'Put yourself to good use, Mr Huff. Go out and build that rabbit of yourn a cage. And it'll need a run, to boot: two by four at the very least I'd have thought.'

'But Mrs Barrow ... I really am determined to ... Mrs *Barrow*!'

Silence.

'Hello?'

More silence.

'Mrs Barrow ...?'

I stand and quietly scrutinize this unfolding scenario for a moment with my dispassionate, journalistic eye. Is Mrs Barrow actually on to something here? Is this not actually about me after all? Am I simply overreacting – lashing out – because I'm so upset ... because I haven't properly processed ... because I won't openly admit to the depth of my real feelings about ...? *Well?* Am I?

Mrs Barrow is standing in the living room as I meekly approach her, gently wafting her duster as she speaks on the phone.

'Hello there, Mrs Bickerton, this is Mrs Barrow up at Mulberry. Yes, hello. I was wondering if I might have a quick word with Rusty if it's all the same to you? Oh. Well, when you sees him will you tell him as I needs him to come and see me up here, pronto? It's a matter of some delicacy. Yes. Yes. Thank you.'

She places down the receiver then glances around the room, deeply gratified.

I fail to see any reason for such high levels of satisfaction. In fact I find myself at quite the opposite side of this emotional scale. I am disgruntled. Momentarily dead-ended. *Stoppered.*

'D'you hear that, Mr Huff?' She places her hand to her ear. I frown. I listen. *Eh?*

'Hear what, Mrs Barrow?' I respond.

'Nothing!' She grins.

'Nothing?' I echo, exhausted.

'They's all gone! See?' She chuckles royally at my mystified expression (is it just me, or has life suddenly become horribly … I don't know … loud? Angular? Bald? Cracked? Convoluted?).

'Buzz, buzz, buzz!' She kindly offers me a clue.

What?! Oh. Yes. *Yes!* The pesky flies! I glance around me. She's right. They're gone. They've vamoosed! All of them. Every single one of the little blighters.

'Never give 'em too many options, Mr Huff.' She taps the side of her nose with her finger. 'My old Mam taught me that. Don't be opening all the windows. Don't spoil 'em. Be sparing. Just open the one – or a door …'

She trots over to the back balcony door and gently pulls it shut.

'Always put something beyond it as a lure, mind. Flies is like livestock, Mr Huff – and some folk an' all, come to that! Skittish, they are, plain skittish! So just give 'em clear directions' – she winks at me, broadly – 'and then they'll do as they's told, right enough.'

10

Miss Carla Hahn

I *am* going to speak to Mr Huff.
I *am* going to speak to Mr Huff.
I *am* going to speak to Mr Huff.
I am. I *am*.

Apologize. Confess. Apologize. I *am*. I will. Yes. I will. It's just that … that after all the drama with the landslip I simply haven't had the … the … you know … the wherewithal … the nerve … the will … uh … no … the *opportunity*. Then I was scheduled on, last minute, for three, consecutive shifts at Mallydams: reception desk, cleaning out cages, hand feeding that snappy young vixen with the broken jaw etc. (they're short-staffed – poor Amy Burrell contracted Rat-bite Fever from a weasel. It's been all the talk in Guestling this week), and of course poor Dad's foot medication ran out yesterday (he forgot to warn me in advance) so I was obliged to charge on over to the Ore Surgery just before closing (ditched the bike, got the bus). Then there was a queue twenty deep at the pharmacy …

But I am going to speak to Mr Huff. Yes. It's an absolute priority.
I *am* going to speak to Mr Huff.
Confess. Confess all.
Yes.

Although … Although no word as yet from Mrs Barrow (and this is a scheduled cleaning day at the cottage, so …

uh ...), so perhaps it didn't all pan out quite so badly as I ... uh ...

Hoped?

Anticipated?

Feared?

No. No. It must've ... It must've been terrible. Awful. The bin hidden in plain view. The little stone through the window (but only a *little* stone, and it's my window after all), the stolen bulb (although – again – it's *my* bulb to steal). And ... and the shark. The dead shark. There's no ... I mean there's no excusing ... no arguing my way out of ... Under the bed! The dead shark! The shark with its guts full of vile, writhing, rapidly pupating ...

Oh Lord!

I *am* going to speak to Mr Huff.

Although (in my defence – I *know* I don't actually have a leg to stand on) he left all the doors wide open! Really! What else did he expect? Honestly!

And he insulted Rogue! Yes! Mortally! And Dad!

And he's an awful, supercilious snoop! He ran over Mum's cat, for heaven's sake!

(That was actually his wife, though, wasn't it? Before she left?)

And then, to compound the injury, he pretty much accused me of lying! To my face! About the poor old boy's age! Followed by the letter! That awful, vain, self-aggrandizing ... *Urgh!* Just thinking about it makes my ... makes my blood ... urgh ... boil.

Such a rude man.

And the subtle way he's gone about ingratiating himself with everyone. Oh lovely, charming, *creative* Mr Huff with his curly hair and his clever, hazel eyes and his cheekbones and his braces and his cosmopolitan life and his artistic hands and his winning ways and his extraordinary sensitivity (*Please!*)

and his shrunken heads and his social conscience and … and
his *amazing* gift – his deep empathy – with macaws!
Urgh.

When I so much as … as *think* about the way he's lied and
connived and conned and … and charmed people. How he's
ingratiated himself (did I say that before?). Ingratiated himself
with everyone. *Everyone.* Even Mrs Barrow! Everyone.
Everyone but … well, but me. Obviously.
The way he's …
Urgh. *Urgh.*

I *am* going to speak to Mr Huff. I *am*. Confess. Apologize.
Although before I can head on over there – here we are …
Phew! Quick left turn. Avoid the puddle. Apply the brake.
Clamber off. Throw down my bike. Remove my rucksack.
Peek inside: tin of pilchards, *check*; pork pie, *check*; iron
supplements, *check*; Deep Heat, *check*; aniseed balls, *check* –
before I can head over there I'm obliged to pop in on Shimmy
to drop off his Dopamine and some other stuff he's asked for.

Of course (nothing's ever as simple as it should be in this
life) when I arrive it's utterly impossible to gain access to the
cottage. Rogue has fallen asleep – as is his perfectly
maddening habit – directly behind the front door. The sheer
weight of that animal, the *heft*, is equivalent (and this is
absolutely no exaggeration) to a large *chaise-longue* or a small
settee. I smack the door into him, repeatedly (Sorry, Rogue!).
I have a full three inches leeway (Oh lucky me!). But he
refuses, point-blank, to budge. I know – I just *know* – that he's
blocking my access on purpose – I'm *certain* of it – purely to
avoid the distinct likelihood of his being dragged out for a
spot of brisk exercise.

And I can't get in through the back, either! Dammit!
Dammit! Security-obsessed Shimmy has bolted the tall side
gate. I knock (obviously – doors, windows), I sit on the bell, I
yell, but all to no avail. Shimmy is listening – at quite
extraordinary volume – to a home-taped recording (off the

TV) of *Fraggle Rock*, his favourite programme. I can hear him singing along to the theme tune, bless him. *Damn* him.

Dance your cares away!
Worry's for another day –
Let the music play,
Down at Fraggle Rock!

Again it plays, and again and again and again. Can he have made himself two separate recordings so he doesn't have to wait to rewind? Has he even got two functional tape recorders? Does he possess the technological know-how for such pointless shenanigans?

I try the back gate for a second time. I return to the front door and smack it into Rogue. *Thud.*
We're Gobo, Mokey, Wembley, Boober, Red!
I return to the gate. I've climbed over it before, but only under extreme duress. There's very little purchase for hand or foot. After scrabbling around for a while I have the brilliant idea of fetching my bike, leaning it up against the gate and using it (the pedal, then the seat) as a kind of portable stepladder.

Everything is proceeding apace. The bike is carefully positioned – a brick wedged under the front wheel, the back wheel pushed against the wall of the house. I climb up. It's a little unstable (a little ungainly, come to that) but everything's going perfectly to plan, until …

It's difficult to describe what happens next. I am almost half-straddling the gate – climbing over boldly, assuredly, very confident – when something catches at my waist, I fall forward, inadvertently – violently – kick out both my feet, and the bike tips sideways, crashing on to the gravel path. I am left hanging over the gate, bent at the hip, a fleshy, top-heavy U-bend, a human peg. To fall back would be difficult – even dangerous (the bike is just below. I'd hate to land on the spokes and potentially injure my foot, my ankle, my leg). I can only move forward. It's just … uh … a question of … of using my hands to … to … And then I find that I'm … that I'm … that somehow I've become … *no*! I'm stuck! The piece of cord in my old jeans (they're drawstring, tautened at the waist with a gentle bow) has somehow become hooked over an irregular piece of … a little wooden chip, a knot. And so I'm … I'm utterly, irrevocably, undisputedly *stuck*! I simply can't …

I struggle. I struggle for what feels like an age to get my hand under my … to loosen the … but it's too taut. In fact it's … it's almost cutting into me. And it's hard to breathe with all this weight – *my* weight – on my gut. So I hang forward, to rest, to inhale, but then – once rested – I find it almost impossible to straighten back up. All the strength has leaked out of me.

I am stuck! Bottom in the air. Legs kicking. Wheezing. Groaning. I am stuck! I am stuck!

The vestiges of my womanly pride restrain me from calling out for help for a full five minutes. Who will come, anyway? It's mid-afternoon on a quiet, unmade road. But after five – or ten – or seven (time loses all significance under such circumstances) minutes, I begin to yell.

At first an informal, undemanding, 'Hello?'

Hello? Hello? Anyone? Hello? Hello?

Eventually a less formal, more desperate, 'Help!'

Help! Help! Help me! Hello? Help! I'm stuck! Is there anyone there? Hello? Hello?

HELLO? HELLO? HELLO?

Oh my bladder, my poor bladder with the gate cutting into it! The chafing. The mortification! The redness of face. The nausea. Hands scrabbling. Feet kicking.

Aaaargh!

I am wailing. I can hear myself. A little, poignant wail. How long has it been now? The wail appears to be coming from the other side of the gate. Although my head is here. And my mouth. How odd! Could it be the cat mewing?

79

In my mind I am singing that silly song by Bananarama. The chorus goes *'Robert De Niro's waiting, talking Italian – talking Ital-i-an. Robert De Niro's waiting, talk-king It-al-lian!'*

I hang in silence for a while, bemused. Singing in my head. I yell for help only every minute or so to preserve my voice for the long haul.

Help!

Help!

Help!

I might be here all afternoon.

In fact I must've yelled this strange word (help – such a strange word! And the more I yell it, the stranger it seems; the hoarser, the darker, the more absurd and despairing) several hundred times when … now this is odd (because my head is hung forward – the blood pounding in my ears, I am almost faint – almost fainting) … I hear sudden footsteps on the gravel and something that seems like a human voice but all muffled and jumbled: like *Aow-aow-aow-aow wah!*

So curious!

Then comes a powerful smell of clementines (I'm not making this up!). An attempt to open the gate. A tentative yank on my foot, a hand on my bottom …

Oi!

And then, *pow!*

The bow on my trousers is untied (how'd he/she/it do that?) and before I know better (or am able to ready/steady/adjust myself) I'm tumbling forward over the gate and landing – *Crump!* (trouserless!) – on my hand/elbow/face/head/back *ow!* on the gravel *ow!* path *ow!* to the other side.

I lie for a few seconds, breathless and winded. *Aow-aow aow-aow?* the strange voice asks, evidently concerned, trying the gate again.

I slowly sit up. Anything broken? Not sure. What I *do* know is that several pieces of gravel are embedded in my forehead.

My legs feel okay … and … oooh … my spine … but my …
ow! … my right thumb is hanging loose.

I've dislocated it! I've dislocated my thumb! Just look at
that! How perfectly ghastly!

'*Oy vey, bubbellah! Ve Gates?* Vat in God's good name are
you doing vith yourself down zere?'
Shimmy appears at the back door with his typical, slapstick
timing.
'I've dislocated my thumb, *Tatteh*!' I wail, holding it out to
him.
'Zat'll have to wait, *Nebekh*!' Shimmy interrupts. 'We got us
bigger fish to fry here. Look at your poor dad! I'm *plotzing*!
Zat damn dog has had hisself another heart attack! Za *putz* is
blocking the front door! I called you a cab already. You gotta
take him to the vet's.'

As Shimmy is speaking I hear footsteps rapidly retreating in
the gravel on the other side of the gate. I try to stand up, but
it takes me slightly longer to find my feet than I'd anticipated.

'Call the vet *out*, Tatteh!' I'm grumbling. 'How're we meant
to lift him into a cab? He's huge. I've dislocated my thumb!
Look! I've got bits of gravel stuck in my forehead!'
'You crazy?!' Shimmy exclaims. 'You know how much zey
charge to call zem out?! It's a disgrace! Be serious, *meine*
Carla! Get inside! Put your trousers on! We gotta do him a
heart massage! *Shlof gikher, men darf di ki kishn*, girl! Stop
your *shmying* about!'

I gaze at him, disbelieving.
'Sleep faster, *bubbellah*,' he repeats, sharply, as a concession
(of sorts), but in English this time. 'We need za pillows!'
Oh – thanks so much for the translation, *Tatteh*.

I click my thumb back into position (gritting my teeth),
grab my trousers with my good hand and follow him inside,
quietly marvelling at his apparently effortless recourse to
poetic sarcasm.

———

11

Mr Clifford Bickerton

I really don't understand why I'm becoming a part of this story. It's not that I'm angry about it, as such, or resentful. But where's the need? I ask this in all sincerity. Because it's obvious (predictable! Even to a registered thicko like me!) how this thing is going to pan out. It's all about them, isn't it? All about Carla and Franklin D.; Hahn and Huff. They're the perfect little double-act. *She* says, then *he* says. Like a relaxing game of lawn tennis. *Phut! – boiiing! – phut!* Polite outbreak of applause. Yawn (that's me yawning. It's a nervous yawn. A defeated yawn. The kind of yawn produced by a sheepdog when you tie it up to its kennel with a length of rope in the heart of winter just as it's starting to sleet).

So what are the actual mechanics of this thing (Yup – *mechanics*. Trust me to get all hot under the collar about the technical stuff!)? I mean how exactly am I meant to … to *fit* into this set-up? Where did I *ever* fit come to that? I'm just way too … too big and awkward and … and *hairy* to seamlessly slot in. Too home-grown, too 'rustic'. Ah, stupid, giant, callus-handed old Rusty – reliable, practical old Rusty – with his pathetic, unrequited crush, his over-long engagement, his over-tight sodding jumper … Soppy old Rusty. An all-round bad fit. A poor fit. The spanner in the works. The hole in the elbow. The tear in the seat. The pesky stone in the lace-up boot.

Perhaps I'll be involved in an accident at work at an especially critical moment in the plot (electrocuted by a malfunctioning school heater – their regular man, the caretaker, is off on a one-day training course *in modern gas-fired central heating systems!*), or get tragically drowned on duty with the lifeboat while saving the crew of a sinking trawler. Yes. I quite fancy that idea. Rusty Bickerton: Mr Brave but Mr Dispensable. A tragic afterthought dreamed up by the mean cow of an Author to add that tiny bit of extra depth, a light gloss of polish – a nice, reliable pinch of snuff (where's the tissue? Eh?! Use your sleeve! That's what Rusty would've done, God bless the poor old bugger! RIP etc.) to the 'main', the important, the real, the actual-grown-up-three-dimensional relationship.

Great.

I mean is that *honestly* the best I can hope for? To be the harmless blameless idiot caught totally unawares in the background of a dramatic photograph of an awful car crash (quietly inspecting the times on a vandalized bus shelter)? Face slightly blurry. Right ear, arm, shoulder ruthlessly cut out. Or the nervous man adjusting his comb-over in a high wind just behind the pretty, buxom woman who is laughing and letting go of a large bunch of red balloons after winning £1,000 in a charity prize draw?

Am I just a little bit of local colour? Is that really the sum of it? Although now I come to think about it, you've already got Mrs Barrow (with her nineteenth-century ways, her housecoat and her – uh, sorry – totally unconvincing Sussex accent) to tick that particular box.

Perhaps I'm suddenly being shuffled into focus to offer a useful – but boring – 'sense of perspective'? An 'outsider view'? Perhaps I'm simply serving as a manly foil – a handy, helpful, humble, *practical* contrast – to the clever but mysterious and (let's face it) slightly uptight and poncy Mr Franklin D. Huff? Fine. *Fine.* Whatever you like. However you want to play it. I might grumble (I *likes* a bit of a grumble, me), but I can't really be bothered getting all fired up about it now. Just so long as I'm back home before milking. I'll grit my teeth and I'll get on with it. Same as I always do.

Although … Although (while I've got your attention – have I got it? Hello? Oh. Yes. Hello) what about that poor parrot? Baldie? Baldo? How's he/she fit into this mess? What did that blessed parrot ever do to anybody? Doesn't seem right – fair – to have his/her/our innermost thoughts – our private feelings and ideas (uninspiring as they most certainly are) – casually picked over (exploited, let's make no bones about it) for the sake of a little light relief.

I remember in RE classes at school (bear with me for a minute) being taught the biblical parable of the 'talents' and thinking, If this parable expresses the moral, emotional and philosophical aspirations of the One, True Religion then there's something badly wrong with it – something horribly … I don't know … *cynical* (I was a precocious boy. Grew out of it soon enough, though). For those of you who don't recall, the parable involves a series of servants being given 'talents' (some kind of coin, I suppose) by their cruel master before he goes away on a long voyage. The servant given the most talents (the most – *ahem* – 'talented' servant) invests them well and doubles his money (slave trade? Opium poppies? Tobacco industry? Who knows?). When the master returns he is naturally delighted by the servant's achievements and the servant is justly rewarded (several rhino horns. A giant, ivory dildo. Something grand and extravagant along those lines). Then there is the servant who has been given *two* talents. Like the four talent servant he doubles his money (slaughtering dolphins, skinning minks) and the master is delighted with him (warm smile, slightly intimidating wink, soft pat on the buttock …).

Finally there's the servant who is given only one talent. This servant is not as clever or as successful as the other servants (one talent, and we don't even know what that talent is. I'm guessing juggling, or unicycling – reading tarot, badly), and he is rightly anxious about stuffing up (the ire of the cruel master might be too much to bear!) so he takes his one talent and he buries it in a large hole in the ground to ensure that it isn't lost or stolen. When the master returns, he promptly digs it up again and hands it over to him (slightly muddy, but still intact).

Is the master happy to get the talent back? Is he heck! The master (fresh from those three, fine weeks in Magaluf) is absolutely bloody *filthy* that the most idiotic of his servants has done so little with his pathetic one talent (gurning. Or possibly the ability to place his leg behind his head. He's oddly flexible).

'Why didn't you just give it to the bankers, you foolish man,' he demands, 'and earn me some paltry interest at the very least?' Of course this is the moment at which that poor, long downtrodden (but basically ignorant) servant can finally take the opportunity to tell his master that all the local banks have been investing heavily in companies supporting child labour (chimney sweeps! That's right! Send the little blighters up those chimneys! Let 'em earn their keep!) and so he (quite naturally, quite rightly) felt compelled to take a passionate stand against it. Yes. That would've been very brave, very principled of him (telling his master *and* the stand). But then could the master be expected to *listen* to his mumbled excuses? Nah! Of course he couldn't! He's just a *servant* – an untalented servant! Why would the master be remotely interested in issues of racial, social or gender equality? Forget it! He isn't. So the servant is bawled at, publicly humiliated and unceremoniously cast out.

'To him that has plenty more shall be given,' the parable ends, 'to him that has nothing, even that will be taken away from him.' (Sarcastic, partial drum roll.)

So there you have it: my pathetic little life in two short sentences. And the worst part? I knew, I just *sensed*, even as a small, snotty, scab-knee-and-elbowed youth, that this would all turn out to be completely true; that I would – of *course* I would! – find myself at the thin end of this parabolical wedge.

Looking back (a great hobby of mine) I can clearly deduce that it was at this precise moment (the reading of the talent parable – pay attention) that I finally lost all sympathy with the Judeo-Christian tradition. There have been others since (other moments, other losses) still more painful. But then that's … Well.

Good. Okay. So I'm not entirely sure why I bored you rigid with that anecdote. I suppose it was a toss-up between this brief Bible-study session or an in-depth breakdown of the journey from Chick Hill to Toot Rock undertaken in a twelve-year-old Ford Transit with no side door, dodgy transmission and a malfunctioning water pump.

Because these are the manifold riches of my life, ladies and gentlemen (the boring parable, the crappy van). No sudden landslips or obscure collections of Soviet memorabilia here, no ancient beefs with the CIA or complex issues of avian gender orientation. None of that. Just practical, gormless old Rusty. Mr Can-do. Mr Happy to Oblige. Mr That's Absolutely Fine, Mrs Barrow, Just Point Me in the Right Direction and I'll Get On With It, Shall I?

'That's fine. Just point me in the right direction and I'll get on with it, Mrs Barrow,' I tell her. Mrs Barrow has kindly provided me with a list. At the top is 'porch bulb' (in all honesty I think she could've handled most of these herself – what am I? Her drudge? Short answers on a postcard, please), then there's 'dispose of shark', then there's 'rabbit?' (her question mark), then 'bin', then, finally, 'bathroom window. Putty?' (putty underlined, twice).

Of course as soon as Mrs Barrow describes the general scenario (rotting sand shark under the bed?!) I am 100 per cent convinced that the salmon-pink paws of Miss Carla Hahn are all over this 'mysterious and completely unprovoked attack'. In truth I think Mrs Barrow suspects as much herself, but worker/employer loyalty (and Mr Huff availing himself of the nearby bathroom) prevents her from confiding in me. All credit to her for that. Although there is a brief exchange of significant looks. Yes. And a slightly raised, under-plucked eyebrow. And she is very – *very* – keen to stop the 'highly offended' ('hurt', 'violated!': *his* words) Mr Franklin D. from getting the local police involved (but what else might you expect from the wife of the local poacher? Eh?).

I know all the signs, though. In fact I'm so certain of Carla's involvement that I promptly head over to an old brass coal-scuttle stored just inside the entrance to the bomb shelter (there is a bomb shelter behind the house – a drab, claustrophobic concrete shed-like thing with a basement nobody ever goes into. Did anyone bother mentioning this before? Nah. Probably not) and I retrieve the porch bulb from this old favourite Carla hidey-hole.

I am smiling to myself (even allowing myself a gentle tut) and straightening up when – Oh bugger! – I see Mr Franklin D. Huff standing behind me, arms crossed, braces dangling ('At ease, *Suh!*'), watching me from the back with a look full of what I can only call 'deep misgivings'.

Sorry if there is something grammatically awry with that sentence. But I think you get what I mean. I respond with my broadest hayseed's smile. This smile is doubly effective because of a missing canine (front top left).
'Hello, Massa. I just be doin' my work here, Massa. No need for the likes of you to be troubling yourself on my account, Massa.'
(Touch brim of pretend flat cap.)

I didn't actually speak that out loud, I just compressed it into a slight bending of the knee and the broad smile, obviously. Especially the smile. Although there's an extra (bonus!) atmosphere of 'I might look like a moron – I *am* a moron – but if you mess about with my Carla – trifle with her – I'm going to … well …'

What might I do?

Bleat like a lamb?

Burst into tears?

Absolutely bloody nothing, same as always?

Oh God, I just had this … this horrible … this shadow-falling-across-my-grave feeling. An icy chill in my … A moment of …

She's going to make me stand up to him, isn't she? The cow Author. She's going to make me act totally out of character – rise to the occasion, give the smug, 'cosmopolitan' arsehole what for – and then quickly kill me off. But it'll be something mundane that does me in – a nosebleed or an infected toenail. Or something completely stupid and embarrassing like … like being squashed under a tractor after diving to save a duckling. Swerving to avoid a weasel and driving off a cliff.

I know that's what she's planning.

I suppose I should just be grateful that the over-tight jumper didn't prove to be my undoing (Ch. 7? Ch. 8?). Although I'm not sure how that would've been managed, technically (I'm always interested in the technical side of things. This isn't much of a virtue in your average romantic hero, I realize. 'Sorry to interrupt you, Miss Eyre, but the axle on your carriage has noticeable signs of wear …'). To be perfectly frank, it doesn't have all that much credibility as an idea (dispatched by an over-tight jumper?!). I mean this is only my second chapter! It's early days yet. To kill me with a lethal piece of knitwear after – how many? – three pages? That'd be so … so clumsy, so amateur. The critics'd have a field day! Although she killed someone in another novel (forget the name of it, offhand) with a frozen, miniature butter pat and then she won a bloody prize. A prize! A big money prize!

What were they thinking?!

In fact there was this very sweet man in her last novel – kind and gentle, a bit of a wimp; rather like me, I suppose (sound the alarm bells!!) – who she hit with a sudden brain haemorrhage just when everything had finally started to work out for him. I don't remember his name or all the circumstances exactly. But she's probably planning something similar for me now. *Right now.*

What a nightmare. What an awful, bloody nightmare.

'... store your bulbs.'

Franklin D. is speaking but I miss the gist of it worrying about all this other crap. There was one character who fed his fingers to an owl and then walked in front of a bus. Or a lorry. But he was the hero. And I don't know if he died or not. I think she left it open so that if the book was successful she could write a follow-up. But the thing bombed.

Ha!

Although – *damn!* – none of this works, logically – logi*sti*cally (Oh great, Mr Technical!). Because I'm thinking these thoughts in October 1984 and she only started writing seriously in 1987 on a student trip to Ireland while volunteering for the Council for the Status of Women. She wrote a wretched piece of teen fiction during that interlude called 'The Perverse Yellow Flower'. It was inspired by three paintings of Christ she saw in a shop window in Windsor and a conversation she had while she was looking at them with a man called Marcus who wanted to make her join a weird cult called Sabud.

What?!

Hang on a second ...

Where the *heck* did all that come from? How could I ...? I ... I just *can't* be having these thoughts right now, about her other books and her sadistic urges and her ... I dunno. It just doesn't make any sense. It's ... it's unnatural, it's *supernatural.*

'... store your bulbs.'

Argh. Am I just sabotaging myself again? Same as I always do? *Am* I? Eh? Mr Bickerton, will you sign on the dotted line

for your regular delivery of a truck-load of self-pity, please?
Oh you've lost your pen. *And* your pencil. Boo-hoo-*hoo*.

There's nothing positive or clever or rational about it,
either, is there? I *know* that. I'm simply *stewing* in all this stuff
– all these regrets. I really need to just try and … I dunno.
Grow a set. Stop over-thinking. Stop making everything twice
as complicated as it needs to be. Heroes don't dither, do they?
Do they? No. Heroes aren't ditherers.
Uh. Sorry. Could you just feed me that line again, please?

'Well that's a very strange place to store your bulbs!'
Uh … Okay. Uh … I already did the smile, didn't I? The
hayseed's goofy smile (my staple)? So how about I just repeat
what he said back to him and then work the rest out from
there?

'A *very* strange place to store your bulbs. Yes. Very strange
indeed. You must be Mr Huff. You were holed up in the
bathroom when I first arrived. I'm Clifford. Clifford
Bickerton. People call me Rusty.'
We shake hands.

'Did you see the shark?' Mr Huff asks, following me over
to the front porch where I quickly re-fit the bulb. 'Yup.' I nod
(Don't give anything away, Clifford!).
'Very convenient being so tall,' Mr Huff observes.
'Great for replacing bulbs,' I affirm, 'but not so great in other
arenas. It's hard to cram myself inside certain models of car.'
Mr Huff nods.
'I sometimes break antique furniture.'
Mr Huff nods again.
'And I play havoc with sofa and bed springs.'

Mr Huff considers this, scowling.
'And everything's dusty.'
Mr Huff looks quizzical.
'I've noticed how women never dust above their own height.
Up here I find everything's dusty. It's sad. I've often thought
how there's something deeply unloved about this altitude.'

91

Mr Huff's eyes de-focus. I am boring him already.

'I mean how are we going to dispose of it,' he wonders, 'with the bin stuck up on the Look Out?'

'Follow me,' I say, and walk around, through the little allotment (Ye Gods! He obviously hasn't fed the badgers) to the front porch where the shark currently abides. I pick it up by the tail, take two steps forward and toss it over the cliff into the mess of rocky gorse below.

'Bloody hell!'

Mr Huff is scandalized.

'Something's bound to eat it eventually.' I shrug. 'I'll go and fetch you that bin now, eh?'

'Will you climb up the little ladder?' Mr Huff is intrigued. 'It seemed a rather precarious arrangement when I went up there the other day.'

'The ladder's not a good option,' I inform him. 'The metal joists are corroded. It has a history of suddenly shearing off – falling out of the wall ...'

Mr Huff blanches.

'But there's a series of thick planks hidden in some nearby bushes,' I add, trying to keep the atmosphere positive, 'and a quantity of corrugated iron. We generally construct a sloping walkway from the edge of the far end of the rock to the roof. It's not especially stable ...'

'We?' Mr Huff asks.

'Local folk,' I say, casually.

I stride out and Mr Huff follows. We retrieve the bin in no time. When we return we find a woman in the garden accompanied by two large red setters, tending the little girl's shrine.

Mr Huff is not best pleased by her sudden arrival. One could almost go so far as to say that he is infuriated by it, and doubly so when one of the dogs menaces him as he opens the gate.

'Do you know this person?' he asks, stopping by the gate as I position the bin in its regular place, scowling.

'Uh … no. But there's a little gang of them,' I say. 'Good, decent Catholic women in the main. Locals for the most part. They aren't too much of a problem. It's the other group – the Romanies – you'll need to keep an eye out for. They come up here in their vans and block off the roadway. Infuriates the people in the Coastguards' Cottages, it does. Causes no end of trouble.'

'But this is trespass, surely?' Mr Huff persists.

'If you try and stop them you'll only make them more determined.' I grin.

'Faith is like bindweed,' Mr Huff snarls, 'an unremarkable enough plant, but give it any kind of leeway and you'll find it pushing its fragile green shoots through thick inches of brickwork.'

'They have Carla's blessing.' I shrug, moving past him.

'Yes. Miss Hahn said as much in her Welcome Pack,' Mr Huff grumbles, following. At the mention of Carla's name he seems profoundly demoralized. I glance back at him as we circumnavigate the allotment to avoid the dogs. He looks ragged. I notice the pinkness of his irises, the bags under his eyes.

'No point railing against it,' I console him (emboldened by the Welcome Pack comment). 'It's going to be a major part of the plot at some point, I suppose.'

'Sorry?' Mr Huff looks confused.

'The plot. The story,' I repeat, 'you know …' I blithely indicate towards the little shrine. 'Orla Nor Cleary. The truth behind what really happened back then. The subject of your book – *the* book. Everything else – the parrot, the landslip, *this* – it's all just incidental detail, surely? Just filler. I mean I can't speak for you, obviously, but I know *I'm* totally insignificant – just a minor character, a handy plot device. That's it.'

Still nothing from Mr Huff, but it's almost as if he starts to … to *fade*.

'I'm very tired,' he says, flickering. Or is it me that's flickering? It's hard to tell.

'Mrs Barrow mentioned a rabbit?' I quickly change the subject.

'Rabbit?' He instantly jumps back into sharp relief.

'Mrs Barrow said you were building it a hutch.'

'Yes,' he sighs, 'I suppose I am.'

'It might be worth popping down to see Shimmy, Carla's dad,' I suggest. 'His wife – Else, Carla's mother – used to keep rabbits when Carla was a kid. She bred some kind of German lop. Huge beasts, they were. They ate them. After the war …'

Mr Huff is staring at me with a strange look on his face. You might almost call it a … a *haunted* look.

'And they kept rescue dachshunds,' I blather on. 'She had about twelve of them, in kennels. It was a long time ago now, obviously. But he's a great hoarder. He might still have something useful tucked away in one of his sheds.'

Mr Huff nods, but he doesn't look especially taken by the idea.

'I mean there's no harm in asking,' I persist.

'It's just that my … my wife ran over his cat …' he starts off, then he frowns. 'Although she's not … she's not … she's not … not actually my …'

He shakes his head and his mouth suddenly contracts. He stops walking as we reach the back balcony, plops himself down on to the bench and covers his lean face with his skinny hands.

'It's all …' he sniffs, trying to retain some vague hold on his dignity (failing dismally), '… all very confused … *confusing*.'

'Can I …? Uh … Would you like me to …?' I don't even know what I'm suggesting I should do. Leave? Spontaneously combust? Gently evaporate? Quietly hang myself? (Oh she'd like that, wouldn't she?! The cow Author? Well then I most definitely *won't* be – hanging myself, I mean. No. I won't be hanging myself. I'm far too *tall* to be hanging myself, for one thing. It'd be so difficult to *arrange*. Although there's always the barn back on the farm, I suppose. Not that I've got any rope strong enough to ... uh ... aside from the blue nylon stuff Eddie's been using to tether the ...

What?!

No!

Why am I thinking like this?! I've never had these kinds of thoughts before – suicidal thoughts. And if I *was* going to kill myself it wouldn't be by rope, it'd be sat quietly in the van with a grand view below me, up near the Country Park, maybe, engine running, blocked exhaust ... Although with all that rust and the missing door there's not much chance ...

No!

I'm doing it again! She's got me doing it again! I *won't* be killing myself! I feel no urge to kill myself! None! I'm very much *here* – larger than life. I am *substantially* here. And I'm not going down without a fight, madam, you can be bloody sure of that! *Bloody* sure!

Good.)

I turn and take in the view. The sea view. This is the most beautiful view in all the world. Just scrubland and then sea. Well, the Channel, really. Just the bit of rough scrub, the ribbon of Sea Road following the sea wall, the pebble beach, the sea, the clouds, the sky.

'Yes. No. My wife died,' he blurts out (how much time has passed? Loads? None?). 'Very suddenly. Three days ago. I'm just ...'

'Sorry?' I turn, surprised (in truth I'd almost forgotten he was there).

'My wife,' he repeats, 'died. Dead. She ...'

I must look shocked – slightly disbelieving. Embarrassed. I mean this started out as a conversation about hutches – didn't it? Didn't it? About rabbits?

'Not the cat woman,' he commences, waving his hand about. 'She wasn't my wife. I was … it's complicated. There's a woman called … You might have heard of … she's called Kimberly. Kimberly Couzens. She's a photographer. We were married. She had the affair with … with *him* … you know. Bran. She was burned. In the explosion – the car – when he …'

'Oh … Oh *wow*,' I stutter, finally making the connection. 'The Canadian? The photographer? She was your *wife?*'

'Yes. Yes. I'm here for her.' He nods, pathetically grateful to be understood. 'I came for her. And I'm broke. Completely broke. I agreed to write the book as a sort of … a sort of favour. I'm not sure how it … I mean I'm not really sure … And then … then she just died. I mean she's been disabled for years – with the burns being so severe … But this was something so sudden … so … so *random*, something to do with a tooth. A *tooth*! I've not eaten in four days. I've not … I've not told anyone … I'm just … The flight couldn't be changed. I can't go back for the funeral. Her mother has dementia. It's been … then the shark … the *flies*. It's been … I've been …'

Still the arm waving.

'… really … really *struggling*,' he finishes off, his voice cracking.

I don't know what to say.

'I don't know what to say,' I say.

I'm furious. In fact, I'm steaming. I can't believe the cow Author has sprung this on me. What a cow. What a *cow*.

I turn and inhale the view again. I refuse, no, no, I *won't* be drawn into this bloody farrago! And I'm angry that I thought I had it all down pat … this … this situation … the set-up … the plot … but now to find out that my knowledge has been

… well, just selective … compromised. *He was married to the photographer!* Why didn't I know that?! I mean if I knew about the *parrot*. Why'd I know about the sodding parrot – all about it! – but nothing about this?

I breathe in deeply and force myself to enjoy the view. The view is still here. The view is still beautiful.
Behind me I hear him sobbing.
Oh God, why? *Why?*

'Well, you still need a hutch,' I maintain. Still looking at the view. Still feeding off the view. I really love this view. I could happily die looking at this view.
'Yes,' he sniffs.

No more thoughts about dying. I reach into my pocket.
'Tangerine?'
I turn and offer it to him.
'Thanks.'
He accepts the tangerine.

'I don't think I actually met her,' I say. 'Your wife. The photographer. But I did see her around and about the place. On the beach with her camera photographing everything …'

He glances up, sharply. 'You were here back then?'
'I'm always here.' I nod. 'That's me. A part of the landscape – a blot on the landscape. In fact I was … uh … Carla and I were …' I shrug.
'Oh. *Oh*, really?'
Mr Huff looks slightly surprised. 'So you were … Oh. So you were here – resident – when everything uh …?' He scowls. 'But why didn't I already know that?'
I shrug (cow Author not doing her job, I suppose).

'That's never been mentioned,' Mr Huff persists, 'I mean there isn't any physical evidence, any testimony … and documentary evidence in all of the … all of the …'

He starts feeling for his pockets (grief briefly forgotten) as if the information relating to my early life in Pett Level might be miraculously contained therein.

Oh, here it is – here's the little bit of paper all about what an insignificant lump of crap you are (cheerfully holds out tiny till receipt with hardly anything printed on it).

'It's my size.' I shrug. 'I'm so huge that people kind of ... they pass me over. It's difficult to engage. They ignore me the way you'd ignore a giant bear.'

'You're the elephant in the room.' Mr Huff grins, weakly.

'Yes.'

'But how odd,' he repeats, shaking his head again, 'that Kimberly never mentioned you, never photographed you. She worked as a war photographer for several years. Her photographs were amazingly ... I don't know ... comprehensive, habitually *copious*, all-inclusive ...'

As he speaks I quietly remember Kimberly and her camera. On the beach, in the garden, the house. Yes. I remember the camera always snapping. I remember – countless times, *countless* times – being briefly blinded by the flash.

'I should go and take a quick peek at that bathroom window,' I say. There are dark feelings in my heart. That's the only way I can describe them – the feelings. Dark. I mean to be so easily ... so ... so routinely *ignored.*

Who's behind this I wonder? Who's at the back of this? Is it *her*? The Author? Has she gone back into the photographer's portfolio, the photographer's mind and just ... just silently *erased* ...?

Oh for heaven's sake!

Just fix the window, Rusty! Just go and fix the window!

I walk through the cottage to the bathroom (ducking to avoid the door lintels, the light fitments). When I get there I realize that I have no tools with me. The ceiling is very low. I can't straighten my neck. And there is a rabbit in the bath. A tiny rabbit. It has a very ... a very deep, a quiet, an almost ... a *mystical* quality about it.

Pink eyes. Pink nose.

I perch on the edge of the bath and I watch it. I look like I am communing with the rabbit (from the outside, in the uncut footage), and I am – but I am also hatching a plan. Yes. Me – I – Clifford Bickerton, Rusty Bickerton. I am hatching a plan. A secret plan. Which I won't divulge here, because it's a secret, obviously.

Every so often I think, Is this her? Is this *her* plan? Or is it me?

And then I expunge those thoughts (expunge? Is that a word I would use, naturally? Is it *my* word or is it ... Oh God, is it *her* word?). I stare at the little rabbit.

Hello, rabbit! It's me, Clifford, the Invisible Man!

The invisible man, eh? *Ha!* Well we'll see about that, shall we, my little pink-eyed friend, *hmmn?*

12

Mr Franklin D. Huff

It's because I'm so over-wound, so damn *tired*. I mean to be
… to find myself intent on building a rabbit cage (a rabbit
cage! A *rabbit* cage!) when I should actually be … I don't
know … arranging the flowers. She loved freesias, hyacinths,
old-variety pinks (those foul, dirty-looking ones), anything
aromatic, anything with a *scent* in other words.

Yes. I should be involved – on hand. Worrying about the
details. I should be selecting the coffin, bearing the coffin.
Choosing the music (something scruffy and pointless and
suitably inconclusive by The Band). I should be planning the
eulogy. Just being … being *there*. But instead I'm here. Here.
In this hell-hole with its maddeningly attractive English view
and its slightly broken-down, chaotic, self-satisfied, bohemian
… And the only solid food I've consumed in the past three
days (that I'm consciously aware of) is a tangerine. Or a
satsuma. Or a clementine.

I'm broke. *Broke!* Kim had promised to send me a cheque
just as soon as the advance came through …
Dammit!
And now she's … she'll be … for ever … indubitably …
incontrovertibly …
Ka-ka-ka-*put*.
Ker-*plunk*.
Doiiiing!

So I go over to Mr Hahn's cottage (it's only a short walk)
to enquire about the rabbit cage … A rabbit cage? This is

ridiculous! *Ridiculous!* And I am approaching the front door when I hear a kind of ... a little wail. A pathetic, little wail. A cat? An injured hedgehog? An amorous fox? So I jink left, to the side of the property, down a badly kept gravel path and I see ... I see ... How to put this politely? A bum in the air. High up. Halfway over a tall gate. Two slim legs kicking aimlessly.

Of course to free up my hands to help (of course – but *of course!*) I am obliged to fill my mouth with the rest of the tangerine – satsuma – clementine. But then I can't ... I can't communicate! Ridiculous! So I ... I kind of ... I pat the bottom gently, to alert it to my presence, move the bike (yes, there's a bike), try and grab the foot to ...

I know. Yes. I *do* know that it's Carla Hahn's foot (who else could it possibly belong to but she?). It is, isn't it? Yes. It is. It's her foot. And (for the record), one of her deck shoes is falling off, revealing an old sock with a giant hole in the heel (so unfeminine! So unedifying!). She kicks out this foot, emitting another curious little yelp. And I see that her awful trousers with the roped-up waist, or another pair just like them – equally unflattering – have become hooked over a little jutting piece of wood. The belt has become hooked, I mean, the rope belt. So I say ... I mean I'm *speaking*, although not especially *well* ... what with the half tangerine (all this is happening very quickly, much more rapidly than I could hope to describe it – a mere matter of seconds) ... I say, 'Brace yourself. I'm going to unhook your jeans from a little ... uh ...'

And I unhook them. In fact I untie them. And then she falls like a bag of potatoes, *out* of the trousers. She disappears from view. The heel of her old white plimsoll almost smacks me in the face.

Oh *balls!*

'Hello? Can you hear me? Are you all right?'

Short silence, followed by a door opening and someone speaking in a thick, German accent, followed by the gate-person, the fallen person (Miss Hahn) yowling plaintively, 'I've dislocated my thumb!'

I'm not sure why, exactly, but I suddenly think that this might be a good time to make myself scarce. I'm not ... I'm not running away, as such, no. I'm just not ... not *emotionally equipped* to engage with all this right now. I didn't ... I didn't *ask* for this to happen. I mean I should be planning a funeral, *attending* a funeral. And if not in *fact*, well, then at least in my fevered brain. The perfect funeral for Kimberly. A fantasy funeral for darling Kimberly, my recently deceased ...

I just don't need all this ... all this ... uh ...

When I return to the cottage (a little out of breath, slightly furtive, perhaps) I find the big man, Clifford Pemberton (Is it Pemberton?) sitting out front on the bench. He is deep in thought. He has the rabbit in his hand. It fits, in its entirety, into his giant palm.

'That was quick!' he remarks.

'Nobody home,' I lie.

'Oh. Well I had a thought while you were gone,' he says, pointing towards a partially dismantled chest of drawers which is lying on its back close by on the lawn. 'I found it in the shed,' he says. 'She was planning to chop it up for kindling – but in the meantime ...'

I go over to inspect it.

'We'll need some kind of ...'

'Already thought of that ...'

'Oh yes. Genius.'

Inside the upturned chest is the cover of an old sewing machine.

'It's a perfect retreat,' he says, 'there's a little hole in the front, the exact size he needs – custom made, almost! I filled the insides with straw. He'll need food and water then he's set up.

Obviously you'll want to bring him indoors at night or the badgers will suck his brains out.'

I wince. The badgers really are – they *really are* – the most awful blight.

'It's milking time,' Pemberton continues, in a loud voice (stiffly, awkwardly, almost as if delivering the lines of a bad play). He stands up. 'But before I head off ...'

He gives me an intense, one could almost call it a *meaningful* look.

'Is there a problem?' I ask. What an extraordinary man he is! So messy. Like he's been drawn with a broken brown crayon by a bored child with an excess of imagination.

'You made Carla cry on the beach the other day,' he tells me (very quickly, garbled, almost). As he speaks, I suddenly feel myself fading (or is it him? Is *he* fading?). Exhaustion. Lack of food, I suppose.

'I don't understand what happened there,' he continues (he almost looks fierce – so big, so decent, all that dark hair, the red beard), 'but I do know that in all likelihood it was Carla who left the shark under your bed. It's just ...' He shrugs.

There follows a period of what I can only describe as 'white noise', 'static', and the most I can decipher is 'Sword of Truth' and 'Web of Artifice'. He gives me a ten pound note and then passes me the rabbit.

'The cow will probably kill me now,' he says.

The cow? Sorry? The cow? Is he referring to Miss Hahn? Someone else? Mrs Barrow? His sister? His mother? Is this simply all about his being late for milking? For milking the cows? I wish I could ... but the sweep of noise ... like a giant ... a giant wave crashing. A Lear jet flying at low altitude. A malfunctioning washing machine perpetually stuck on its spin cycle rocking its way across the kitchen tiles.

Uh ...

What a strange man he is! Look at him! Look at his lips working! Like the mouthparts of a giant wasp – a bee – in astonishing close-up! So hairy – huge – confused ...

Bumbling! Yes. Intense! Certainly. Deluded? *Hmmn*. But he seems decent enough (journalist's first instinct. Gotta try and trust my initial gut ...), uh ...

Okay – okay, yes, the way he *immediately* knew where that missing bulb could be located. *Highly* suspicious. And the custom-made planks in the hedge by the Look Out? Strange. His desperate need to get shot of me for a while (Miss Hahn's mother and the giant, German rabbits? I know for a fact – a *fact*! – that rabbit isn't even *kosher*). Yup. He's got an agenda a mile wide, I'd have thought.

Did Miss Hahn ever actually date him? It seems an improbable union. And what about the signal lack of *any* documentary evidence (photographic, earlier testimonial etc.) to this effect? And the parrot? Which parrot? *Whose* parrot? What *is* he? Who *is* Clifford *né* Rusty Pemberton? What does he amount to, narratively? Is he a mere nothing? A nobody? Is he a missing link or a red herring? A loose cannon? A pointless distraction? A blind alley? A freak? A fanatic? A fantasist?

Because why would he be so determined to push Miss Hahn into the fray if he wasn't (all of the above – none of them)? By outright accusing her? Why would a friend – a protector – feel the urge to behave in that way? So disloyal – so ungentlemanly. I mean I won't pretend that I hadn't suspected her myself – before. But now? No. Now, she's the only person I *don't* suspect! Our dear Mr Pemberton on the other hand ... Oh-ho! With friends like these, Miss Hahn, who needs ...?

Perhaps I've been slightly rash in confiding in him? Should've kept up my guard. Stiff upper etc. Although if he's as strange and as skittish as he appears, then why would local people believe anything he says?

He prepares to leave.

Oh dear. Did I *really* make Miss Hahn cry the other day? On the beach?

We attempt to shake hands but this is rendered impossible by the ten pounds and the rabbit. So instead he kind of ... he sort of *curtseys.*

Once he's gone I sit down for a minute to try and gather my thoughts together. After about ten or so seconds the white noise diminishes. Well thank God for that! But then another sound neatly replaces it. Barking. Yes – barking! – followed by a series of profuse apologies. A woman's voice. Then Mr Pemberton – Rusty – saying, 'It's fine. It's absolutely fine. It isn't deep. I actually ... I ... I sort of *expected* it, to be perfectly honest.'

13

Miss Carla Hahn

Poor old Rogue is no more. Which is terribly sad. But worse still is the knowledge that I – yes, *me*! – am going to be chiefly responsible for burying the body. *Tatteh* is too busy focusing on the onerous task of preparing a brief funeral oration and gathering together Rogue's favourite toys to be buried alongside him (I note that several of these are items I have given to *Tatteh* myself – among them a Clarks' sandal, a Johnson's cashmere scarf and a little, plastic flamingo which I bought to commemorate the arrival of a lone bird of that species on Pett Pools in 1978, 1979 or some time thereabouts).

I have a fork and a spade, but the ground is pretty hard. And space is limited because numerous other dog corpses have been deposited here in years past. Upwards of thirty and counting, I'd have thought.

And Rogue was so huge! The sheer depth required to cover his bulk, and the terrible likelihood that if he isn't buried deep enough the foxes will dig him up again haunt me as I work. I have bound up the thumb which aches horribly. In fact I am unwinding my makeshift bandage (consisting of a mesh washing-up cloth) and attempting to reapply it when Clifford Bickerton comes charging into the garden.

'I saw your bike out front as I was driving past,' he puffs. 'Your dad says you dislocated your thumb.'

'Rogue had a heart attack,' I explain. 'I was climbing over the side gate and my pesky belt got snagged on a piece of wood ...'

Rusty takes off his work coat, folds it over his arm in order to put it down and grab the spade and commence digging, but as he does so a clementine (satsuma? Tangerine?) falls out of the pocket and rolls into my partly dug hole.

I stiffen.

'Then after I'd been hanging there a while,' I continue (more halting, now), 'some big goose ... some ... some Smart Alec happens along and ... and without warning ... they untied my trousers. I fell head first on to the gravel below. Dislocated my thumb. Then they buggered off.'

'Bloody hell!'

Rusty looks shocked, then ruminative (not quite the reaction I'd have expected). His eyes briefly de-focus.

I reach down and retrieve the satsuma, once again remembering – quite clearly – that very strong smell of tangerine. Or clementine. Or satsuma. From earlier. I proffer him the fruit.

'Keep it,' he suggests, 'I've been eating the bloody things all morning. Mum bought a giant sack of them for the B&B-ers. I've actually got a little ulcer on my tongue.'

As he speaks, I notice a patch of dried blood on his forearm.

'What happened to your arm?' I ask.

'Uh ... I was bitten by a dog.' He scowls. 'Up at Mulberry. A setter. It belonged to some woman who was tending the girl's shrine.'

'What were you doing up at the cottage?' I ask, scowling.

'Uh ...'

Again the uncertainty. 'Uh ... Mrs Barrow called me.'

He starts to dig, chin burrowing into his breastbone, almost ashamedly.

'Why?' I wonder.

'Because ...'

As he begins to respond (still digging) a hedge-cutter roars into life in a neighbouring garden.

'Sorry?' I place a hand to my ear.

'Mr Huff's wife died,' he roars, just as the hedge-cutter is turned off again.

'What?' I take a small step back, blasted (in two senses) by this news.

He continues digging but offers no further information.

'When did she die?' I ask, shocked. Oh Please God Let It Be Today! Let It Be Yesterday!

'About three or four days ago.'

I do the sums. My heart plummets. He continues to dig.

'But then why would Mrs Barrow ...?' I persist, struggling to piece the thing together to my complete satisfaction.

'I don't know,' he says, still digging. 'I don't think she wanted to bother you. After the landslip and everything. The underlying tensions with Mr Huff ...'

'But then why ... why would she call *you* of all people?' I finish off. I mean why wouldn't she just call *Mr* Barrow? Is Clifford Bickerton now part of some new, UN-sponsored Pett Level Peace Initiative I know nothing about?

'To help,' he says (as if this is the most obvious thing in all the world).

'With what?' I ask.

'A missing bulb.' He shrugs. 'A broken window. The rabbit hutch.'

'Rabbit?' I echo.

He nods. He digs. I watch, rotating my sore thumb, thinking about Mr Huff. Thinking about his dead wife. At the same time, I try and imagine Clifford Bickerton unfastening my trousers and letting me drop like that. Making those weird noises. Running off. No. No! I just *can't*. I can't imagine it.

Clifford pauses for a moment to catch his breath. 'He was married to that photographer,' he explains, 'the one who ... the one who got burned.'

'Sorry?'

'The photographer. His wife. Kimberly someone. He's her husband. Although I don't think ...'

'Kimberly Couzens?' I gape. 'Are you sure about that?'

He nods.

A short silence follows.

'But why wouldn't he have ...? Kimberly Couzens? Mr Huff was *married* to Kimberly Couzens? He was the ... the *husband* of ...?'

'Yup. And – for the record – it was probably him ...' he adds (just at the precise moment that damn hedge-cutter starts up again).

'What?' I yell.

'The gate. Mr *Huff*. Who ran off. I sent him down here earlier to see if your dad had a spare hutch.'

'Sorry? You ... you actually think ...?' I scowl, trying to work out if I've heard him correctly. 'You actually think it was ... that *Mr Huff* dislocated my thumb?' I yell.

He nods, fiercely. He gestures towards the hedge-cutter.

'There aren't any hedges!' he yells.

'Sorry?'

'No hedges!' he yells. 'I can see. From up here. There aren't any. Only fences. It's a farce. This is all *her*. It's just so ...'

He gesticulates towards the fences, then towards his head in an uncharacteristic gesture of 'has the world finally gone mad?' or possibly, 'Crazy, eh?'

'... so *embarrassing*!' he concludes. 'I mean how *stupid* does she think we all are?'

As Clifford completes his little diatribe, he steps back slightly (recoiling with the sheer force of its delivery, I suppose) into a small heap of soil and almost loses his balance. I grab his arm to steady him (can't have him collapsing backwards into that shallow hole!), but in the act of grabbing him (and him automatically steadying himself), he somehow manages to let go of the fork he's holding (I could've sworn it was a spade – that he was holding a spade) and the thing drops from some height, straight down on to his foot and pierces his leather boot (his old cherry-coloured Doc Martens).

The hedge-cutter falls silent (in awe, almost – in shock) at that exact same instant. We both stare down at his foot, aghast.

'Oh God,' I murmur.

'It's okay,' he insists, slightly tentative, not moving, still just looking. 'It's only a warning this time. I don't think it's actually … uh … actually … uh … pierced the flesh.'

He gingerly pulls the fork out. There are three clean holes in the leather. I fall to my knees and start untying his laces as he lowers himself down – white as a sheet – into a sitting position. We carefully remove the boot together. His socks are also pierced! But no blood, as yet. I gently remove the sock. We inspect the foot together. Nothing. Nope … Nothing! Not a scratch on his skin! The prongs have somehow contrived to fall in between his toes!

I am in awe. I am flabbergasted. 'You were so lucky,' I mutter. 'That was just so … so … so incredibly *lucky*.'
And as the last 'lucky' is leaving my lips, a couple of swans come flapping across the line of back fences and swoop overhead (that extraordinary, gasping-pounding-wheezing sound the wings make! The huge, ungainly grandeur of the bird itself with its utterly un-aerodynamic-seeming, almost comically distended neck! So big! So white! So rhythmical! So close! The strangely holy-spotless-miraculousness of it all!) and a giant bird poo hits him on the head.
Whap!

Giant! A *giant poo*! Square on the head! As he quietly sits there! In one sock! With his bizarrely undamaged foot!

I am still holding the satsuma – tangerine – clementine in my one hand. His sock is in the other. I look down at these two objects and something strengthens within me (my nerve? My resolve?).

'I must go and see Mr Huff!' I announce, breathlessly. 'I *must* go. Right now. This very instant. Yes.'

Then I pass him his sock, with my heart … I don't know … my heart kind of … sort of … almost … Oh God … *exploding* in my chest, and I clamber to my feet and run – run like the bloody clappers – into the house.

14

Teobaldo

Baldo! Baldo! Baldo! Baldo! WAH!
WAH!
Yay!
[*Shrill whistle.*]
Pretty boy!
Bob! Bob! Bow!
Bob! Bob! Bow!
Yay!
[*Shrill whistle.*]
Pretty boy!
Bow!
Happy!
Bow!
   Yay!
Look! *Look!*
Jingle 'bell'!
[*Baldo jingles his bell.*]
Tra-lah!
Baldo jingle 'bell'!
Yay!
H-A-P-P-Y!
H-A-P-P-Y!
Jingle!
[*Another jingle.*]
   Look! Look! *Look!*
See? *See?*

Bounce! Bounce!
'Sun' in 'cage'!
Yay!
'Sun' in 'cage'!
Yay!
Bask in 'sun'!
Joy!
Preen in 'sun'!
Joy!
R-r-r-r-r-uffle feathers!
Brreuuagh!
Blink! Blink in 'sun'!
Bask in 'sun'!
Preen in 'sun'!
Happy! Happy! Happy 'sun'!
      Rock, rock, rock.
Happy!
Yawn.
[*One eye closed.*]
Bird 'smile'.
[*Other eye closed.*]
Bird 'smile'.
Aaaah!
Happy moment!

Silence.

  Hup! Eh? *Whassat?*
[*Eyes fly open.*]
Alarm!
Eh?
[*Twizzle head.*]
Whassat?!
Eh?
Where'd 'sun' go?

Where'd 'sun' …?
  Urgh!
It's Bitch! Bitch is blocking 'sun'!
Raaaughh!
Baldo *rage*!
Bitch is blocking 'sun'!
Raaaughh!
[*Bounce!*]
Double rage!
  Eh?
Whassat?
[*Bounce! Bounce! Bounce! Bounce!*]

'*** *** * ****** *** **** ** *****, Baldo? Hmmn?
** ** * ****** *** **** ** ***** *** ***, ** ****?
***** * ***** *** ******** *** ***, ** ***?'

['*Are you a little bit warm in there, Baldo? Hmmn?*
Is it a little bit warm in there for you, my love?
Shall I close the curtains for you, my boy?]

Eh?
Eh?!
What Bitch do?
What Bitch done?
Where 'sun' go?
Baldo want 'sun'!
BALDO WANT… WANT …
BALDO WANT SSSSS … HAPPY!
AAARRGH!
Baldo RAGE!
  Why no 'sun'? Eh?
Where Bitch …?
[*Bounce! Bounce! Bounce! Bounce!*]
Eh?

[*Anxious head tip.*]
WAH!
WAH!
[*Bounce! Bounce! Bounce! Bounce!*]

Brief pause.

Hmmn. Why Bitch move 'table'?
What Bitch do?
Brreeeuugh!
[*Feather ruffle.*]
[*Disquiet.*]
Why Bitch move 'table'?
Baldo *hates* change!
Hates, *hates* change!
WAH!
WAH!

Where 'sun' go?
[*Bounce! Bounce!*]
WAH!
Baldo itch! Baldo itch! Baldo itch!
Scratch. Scratch.
[*Frenzied scratching.*]

'*** ** **** ***** **** *** ******* ** ***** *********,
Baldo. *** ********* **** **** *******. *** ** * good boy
*** *****, Baldo. ** **********! ****! ******! **! **
*********! **** ****!
** **** …'
Voice fades.

[*'Now I'm just going into the hallway to fetch something, Baldo. It's something very, very special. You be a good boy for Mummy, Baldo. No scratching! Okay! Enough! No! No scratching! Stop that!*

———
116

I'm just …']

Voice fades.

Eh?
[*Head tip –*
Inches short way up perch. Peers towards door –
Head tip.]
Eh?

'****! **** ** **! *** **** ***** *** ***** ** *** * ***
******* ** *** *** ***********. *** * *** ******** *****
*** *** *****. *** **** … ***** ** ** … ** ** *** *****.
Ooops! **** * ***** *** ** *** ***** ****! ***** ****.
    ***** *** ***** **** *****, ****** Baldo? Hmmn? ***.
** ** **** ********. *** ** **. *** *** **** *********.
**** ***** ***** ** ** *******. *****. ****. *** *** ****
*** *** *** **** * *** ** *** … Phew! **** *** *******
**** * *******. ******** **!'
Voice fades.

[*'Okay! Here we go! I'll just leave the cloth on for a few minutes*
to let him acclimatize. He's a bit stressed after the car drive. I'll
just … There we go … on to the table. Ooops! Hope I didn't tip
up the water bowl! Right. Good.
    How're you doing over there, little Baldo? Hmmn? Yes. It is
very exciting. Yes it is. But it's only temporary. Only while
Alice is in Majorca. Right. Good. Now I'll just pop off and make
a cup of tea … Phew! That was heavier than I thought. Gracious
me!']

Voice fades.

Eh?
Eh?

[*Head tip.*
Shifts on perch.
Head tip at other angle.
Crest rises.
Eyes new object on table.
Crest lowers.
Slight muttering under breath.
Disquiet.
BIG feather ruffle.]

BEEEUUURRRGH!

Silence.

[*Baldo closes his eyes and attempts to regain his equilibrium.*
Baldo listens to the sounds from the kitchen.
Kettle boiling.
Baldo waits, impatiently, for the whistle.

Then ...

Small cough from new object!]

Eh?!
[*Baldo's eyes fly open.*]

'Namaste!'
[*Sound from inside new object!*]

'Ksama Kijie!'

[*'Excuse me!'*]

Pause.

(Baldo is an African Grey Parrot, hailing from four previous generations bred in captivity. He is not fluent in Hindi.)

'Hullo! Hullo!'

Pause.

'Madad!'

[*'Help!'*]

[*Shrill whistle – from object –*
Followed by …
Kettle whistle – from kitchen, pitched on a comparable metronomic scale.]

'Lor 'av Mercee! Merimdarane luvlee vali nav sarpaminom se bhari hain!'

[*'Lord have Mercy! My lovely hovercraft is full of eels!'*]

Silence.

WAH!

Crump.

[*Baldo falls off his perch.*]

15

Mr Franklin D. Huff

Miss Hahn arrives, unannounced, one hand swaddled in a white(ish) cloth, bearing a large pork pie. I am sitting on the front porch, knitting her a pair of socks. It's been months since I've felt like getting my needles out.

'Why on earth didn't you tell me you were married to Kimberly Couzens?' she demands. 'That changes everything.'
'Does it?' I ask. I mean, forgive me for being a tad haughty and suspicious, but she's still the same Carla Hahn who cuts her own hair, has an extraordinarily overweight dog, cries openly on the beach, dresses like a tramp. And lies about her mother's cat's age (please God, let's not forget about that!).

'Of course!' She nods. 'Don't be ridiculous. It means you're one of us.'
One of us?
'I suppose you intend that as a kind of compliment,' I murmur.

'I brought you a pork pie.' She smiles. Ah. She gets my sense of humour! Well that's refreshing. People sometimes struggle with it. I struggle with it myself, on occasion. Hmmn. Was I actually being funny, though? Or was I simply being rude? I must confess that there is something about our dear Miss Hahn that brings out the spiteful in me, poor creature. Should I mention at this juncture that her ex-partner is a giant, delusional maniac? Or that I hate pork pies because of an infantile terror of the layer of aspic?

It's a magnificent-looking pie, admittedly. And I'm all but starving. I put down my knitting, take the pie from her and transport it through to the kitchen.

'If only you'd been straight with me from the very start – phoned me, sent me a letter – this all could've been so different,' she persists.

Is she actually being sincere? If I'd *sent her a letter*?! Nah. I'm not convinced.

'I can't stay long …' she adds, sniffing the air, anxiously.

'There's a very strong smell of eucalyptus …'

Ah yes, the much-touted disinfectant allergy!

She frowns and clears her throat, almost nervous, as if preparing herself for something, then sneezes, twice. 'Do you smell it?'

'Sorry?'

'Eucalyptus.'

'Nope,' I lie.

I place the pie on to the breadboard and take out the bread knife.

'That isn't the proper board for meats,' she says.

'This isn't meat,' I answer. 'It's pastry. It's a pie.'

'A pie containing meat,' she corrects me. 'A meat pie.'

I cut into the pie, nonetheless. She winces.

'Your rules about cutting boards in the Welcome Pack are certainly voluminous,' I say (keen for her to know that I am *aware* of the rules; in fact I recall that there are almost *two whole pages* on this subject in the aforementioned tome. Nothing – *nothing* – not so much as a paltry *line*, about the temperamental toilet flush).

'Jewish/German heritage.' She shrugs. 'And I'm a trained nurse. I did an entire nodule on basic food hygiene.'

An entire *nodule*?!

'I believe the fall of the Holy Roman Empire ultimately hinged on a badly prepared prawn,' I quip.

'I'm very sorry she's dead, Mr Huff,' Miss Hahn murmurs.

I pull out a slice of pie and notice that there is hardly any aspic in it at all. My hunger is suddenly quite overwhelming. I forgo the luxury of a plate and take a bite. It is delicious. It is utterly delicious. It is the most ... the most ... the most succulent, flavourful, rich, moist, sweetly porky ...

I idly notice that Miss Hahn is watching me with an expression akin to alarm. Some time has passed, but I couldn't say how much exactly.

'You seem alarmed, Miss Hahn,' I note.

'How long since your last square meal?' she asks.

'Three days,' I say, 'four days.'

'Pace yourself,' she suggests.

I help myself to a second, larger slice (almost on principle, I suppose).

'Was it very sudden?' she wonders.

'No. I just gradually ran out of money, over time. I ate less and less. Then finally I stopped eating altogether. Starvation generally follows a fairly predictable arc, I find.'

'Well there's still stuff on the allotment,' she gently chides.

I don't respond. A handful of blackening *chard*? Three soggy *leeks*?

'There was something so ... so terrifyingly *competent* about her,' she continues, gently adjusting the 'bandage' around her thumb (Are we actually talking to *each other* here, I wonder? I glance over my shoulder, just to make sure. Yup. Only us). 'I mean nothing ever seemed to faze her.' She grins, remembering. 'She was prepared for every eventuality. So able. So *experienced*. I never saw her in any colour other than black. But everything spotless. It was so intimidating. That shock of white-blonde hair and that amazingly luminous ...'

She is going to say 'skin', but she stops herself just in time. I start a third slice.

'Sorry,' she says, gathering up a little chunk of pastry that has fallen on to the floorboards, before shoving it, unthinkingly, into her pocket, 'that was ...'

Tactless?

Yes. Yes it was.

'Kimberly suffered 78 per cent burns,' I say, through a giant mouthful. 'People rarely survive with even a fraction of that percentage. But there was a South African doctor working at the hospital she was taken to in Derry. He was a burns specialist and a plastic surgeon. He shouldn't have been there – I won't bore you with the details ...' (Or myself, for that matter.)

I cut another slice. 'I mean he was meant to be in Singapore. He was on a lecture tour. But then the toddler of the couple he was B&B-ing with ate two pages of his passport. And Kimberly shouldn't have been there, either, come to that; her flight had been cancelled the day before. The ambulance driver suffered a seizure and the assistant driver who took over the wheel – and received a formal warning, after the fact, for his trouble – got lost. But if she'd ...'

I pause. It's such a convoluted story. Yet Miss Hahn seems rapt.

'We worked out afterwards that there were approximately twelve or thirteen coincidences which all led, *en masse*, to her ultimate survival. If any *one* of them hadn't taken place ...' I pause. 'All these strange coincidences – a comedy of errors, one after the other. We often laughed about it.'

'What a beautiful story,' she says, somewhat fatuously, as I cut my fifth slice. 'And what a sad story,' she adds, carefully, as an afterthought.

'She survived another twelve years,' I say.

Was it twelve years? Suddenly that doesn't seem very long at all.

'She survived for a reason.' Miss Hahn nods.

'And every day – *every day* – she wished that she hadn't,' I continue. 'Every day she wished she'd just died in that fire. Every day she cried – with the sheer *frustration* of it all. I mean the pain she was in. She was virtually blind. This

---

124

incredible … *inconvenience*; the sheer … sheer *effort* … the *laboriousness* of a life with severe burns. The infections. The ulceration. Some of the scars never fully healed. On those pressure-points of the body: the elbows, the buttocks …'
I gaze down at the pink pork-meat, then over at Miss Hahn's crimson hands. Miss Hahn is also gazing down at her hands.

'And when people say things like … like … "She survived for a reason" …' I throw out my arm and another small chunk of pastry ricochets off the hood of the oven (Miss Hahn goes to retrieve it). 'For a *reason*! I just think – no harm intended, of course – I just think: You misguided bloody idiot, you cliché-toting well-meaning but misguided bloody *idiot*. You sanctimonious fool. You *moron*. I mean how *dare* you simply *presume* to …'
I run out of words, so I finish my slice of pie and then hack off another chunk. I eat this one, too.

Miss Hahn says nothing. After a minute or so she cuts herself a thin slice of pie and carries it through to the little sitting room. She stands by the window and peers out of it as she eats. I wonder what it is that she's staring at out there. A cat regally defecating down by the cut? A bus disgorging its occupants over on the main road? The black shadow of a giant tanker on the far horizon? I suddenly feel a slight pang of … what? Guilt? Empathy? Nausea?

'That was good,' she finally observes, brightly, on completing her last mouthful. 'So what about the book?'
'The book?'
The *book*?! Is this any time to be talking about *books*?
'Well I guess I'm off the hook.' I shrug.
'Oh – you were on a hook?' She looks surprised. 'I didn't realize.'
'Yes. No. Uh.'
Arrgh. You know what? I wish I could just … I wish I could just put all these feelings I have inside me – this mass of tiny peppery black dots which march around in my stomach,

behind my eyelids, over my shoulders, like … like *ants* – into coherent sentences. I wish I could just print them out on to clean, little slips of paper – in neat, densely printed lines – like a till receipt. Then take that damn receipt, screw it up and throw it into a wastepaper basket. Dispose of it. Dispose of *them*. Responsibly. Then calmly move on (machismo – *pride* – still abundantly intact). Yes. I wish I could just … I wish I could just stop *saying* things and *doing* things and then not knowing why I did them or why I said them. Or knowing really – underneath – and wishing that I didn't. Yes. Wishing I could just graciously accept what I know. But I can't. Because what would be left of me, then? How might I be expected to drag myself out of bed in the morning? Look in the mirror? Blanch? Look again? Pluck the odd stray hair from inside my nostril? Apply shaving foam?

'Will you be returning home for the funeral?'

Miss Hahn has returned to the kitchen again. I find her gaze very intimidating, all of a sudden.

'Kim lived in Canada. My flight was to Monterrey.'

'You couldn't change it?'

I just … I just wish I could be slightly more in control of this entire … I wish I was more in *control* of my entire wretched, tilting, wonky self. If only my feelings – my impulses – my actions were an orchestra which I – *me* – was able to conduct. They *are* an orchestra, to all intents and purposes – but my conducting? A disaster! Chaos! A deafening cacophony! Horns parping! The percussionist rolling around on his back, legs in the air, having a riot on the maracas! Violas being plucked by teeth instead of fingers! A chronic excess of flugelhorn!

'You couldn't change it?'

Because I honestly don't know – really and truly – I don't know *why* I was knitting her those socks. Why? When I think about it – logically – my having succumbed to this silly impulse – this improbably tender urge – I just … I'm just

126

bewildered. Yes! Bemused. Nonplussed. Are they even *for* her? The socks? The three paltry rows so far completed? These non-socks? These 'idea of socks'? These 'contended' pieces of un-knitwear?

Is it guilt? Over the satsuma incident? And if it is, then why am I behaving so objectionably now, when she's so kindly brought me over a conciliatory pie? A Pie of Peace? *Eh?*

'Maybe I could help? If it's the money? I could refund you the rent you paid ...'

No. *No.* I don't know *why* I agreed to write the damn book! Or maybe I do. To get my own back. On them. On our dear Miss Hahn here with all her disgustingly kind suggestions. On ... on Kimberly, even? By scapegoating Bran Cleary (an arch-seducer! An adulterer! A political neophyte! And *artist* for heaven's sake!) and then diminishing my own humiliation? But I was already humiliated – wasn't I? My reputation in shreds? After Tlateloco? After I got it all so wrong? And the dalliance with Win Scott? The way I trusted him to a fault. Not just once, but twice! *Twice!* The way he drew me in? Led me on?

'I was planning to refund it anyway, I mean after I found out ...'

Oh God I don't know why Kim and I were never divorced. Or maybe I do know: she was my shield, my excuse – but for what? No. I don't want to think about it. I just ... I just ...

'It seems like the right thing to do.'

I don't understand why the import/export business won't really take off. Why can't I make it work? Because I'm not an importer/exporter, I suppose, not a businessman, just a journalist. A discredited journalist! A laughing stock. And only Kimberly truly understood. The subtle pressures. The necessary compromises. The gentle log-rolling. Only Kimberly ...

'I'll go into Rye and withdraw it from the bank. First thing in the morning.'

But there are plenty of people – plenty of expats – in Mexico in desperate need of reliable supplies of Robinson's Barley Water, and Marmite and Colman's Mustard and Oxo Cubes and Bird's Custard Powder and Lyle's Golden Syrup and McVitie's Digestive Biscuits – a choice of plain, milk or dark chocolate (just tick relevant box).

There are plenty of blathering idiots. Moronic expats. Plenty of them.

Miss Hahn is speaking again. Kind Miss Hahn. *Helpful* Miss Hahn. I turn – without answering – and trot (like a little pony) through to the bathroom. As I do this I play back in my mind what she's just said and realize that it's: 'Mr Huff, you're a pale shade of green. You are going to be sick. Don't use the toilet. It'll block. There's a perfectly good bucket here – there – under the sink.'

Later, hanging over the toilet bowl, exhausted – I don't *want* your damn money, woman! You castrating bitch! Not a penny of it! – I hear her in conversation with the rabbit. If the rabbit responds – as I'm sure that it will, that it must – its replies are tragically indecipherable (to my ears at least).

16

Miss Carla Hahn

I had one of my special dreams – could you call it a nightmare? – one of my special, terrible, Orla dreams. It's been a while now since I've dreamed about her. Was it the smell of eucalyptus that set it off? Did it awaken something hidden – suspended – deep within my synapses?

I was at Mulberry Cottage – in my dream – and I was in the garden gathering the fallen leaves from the old tree (the long defunct old mulberry tree). I was raking them up, anxiously. And there was fruit, too. A host of fat, purple berries. They were dropping from the branches overhead. Soft, ripe fruit. And as I gathered the berries up and crammed them into the pockets of my coat, I noticed that my hands were stained – all red. From the juices. And I felt an encroaching sense of panic – a strong resistance. An urge to hide, to flee. Then the fruit started to fall more heavily, like hail. It hit me, like hail. And it left red welts where it landed, but I couldn't tell – wasn't certain – whether they were real wounds or just remnants of pulp. It didn't hurt. There was no pain.

I blinked, in the dream, and I was transported inside the cottage. I was still gathering leaves, on my knees, from the floorboards, but these were eucalyptus leaves, and I was fearful, because I remembered that I am allergic to these leaves, that my hands would blister if they made contact. And so I looked down at my hands. I held out my hands – which only seconds ago had been a vicious shade of puce – and they were clean; healed! A pure, milky white!

Then Orla spoke to me. Orla was there. She was among the leaves. She is the leaves.

'Gather them up for me, Carla,' she whispers, her voice just a gentle rustling. 'Don't be scared. Gather them up for me, please.'

And she held out her little arms. 'It is time, *meine* Carla,' she says.

'Watch out for the mulberries!' I warn her. Because although I'm inside, I'm still afraid of the mulberries, and I can't be certain they won't harm her. And I'm right to be afraid, because her skin is suddenly marked by a series of crimson spots – like she's been peppered by shotgun pellets. But she is still holding out her arms. Her tiny arms. And I can't lift myself from my knees, I can't help her. There is nothing I can do to help her. But I can gather up the leaves for her. So I start gathering them together, crying, helplessly, my face a mess of tears and snot. And the more I gather them the more there are. And every time I clear a section, a gust of wind hits the little pile I've amassed and sends them flying. I am muttering something under my breath: 4004. Four thousand and four what? Leaves? Yes. 4004. I am counting the leaves; one, two, three, four ... Counting the leaves, anxiously. And I need to reach the total, very precise number. 4004. I am muttering it obsessively: '4004. Orla's number.'

I wake up, suddenly, in a cold sweat. 4004! I roll over. 4004! I throw out my arm and feel blindly for a pen or a crayon or a stub of pencil on my bedside table. I am sleepy – clumsy – knock over the alarm clock, almost up-end a glass of water, hear my wristwatch go flying. But I quickly locate a felt-tip and pull off the lid. Paper. Uh ...Uh ...

I turn, automatically, towards the wall next to my bed, reach out to touch it and prepare to write on it, but there is a poster, one of my new, Russian Propagandist collection, recently hung …

Uh …

4004! I quickly scribble the four digits on to the soft skin inside my arm and then – overwrought, exhausted – lie there, shivering, as the poster (its supporting balls of Blu-Tack disturbed by my blindly grappling hands) suddenly drops from the wall, half on to the floor, half over the bed and sets my heart frantically pounding. Oh God. What did she mean? 'It is time, *meine* Carla?' My skin starts to crawl. I attempt to distract myself by guiltily pondering the apology which I really should have made to Mr Huff – which I fully intended to make – which I really wanted to make – but which I never actually … never actually … somehow … never actually somehow quite got around to … uh …

'It is *time*?'

Time for what, exactly?

There just never seemed an appropriate *moment*. Can there ever be an appropriate moment to gently alert a person to the fact that you knowingly – *calculatingly* – hid a rotting shark in a suitcase beneath their bed? Out of pure spite? Pure bile? No. No. No. No. Probably not.

I tried to be nice, though, didn't I? Took the pie? I was full to the brim – bursting! – with good intentions. But the smell of eucalyptus. *Orla's* smell. And the way he devoured the thing – slice after slice. Hacked into it with the bread knife. Bolted it down – almost vengefully – like a spiteful baboon cannibalizing the live young of a weaker species, all grabbing hands and gnashing teeth and flashing, bloodshot eyes.

Unsettling.

Poignant.

Unsettling.

What was that other thing she'd said? Orla? About gathering? Gathering the leaves together? The *leaves*?

Oh why has this all become so complicated?! Why couldn't we just be ... I don't know ... *civil*? Why all the mischief and the rancour and the game playing? If he'd only just ... if he'd just *approached* me, cordially, from the off, explained himself – the project, in detail.

Yes.

I'd have run a mile.

Oh God!

A mile.

Is it possible – vaguely, even *remotely* possible – that he wasn't ever actually interested in my account of events? Like Alys said? That my feelings of guilt may have exacerbated – inflated – my sense of my own significance? I mean it's not entirely beyond the bounds of ...

Is it?

But then didn't he say he was 'off the hook'? As if the whole thing had been forced upon him? Against his will? By ... by Kimberly, I suppose?

But couldn't that just be yet another one of his cunning wiles? To befuddle me? To set me off track? To draw me in? *Am* I being drawn in?

Oh God.

And now the dream?

If I can just ... just ... *yes*. If I can just *get* rid of him, somehow. Pay for his flight. Ship him off. Return his rent. Yes. If I return his rent surely that'll help to even things out? Morally? And if he leaves very quickly – packs up and leaves, very quickly (like he says he wants to, like he plans to) – then surely everything can just be quietly ... *discreetly* swept under the carpet? Resolved. Tied up. Finished off. Forgotten about. If I can just ... Uh ...

Eh?

If I can just ... Uh ...

Eh?

★ ★ ★

I awaken, abruptly, in a state of marginal discomfort. What is that? In the bed? I reach down, blindly, and discover the pen – the felt-tip – pressing into my leg. Ow. And I can tell, simply by testing with the pads of my fingers as I extract it, that the lid has come off.

Urgh.

I throw back the sheets and sit up; the fallen poster slithers under the bed. On the wall – where it once hung – are approximately a dozen 4004s, in different sizes, colours, hands. I scowl and look down: good heavens! There are tiny spots of ink everywhere! Everywhere! On my skin, my pyjamas, all over the bed linen! A riot of felt-tip ink! As I register the mess, I straighten the objects on my bedside table – my alarm clock has tipped over, my watch has … And two things strike me in rapid succession: it is one fifty! One fifty! I shake the clock, start looking for my wristwatch to confirm, but it's fallen behind the headboard and as I reach out to lift the mattress I see that my hands …

Good God! My *hands*! My hands are all faded! The redness! The chapping! Quite faded! My hands are healing! But instead of a natural sense of joy (awe? Surprise? Gratification?) I feel an awful, dull, thudding sense of … of what? Disappointment? Aversion? Gnawing guilt? Can that be right? Can it? And … and … and it is one fifty! In the afternoon! Yes. And I'd promised to go to the bank to withdraw … to set right … to get rid of …

I throw on some clothes, grab my wallet and my cheque-book, and slam my way out of the house. I jump on to my bike, sprint to the bus-stop, chain it up and then wait for the bus, cursing. I wait for the bus. It finally arrives. I jump on to the bus. It's almost empty. I sit down, look at my hands, marvel at them (that strange feeling again – in the pit of my stomach). I try and rub off the worst of the felt-tip (spit on an old tissue), but the ink is all but indelible. I curse again. I wipe the sleep out of my eyes and rub my index finger across my teeth. I make some basic financial calculations. We arrive in Rye. I clamber off the bus and sprint for the bank. I arrive at the bank and try the door. The bank is shut. Am I too late? The High Street is virtually empty. Across the road a man is delivering bread from a van to a little teashop. I ask him the time (why might he be delivering bread in the afternoon?). He gives me a curious look then inspects his watch. 'Ten past seven.'

Ten past seven.

Ten past seven?!

Even the *library* won't be open yet! What an idiot! After several minutes of pointless indecision I wander down to the quay and sit there for a while watching the gulls promenading up and down angling for food scraps, the boats bobbing, my healing hands clenched – all the while – into defensive fists, thrust deep, *deep* inside my pockets.

Please don't do this to me, Orla! I stamp my feet – perform a little seated tap-dance of anxiety on the tarmac. Yes, I've made my mistakes, I've been weak – sullen, *petulant* – but I've tried my best to set things straight, so please, *please* don't do this to me, Orla! Don't draw me in again! No more of the pyrotechnics, the miracles, the wonders. Because I'm not a spiritual person, Orla – remember? Not remotely. You know that. I find it hard enough to understand *this* world – the sticky mess of it, the strangeness – let alone trying to factor in the darkly hollow and woolly hereafter; all those awful consequences beyond awful consequences. No. *No.* There's no space in my cramped, lonely little life for faith, for the straitjacket of religion. I'm already a square peg in a round hole: a crazy mishmash, an outsider, conceived in war, born out of misery. I was always – *always* – a troublesome imposition, a 'darling mistake', always dependent on the kindness, the forbearance of others. Nothing was ever unconditional. Or maybe it was, but I never felt like it was. To be so deeply alien and yet not free ... never free to ... to be as good or as bad as I longed to be. Nothing was ever unconditional. Nothing. Except … well, except your love, Orla, I suppose.

And then I had to go and destroy that.

Inevitably.

Oh Orla – please, *please*. Can't you see? There's barely enough room for me here as it is. It's all so … so boxed-in, so close and airless, so cramped. Take pity on me! Leave me as I am: quiet, plain, decent (as I possibly can be). Unobtrusive. Repentant. I paid the price, didn't I? Last time around? And I kept my mouth shut. I made the necessary adjustment. So please, *please* don't stir everything up again – just for the sake of it, just because you can – don't do this to me, Orla! *Urgh.*

I shove a stray strand of hair behind my ear and focus – ferociously – on the boats! Yes! The gulls! Yes! But … but here is the evidence, surely? I glance down at my lap. Right here, in my hands. Here is the evidence made concrete in my very flesh. Is this miraculous? I hold the hands out, horrified. No! *No!* No more miracles! I've no *time* for miracles! Because I've learned, from hard experience, that when something is given, then something bigger, something momentous, is also – invariably – extracted. And what else do I honestly have left to give?

A commotion suddenly erupts on the road behind me where a large delivery lorry accidentally reverses into a stationary car (an old Capri). Horns are sounded. Both parties leap out of their vehicles. I quickly stand up and walk off, head down (determined not to get caught up in it).

Yup. That's what *Mame* always taught me. Never get involved. Okay, she didn't teach it so much by word as by the worst possible example. Fearless *Mame!* Always at the heart of any commotion, with her red lips (spewing a constant stream of peerless vowels and brutal consonants), her impeccable blonde curls, her neat little suits and pristine gloves.

135

Mame's gloves! That was the formal face. And the informal? Equally pristine, but tough. Those same, perfectly manicured fingers would wring a chicken's neck, shoot a rabbit, disembowel a deer, mend a radio, fix a lawnmower, paint a house, grab a hammer and build a shed. Fearless *Mame*! Pitiless *Mame*! Indomitable! Irresistible! Implacable *Mame*. With her passion for the rules and her unutterable *horror* of encroachment!

It sometimes felt – and this was the unsayable, the truly unthinkable – as though she was determined to dedicate the rest of her life (after my disgusting conception) to making up for that one, terrible occasion on which she simply *could not* say no. Storming into battle at the slightest provocation. Searching out trouble. Routing all – *any* – opposition. Righteous. Opinionated. Hungry for justice. But at what cost? And for whom, precisely? Herself? Me? Us?

But where was I, meanwhile? Where's cripplingly shy and unassuming, little Carla to be found? Quiet, little Carla? Hiding among *Mame*'s skirts? Cringing behind the sofa? Fleeing on her bike? Skimming stones on the beach? Perpetually ducking? Perpetually wincing? Standing at her shoulder, mesmerized, as she sits at her old dressing table, carefully applying her lipstick, her 'warpaint' – a special red, *Mame*'s red – before grabbing her purse and marching out? Oh God, just wishing she sounded a little more like the other mothers! Wishing she could *act* a little more like the other mothers! Be *normal, Mame*! Why did she always have to be so brave? So proud? So exceptional? So confident? So straight? So practical? So extraordinary? So unbowed?

Is that how she ended up with poor, old *Tatteh*? Out of sheer contrariness? Just kicking against the pricks? Out of habit? Always different. Always difficult. Engaged to a Jew? A shiftless musician? A piano tuner? In wartime Berlin? Was it simple bloody-mindedness? Or was it … was it actually heroic? Noble *Mame*!

Fearless *Mame*!

How different they were. *Mame* so unflinching. *Tatteh* so careless. So jolly! So ... so deliriously selfish.

Was that me? Did *I* do that to them? Or was it simply the war? Was what happened *his* fault – pure cowardice – for getting out when he could, abandoning her, his darling fiancée? Or was it hers: cancelling the wedding, staying behind – out of sheer necessity, she insisted – to support her consumptive younger brother, just sent home, broken, raving, from the front?

My mind suddenly switches back to the dream. Orla's dream. Aren't objects in dreams always something other than how they appear? So the tree? That old mulberry tree? How long since I've thought of it? Does it represent the past? Does it represent *me*? My fear? Or ... or my *Mame*, perhaps? The red, remember? *Mame*'s red?

I consider the actual tree – the old mulberry. I remember gathering fruit from it as a child. Miss Vaughn (Hungarian by birth), who owned the tree back then, was best friends with *Mame* – *Mame*'s only friend so far as I can remember. She'd lay out a sheet and then shake the branches. The fruit would come raining down. *Mame* made jam, cordial, syrup, curd, cobbler, custard, dumplings, sorbet, pikelets. She even glazed the odd chicken and rabbit.

When did that old tree finally die? I don't remember. Was the tree still fruiting when the Clearys came to stay? Wasn't it already dead by then?

Still, I don't remember.

But the hands ...

'It is time, *meine* Carla.'

I find myself standing outside a nearby café. I enter, order a poached egg on toast and a pot of tea at the counter, grab some cutlery and a paper napkin, then sit at a table by the window and gaze out at the quay from this new, slightly more obtuse angle, until the waitress brings me my cup and teapot.

I pour out my tea (don't look at the hands! Don't focus on the hands!). It's in one of those squat, familiar, stainless-steel pots (typical of rough and ready catering establishments) and as I lift it to pour I inadvertently catch sight of my reflection in its silver-angled surfaces.

Eh?

I stop pouring, alarmed, and adjust the pot to try and see my cheek in it. Is that …? *Ow!* A little stream of tea pours out of the full pot and on to my lap. *Ow ow!* I put the pot down and dab at my trousers with my serviette, then grab my knife and try to see my reflection in it. Useless. Back of a fork. Nope. Teaspoon …?

Uh …? Is that …? I throw down the teaspoon and angle my cheek towards the windowpane. There's a light on overhead, so perhaps if I …? If I …?

Good heavens! Is that …? Is that a large, black felt-tip mark right across my left cheek? But … but how the heck …?

Argh! *Of course!* The numbers on my arm! I push up my sleeve. There they are – the four numbers – slightly blurry now. I must've slept with my cheek resting against them at some point! And now there's a giant, black, back-to-front …

I grab the damp serviette and start rubbing away at the mark, focusing very hard, trying to …

Eh?

I de-focus with a slight jump. Someone is … no, no, not *someone*, Mr Huff – MR FRANKLIN D. HUFF! – is standing at the other side of the window peering in at me! He lowers his knuckle. He has just knocked on the window.

What? *No!* Why? *Why?* Why? Why Mr Huff? Why here? I cover my cheek, mortified, as Mr Huff stalks towards the door and enters.

'I've been standing at the other side of that windowpane for several minutes, Miss Hahn,' he chronically exaggerates. 'What on earth are you up to? What *is* that?' He points. 'On your cheek?'

I drop my hand from my face.

'What *is* that?' he repeats, drawing closer. 'Are they digits?'
I nod.

The waitress brings over my poached egg and places it down, looking at Mr Huff enquiringly.

'Flying visit,' Mr Huff informs her, with a flap of his ludicrously skinny grey-suited arms.

He then pulls out a chair and sits down.

'Feeling a little better this morning?' I ask.

'I think that pie might've been slightly off,' he confides.

'The pie was perfectly fresh,' I snap. 'I ate a slice myself – remember? – and have been absolutely fine.'

'I have a ludicrously delicate constitution,' Mr Huff sighs, 'very sensitive.'

'Like a girl's,' I mutter.

'4004,' he reads, eyes slitting, mystified.

'A delicate constitution hardly tallies with your reputation as an international jet-setter,' I murmur.

'Well observed,' he concedes. 'It's my Achilles heel,' he continues. 'I feel things through my stomach – stress, unpleasant emotions. It's a nervous thing. And yes – I openly confess – it's perfectly risible in an adult male.'

I am signally nonplussed by this sudden show of humility on Mr Huff's part – this unexpected show of vulnerability. Chiefly because I don't want to share personal details with this man. I don't want intimacy. I can't afford for Mr Huff to become dimensional. That would be difficult – uncomfortable. I gaze over at him, perplexed.

Bad stomach aside, he seems to be in a state of high good humour; his face is shining, as if he's delighted by something (my patent unease, perhaps?). It's almost as if a great – an unendurable – weight has suddenly been lifted from his stupidly puny grey-suited shoulders.

'Did you come into Rye on foot?' I wonder, suspicious – almost jealous – picking up my knife and fork.

———

'I found the rabbit sitting in a colander,' he says, eyeing my plate. 'Last night. It seemed a rather strange place to …'

'I didn't put it in a colander,' I say (I did put it in a colander. It was that or the washing-up basin which was choc-full of dirty crockery).

'Your friend, Pemberton, had set up a nice little home for it in an old sewing-machine cover.'

'Bickerton.'

'Sorry?'

'Bickerton. Clifford Bickerton.'

'Really?'

'Yes. And the sewing-machine cover has a certain sentimental value.'

'*Really?*' Mr Huff's eyes widen.

'Yes. It belonged to the cottage's former owner, Miss Vaughn.'

'Oh.'

I pour myself some tea.

'Sentimental value,' he muses (almost under his breath).

I don't respond. It was petty of me to object, I know. But that rabbit (as I explained to it, at length, in person, last night) is a tiny, unwelcome impostor at Mulberry. Just like Mr Huff.

'Turns out your pal Bickerton was resident in the area way back when the Clearys were hereabouts,' Mr Huff informs me (as if this will be breaking news to me). 'At least that's what he claims.'

'Clifford *is* a local,' I confirm as Mr Huff's hand snakes out and purloins a half-slice of my toast. 'He and I were at school together.'

'Huge!' Mr Huff exclaims, taking a bite.

'Yes.' I scowl (the impudence!). 'Very tall.'

'And possibly a little unstable,' Mr Huff continues (on finishing his mouthful).

'Clifford?' I snort. 'Don't be ridiculous! Clifford's *ridiculously* stable – trustworthy, reliable – almost to a fault.'

Mr Huff takes another bite of the toast, grimaces then points at my cheek. 'It looks very odd,' he says.

I rub at it, reddening.

'4.0.0.4,' he re-reads, then, 'Gracious me! Just look at your hands!'

I glance down at my hands. My hands seem to be improving in texture and colour with virtually every passing second.

'What brings you to Rye so early?' I ask.

'Why are you changing the subject?' he responds.

'Am I?'

'Yes. You seem very … very *shifty* this morning. Quite ill at ease.'

'Shifty,' I echo.

'I've been invited out to breakfast,' he swiftly moves on.

'Really? Where?'

'With a woman called Sage Meadows.' He finishes off his slice. 'She's the widow of a local doctor.'

'Dr Meadows.' I nod, eyes slitting. 'Of course.'

'Ah, so you're familiar with Mrs Meadows?'

It irritates me in the extreme the way he automatically presumes that I have no social circle in the area. He's been here for a matter of *weeks*. I've lived here my entire *life*! It's so patronizing! Do I know Mrs Meadows? Do I know Mrs Meadows? This is the sort of thing a person simply shouldn't need to *say* – or to *ask*. It should be … It should be patently *obvious*.

'No.' I shake my head. 'Not personally. I knew Dr Meadows though, of course. And I know *of* her. I mean I know her by sight. I must confess that I've always thought her name a little … ridiculous.'

What I don't say is that I've always thought *her* a little ridiculous, too. Full of herself. Stuck-up.

'A redhead.' He nods. 'Beautifully groomed. Got a first-class honours degree in English and Philosophy from Durham University. Lives up in Henry James's old house. Aspirant poet. Has an amazing walled garden – the most lovely in Rye, I'm told. It's won awards. Classic borders bursting with elegant white annuals. She's very green-fingered by all accounts.'

'The gardens are beautiful,' I concede, 'although I believe some of the credit must go to the full-time gardener, Richard Stanley. Dick and I were in the Sea Scouts together.'

'Girls aren't permitted in the Sea Scouts!' Mr Huff barks.

'My mother made a deal with the head of the local troop.' I shrug.

'Ah, the legendary Else Hahn.' Mr Huff smirks. 'The *bête noire* of local squatters, I'm told. Punctilious and unbending to the point of pure insanity in her application of local planning laws.'

'I was officially there as "cook".' I glower.

'Sage has no inkling of *your* identity,' Mr Huff confides. 'I suppose that's to be expected,' he adds, idly, 'with the generational difference.'

'Generational?' I echo, bemused.

'I concede that the name *is* a little twee.' He grins.

He grins. Yes, he *grins*. Mr Huff grins. At me. And while I'm still confused about what it is that he's saying, exactly ('generational difference'? And … and *how* exactly did he get to be so well-informed about my beautiful *Mame*? Alys? Mrs Barrow?), I'm struck – yes, struck – by how very handsome he is when he smiles. It's not the teeth. Although the teeth are fine – for a smoker. The teeth are good enough. But something in the jaw, the cheekbones. A fine-ness. A fragility. And the eyes: a wide-spaced hazel behind his little wire-rimmed spectacles. Warm. Shy. Humourful. And the delicacy of his features conjoined with the light, careless tangle of pale, brown curls which hang across his forehead, around his ears …

A *different* generation?!

'Is this meeting connected to the book?' I wonder, and then before he can respond: 'Because I thought you'd already made up your mind to abandon all—'

'Not that it's any of your affair,' Mr Huff interjects drolly, 'but I took Mrs Meadows out for lunch at the Mermaid when I first arrived in the area. The food was execrable, but we got on terribly well. She promised to show me around Lamb House on a reciprocal date but then was suddenly obliged to journey up to Coventry for a few weeks to assist her younger sister in launching her latest venture: a butterfly farm – a kind of zoo for exotic butterflies. The sister's quite the impresario, it seems.'

Yes. Mrs Meadows *is* very well preserved. I openly concede the point (to myself). But a *different generation*? I honestly can't imagine that there's more than a couple of years in it.

'She apparently had an infestation of ants in her larval rearing house,' Mr Huff continues. 'Ants always pose a serious threat to the larvae. She panicked. And Sage flew to the rescue.'

'Hurrah for Sage!' I cheer.

Mr Huff lets this pass. 'I'd pondered setting up a butterfly farm in Monterrey at one stage,' he continues, 'so we naturally had a very fruitful exchange on the subject.'

'I don't know why,' I murmur, 'but I've always thought it a little embarrassing the way ...'

I peter out.

He honestly thinks I look *older* than Sage Meadows? With her awful, static hair and her green eye shadow and her brittle laugh? Not just older – of a 'different generation'?! I mean how many years *are* there between generations? Five? Ten? Sixteen?

'The way what?' Mr Huff demands.

'Sorry?' I blink.

'You said you always thought it a little embarrassing the way ...' he rotates a graceful hand.

143

'Oh. Yes. The way aspirant writers seem to think that simply by living in the former home of another successful writer their allure will somehow, miraculously, rub off.'

'Surely it's just a matter of aesthetics?' Mr Huff snaps, plainly riled. 'Sensitive writerly eyes are naturally charmed by the same qualities in a home: the layout, the seclusion, the sense of quiet ...'

'Possibly.' I shrug.

Hang on, though ... Hang on. Shelf the negativity for a moment, Carla. Maybe he thinks Sage is of an *older* generation? Dryer, fustier, careworn? It makes a strange kind of ... *Can* he mean that? I furtively glance over.

No.

No.

He is staring at my cheek again.

'Are they fours, or are they little, primitive crosses with a diagonal line going from the top to the—'

'Charming as the widow Sage undoubtedly is,' I quickly interrupt, 'I'm hazarding a guess that it was her former connection to Dr Meadows that initially drew you to her.'

'I hear Dr Meadows kept extensive private diaries,' he twinkles (infuriatingly).

'And did Mrs Meadows show you the diaries?' I wonder.

'Nope.'

'Why ever not?'

'Because I didn't presume to ask, Miss Hahn.'

He checks his watch and then reaches for his jacket. Did he take *off* his jacket? I have no memory of that. But I like his cream shirt and his thin tweed tie and his old-fashioned corduroy waistcoat. I suppose – to all intents and purposes – he's quite dressed up.

'Well I'd hate to keep you.' I smile.

'I got a lift in with Mr Barrow.' Mr Huff casually returns to one of my earlier enquiries. 'An interesting man. No conversation. Watery eyes. Like he's always teetering on the verge of bursting into tears.'

'I've always felt as though Mr Barrow's superficially unprepossessing exterior actually conceals hidden depths,' I murmur. 'Like he's ... I don't know ... an old soul.'

I have no idea why I feel this (there's no physical or anecdotal evidence), but I always have.

'Really?' Mr Huff demands.

I nod.

'Because I've often found myself thinking the exact same thing!' he announces, apparently utterly astonished by the parity in our thinking.

'Oh,' I say.

Just 'Oh.'

'I do believe that's the first subject we've ever actually agreed upon, Miss Hahn!' he exclaims, rising to his feet.

I desperately try and think of another (another thing we've agreed upon), but I can't. No. There's nothing. Simply nothing.

'That's very possibly true,' I grudgingly concede.

'And there's number two!' Mr Huff holds up his arms in a gesture of sporting celebration. 'We're on a roll, Miss Hahn! *Dios de ni Vida!*'

Then off he saunters.

Urgh. I stab into the yolk of my poached egg with my fork. So irritating. So ... so *irritating*. He is. Him. That awful man. That awful, *awful* man. Mr Huff.

17

Mr Franklin D. Huff

It was what I was actually *thinking* as she did it that shocked me. Sorry – I'm running ahead of myself. 'She' (aka the Cat's Mother) aka Mrs Sage Meadows, widow; and what she did: pressing my thudding head into her (perfectly) ample bosom. And what I was actually *thinking*, meanwhile? I was thinking: Oh our dear Miss Hahn would have a *field* day with this! I can just imagine her expression. Or her signal *lack* of expression. Those careful, bleached green eyes with their strange, dark grey surround full of a *complete absence* of malice which is actually a *profound expression* of malice. Yes. It's all in the brows, I suppose. A tiny movement of one brow. Yes. I can just imagine how …
Enough!

It shocked me. As a man. To be thinking about how another woman (Miss Hahn! With her bizarre skin condition and the inked digits scrawled carelessly across her cheek) might register this sudden (not entirely unexpected, but then not entirely expected, either) act of intimacy on the part of another (much better maintained) female.

It's always been difficult for me to live in the moment. I'm horribly prone to over-analysing everything. Spontaneity isn't really my strong suit. And this heartfelt embrace (the aforementioned – quite – ample bosom) of Mrs Meadows had taken me somewhat by surprise. Did I lift up my arms (which were glued to my sides) and curl them around her waist (Does Miss Hahn even *have* a waist? Certainly not one I've ever knowingly apprehended)? Did I burrow my nose into the cleft (*is* it a 'cleft'? Might the word 'cleft' be principally attributable to the partition of a pair of buttocks?)? Or did I simply remain perfectly still, stop breathing through my nose (my nostrils were slightly impaired by the ... the intense *fleshiness*) and commence breathing through my mouth while bearing in mind that it would be completely inappropriate to move my lips excessively or, worse still, drool?

Oh she's perfectly right – *damn* that Miss Hahn! – it *is* a silly name. Sage Meadows. Affected. Ridiculous. And I suppose the gardener *was* chiefly responsible for that wonderful garden outside. And while I'm on the subject (I am on the subject, aren't I?) wasn't Mrs Meadows perhaps slightly – very slightly – over-perfumed? Twixt the aforementioned 'cleft' of her quite charming bazooms? Was that a heavy (and rather predictable) dusting of Crabtree and Evelyn Lily of the Valley talcum powder upon her *embonpoint*? I idly wondered (palms now gently resting on her curvaceous hips) if Miss Hahn has any discernible scent. Something peppery, I'd expect. Something grassy. Warm sand with a slight tinge of sump oil. The kind of smell a piece of crushed kale might exude from under a square-booted heel ...

Enough! *Enough!* Why should I give a fig about Miss Hahn's smell or what her ridiculously uptight take on this curious little situation might be? I hardly know what *my* take on it is. Part of me was too embarrassed to object (as her hands moved down to my waist and started fiddling with my belt), part of me was victorious (what red-blooded male wouldn't be?), part of me suspected that Mrs Meadows might be (i) taking things a little far (for a well-bred female), (ii) taking things a little for granted (complacency is not a quality I am much given to admiring in womankind in general. Treat 'em mean and keep 'em keen has always been my romantic philosophy), (iii) taking advantage of *me* (of my 'grief', even) to further her own mysterious agenda (I have no idea what that might be – and don't much care to speculate, either).

Another part of me (an opportunistic part, I openly confess) senses that an unexpected increase in intimacy between myself and Mrs Meadows might inch me yet closer (slowly, ineluctably) towards Dr Meadows's private diaries, which, for the record (whose record?), I no longer actually want or need. Because I'm fully intent on abandoning the Cleary project forthwith.

Or am I? Hmmn. I suppose it might be useful/honest/ helpful at this juncture to share the contents (or just the pith, the nub) of a very lengthy telephone call (which was received – due to that pesky time differential – late last night) from Kimberly's attorney (no less) pertaining to Kimberly's last will and testament. Or the lack of one. A search of her home had been undertaken (by a greedy niece) and nothing definitive had been discovered. Which meant that I, as her 'husband', would be first in line to inherit … to inherit … well, the whole kit and caboodle. Everything. Everything Kimberly. Bills, debts, standing orders, funeral expenses. The house. What remains of her insurance payout. A prospective lawsuit against her useless dentist. The photos. Oh yes, the photos. Please, *please* don't let us forget about those.

And how did I respond to this news? Shock! Yes. Complete shock! A swift backhander-across-the-chops – *bwuuh!* – kind of shock. Then a measure of deep anxiety (not entirely dissimilar, in fact, to how I responded to Mrs Meadows's legendarily green fingers trespassing upon my fly) followed (quite hard-upon) by … by a gradual sensation of … well, like a gentle *defrosting* (imagine clutching on to a hot-water bottle but your hands are freezing. At first you are too cold to feel anything and then suddenly this gentle, this profound and incredible feeling of … of extraordinary, comforting, low-level *warmth*), finally followed by what I can only describe as a sensation of pure, unexpurgated, unadulterated joy. *Joy!*

JOY!

I was a part of it! I was remembered! I actually mattered (for once)! It was real! It wasn't just one-sided or in name alone! I was of significance! Yes! I was ... I was regarded! Liked! Respected! Included! I was ... I was loved!

I WAS LOVED!

AND ... AND CHERISHED AND ... AND HONOURED!

I WAS TRUSTED!

SHE TRUSTED ME!

STILL! AFTER ... AFTER EVERYTHING.

But *am* I trustworthy? Eh? Wasn't I fully intending on ...? *Am* I trustworthy? Miss Hahn probably wouldn't—

Enough!

JUST BREATHE, FRANKLIN! JUST ... JUST BREATHE!

This was followed (sixty seconds later) by: 'Did Kimberly actually *want* me to inherit? Isn't it all just a terrible mistake? An almighty screw-up?'

And this, in turn, was then followed (two, three minutes later) by: HAAAAAA! THEY'RE ALL MINE!

MINE!

MINE!

MINE!!!

(Not my greatest moment, I confess.)

Miss Hahn (as an inheritor of property herself) would probably find it difficult to imagine that I hadn't already pondered this extraordinary eventuality at some considerable length: you know, the will, my inheritance etc. (Good heavens! Was *that* why she brought over the pie? As a pastry-encrusted negotiating tool?) But I honestly hadn't – *honestly* (too sad? Too hungry). And who cares what Miss Hahn thinks anyhow? Ha! The *Sea* Scouts! Miss Hahn in the *Sea* Scouts! Absolutely bloody typical! That woman has a rare genius at turning up where she isn't wanted and then promptly tying everything into knots ...

As I ponder Miss Hahn's tactile dexterity, Mrs Meadows is quietly and methodically relieving me with her hand. I couldn't say that this was a bolt from the blue – no ... – but it certainly wasn't inked in on my morning's itinerary. The jury is still out as to whether a bout of somewhat mechanically administered hand-relief is actually an appropriate response to the candid expression of feelings of profound loss, sorrow and grief.

(Okay, so half of the jury are now in, and they're all lolling around in the box grinning like a bunch of idiots.) Although (I'll be frank – you deserve that at the very least) the feelings (of sadness etc., that awful, hollow sensation in the pit of my stomach) aren't nearly so profound now – now that I have been made the chief (fine, the *only!*) beneficiary of Kimberly's small estate. I feel light-headed, almost. Yes. Very odd.

Of course silly, frumpy Miss Hahn (newly shelled walnuts, washed gravel, a field mushroom lightly frying in sunflower oil) can have *no concept* (none!) of what a weight of responsibility this inheritance may ultimately prove to be. I mean there's Trudy (Kimberly's mother) to be considered (her declining mental health was the main, contributing factor towards the photos' publication in the first place). Trudy was always (in my view) quite doolally – completely bats; cranky, dotty, dizzy. An artisan, she turned up at our wedding shoeless, in a home-made goat-skin dress. Followed a strict raw food diet for seventeen years. Hasn't washed her hair for over two decades (hair is designed to 'self-clean', apparently). Thinks coffee is a kind of poison. Once tried to knit a hat for her dog (a basset) out of spider's webs.

Dear old Trudy.

And now this is all *my* problem? Now just hang on a second ... I have seven recovering drug addicts with their terrifyingly large and touchingly hopeful Catholic families in tow jamming up my workshop in Monterrey, being taught wood-carving, hide tanning and – ha! – *life* skills by another recovering drug addict called Honesto Soto Salazar (who is anything but), while his loyal wife Juana, my housekeeper, plays her part, training the other wives to hand-weave classic long silk *rebozos* with their spectacularly tasselled fringes at the far end of my back porch. All these honourable endeavours are supported by an astronomical bank loan (mine, of course).

I suppose I should just sell the house (which Kimberly no longer needs, obviously) and use the proceeds to set up Trudy in a care home (but who would be willing to take her?). Unload those infernal photos to the highest bidder and damn the consequences. This isn't what Kimberly wanted, no, but then this isn't what *I* want. By 'this' I mean to be here. Back in England. East Sussex. Rye. Lamb House. The beneficiary of a brief, unasked-for interlude of hand-relief from Mrs Sage Meadows (widow) (poet) (gardener) (chef).

Now I come to ponder it, that breakfast was alarmingly high in iron and protein. Eggs Benedict followed by fried liver, kidney and bacon? One might almost think Mrs Meadows was priming me for something.

I wonder what she stands to gain from this curious transaction? Oh I do hope I don't … *you* know … all over my clean suit. Should I pass her the handkerchief in my waistcoat pocket? Or would that be ungallant? The social politics of these situations are quite literally a minefield. A minefield! And she a poor widow! And *me* a poor widower (come to that)! I need to be immensely sensitive – kind – charitable. This situation wants – needs – *demands* prodigious levels of tact.

I confess to having had quite mixed feelings about this whole torrid/intimate exchange from the outset. But what was the alternative? A polite rejection? And how to time it? And what to say? And how to maintain eye contact afterwards? And what then the likelihood of tears/bitterness/recriminations/suicidal urges (she calls herself a poet for heaven's sake!)? She would have been *mortified*, surely? Utterly *mortified* (Just wave

those fascinating private diaries – which you don't even want
– a quiet toodle-oo, Frankie-boy). I mean to reject her, curtly,
brusquely, out of hand. Is that gentlemanly? For it to be made
so … so *abundantly clear* that she'd overstepped the mark?
Which she so patently had?! Human decency alone forbids
this course.

I suppose Miss Hahn *did* have a point about the whole 'I'm
moving into Henry James's old house and therefore my awful
poems about bluebells and *feelings* and lace and chiffchaffs will
somehow be magically transformed – transubstantiated (is that
an appropriate use?) into Serious Art' thing. 'Embarrassing'
(was that the word she used?) is certainly a little harsh. But
'suspect'? 'Gauche'? 'Naive'? 'Utterly unfounded'?

In terms of our future relationship (Ha! *What* future
relationship?) (To be absolutely brutal) I think I can probably
get away with acting as if the entire, curious interlude has
been a strange – almost psychedelic – dream. My grief is my
shield in this regard. I'm not thinking straight. How *could* I
be? I am vulnerable. Poor Franklin. Poor, dear Franklin. So
giving. So open. So kind. So generous. But so … so
immensely vulnerable.

If Miss Hahn (damp cardboard, dead starfish) would just
… Oops!
Gracious me!
There we go!
Oh, very well managed, Mrs Sage! What a pro!
Uh … Right. Good. Wonderful.

Another cup of your delicious espresso, my dear? Might I
possibly … uh … use the bathroom? First door on the right?
What an amazing shine on the parquet! Is the panelling
original?
Ah. Yes. Uh …
Wasn't it *The Ambassadors* he penned here? In this very room,
you say? *The Golden Bowl*? Oh. I must confess to never
having got around to …

Lord Give Me Strength! How soon before I can make my excuses and head home?

18

Miss Carla Hahn

An awful catalogue of catastrophes! For starters I left the money (for Mr Huff, like a *fool*) on the bus. In my purse. In my string bag. Luckily, another passenger, the wife of the nice man who fixes electricals in Ore (the seventh person today to say, 'Excuse me, but did you happen to know that there's something ... uh ... a dark mark/a blotch/a smudge on your ...?' Oh yes, *yes*. I *do* know. And it's indelible, I'm afraid. Thank you so very much for telling me, though ...), kindly alerted the driver and he promptly stopped the bus (a breach of *all* regulations, apparently), jumped out and bellowed after me. I ran back over the Sea Road to retrieve it (puce-cheeked) and was almost hit by an oncoming cyclist. 'Clipped' I suppose you'd say. He swerved so violently to avoid me that he came flying off his bike and skidded several feet across the tarmac on his side. I was slightly winded (it was more the shock of it than anything) and sustained (at worst, in all likelihood) a tender, little bruise on my shoulder.

I grabbed the bag, white as a sheet (the driver said, 'This is a breach of all regulations! You're white as a sheet!'), while inanely garbling a thousand apologies ('Oh I'm *so* sorry! Sorry! Very sorry! So sorry!'), and then ran back (was almost hit by a *car* this time – he sounded his horn, furiously) to help the poor cyclist. He was already on his feet and picking up his bike. There was a small tear in the back of his trousers. Right in the middle. Which was rather embarrassing. His palms were grazed. 'It's fine, it's fine,' he growled. He wouldn't even look at me as I offered to … oh I don't know; take him back to Mulberry to clean his wounds, sew up his trousers, make him a cup of … He just seemed utterly determined (at *any* cost) to escape my pointless ministrations. I asked him if he'd noticed an overwhelming smell of eucalyptus (there was one), then spat on my hanky and proffered it to him. He glowered at it shaking his head, almost incapable of speech, then clambered on to his bike and rode off (not another word – he *hated* me) looking slightly wobbly, the pedals (or was it the back mudguard?) producing an awful, metallic, keening sound which alerted several gulls from the adjacent marsh (the tide was fully in) who flew along behind him (quite maddeningly) for several minutes, squawking wildly.

I turned and headed up Toot Rock; shaken, almost tearful. After blowing my nose a couple of times (I often find blowing one's nose has a positive psychological impact), I was casually shoving my previously rejected (but now used) hanky into my trouser pocket when it was caught by a sudden gust of wind (which, from a purely rational perspective, seems somewhat ridiculous: it's been warm and slightly airless all day, and the hanky is a large one, 100 per cent cotton, quite heavy). Away it blew, straight into a large clump of brambles on the side of the road. Of course I reached over to try and retrieve it, and in the process my cardigan became snagged on a series of little hooks and thorns. I released my string bag to free up my hands and the next five minutes (I don't exaggerate) were spent disentangling myself, then my hanky, then myself again (June Seelinger's idiotic spaniel standing poised at the kerb, meanwhile, watching me incredulously, apparently *very* entertained by my total folly), during which freeing-up process I re-hooked the hanky (argh!) so then I just … I simply withdrew. I left the damn thing *in situ*, quietly observing, once again, that powerful eucalyptus smell (is it … is it *me*? Have I …? Have I somehow managed to …?), before cursing furiously, gathering together the contents of my bag (I had inadvertently kicked the damn thing with my foot during the extraction process and the meagre contents were now spread all over the road) and marching off.

Someone more credulous – more given to superstitious thoughts, I suppose – might suspect the involvement of supernatural forces in the seeming sabotage of this superficially uncontentious delivery process. Or perhaps, I pondered (falling back instead, rather more keenly, on the teachings of science), it's merely my unconscious mind trying to trip me up ... But then why ...? What could I possibly ...? Uh ...?

I had walked approximately twenty steps (was still only just approaching the Coastguards' Cottages) when I began casually fishing around in my bag for the little envelope of cash. For some reason, I didn't remember scooping it back into the ... or maybe it ... when the ...?

The envelope was gone. Of course it was. It was gone. The envelope of cash was gone. It was gone. This discovery was followed by another strong whiff of ... oh *you* know.

Okay, so now I *was* beginning to feel a tiny element – a minuscule tinge – of paranoia. I ran back to the bramble bush (distinguished from all the others by its glorious raiment) and hunted for the envelope. Nothing. Had it been taken out – stolen? – or ... or dropped while I was in Rye, perhaps, or on the bus? No. *No.* Surely not.

I headed back towards the Sea Road in a panic. It was here – at the halfway point, just before the little bridge – that I re-encountered Joyce (the spaniel). But only his (yes, he's a boy) fluffy brown and white rump. He was rooting around between some tall banks of nettles, digging for moles (as is his habit). I just ... don't ask me why I thought this or did this, but I noticed a large molehill right next to the spot where Joyce was digging and I felt a profound need, an *urge*, to march on over and kick at it with my foot. This I duly did, and there, hidden under several centimetres of fresh soil, was the envelope. Muddy, but still miraculously intact.

Extraordinary! I bent down to retrieve it, quite astonished by my good luck (or bad luck, depending on your take on it) at the exact moment at which the digging Joyce uncovered a mole in an adjacent hole. The spaniel drew back on his haunches for a split second, with sheer surprise (I expect). And oh! It was the most beautiful, handsome, blackly velvet mole! Unearthed! Horror-struck! Pink hands (inside their giant boxing gloves) flailing in the air. Magnificent bewhiskered winkle-picker snout vibrating wildly, sending out little Morse code messages of shock and alarm to any creature sensitive enough to receive them. Ah, and that wondrously hypnotic hairless spot on the sides of the head where the eyes should be, but where they aren't, still blinking, somehow, instinctively blinking, sightlessly at … at …

I lunged towards Joyce to thwart his initial attack, grabbing him by the tail. Joyce was not best pleased and turned to snap at me, I rolled to avoid his teeth and crashed, head first, into the bank of nettles.

Ow! Ow! Ow! Ow! *Ow!*

Ow!

But I held on fast.

Joyce and I then wrestled away dynamically for a brief duration (it was dreadfully undignified – for both parties). Thirty seconds passed, at most, before I released his tail (so *glad* Mrs Seelinger didn't see fit to dock it), by which time the miraculous little mole had sensibly withdrawn.

Joyce was livid and returned to the hole to recommence digging with a renewed (if slightly grim) enthusiasm.

I was covered – *covered* – in nettle stings: face, neck, hands, stomach.

Ow!

I grabbed the envelope of cash, shoved it into my bag and began hunting around for some dock. There's always a clump of dock near a patch of nettles. Always. *Always*. It's ancient country lore. But ...

No. Nope. No dock. Not so much as a whiff of it. Although very much a whiff of ... (Urgh. I can't even bring myself to say it.)

Smarting, stung, defeated, I started back up the road again. No further misadventures (at least that I was aware of) took place in the following few minutes (no lightning-strike, no Martian abduction, no puma attack). I entered Mulberry through the little, cast-iron gate. The bin and an ancient (bad) apple tree to my right obscured the old mulberry (the cottage's namesake) which I suddenly (*No!* No, Carla! Stay focused, you idiot!) had the strong desire – in the light of my recent dream – to take a proper look at.

I squeezed past the bin, ducked under the branches of the apple and found the trunk of the old mulberry right up close to the fence, almost obliterated by ivy. I pulled idly at a couple of strands and they came away easily, so I yanked at a couple more, until eventually I was attacking the stump like a madwoman, pulling and ripping, tearing it from the bark.

How long it took me to clear the trunk I have no idea. But eventually it was done and I stepped back to appraise my work, slightly breathless. The tree was dead. Very dead. As a doornail. I tried to recall Mrs Vaughn and her spread-out checkered blanket; that magnificent fruiting tree in its prime, the giant spearmint-green leaves, the succulent berries, but it was difficult to visualize that scene here, where the tree currently stood, so close to the fence. So cramped.

I took a further step back to try and imagine the apple smaller or gone (but it's an old tree, too – or perhaps simply aged by disease ...?) and as I did this, I was stabbed, savagely, violently, in the back of the neck. I screamed. The impact of this tiny, awful blade was so sudden, so vicious: a blinding, bright white pain. I turned around, panicked, and saw a dark, flashing entity which hung in the air before me and then dropped like a tiny stone. A hornet. A hornet! Stung by a hornet on the back of the neck!

No! *No!* This was too much! This was way too much now! 'Enough, Orla!' I yelled. 'You're scaring me! Enough now! Enough!'

I leaned forward (resting my palms on my knees) and breathed deeply, slightly dizzy, my neck burning and throbbing remorselessly. And as I breathed I waited – resignedly – for that all too familiar aroma …

But … No. Nothing. I sniffed again, actively, glancing up, scowling. And as I glanced I could've sworn I saw something: three … no … *four* digits, scratched into the trunk …

'Jesus wept! *Carla?!* Is that you, child?'

I inhaled, sharply. It was Mrs Barrow, presumably alerted from next door by my histrionics as she hung out her washing (Mrs Barrow can invariably be found – rain, sleet or shine – in the act of hanging out her washing).

She was leaning over the fence.

'Good gracious me! What have you been an' done to yourself, you foolish creature?' she exclaimed. 'Your face is all up in hives!'

I explained about the nettles. And the hornet. I moved closer to the fence and Mrs Barrow carefully appraised the back of my neck like one primate fastidiously inspecting another's shaggy pelt for edible parasites.

'Oh it's got you good an' proper!' she muttered. 'You must of upset its nest mucking about with that old mulberry stump. Up like a quail's egg it is! Red as a beet! No sting more painful than a hornet's in all the English countryside,' (she helpfully added, with a smidgeon of patriotic pride) 'not even your poison adder.'

I explained (still wincing at the discomfort, sniffing, eyes watering, moving gently from foot to foot) that I had come around to deliver an envelope to Mr Huff.

'First things first …' Mrs Barrow brandished a yellow, plastic peg-bag at me, opened it and withdrew a blue, plastic peg. 'We needs to extract us that there sting.'

'With a peg?' I wasn't entirely convinced.

'Knock at it with a flat edge, that's the secret. Never tweeze a sting, Carla. If you tweezes a sting you runs the risk of pushing yet more venom into the flesh. Mr Barrow was once bit twelve times by the same creature. Insides of his thigh. Come an' stand by the fence a'gin and lean yourself slightly a-forward.'

Mrs Barrow then proceeded to remove the sting with the flat edge of the peg.

Ow.

I thanked her gratefully, in spite of the discomfort.

'Now the next thing as we'll be needing us is …'

I thought she might say 'ice'.

'WD-40.'

'Sorry?' I performed a little double-take.

'Works a treat on bites, it does. Mr Barrow swears by it. I'll go and fetch it from the shed, shall I? Won't be more'n a minute.'

She promptly headed off towards the house.

'You happen to notice that there shrine of yourn?' she yelled over her shoulder, as an afterthought, as she rapidly retreated.

'Sorry?'

'I thought as you might've seen it.' Mrs Barrow's voice faded. 'Quite marvellous, it is.'

'The shrine?'

I grabbed my bag with my free hand (the other still affixed to the throbbing lump at the back of my neck) and waded through the long grass towards the side of the cottage, idly remembering Clifford's words from the previous day about the woman with the two setters tending to the thing. As I approached it from a distance my nostrils were assailed, once again, by the powerful scent of eucalyptus.

The ground around the shrine (which, in itself, was only a modest construction – two foot by three, at best) I could tell – even from some way off – had recently been weeded and the grass cut flat. There was a tiny, purplish-leaved hellebore in a plastic pot placed reverently alongside it (tag of dedication reading, *My Dearest, Sweetest Orla, who Suffered for Us all, Most Beloved confidante of The Most Blessed Virgin Queen, you* know *the secret agonies of my heart. Please,* please *help me to resolve them now, as you have done so often in the past. J*) and the standard (slightly irritating) collection of plastic roses, mouldering dolls and teddy bears. But the shrine itself, which consisted of a mid-size concrete statue of the Virgin Mary (poorly executed, her cloak covered in somewhat lurid peeling turquoise paint; several faded wreaths of paper flowers draped around her neck), and a smaller concrete angel – of a later, but no more tasteful generation, mercifully unpainted – kneeling in prayer, facing her (slightly lopsidedly), both encircled – or en-squared, to be precise – by a greening, brass surround with a small, rotting, wooden plaque (installed by dear Mrs Vaughn herself, somewhat under pressure from various visitors and pilgrims over the years), which simply read: *Orla Nor Cleary, 1960–1972, One of Holy Mary's Most Fragrant Flowers, Plucked too Soon, may she Rest in Peace* (the mixture of upper- and lower-case letters had always been a source of considerable wonderment to me) and was now absolutely covered – smothered – in an exquisite, dense mass – a carpet – of tiny, white forget-me-nots.

But where on earth had they all come from? Did the woman with the setters …? I drew up close to the shrine and knelt down, slipping my fingers between the mass of blooms to inspect the soil beneath. Nope. There was no evidence of any recent disruption. These flowers had grown naturally, of their own volition, presumably from seed (I reasoned).

But then didn't I ...? How long ago? Not yesterday – no, not properly, not consciously – but ...? And hadn't it been ...? Uh ...

Still the smell of eucalyptus! I suddenly remembered how Orla would chuckle about it – she always seemed to find it hilarious. But then Orla would laugh about pretty much everything; every difficulty, every setback, every trial, every problem was viewed through a permanent filter of ... well ... *joy*. Everything. *Everything*.

And she insisted that it wasn't *her* scent at all, but the scent of Mary that surrounded her (at first only intermittently, but constantly by the end), claiming that Mary always carried the sweet perfume of flowers with her – roses, violets. But it got lost in translation, somehow, and to our rather more practical, slightly less elevated senses Orla was surrounded by the scent of eucalyptus. Not roses, no. Nor violets. It's a clean smell, and warm but ... well, acidic – *sharp*?

Was I allergic to it back then? Why can't I remember? Or did that come ... was it after?

Kalinda (aka 'Lonely', her mother) always found the smell unbearable. That much I *did* know. It reminded her of her childhood home: the Australian Rangelands. I grinned as I remembered the first time she casually mentioned the name of the place she originated from. 'Rage-lands?' I'd repeated, struggling to translate her heavy accent. '*Rage? Rage*-lands?' Orla had burst out laughing. 'What do you think, Ma?' She'd grinned. '*Rage*-lands? Is that home? Is that where you come from, Ma?'

Kalinda railed against everything – *raged* against everything. I'd never met a woman who ... who *burned*, who glowered, who *smouldered* so ...

'Not a thing there yesterday,' Mrs Barrow (who had suddenly appeared at my side) cheerfully observed, shattering my brief reverie: 'Then this morning, stone the crows: all a-flower, they was.'

She sniffed the air. 'You smell that?' she asked, suspiciously. 'The girl's room was full of it the other day. Kept all the flies at bay, it did. Now it's here.'

She shook the little can of WD-40 (as if intending to use it to defeat an invisible adversary).

'Forget-me-nots,' I mused. 'And they haven't been freshly planted. They must've been growing here all along, hidden amongst the weeds.'

'It was cleared yesterday; top to toe. Nothing left – not so much as a scrap of *any*thing,' Mrs Barrow reiterated. 'How's the sting?' she finished off.

'Sorry?' I looked up, frowning.

'The sting,' she repeated.

'Oh.'

I lifted my hand to the back of my neck and felt around, blithely. Dissatisfied by the findings of this first hand, I dropped it and used my other … Uh … *Nope*. The bite had disappeared. It was gone!

Noticing my bewildered expression, Mrs Barrow shifted around to take a look herself.

'Gone,' she intoned, slightly ominous. 'An' your face – the nettle stings is all a-faded.'

I put my hand to my cheek.

'But you got yourself a big smudge of something or other right the way across—'

'I know,' I snapped. 'It was an accident. Permanent marker pen. It won't—'

'And see your poor hands!' Mrs Barrow interrupted, aghast. 'White as milk they are!'

As she spoke, she took a precautionary step back. 'Crikey! Mr Barrow won't like the sound of this one bit,' she continued. 'Maybe those Papists and all them filthy Romanies and whatnot aren't nearly so backward as how they seem to us normal folk.'

She took a further step back.

Eventually I murmured, 'I'm sure there's got to be a sensible explanation …'

'Mr Barrow won't like it one bit,' Mrs Barrow repeated.

'Then don't tell him.' I smiled, trying to make light of it. I clambered to my feet.

'Forget-me-nots,' Mrs Barrow mused. 'But them's white-uns …'

'A common enough strain.' I shrugged, grabbing the envelope of cash from my bag and heading towards the front door. Mrs Barrow followed.

'I'm still smelling it,' she grumbled. 'Very strong. Like a fancy disinfectant.'

I stood on the front porch and tried to push the envelope through the letterbox, but the flap – which had always been stiff – wouldn't shift *at all*.

Eh? I peered at it closely. It almost looked … well … *rusted* shut. I smacked at it with the side of my palm. No movement. So next I tried the door handle. The door was locked.

'It ain't locked,' Mrs Barrow insisted, 'he never locks nothing, that one. I suppose it's 'cos he's got nothing worth the taking of.'

I tried the handle again. It came off in my palm.

'This is ridiculous!' I exclaimed, finally losing patience. I planted the handle into the front pocket of Mrs Barrow's housecoat and stomped around to the back. Mrs Barrow followed, slightly affronted. 'What're you expecting *me* to do with it?' she demanded.

I climbed up on to the back porch and tried the back door. Again the door was locked.

'I'm delivering this damn thing if it's the last thing I do!' I muttered, flapping the envelope, slightly hysterical now.

'It isn't locked,' Mrs Barrow insisted, 'I was in there not half an hour since.'

I knelt down and attempted to push the envelope under the door, but the gap – much as I'd suspected – was too narrow.

I scrambled to my feet and tried the handle again. Still locked. Mrs Barrow (losing patience), shoved me out of the way and tried the door herself. This time the handle came away in *her* hand.

'Now I'm getting myself proper spooked,' she growled. 'What exactly have you got in that envelope of yours, Carla?'

'Only cash,' I answered, slightly defensive.

'An' what's it be *for*, precisely?'

'Uh … I'm paying Mr Huff back his rental money.' I shrugged.

'Guilty conscience?' Mrs Barrow snorted.

'Because his wife died!' I hotly retorted.

'Mrs Ashe?' Mrs Barrow was suitably horror-struck. 'Dead, you say?'

'Uh …' I floundered, unsure how precisely to answer this question without begging several dozen more.

'No. *No*. His *first* wife,' I eventually settled for. 'Not Mrs Ashe.'

'Oh.'

Mrs Barrow mulled this over.

'And he might need to return home for the … you know … funeral,' I added.

'Ah.' Mrs Barrow nodded.

'So I thought I'd refund some of his rental money, as a gesture of …'

'Poor soul's broke as the Ten Commandments,' Mrs Barrow interjected.

'Yes. Apparently so.'

'Well …' Mrs Barrow inspected the newly detached handle. 'I think as it would be fair to say that some body – or some *thing* – ain't too keen on you delivering that there envelope.'

'Don't be silly,' I pooh-poohed her, jumping down off the porch and heading towards the air-raid shelter where a selection of old tools was generally stored.

'You can scoff alls you like, girlie …'

166

Mrs Barrow followed. '… but don't you reckon as it might …?'

I emerged from the shelter holding an old screwdriver. First I tried to re-affix the back door handle (to no avail; the screwdriver was too small to mesh with the fitments), next I tried the front door (featuring the same generation of old, Bakelite handle; but the screwdriver was too large this time). I returned to the shelter and re-emerged, thoroughly exasperated, with a nail and a hammer.

'For the love of God, Carla!' Mrs Barrow exclaimed. I marched back up to the front door, placed the envelope against its wood, positioned the nail in one corner, drew back the hammer and the head flew off. Mrs Barrow (standing – somewhat ill-advisedly – at my shoulder) quickly ducked and only narrowly avoided being hit by it.

'Okay. Fine. Perhaps you should call in Mr Norwood,' I compromised. 'Explain to him about the doors. And the screwdriver. Get him to pop over as soon as he possibly can.' (Mr Norwood was our local odd-jobs man.) I placed both handles on to the doormat, side by side.

'And what about your envelope?'
'Uh … Oh.' I turned. 'Well I thought *you* might possibly consider …?'
Mrs Barrow leapt back (by approximately a foot) as I casually proffered it to her. Nope. This plainly wasn't to be an option.
'Right.'
I tore the envelope open, withdrew the cash, then knelt down on the front step and proceeded to feed the money, painstakingly, individual note by individual note, through the minute gap under the bottom of the door, culminating, finally, with the envelope itself.

Mrs Barrow watched me (from a safe distance), wincing theatrically, as if waiting for some dramatic consequence. But there wasn't one (no unexplained gust of wind forcing it back out again, no flickering flame, no sudden flood). The money was delivered. It was done.

'Goodbye, Mr Huff,' I murmured softly, thoroughly satisfied – even a little smug (a tiny, impertinent fist, tightly clenched, shaking, defiantly, against the gods).

Goodbye, Mr Huff.

Yes. Yes. *Yes*. And a very good riddance to you, too! I thought.

19

Mr Franklin D. Huff

I swear I had no idea that it was actually a sauna. Absolutely none. It was an honest mistake. I thought it was just a shed – that our dear Miss Hahn was simply rootling around inside a shed (something that I don't doubt she is often – *very* often – wont to be found doing). In fact there were other sheds in the vicinity. Several of them. In various stages of collapse. One of which appeared to be hanging off a small precipice.

Although what kind of an idiot – an *idiot* – would you have to be to persist in inhabiting a place that is so patently unsafe? Not out of dire need. Or poverty. Or mental illness (at least not so far as I am aware). But to actively pursue it – to … to *celebrate* it, almost like it's some kind of wild and crazy lifestyle choice! A place where the ground might slip right out from under you at *any* given moment?

What kind of a stupid, arrogant, bumptious, over-confident *fool* would you have to be to actively pursue a life on the edge of an unstable cliff? Not even on the edge – *beyond* the edge (a significant section of Miss Hahn's 'garden' was in 'tiers', *below* the drop!).

No. It simply made no sense to me. None at all. It just seemed so … so unbelievably … complacent. Yes. That's it. Such … such *complacency*. To be so … so cocky, so *complacent*. Even uttering the word. Even uttering the word – 'complacent' – made my hackles start to rise. Even so much as … as *uttering* the word. Even engaging with the concept. To be so complacent. To be so … so *complacent*.

These (the above, but artfully edited here of swearing etc.) were (approximately) my thoughts as I wandered through Miss Hahn's strange, little bungalow (the front door was left wide open!), calling out her name, then (having had no success in discovering her actual whereabouts), into the back garden which was a huge, ramshackle affair with astonishing views (*natch! View-schmiew!* Yeah. Change the damn record why don't cha?), the shabby lawn peppered with a succession of visible faults (well, to the knowledgeable eye, at least), and then falling, in a succession of dramatic (and patently unstable) steps, down, down, down into the sea far below.

These, in fact, were my thoughts as I tiptoed, very tentatively, across that fractured lawn, finally detecting a very slight and vague – almost inaudible – answer to my call. I was thinking: To be so ... so arrogant, so *complacent* as to believe that it simply won't happen to you, that it simply *couldn't* happen to you. As if all those other poor buggers in the world who ...

I'd already decided to tear her off a strip. Yes I had. I really had. I was suddenly livid – perfectly furious. Almost disproportionately so. Was it the ...? I glanced around me, tensed, as if waiting for some terrible impact ... There was something about the vista, the view, the ... the ... which suddenly brought to mind ... which filled me with a perfectly explicable (yet correspondingly inexplicable) sense of ... Foreboding? Fear? Awe? *Déjà vu?*

I knew why.

When I finally routed Miss Hahn I planned to tell her about a tragedy I once covered as a reporter in Yungay, Peru, where the whole town had been decimated by a giant landslide of mud and ice and glacial rock after the Ancash earthquake sent a giant chunk of the north section of a nearby mountain crashing down on to it. An American scientist friend of an American scientist friend called Charlie Sawyer had warned the Peruvian press almost ten years before that a giant slab of rock was being worn away by the glacier and threatened to obliterate the town. He and his research partner were promptly driven out of the country under threat of arrest.

Fast-forward to 1970, and 25,000 people were buried alive under that same giant slab. A grand total of ninety-two survived. They didn't even bother to excavate Yungay in the end, just left it as it was, planting a giant statue of Jesus on top of it, like a demented, Catholic cherry on a stupendous – and completely avoidable – cake of death. In fact I travelled back a few years ago for the ten-year anniversary. I'd made a great Peruvian friend in the area – a wonderful man called Mateo Amaru Mamani Martinez – whose mother actually ran the little boarding house I stayed in on the trip. He was training to be a geologist. His girlfriend (later his wife) and her entire extended family all lived in the town. Every single one of the girlfriend's relatives (twenty-seven family members, in total) was killed.

Like I say, I'd decided to tear Miss Hahn off a strip but it was just a question of ... of *finding* the damn woman to facilitate this process when ... uh ... that curiously muffled response originating from ... uh ... was it ... uh ... was it ...? I delivered a sharp rap to the shed door and then yanked it open. Even as I did so I was reprimanding the poor creature in no uncertain terms (I'd built up quite a head of *steam* by this stage – which, in retrospect, was rather appropriate given that Miss Hahn was sitting, all but naked, inside a tiny sauna).

'I'm *astonished* by your complacency, Miss Hahn!' I snapped, and then ... Oh yes. Then the awful, dawning realization that ... uh ... As I already mentioned. Ho-hum.

Miss Hahn was tying a towel around herself. My glasses immediately fogged up. But not before I'd had the chance to note, internally, that she was slightly pink, all over, and that she had very beautiful shoulders. The particular jut of her pinkened collar bones was extraordinarily ...

171

'*My* complacency?' Miss Hahn sprang to her feet. I took a couple of steps back (quite risky in this location with absolutely no – zero, zilch – visibility).

'Yes,' I persisted, slightly losing the thread of my thoughts, 'to voluntarily set up permanent camp in such a ...'

'I'm having a *sauna*, Mr Huff.' Miss Hahn's voice was quite clipped (Germanic. Even more so than normal – although it isn't that clipped normally. Nor Germanic). 'Do you honestly think it's *appropriate* behaviour to barge in on a lone female while she's ... while ... in the privacy of her *own* home and then accuse her of ... of ...'

She waved her pinkened arm.

'Complacency,' I repeated.

'Complacency,' she finished off. But there was a slight question mark in her voice. This was probably because there is nothing specifically complacent about the act of taking a sauna, I suppose. Although saunas strike me as such ridiculous things. To sit in a tiny room and sweat. It's so ludicrously *Swedish*. And the Swedes are – by and large – a somewhat supercilious, ridiculously reasonable, utterly dull and, one might easily say, maddeningly complacent tribe. Although not so bad as the Norwegians with their sanctimonious Peace Prizes and their pesky trolls and their endless bucket-loads of North Sea oil.

'Now if you'll kindly excuse me,' Miss Hahn continued, 'the sauna is all fired up, so I must head back inside.'

Well the sauna wasn't the *only* thing that was all fired up! What a prickly woman Miss Hahn is! And slightly humourless, to boot. Ha! So much for her determinedly bohemian exterior. Didn't take very long to scratch the surface of *that* particular paper-thin badly glued-on walnut veneer.

'There's a hole in your towel,' I informed her.

It was perhaps the oldest, tattiest towel I had ever set eyes upon. Of indeterminate hue and – worse still – of questionable hygiene.

Miss Hahn looked down at herself. The large hole in the towel corresponded with her pinkened lower thigh area. She emitted a growl (Yes, an actual growl. She really was quite incensed!), and then snatched the towel away from her body (she was naked. Underneath. And pink. I think I may have already mentioned that), bundled it up at one end (I thought she might be planning to whip me with it!) and then draped it (well, *slung* it, more like) over my shoulder.

'That's because it's the *floor* towel, Mr Huff,' she snapped. 'It's intended to be used for the *floor*. It may have escaped your notice, but you've caught me somewhat on the hop.' Then she slammed her way back inside (the imprint of a slatted, wooden bench indenting her pinkened thighs and buttocks as she angrily retreated).

I gingerly removed the floor towel from my shoulder. How odd. Did she grab the floor towel by mistake, I wonder? Doesn't she bring her *own* towel to the sauna? Or a robe? A towelling robe? Or – perish the thought – does she never actually *use* a towel in the sauna? Does she just … Does Miss Hahn simply saunter about the house and the garden (I glanced around me. Nope. She wasn't *noticeably* overlooked by any neighbours; possibly because their properties had all fallen into the sea by this stage), getting in and out of the sauna, at will, completely and utterly – *unapologetically* – starkers (and by that I mean with *no clothes on whatsoever*)? Might this be her Russian-German ancestry coming into play here?

'Miss Hahn?'
I knocked on the door.
No response (Well, perhaps a gentle harrumph).
'Miss Hahn?'
Another knock.

'Either join me in the sauna,' she yelled (irate! Plainly irate!), 'or *please* go away, Mr Huff!'
'But Miss Hahn …? Might we just …?'

'I am *having* this sauna, Mr Huff, come hell or high water. It takes several hours to fire it up and I'm *not* going to let it go to waste on *your* account.'

Pause.

'On *anybody's* account' (she modified).

Pause.

'It's nothing personal.' (Almost regretful, now.)

'Miss Hahn, might we just …? I don't …'

No response.

'I can't possibly come into the sauna in my woollen suit, Miss Hahn,' I informed her (quite strictly). 'And are you aware of the fact that there is a small fissure, a crack, running right across your lawn which disappears directly beneath this structure?'

No response.

'I just wanted to return … to *talk* to you about the money you left scattered all over the floor at the cottage, Miss Hahn.'

No response.

'Look, I'm very sorry to have walked in on you like that. Unannounced. It was rude – ungentlemanly. And I didn't mean to call you complacent, either … Well, I *did*, but that was simply when I thought this was … that you were …'

No response.

'How long does a sauna generally take, Miss Hahn?'

No response.

Oh for heaven's sake! I took off my suit and shirt and placed them (neatly folded), on to the warping seat of a dilapidated wicker lawn-chair. I pulled off my shoes and slid them underneath. I then removed my glasses and slipped them into the top of my sock (for speed of access). I cleared my throat. 'I'm coming in, Miss Hahn!' I announced. A noise emerged from within which I would struggle to describe (worse still interpret). I then knocked on the door (as a final precaution) and entered.

Urgh! A dense wall of steamy heat! It was terribly close –
terribly, *terribly* close – in there. And very small.
Claustrophobic. And dark, just a tiny, sullen, red bulb blinking
in one corner. And the air – what little remained of this most
precious of commodities – was redolent with herbs (sage?
Marjoram? Mint?). Miss Hahn was sitting bolt upright with
her knees together and her arms crossed. I sat down next to
her on the tiny, slatted bench.
'I haven't got my glasses on,' I said (by way of defending her
honour – such as it was).

'Are you seriously thinking of taking a sauna in your socks,
Mr Huff?' Miss Hahn barked.
'I'm not what you might call an habitué of the sauna,' I
confessed.
'Well do you make a habit of wearing gloves in the bath?'
Miss Hahn demanded (in a flawed attempt to draw some
ridiculous kind of parallel, I suppose).

'I've always thought saunas a little sordid,' I confided.
'I imagine even the innocent Snowdrop might be considered
"sordid" if apprehended by a sufficiently warped mind!' Miss
Hahn retorted.
'I can't entirely go along with your logic.' I shrugged.
Silence.
'And I can't pretend that I don't feel a measure of anxiety
about remaining in here – such a small space, such a tight
space – partially undressed, when there's a giant crack, a
fissure, running straight across the lawn which finishes up
directly beneath …'
I gazed down at the concrete floor. It was very dark (like I
said), but wasn't that a … a …?

'I didn't think you'd actually come in,' Miss Hahn informed
me, stiffly.
'Oh. Oh dear,' I muttered, still inspecting the floor, running
my be-socked toe over the perceived 'fault' and realizing that
it was just a water-mark.

'I mean it's only a tiny sauna,' she explained.

'Yes,' I conceded. 'It's certainly small, extremely small, but is it structurally sound? I wonder.'

'Probably not,' she sighed (as if this was the very least of her concerns). 'Although now that you *are* here,' she continued, 'I think it only fair that you remove your underwear. Otherwise you run the risk of placing me at a psychological disadvantage.'

'I've always been led to believe that the dynamics of power in a situation in which one party is naked and the other dressed, generally tend to favour the naked party,' I confided.

'*Who* led you to believe that?' Miss Hahn enquired.

'I think it's an idea that's quite commonly accepted.' I shrugged.

'People used to think the earth was flat,' Miss Hahn opined.

Silence.

'But it's round,' she eventually added.

'I fear we may be getting a little bogged down in the details.' I smiled.

'Speak for yourself,' she muttered, and as she was speaking her words were all but obliterated by a loud creaking sound.

'Do you think this structure is safe?' I bleated, knuckles whitening as I clung, for dear life, on to the rickety bench.

'Probably not,' she repeated, 'but I had to try and do something to get all this indelible ink off.'

She touched a hand to her cheek.

'Have the cracks running across the lawn been there long?' I wondered.

'About as long as I can remember,' she snorted, 'but if you're too scared to risk it, Mr Huff, then by all means ...'

Scared? *Scared?!*

Typical of our Miss Hahn to cleave so quickly, so readily, to the lingo of the schoolyard!

'I'm not remotely "scared", Miss Hahn!' I snapped.

Oh but I was! I was! I kept stopping myself from looking up. Into the dark rafters above. I'm not sure why I felt this sudden urge, or the corresponding need to counter it. But if I gave in to it and looked up I was convinced I might scream. Like a girl. Or that I might simply collapse. In a heap.

'Then just too bashful, perhaps?' She smirked, pityingly.

'You should probably know that one of my first jobs as a rookie reporter was covering the Ancash earthquake in Yungay Province, Peru,' I tartly informed her (focus, Franklin, *focus* man!), 'where an entire town was decimated by a giant landslide of mud and ice and glacial rock ...'

As I continued to speak Miss Hahn calmly placed the flats of her hands over both her ears. Interestingly, she performed this manoeuvre without fully uncovering her breasts (by leaning forward slightly, and compressing them between her elbows).

'Miss Hahn?'

The hands remained in place.

After a minute or so – she's impossible! Quite impossible! – I removed my vest.

(Can't breathe! Can't ... Can't *breathe!*)

'Happy? See? I'm not remotely scared – *or* bashful! It's simply that I ... I ... I have an important meeting which I'm supposed to be at ... at ... a ... a *phone* call! Yes! An important, international phone call. About the will. And the book deal. From my lawyer. So I need to ...'

The hands remained *in situ*.

After another minute I removed my underpants.

Hands shaking, uncontrollably.

'I've removed my underpants.'

No change.

'I *can't* remove my socks, Miss Hahn,' I hissed, 'I'm storing my glasses—'

'Then remove one sock,' she interrupted (thereby proving that she *could* actually hear me, all along). I removed one sock. It was soaking wet.

Miss Hahn promptly took her hands away from her ears.

'You were saying?' she asked, perfectly civil, now.

'Sorry?'

(Need to look up! *Want* to look up! *Must* look up!)

'The Peruvian earthquake?'

(And I *do* know why! I do! To see those strange, black birds circling, high above ... remember?)

'The Peruvian earthquake, Mr Huff?'

'Oh. *Oh.* Yes. The entire town was decimated,' I panted, 'there were casualties totalling over ...'

While I was speaking Miss Hahn leaned forward, dipped a tiny, handle-less china cup into a small, dented enamel bucket of water and then tossed this liquid on to some hot coals which were suspended in a little grate directly to the right of her.

The coals hissed furiously, and a cloud of scalding steam billowed up, enveloping us both. I instantly began to cough (to be asphyxiated in a sauna! How ignoble an end!) and it was as much as I could manage not to slam my way out of there in sheer panic. Miss Hahn, on the other hand, seemed to find the billowing steam deeply therapeutic. She pulled up her legs, wrapped her arms around her knees and threw back her head. It was a curiously closed-up and yet deeply expansive pose, putting me in mind of a figure – perhaps a nymph or an angel (real or possibly imagined) – from a William Blake watercolour.

We were silent for a while (my mouth dry as the Gobi Desert) and then Miss Hahn sighed. 'I'm dreadfully keen for you to return to Montserrat, Mr Huff ...'

'Monterrey,' I corrected her.

'... but the bad news is that Orla seems to have very different ideas. And for reasons which I can't even pretend to understand ...'

'Sorry?'

I knocked a drop of sweat from the tip of my nose.

'She doesn't want you to leave, Mr Huff. She tried every trick in the book to stop me from returning you that rent money this afternoon.'

She paused.

'Please, *please* tell me you haven't gone and brought it back again?'

'The envelope's on your kitchen counter,' I confessed. 'Sorry about that.'

Another creak! I almost sprang to my feet, but then the urge to pursue this line of enquiry, this sudden chink in Miss Hahn's previously steely armour (a chink aided, even abetted, I presumed, by the dizzying abundance of scalding steam) proved too much to resist.

'When you say "Orla doesn't want you to go,"' I muttered, 'are you referring to the ... to what I might be given to understand is the ... the *ghost* of Orla Nor Cleary?'

'Heavens no!' she exclaimed, horrified, and then, 'Well, *yes*, but not ... More the ... the spirit, the ... the *essence* ...' She grimaced, irritated. 'I'm no expert in this area, Mr Huff, I can't pretend to understand the technicalities of the thing.'

'But then ...'

(Breathe from the stomach, Franklin! That's right. Yes. That's better.)

'... isn't it possible you just ...?'

Uh ... How to put this politely? How to un-jumble the kaleidoscope of tumbling words inside my head? How to straighten them out into something approximating a straight line and then slowly, *slowly*, teeter my way along it?

'Isn't it possible that what you *take* to be a ghost,' I finally gasped, 'a ... a ... a spirit, an ... an *essence*, as you say, is simply the expression of some ... some deep-seated, unconscious desire of your own which is somehow compelling you to ... uh ...?'

'Yes. I already thought of that.' She nodded. 'But it makes no real sense. Because I don't *want* you to stay, Mr Huff. No offence intended, but at best you're a problem to be solved, at worst you're a threat. It's nothing personal ... well it *is* personal because you lied to me about your identity – you ran over my mother's cat ... Although of course that's all water under the bridge as things currently stand.'

'I'm not sure if you fully comprehend the meaning of the phrase "unconscious desire",' I still persisted (very bravely, slightly piqued). 'And in point of fact I *didn't* run over your mother's cat—'

'What you need to realize,' she interrupted, 'is that quite contrary to what you seem determined to believe, I'm not heading a passionate campaign to defend the honour – or otherwise – of Orla Nor Cleary against the cruel assaults of a secular world. This isn't about that for me. It never was. What I'm actually doing is defending myself – and those I love. I'm maintaining a distance. I'm protecting myself *from* Orla.'

'From the ghost of Orla?' I was confused.

'I *can't* surrender,' Miss Hahn murmured, rubbing distractedly at her cheek with the back of her fingers. 'I saw what happened to that poor girl close at hand. Just being *near* her ...' She shuddered. 'At the end. I saw how ...'

She was silent for a while. I waited, nerves jangling.

'Religion – *faith*, for Orla – was, *is* all about forcing yourself to do the things you don't want to do,' she finally continued, 'for God. For souls. All about suffering, guilt, surrender. And I can't. I *can't*. Not more than I already have. I won't. Because ... Because it scares me. To obliterate the self, so joyously, the way she did. The way a child does. Can an adult do that? *Should* they? Because when will it ever end, Mr Huff? What are the boundaries? When does it ever stop?'

'Are you ... Are you suggesting ... Are ... Are ...'
(Hold it together, Franklin!)
'Are you saying that you think we may have common cause
here, Miss Hahn?' I stuttered, slightly breathless. 'Because I'm
not entirely sure ...'

'There was this passage from the Bible Orla always loved to
quote.' She smiled as she remembered. 'Whenever her actions
provoked any kind of an argument, she'd murmur, "Our Lord
said, 'Do you suppose that I came to give peace on Earth? I
tell you, not at all, but rather division.'"'

She slowly shook her head. 'I always found that so ... so
confusing. I honestly used to believe – before, *before* Orla –
that the New Testament was all about everybody just ... just
loving one another! Jesus suffering so that the rest of us didn't
really *need* to.'
'Jesus as the Get Out Of Jail Free card!' I panted, grinning,
slightly ghoulishly.
'The truth is that when God *gives* you something' – she
scowled – 'it's a kind of ... a kind of ... I suppose the word
I'm thinking of is *bribe*, but it's not quite so ...'

I quietly watched her talking – struggling to amass her
thoughts – in profile. She looked straight ahead of her. She
seemed almost ... almost compelled to speak. To explain. It
was as though my abundant discomfort, my strange, pulsing
anxiety (I was deafened – utterly deafened – by my own
heartbeat!) had somehow released (untapped!) this little geyser
of words from within her. But the more she spoke the more
intense my claustrophobia grew. As if the very information I
had craved all along was acting as some kind of ... of *tinder* to
my soul. It wasn't quenching me, satisfying me, but rather
setting me on fire. Lighting up my fear. But of ... of *what*
exactly?

'"For everyone to whom much is given,"' she finally
quoted, '"from him much will be required: and to whom
much has been committed, of him they will ask the more."'

She turned and gazed at me, intently.

I was perplexed. Confused. Terrified. I slowly shook my head.

'Orla appeared in a dream and healed my hands,' Miss Hahn sighed. She held them up for me to inspect. My vision was slightly blurry. But I blinked at them, nonetheless, quite gamely.

'So ... so you think ...?'

'And she definitely doesn't want you to go,' she insisted.

But I *must* go, I thought. I must. I *must.*

'Perhaps you ... perhaps you healed your own hands?' I volunteered.

'Then she adjusted my alarm clock so I'd think I couldn't make the bank ...' Miss Hahn paused, scowling. 'Although that could've just been me, like you say ... A simple mistake – an accident. I might've knocked it over myself, after the dream, in a panic.'

She cradled her head in the crook of her arm for a minute, plainly in conflict.

Another loud creak.

I yelped (inadvertently masking my genitals in my panic).

'Then I left my bag on the bus,' she continued, perfectly oblivious, 'something I'd never normally do. With the money in it. But the driver stopped the bus and returned it, which is a breach of all regulations, apparently. And as I was crossing the Sea Road to fetch it I was hit by a passing cyclist.'

'Hit?' I was concerned (and furtively removed my shaking hands). 'Were you hurt?'

She straightened her head, shook it, and indicated, dismissively, towards a small bruise on her shoulder. I blinked at it, owlishly.

'Then I was almost knocked down by a car, seconds later.'

'But wasn't that just ...?' I started off.

'Sheer stupidity on my part?' she snorted. 'Very possibly.'

'Mrs Barrow said ... uh ...' – I struggled to focus my thoughts – 'something ... something about a hornet sting. On your ...'

'So then I headed up Toot Rock,' she continued (ignoring me), 'and my handkerchief was suddenly snatched away by a gust of wind. It landed in some nearby brambles ...' She paused. 'It was an airless day – I don't know if you ...? If you noticed that at all?'

'Your ...?' I echoed, blankly.

'Yes. And while I was retrieving it – which took an *age* – Joyce got into the bag and took the money.'

'Joyce?'

'Mrs Seelinger's spaniel.'

'Oh. *Oh.*'

'I found it – the envelope – after a short hunt, buried inside a mole hole.'

'Okay ...'

(I was starting to think Miss Hahn – and possibly even *I* – might've been indulging in hallucinogenic drugs by this point.)

'But then Joyce managed to dig up a mole – in a different hole – so I grabbed him by the tail ...'

'Do moles actually *have* tails?' I gasped.

'The dog's tail' – she grinned – 'Joyce's tail.'

'Joyce is a ... a ... *boy* dog?'

Boy dog?!

'Yes. And I fell into some nettles to save the mole and was stung all over.'

'*Ouch,*' I murmured. For some reason ... for some inexplicable reason, the hair on my body was all beginning to stand on end. As if alerted to something ... As if my body had become aware of something that my eyes, my nose, my *ears* hadn't even quite yet ...

'I couldn't find any dock, but there was this powerful smell of eucalyptus,' Miss Hahn continued, 'Orla's smell. In fact

183

every time something bad happened, there was the smell, that sweet, fusty smell, all around me.'

That was it! Eucalyptus! It was eucalyptus! In the air! Not mint or sage or marjoram! It was eucalyptus!

It was eucalyptus!

It was eucalyptus!

The girl was here!

The girl was *here*!

With me! With Miss Hahn!

Eucalyptus!

And the more I heard the word echo in my head the less sense the compound sounds made to me: *You-Cal-yip-tus!*

I just … I just really *had* to stop her from talking! Surely it was her words that were releasing this … this intoxicating … this asphyxiating … this dreadful vapour! But the urge to discover and then … If I could only … But without … If I could only … But these conflicting impulses … How to …?

'Eucalyptus,' I repeated, just repeating things, now, quite eradicated, now.

'So I went up to the house and when I got there I went to see the old mulberry tree, just to take a look. And then I found myself pulling all this ivy off the dead trunk …'

'Well this has been … uh … great. Very … uh … illuminating. But I should …I should probably …'

Did I say that? Or did I actually ask, 'Which old mulberry?' I started scrabbling around for my clothes.

'The old mulberry that the cottage originally got its name from. It was in my dream – last night. But in the dream it was still in full leaf, shedding leaves. And I was gathering them up. And then I was collecting up the fruit – the mulberries. They were falling down … so … so hard … almost *pelting* down on me. And I thought my hands would be all crimson – from … with the juice. But my hands were a pure white, and I felt …'

She shook her head. 'Suddenly I was inside the cottage, but I was still gathering up the leaves. Although now they were eucalyptus leaves; you may remember I'm *allergic* to disinfectant, so I was feeling a measure of anxiety. Then Orla appeared and—'

I drew myself up straight. 'Is there anything more ... more *boring* ... more ... more ... *boring* than other people's boring dreams?' I interrupted, determined to silence her, to shut her up, before her porous words drained away all final vestiges of peace, of ... of quiet, of *air* ... or ... or ... before they released any more of this ... this terrifying vapour ...
Which was it?
Neither?
Both?

She turned to glare at me, balefully. 'I'm as infuriated by all this as you are, Mr Huff,' she grumbled. 'I think it's ridiculous. I honestly do. I just want it to stop. It *had,* stopped, to all intents and purposes, before you arrived here. That's why I wish you'd never come. That's why I long for you to leave and head back to Montserrat. For my sake. And for yours. It's nothing ... nothing personal.'
'Monterrey, Miss Hahn,' I croaked. 'Montserrat is ... is ... is an island in the Caribbean.'
'I know,' she sighed.
Another creak. But was it from without, or ... or – Oh God! – from within?

'Do you hear that?' I asked.
'Sorry?'
'A creaking sound?'
'Uh' – she cocked her head – 'it's probably only the gulls ...'

She listened harder. 'Or it could be the shed, creaking. The surveyor said it would probably come down at some point.'
'It's very ... very hot,' I noted.
'There's always a slight risk of more land slipping,' she conceded, 'but we generally find the biggest problems develop after heavy rain – sustained periods of wet – when the soil becomes saturated.'

Another creak. My hands gripped on to the bench.

'I'm not sure if you're familiar with it,' she murmured, 'but I once heard a recording of the noise glaciers make. It was such a strange, haunting, almost ... almost *intelligent* sound. Huge chunks of ice just moving and shifting and freezing and melting. Lost in their own abstract conversations. Just giant slabs of inanimate matter but so ... so ... *burdened* somehow ...'

'To cut a long story short,' I said, grabbing for my vest, 'I've brought you back the rent money. I can't possibly accept it. Thanks – and everything – but no thanks. That's it. That's all I wanted to say. Good. Great. So now I'd better ...'
She grimaced. She was looking down at her arm.
'Nearly gone,' she mused. 'See?'
She showed it to me.
'I'm ... What ...?'
I wiped the sweat from my eyes.

'The number. From my dream. It's almost gone. I've sweated it out. How's my cheek?'
She turned her cheek towards me.
'Uh ...'

'She tells me the number,' Miss Hahn patiently explained (each word sucking another ounce of precious calm away from me, each word splitting the wood inside me – my core – with the cruellest of linguistic axes), 'she tells it to me in my dreams. Or maybe you're right and I just tell it to myself. Sometimes I don't even remember having dreamed it, but then, when I wake up, I've written the number down; on the back of a book, a piece of paper, on the wall next to my bed. Once in a pile of flour on the kitchen counter. On my hand, my arm ...'

That creak again!
'4.0.0.4,' she murmured, 'I suppose I ...'
She passed her hand across her cheek.

'I must've accidentally pressed my face against my arm while I was sleeping, and the ink got transferred ...'

I nodded. But I wasn't really focusing. I was listening out for the creak, and I was wondering how straight the floor was, and I was staring at Miss Hahn's breasts which seemed perfectly uncontentious – in size and quality – for a woman of her age and physique. They were very well positioned on her ... her ribs, her ... her diaphragm. Either side of it. In the ... in the manner of most woman ... female ... woman breasts, I suppose.

Woman breasts?

I pulled on my vest. It was soaking wet. I was soaking wet.

'But when I stripped all the ivy off the old mulberry this afternoon,' she continued, 'moments before I was stung, I thought I saw it there – the number. Etched deep into the bark.'

She grinned. 'You probably think I'm stark, staring mad, Mr Huff!'

'You?' I echoed. Although I meant me, obviously. The you that was me. *Her* you. *Me.*

'But no matter what we happen to think of each other,' she chuntered on, doggedly, 'the fact is that we *do* actually have something important in common: neither of us really wants to take this thing any further.'

'This?' I echoed.

Thing?

'This story.' She frowned. 'This situation. And for our own perfectly good reasons, too. Neither of us truly believes, for starters. At least you won't. And I can't. Neither of us really wants to engage. You find the whole thing ridiculous – all of it, all of us. I just want to ... to erase it ...' – she shuddered – 'to keep my head down. To quietly get on with things. Because I simply can't ... I can't *give* anything more to it, Mr Huff. I won't surrender to it. Not again. I just ... No. No. I *can't*. I've suffered enough. In my own, very shallow way. And

I suppose I've grown – without even realizing it – I've grown very … very *cynical* about it all. About everything. Same as you have. Same as you *are*. So that's … that's another thing we share – another thing we both have in common, Mr Huff.'

I pondered this for a while – this professed commonality between us – as I pulled on my underpants, my eyes – my vision – swimming with a succession of giant, orange-yellow blotches. And the urge to look upwards! It was so strong! Away from the … into the … Oh! Up into the …

When did I last *breathe*? Was I still breathing?

'Gotta go,' I whispered, but it sounded horribly like, 'You were her nurse?'

(Is it … Is it possible to say two things at once? To project two, diametrically opposed impulses in a single linguistic thrust?)

'No. *No.*' She shook her head. 'Not her nurse. No. I just … I sat with her. I was just a student back then. I sat with her at night. And on some days.'

Oh God. I honestly think she would tell me everything! *Everything!* But would it matter? Does it matter? Here? Now? Is it …? If I could only … If I could simply … but the … I grabbed my glasses out of my sock. A feeling of such powerful, such intense and unspeakable claustrophobia enveloped me in that moment. I really had to leave. I really needed to leave, before …

Right now.

Yes.

Right then.

Yes.

Right this/that minute.

'So she was very ill by that stage?' I garbled.

Was I trying to *kill* myself?!

'Not too ill. No. Not at first. But her parents wanted to stop her from praying. She had a special, little prayer that Father Hugh had taught her which she liked to say. But literally all the time. *All* the time. To save souls. Every time she said it she saved a soul. They thought it was ... they thought she was mentally ill. Fixated.'

'Goodbye!' I announced. But I was actually saying, 'And they *both* thought that? Bran? Kalinda?' I reached for the door. I tried to turn the handle, but my fingers kept slipping, the mechanism wouldn't ... My fingers couldn't ...

'I think it was one of the only things they ever actually agreed about.' She chuckled. She clambered to her feet. 'Here, let me ... It sometimes tends to ...'
She drew close and reached for the handle. Her mouth was still moving. If it moved any further ... if she said anything else ... if she ... if I couldn't ... But it did ... It *did* ... And so I ... So I ... simply to shut her up ... I just ... Soaking wet ... I just ... With my mouth ... I ... I pressed ... On ... on ... on her mouth. She gasped.
Then the door was open and I ran out. I simply fled. I ran. Out.

20

Teobaldo

[*Baldo speaks.*]

Baldo! Baldo! Baldo! Baldo! Baldo! W—

[*King suddenly interrupts.*]

WAAAAAAAAAAHHHHH! WAAAAAAAAAAHHHHH!
WAAAAAAAAAAHHHHH! WAAAAAAAAAAHHHHH!
WAAAAAAAAAAHHHHH!
WAAAAAAAAAAAAAAAAAAAAAAAAAAHHHHH!

Baldo stares over towards King's cage in stunned silence.

[*King ...*]
WAAAAAAAAAAAAAAAAAAAAAAAAAAAAAAAAAA
AAAAAAAAAAAAAAAAAAAAAAAAAAAAAAAAAAAA
AAAAAAAAAAAAAAAAAAAAAAAAAAAAAAAAAAAA
AAAAAAAAAAAAAAAAAAAAAAAAAAAAAAAAAAAA
AAAAAAAAAAAAAAAAAAAAAAAAAAAAAAAAAAAA
AAAAAAAAAAAAAAAAAAAAAAAAAAAAAAAAAAAAA
AAAAAAAAAAHHHHHHHH!

Pause.

WAAAAAAAAAAAAAAAAAAAAAAAAAAAAAAAAAA
AAAAAAAAAAAHHHHH!

Bitch comes sprinting into the 'living room' in a complete flap.

'Baldo! **** ** ******* **** ** ***** **** ***? *****
*****, Baldo? *** *** ***? *** *** ** **** **** ** ****?
**** ** **, ****** ***? ** ** *** ***? *** *** *** *** ***?
******** ****** ** *** ****** *****? ****? ***** *****,
Baldo? **** *****.'

['*Baldo! What in heaven's name is wrong with you? What's wrong, Baldo? Are you ill? Are you in some kind of pain? What is it, little man? Is it the cat? Did you see the cat? Prowling around in the garden again? Hmmn? What's wrong, Baldo? Tell Mummy.*']

Pause.
Bitch turns.

'King? *** ***** ***, ****** ******? *** *** ** *****,
*****? *** Baldo ***** *** **** *** **** ***** ******?'

['*King? How about you, little fellow? Are you all right, there? Did Baldo scare you with all that awful racket?*']

King commences preening. Then stretches out his wing. Then gives Bitch 'the glad eye'.

[*Bitch speaks.*]

'Awww! **** ***, King! ***** *** ******** **, eh? *****
*** *****, King? ****?'

['*Awww! Good boy, King! How're you settling in, eh? How're you doing, King? Hmmn?*']

King produces a little, tender trilling sound. He triple-blinks at
Bitch. Then turns. Then shits. Then turns back again.
King glances casually towards Baldo.

[*King speaks in a simpering voice.*]

'Tumhara nam kya hai?'

[*'What's your name?'*]

[*Bitch responds, thrilled.*]

'*****, King! **** * ****** ***, eh?'

[*'Hello, King! Who's a clever boy, eh?'*]

[*King repeats.*]

'Tumhara nam kya hai?'

[*Bitch responds.*]

'***** **** ***** ******, King? ****?'

[*'What's that you're saying, King? Hmmn?'*]

[*King speaks in a 'tender' voice.*]

Hullo! Hullo!

Bitch is now beaming from ear to ear.

[*Bitch speaks.*]

'****, *****, King! *****, King! ***** ***, King?'

[*Well, hello, King! Hello, King! How're you, King?*]

Bitch pushes a finger into King's 'cage' and gently tickles his 'chest' with it. Much to Baldo's astonishment, King does not jump away, squawking, or attempt to bite Bitch. King merely simpers and emits yet more of the tender, trilling throat noise. King actually seems to *like* Bitch!

[*Bitch speaks.*]

'********* King! Eh? ****** King! ***** *** * ********, ****** *********? Eh?'

[*'Beautiful King! Eh? Lovely King! Aren't you a friendly, little gentleman? Eh?'*]

[*King speaks.*]

'Hullo, King! Hullo, King!'

Baldo's crest slowly rises as he observes the oleaginous King in action.
Baldo sneezes.
Baldo's crest slowly falls.
Baldo's feathers gradually start to inflate until soon he looks almost double his original size.

Silence.

More gentle chest stroking between King and Bitch.

[*Bitch sighs, regretfully.*]

'**** ** ****** ** *** ****** ** ******* *** *** *** ***, King!'

[*Well I'd better go and finish my ironing. Bye bye for now, King!*]

Bitch slowly withdraws her finger, turns and heads out of the room ... But – horror of horrors! – Bitch has only gone and forgotten to bid a tender farewell to the hugely irked and inflated Baldo! Baldo remains glued to the spot, plainly stung by this terrible omission.

King eyes Baldo's inflated torso with evident amusement. He smugly preens again. Then he saunters to the far end of his cage and partakes of a choice piece of chopped mango from his bowl. He seems very pleased with himself.

The silent Baldo is incandescent with rage.
Why?
Because this is Baldo's 'living room', stupid!
And King is an interloper!
Yes!
And King is a sly, evil, cunning interloper!
Yes!
And ... and King is a ... a ... a thief!

Baldo, Baldo, Baldo, Baldo, Baldo *hates* King!
He finds that he ... yes, that he, that he *hates* King!

WAAARGHH!
[*Expressed interiorly.*]

King is a sneak!
King is a brown-nose!
King is a dirty, calculating *thief* of Baldo-sounds and Baldo 'air' and Baldo 'table' and Baldo ... Baldo ... Baldo-*bitch*!
Even Bitch! Who Baldo *hates*! For ... for 'cage' and no 'sky'

195

and … and no 'egg' and being … being 'he' instead of 'she'
… yes!
Baldo *loathes* King. But Baldo lacks the necessary proximity
and vocabulary to fully express to King how much he (she)
hates him.

Baldo stares at King, enraged.

(?)

(!)

A tiny fly buzzes around Baldo's cage and then enters
between the bars. The fly buzzes around Baldo's head while
Baldo stares at King. The fly lands on Baldo's beak. Baldo
stares at the fly. Baldo stares at King. Baldo stares at the fly
again. His/her feathers remain immensely inflated with air.
This display seems to be demanding extraordinary levels of
effort and concentration on Baldo's part.

Baldo notices that 'sun' is moving into the vicinity of King's
'cage', while his/her own cage is in full shade.
King is a thief of 'sun!'

WAAAAARGHH!
[*Silent.*]

King finishes eating his piece of fruit. He fake-'burps' then
says, 'Oh pardon nee!'
He giggles like a girl before repeating, 'Oh pardon nee!'

Slowly, slowly, Baldo's feathers lose their inflated quality. The
fly is now walking around in Baldo's food bowl. Baldo
continues to stare at King as 'sun' slowly, slowly enters King's
'cage'.

King is the thief of 'sun'!
King is the thief of 'sound'!
King is the thief of 'fruit'!
And of Bitch!
Even Bitch!
Baldo *hates* King.
Baldo toddles rapidly along his/her perch and then –

(?)

Snap!
He/she chops that pesky fly in half.
Ha!
All flies and other pests would do well to fear the devastating wrath of Baldo!
Ha!
Ha! Ha!
Ha!

21

Miss Carla Hahn

Alys answers the telephone sounding hoarse, panicked and out of breath.

'Hello?' she pants. 'Hello? Hello? Who *is* that? What do you want? Is anybody—'

'Alys – *Alys*,' I interrupt, 'calm down! It's only me!'

   'Me?'

She's suspicious.

'*Me*, Carla!' I exclaim, slightly wounded.

'Oh. *Oh*. Oh I *am* sorry, Carla,' she murmurs, embarrassed, 'it's just that I've been having … There's a problem with the phone. Someone keeps ringing and then hanging up. *All* the time. I know it doesn't sound like much, but it's got me really … really spooked.'

'Just kids, maybe?' I speculate.

'Yes. *Yes*. Probably. I mean I don't often give the number out – I'm usually very … very circumspect. After all the problems ten years ago. People wanting … *You* know. So I changed the number and since then, like I say, I've been extremely circumspect …'

I adjust my towel and ponder the issue for a moment. 'Well has there been anything … I don't know … anything out of the ordinary happening recently? An argument with a neighbour, perhaps or …?'

Alys considers this for a second. 'Nothing I can think of, no.'

'And the caller doesn't speak? They don't say anything? They don't … No heavy breathing or …?'

'Nope. They just hang up. Straight away. As soon as I place the receiver to my ear. Before I can even ... And I know that might not *sound* like anything much' – she sighs – 'but it's quite literally *all* the time. I'm ... I'm completely jittery. I'm turning into a nervous wreck.'

'Unplug the stupid thing, then!' I exclaim.

'I can't, Carla. I need it for Mother. Just in case she gets into any kind of ... of bother ... And Jenny often rings if ever she needs a quick hand with Sam.'

She's plainly exasperated.

'Okay. *Okay.* And you have *no* idea who might ...?'

'None.'

Silence.

'Although I suppose ...'

'What?' I demand.

'No. No, it's just way too ...'

'*What*, Alys?' I repeat.

'Well the only person who I gave the number to recently was your friend Mr Huff.'

'*My* friend?!' I echo, my free hand rising, unwittingly, to my mouth, my cheeks reddening. And then, straight after, 'Oh, I don't think Mr Huff would ... I really can't think he'd stoop to ...'

(Yes! *Yes!* Exactly! *Defending* him! To Alys. After ... after ... Quite extraordinary!)

'He's the only person I can really think of,' Alys persists. 'In fact, if I remember correctly, he *asked* me for it – the number. And I just ... I reeled it off. I gave it to him without so much as a second thought.'

'But why would Mr Huff ...?' I wonder, perturbed.

'I don't know,' she muses, 'but after our conversation the other day – yours and mine, I mean – I sat down for a second and I had a good think about it – about what you'd said – and I realized that ... I don't know ... maybe I *had* been a little taken in by his charm. Maybe I *had* been a little bit too ... too forthcoming. I think it was just … just seeing all those amazing photographs. This feeling of such … such enormous *well-being* engulfed me. Of recognition. *Yearning*. To suddenly be presented with all this tangible evidence of … I don't know … something that seems like a kind of a … a … a *dream,* almost. Something I've thought about so much over the years, and nurtured and analysed and protected and … and defended. And doubted. Even doubted! Really doubted, sometimes – as a faithful Catholic! It just brought the whole … whole experience crashing back into this extraordinarily clear focus again and I … I suppose I got a little carried away. I let my guard down.'

'Did you hear about Kimberly Couzens?' I ask.
'Sorry?'
'The photographer. Kimberly Couzens. She died. She's dead. Last weekend, apparently.'
Alys inhales, sharply.
'It was all very sudden,' I continue. 'It was actually on the day that I … When we last spoke. Which I suppose was why he – Mr Huff – was so strange and rude when we bumped into each other on the beach that afternoon.'

'Heaven forbid! Not on the same day you …?'
'Yes.'
'Oh my goodness! Oh my goodness! So what did you …? How on earth did you go about—'
'Apologizing?' I interrupt. 'I didn't.'
'Sorry?' She's confused.
'I didn't.'
'You didn't actually *tell* him that …?'
'No. *No.* I *couldn't*, Alys. Not once I found out. I mean there was the landslip – as you know, and then everything went a bit … a bit crazy for a while. A certain amount of time passed by – too much, really. And so I just … I decided that I might as well just—'

'Oh poor Carla!' she interrupts. 'What a mess!'

'Yes.'

'And poor Mr Huff!' she adds. 'Were they close? I don't actually remember him mentioning what the connection between them was ...'

'They were married.'

Shocked silence.

'Kimberly Couzens was Mr Huff's wife,' I expand.

'But ... but ...' – Alys is perplexed – 'but what about his ... the other woman? The one who rented your ...?'

'I don't really know. His girlfriend, perhaps? He and Kimberly obviously lived separate lives; she was based in Canada. He lives in Montserrat.'

'Monterrey. In Mexico,' she corrects me.

'On different continents,' I continue, 'so far as I can tell. But they were still ... still connected, I suppose. I mean whenever she mentioned her husband that summer it must've been ... well *him* that she was referring to ... And when she was burned after the car-bomb a couple of months later, obviously ... In Ireland. With Bran Cleary. When they were having the ... the ...'

I can't say it. I *can't* say it.

'... he was still her husband then, presumably.'

'But why didn't he mention that?' Alys is confused.

'That they were married?'

'Why didn't he mention it?' Alys repeats. 'It just seems ... It just seems so *odd*.'

'Maybe he thought it might work against him.' I shrug. 'In terms of getting people to open up. The point is he was—'

I suddenly stop what I'm about to say. I am about to say, 'betrayed. Like me.'

But I can't possibly say that. Not to dear Alys. Not to anybody. Except ... Except perhaps ...

'But that's such a *curious* omission, don't you think?' Alys persists. 'I mean do we actually have any concrete *evidence* that they were married?'

'A great moment to return to first principles, Alys!' I snort.
'But how do we ...?'
'We don't! It's simply what he told Clifford.'
'Clifford?' Alys echoes. 'But how on earth did Clifford ...?'
'Clifford said he was in a really terrible state about it all. So I went around with a pie last night, fully intending to come clean and apologize ... Although I kind of ...'
'A pie?'
The pie is one detail too many for Alys.

'Yes. A pork pie. To apologize. But he behaved very oddly. He virtually devoured the whole thing in one sitting. Then he was sick. He was starving. Turns out he's completely broke. He can't even afford to fly home for her funeral.'
'How awful!'
'Yes. Which is why I tried to return him his rent money ...'

'But you'd think that if his *then* wife and Bran Cleary had been ...' – Alys politely clears her throat – 'he'd have really mixed feelings about the whole thing. I mean that puts a totally different slant on the situation. On the book. Do you happen to know if he ... Did *he* know the Clearys? I mean if he was married to Kimberly and *she* was so tight with them all – with Bran, specifically – then surely ...?'

'But *were* she and Bran really that close?' I demand, somewhat irritably. 'We have no concrete evidence of that. It's just idle speculation for the most part ...'
'Well they *must* have been, Carla!' she insists.
'I'm just ... I'm just not so sure that they really were. She was more ... It was more ... Almost a *professional* ... I don't know. He always seemed to find her rather irritating. At least from my perspective—'

'Well the affair must have started at Mulberry,' Alys interrupts, continuing to worry away at the facts, 'because the turnaround between then and ... and ...'
I just can't let this go on any further.

'Poor Mrs Barrow seems to think that Mr Huff is under surveillance by the CIA!' I chuckle (almost convincingly). 'She told me he actually said he thought *they'd* put the shark under his bed!'

'He was just pulling her leg, surely?!' Alys snorts.

'Maybe, but Mrs Barrow certainly swallowed it all hook, line and sinker.' I grin. 'In fact she's so paranoid now that she'd probably think it was the Secret Services messing around with *your* phone ...'

'Why? Because I'm half Irish?' Alys snaps (suddenly quite failing to see the funny side). 'Because of the IRA angle?'

'I'm just kidding!' I protest.

'D'you think I should contact Father Hugh?' she wonders.

'I was just *kidding*, Alys!' I maintain.

'Because nothing really adds up, Carla. I mean the more I think about it the more ... And I know for a fact that Mr Huff had been making strenuous attempts to get in touch with Father Hugh at Douai ...'

She sighs, worriedly.

'But Father Hugh isn't ...' I murmur.

'I have special privileges,' she confides, almost apologetically, 'as his Spiritual Child. And I may have encouraged him to look on Mr Huff's recent requests more favourably than he naturally ...'

'But I always thought ...?' I start off, confused.

'He's not allowed to talk about it. Not on *record*. No. But he still has ... He still thinks – same as we *all* do – that ... *you* know. That Orla deserves recognition. But it needs to be carefully managed – the right *kind* of attention. Not sensational and exploitative. I told him I thought the photos were just ... Photos are truthful things, Carla. And several of them feature Father Hugh himself. There's one of him in the garden at Mulberry, laughing, covered in daisy chains. It's just beautiful. And you're there, in the background, with Bran, wearing that little, red beret you always loved to—'

'I was probably stringing the chains,' I mutter. 'Orla sometimes found it hard to ... to string the little stalks together – with her poor arms being so ...'

My eyes fill with tears. I blink, fiercely.

Don't let her ...

Don't ...

'So I just wanted him to know,' she continues, 'to prepare him, up front. Just in case he might get into strife with his superiors.'

'Do you remember the actual words of that special prayer?' I murmur. 'The one about sinners being daisies? The one Kalinda wouldn't let her ...?'

'Sorry?'

'There was a special prayer. About the garden. And weeds. Daisies. To save souls. Orla's little prayer to save souls. I was telling Mr Huff about it earlier, in the sauna, and then I suddenly realized that I didn't ... I couldn't actually remember—'

'You were talking to Mr Huff?' Alys interrupts, sharply. 'About Orla?'

'No. *No.* I was just ... I was having a sauna and he dropped by at the house to return the rent money. I was just ... It was all very ... very *odd*, really.'

How to explain it?

'Mr Huff was ... You were ... Are you saying that he was *in* the sauna? With you? You were in the sauna *together*?'

'No. Well, yes, but it was ... it wasn't ... he was behaving very strangely, Alys. That's actually why I—'

'You, in a sauna, stark naked, with a virtual stranger?!' Alys finds this difficult to digest.

'He just barged on in there. I don't think he quite realized ...'

'This just suddenly feels all ... all *wrong*,' Alys mutters. 'I'm going to get in touch with Father Tierney again and warn him off. In fact I truly, *truly* regret giving Mr Huff his address now.'

'You gave Mr Huff Father Hugh's address?' I'm shocked.

'Yes. And by way of thanks he's phoning me at all hours and taunting me. Who knows why?'

'I *really* don't think …' I start off.

'You mustn't be taken in by him, Carla,' she warns me, 'you've held out all these years. Kept schtum. There must be a good reason for that, surely? Why suddenly change the habits of a lifetime now?'

'But I really don't think … it's just not *like* that, Alys,' I insist. 'Mr Huff told me that he'd only been persuaded to write the book in the first place because Kimberly had begged him to. He wasn't at all keen on the idea to begin with. So now that she's dead he'll probably just … And if you remember, he *didn't* approach me. He *hasn't* approached me. In fact when I mentioned the Clearys earlier – in the sauna – it was like … it was as though he couldn't bear to hear anything about them. It was like it almost made him … made him panic. It was very odd, Alys—'

'But that's what he does, don't you see?' she interrupts. 'That's *precisely* what he did with me! He kept pretending that he didn't actually *want* to know anything, that I was just … just *unburdening* myself to him, unnecessarily, but in actual fact he was …'

'But now that Kimberly's dead …' I persist.

'Are we sure of that?' Alys demands. 'We don't even know for certain that she *is* his wife, God rest her poor soul.'

I can hear Alys crossing herself.

'But, Alys, she must've given him permission to use the—'

'He could've stolen the photos, Carla!' Alys speculates, wildly. 'Mr Huff might be a refugee from justice for all we know! On the run from the FBI. And that's why they're leaving rotting sharks under his bed!'

'Alys, *I* left the shark under his bed.' I laugh, amused but still quite shocked.

'Well good for you!' she exclaims.

Slight pause.

'I think my soup might be splashing over on to the hob,' she mutters.

'Well you'd better go and ...'

'Yes.'

Pause.

'Although I'm quite worried about you now,' she sighs.

'Don't worry about me!'

(I'm very eager not to be worried about.)

'I'm just worried that your resolve might finally be loosening, and at the worst, possible time ...'

'*Don't* worry about me!' I repeat.

(Although – to be perfectly frank – *I'm* slightly worried about me, now.)

'Ah. Smoking candles,' she says, enigmatically.

'Sorry?'

'That's what she called the bad people. The sinful. Smoking candles. I always thought it was quite ... quite lovely.'

'Smoking candles,' I repeat, remembering.

'Your initial impulses were right,' she commends me, 'I really do think our Mr Huff might be a serious threat to little Orla's legacy: a con-artist; a bad egg; a smoking candle. I'm only sorry that it's taken me so long to realize – to follow your lead. Just remember that he's extremely clever and subtle, Carla. So be very, *very* sure you don't get ... get ... blinded – overpowered – by all the fumes. Promise me that. *Please.*'

'Of course,' I promise (who can deny sweet Alys anything?).

'I'll be very careful. Don't worry. Not on my account.'

Having exacted her promise, Alys rushes off – slightly mollified – to rescue her supper.

I put down the receiver. I stand still for a moment, scowling, and then quite suddenly I open my mouth and I'm saying:

Holy Queen, Most Joyful Mother, we are sinful weeds in your fragrant garden. Please bind us in your gentle hands and offer us all in a daisy crown of love to your merciful Son, and to God the Father.

It's come back to me! The prayer! Orla's prayer. For sinners. I say it again:

Holy Queen, Most Joyful Mother, we are sinful weeds in your fragrant garden. Please bind us in your gentle hands and offer us all in a daisy crown of love to your merciful Son, and to God the Father.

It's as though I have been saying it all my life! The way it rolls off the tongue! It feels so ... so *good* ... so familiar! And I start to imagine ... to wonder whether just saying it twice like that, quite casually, quite idly, might have saved a poor, lost soul – suspended somewhere, like a trapped butterfly – from immortal agony. But then I counter-wonder whether I even believe in souls. Or immortal agony. And then another part of me starts to argue that even the ... even the slightest hope ... the *vaguest possibility* that it might have ... that it might be ... that it might possess the tiniest bit of power to save someone – a *lost* someone – from unspeakable torment ...

So I say it again. Then I say it again, emphatically. And the more I say it, the more readily it comes. And then I begin to wonder whether the soul I am saying it for is actually my own. I start thinking about my *own* soul. And I remember Orla telling me about how the soul is like a tiny, beautifully mirrored globe situated somewhere close to where the heart is, and that sometimes the mirrors are darkened, as if by smoke (The smoking candle! The smoking candle of sin! But of course. Of *course* ...), and that each time you pray for your own soul – or, better still, for someone else's – Jesus sends down an angel to shine one of the mirrors. But the stain of the smoke is very dense, very thick. So sometimes the angel needs to rub at the mirrors very hard so that they can ... so they can truly shine, and clearly reflect back ... reflect back all the ... all the ...

What?

As quickly as it arrived, the prayer leaves me (the words, the urge to say it, the reason, the *will*). And I put my hands up to my lips. Both hands. Damp hands. Clammy hands. And I suddenly feel quite ... quite *sick*.

22

Mr Clifford Bickerton

I think some kind of tacit deal's been struck between me and
the Author (*Oi!* Hang on a sec … Is that an actual word?
'Tacit'? *Eh?* Tacit?! A 'tacit deal'?! … What's it even mean?
Okay, fine, I *do* know – at least I can guess – what it means,
thanks very much, but why would I – *she* – make me say these
things, these arty-farty, stuck-up, *pretentious* things – shove
words and ideas into my head and my mouth – which I don't
honestly have the first clue about? *Why?*).

And the deal (you ask, eyes rolling)? The 'tacit' deal? That
she will promise to leave me the hell alone (remember the
dog bite? The swan attack?) just so long as I don't go sticking
my giant hooter in anywhere that it isn't wanted (you may
need to re-read this sentence a couple of times; not *this*
sentence, the opening sentence. Then the other one – the one
after the bracket – to make any sense of it. Sorry. I'm
currently stuck behind the wheel, and half my mind is
focused on the road ahead. Which leaves precious little to
conjure with, obviously). (*'Precious little'*? *'Conjure'*? I'm a
farmhand, woman! A country bumpkin! An odd-jobs man
with a talent for plumbing! Okay, and I can change the odd
light fitment, if push comes to shove. That's me. That's who
I am. That's Clifford Bickerton. And you? A 'professional'
writer – a 'wordsmith'! So raise your pathetic game, why
don't you? Set a standard and stick by it. Because you're not
making an idiot out of *me* right now, so much as a fool out of
yourself. You're way out of your depth. You're drowning. It's

all falling apart at the seams. Not that I really give a monkey's. This is *your* story. But a man has his ... his *integrity* ... his ... his *pith*, and it's your job, your duty, as 'Author' (as 'Author'?! I would never, *never* use that phrase! Never! And yes, I do understand that what we are currently dealing with here is a bracket inside another bracket directly following another bracket) to represent this fact in as honest – as *sincere* – a way as possible. Isn't it?)

Just so long as I don't get in the way – destroy her carefully arranged plot with my shining sword of truth etc.

etc.

etc.

That's why when I saw Mr Huff standing by the bus-stop in Fairlight, with a bright red face, flapping his arms up and down like a caged bantam, I seriously considered not pulling over to offer him a lift. But after I checked my watch I calculated that it was a full fifty minutes until the next bus arrived.

I then smiled wryly to myself because I actually have *no idea* – none! – what times the buses run. I also noted (in passing) that I was driving up the wrong road and in totally the wrong direction for the job I am currently on (a blocked drain in Westfield). But then why should we (me, I) let these boring little details stand in the path of great literature, eh?

So I pulled over. She obviously *wanted* me to pull over. And I am her spineless, over-sized, ginger pawn. She has stripped me of all dignity (I didn't have that much to begin with, did I? Nope, Rusty old man. No you didn't, as it happens). So I pulled over.

'Can I offer you a lift, Mr Huff?' I asked.
'That's very kind of you, Mr Pemberton,' he yelled back (I can see how the Reader might find his habit of getting my name wrong pretty bloody amusing. But if you think about it carefully this seems like an unlikely trope (I would *never* say 'trope'! *Trope?! Tripe!* Complete and utter *tripe!*) (Uh, yes, I

am aware of the fact that we are currently stuck in the middle of yet another, complicated treble bracket pile-up. But blame *her*. She hasn't bothered leaving enough room on the page for my internal monologue (I would never, *never* use the phrase 'internal monologue'!) so I'm just doing the best that I can within the limits of what's currently on offer) in a man who has worked as a journalist for many years (are you still following this? Have you kept the brackets strictly compartmentalized? Think 'inside of a plug'; you know, with the different wires all leading to different places – because that's the only way you'll keep any kind of a handle on this pathetic botch-up). Unless it's all just a big lie (the 'journalist' pose) and he's going to turn out to be a spy or … or an astronaut or a … a time-traveller! In which case this book might actually turn out halfway decent. There's always a first time for everything, I suppose). Remembering names is his business – as unblocking drains is mine. Although – by and large – I don't generally unblock a drain close to the drain I need to unblock. I unblock the drain that needs unblocking. So why would Mr Huff repeatedly forget my name? Eh? Unless he is trying to humiliate me, I suppose. But then why would he want to humiliate me? Because he is actually falling in love with Carla Hahn and knows, in his heart-of-hearts, that Carla and I are … are … (What *are* we, Bickerton, you big pansy? What are we? Huh?).

'… But I'm perfectly happy to wait for the bus.'

Screw him, Rusty, I thought. Just wave and drive on. But instead I said, 'The next bus is over fifty minutes off, Mr Huff.'

(Complete hogwash.)

'I know,' he said.

(Is he lying too? Or *is* the bus actually fifty minutes off? If it is, then she's clearly feeding me 'lies' that are – in some crazy way – 'true'. And I hate that idea. No. I don't like that idea at all. Because it makes me seem almost, I don't know, supernatural. Psychic. Which is silly. Because there's enough mystical mumbo-jumbo in this book already, and I should probably state – up front – that I am not sympathetic to it (mumbo-jumbo etc.) in any way, shape or form. This is a rational age, a cynical age (yes, these *are* actually my thoughts; not simply some half-arsed pre-digested crap she's plopped into my head. Although it could still be half-arsed. And crap, come to that).

The Cleary story is definitely a strange one. 'Haunting', even (*woo-hoo!*). But will she ever get around to telling it? Eh? Does she *ever* get around to telling a story? And aside from that (how can you write a story without actually *telling* a story?) I just feel like she's really over-egging the pudding this time around. I can't seriously imagine her Average Reader would approve (is that you? Or are you just flicking through this at your mother's house during the Christmas holidays – bored out of your tiny mind – because it's something she's been forced to read by her book group?) (I don't have a clue what a book group *is*. So I don't even know why I mentioned that). I think they'll all say she's losing the plot. The book'll bomb. It'll be remaindered two days after publication and I'll be remembered as one of her most unsuccessful characters, ever. Better still, one of the most unsuccessful fictional characters *of all time*. Great! Thanks a bunch! Yet further humiliations on the cards for Mr C. Bickerton Esq.!

Although … Although I've got no issues – none – with Orla. The Cleary girl. She was always very sweet. And brave. And pretty messed up, I suppose. By the slutty mother. The creepy priest. Her filthy bastard of a dad.

What other options did she have? Honestly? Being raised in such a crazy hothouse atmosphere? I've never … I don't understand how … I mean all those pointless arguments – those constant, high-flown 'discussions' – about politics and money and religion and *art*. But she was a sweet kid, just the same. With that big old smile. Those tiny arms. Those funny little flippers instead of hands. Way too special (in my opinion) for someone like *her* to muck around with (why didn't Edna O'Brien get involved? A *real* writer? The kind of writer who can always be depended upon to spin a good yarn?). But then nobody gives a damn what *I* think. Nobody. *Nobody*. Not Carla Hahn. Not Mr Huff. Not you. Not *her*. I am the Great Unheard. Clifford-Rusty Bickerton-Pemberton. The Giant Hairy Ignored.)

'So get in the van,' I suggest.

'Okay.'

He climbs in (there's no door on the passenger side, remember?) and puts on his seat belt.

'Good idea.' I smirk. 'I'd really hate to lose you on a stiff corner.'

(The seat belt doesn't actually work.)

In fact, the seat belt *does* work, but I'm wondering whether just *saying* it doesn't work means – because of my supernatural powers etc. – that it *won't* actually work. I'm not lying (these aren't *lies*, as such – who could forget the 'tacit deal'? Who would dare? Who would be stupid enough?), just … just experimenting with a couple of harmless, little … uh … improvisations. There's nothing nasty or … or mean in it (I swear). It's just an innocent experiment. And completely off the cuff. Not pre-planned in any way, shape or form. I am not (I repeat, *not*) messing about with what you might call the 'building blocks' of the plot. These are just silly details. Pointless little details.

So he fastens the (fully functioning) seat belt (I even leaned over and double-checked it! It was firmly locked!) and then we pull off. I start the conversation by referring to the weather.

'Nice, warm day,' I say.

Mr Huff looks completely paranoid. 'I didn't kiss her,' he pants, 'whatever she tells you – told you. I was just trying to make her stop.'

'Sorry?'

It takes me a few seconds to catch up.

Kiss her?

Kiss her?

'It was unbearably hot in the sauna,' he continues. 'Close. Dark. Airless. She practically forced me to join her in there. I was just returning the money – the rent money. I put it on the kitchen counter. I was calling her. I didn't even know that it *was* a sauna. I thought it was simply a shed. Then she came out – stark naked – and insisted that I took off my vest and my pants, and I ...'

He swallows, nervously. 'I am not a natural habitué of the sauna, Mr Pemberton ...'

Mr ...? Oh ha ha *ha*.

'I told her that, quite plainly. I find them a little ... well, sordid. I *told* her that. But she insisted. She really was quite determined to ... I mean I really am ... to all intents and purposes ... I really *am* the wronged party here.'

'Hold on. Could we just ...?' I stutter. 'You're saying that you and Carla – *my* Carla ... that you ...?'

Stark naked?

Kiss?

Sauna?!

No! No! *No!* I can't get a handle on this! It's not ... it just doesn't ... *My* Carla? *The* Carla? No! It must be a joke. A lie. I can't ... I just don't understand how the Author could have ... could have got her into ... manipulated her into ... I simply don't understand how ...

'She practically forced me!' Mr Huff squeaks. 'I'm just ... It's been one of those days. First Mrs Meadows putting her hands down my ... down my ... down ...' He indicates, horrified. 'But what could I do, Mr Pemberton? Without mortally offending her? After all that protein? And me a ... a recently ... just ... just *widowed* ... Vulnerable! Then a couple

of hours later, Miss Hahn. With her ... her ... I really *am*
quite ...'

We are now travelling at approximately ten miles above the
National Speed Limit. My foot feels very heavy, all of a
sudden, as if my ... my frustration, my ... my rage, my ... my
despair (I don't think that's too dramatic a word under the
circumstances) finds itself perfectly focused (all this black
helpless fury) directly above the arch and deep, deep inside
the pad ...

Mr Huff double-checks his seat belt.
Ha!
It holds.
I am perfectly calm.
Perfectly. Calm.

Although why the heck didn't I know anything about all
this in advance? Why wasn't I 'forewarned'? That sixth sense
I've recently developed? I knew about that other stuff (the
parrot, remember? The Author's other works published – in
some cases – several decades after the current year of 1984?).
So why didn't I know about this? Why keep me in the dark
till now? Huh? Just to ... just to *humiliate* me, maybe? Or
perhaps (twenty miles over the National Speed Limit!
Weeeeeeee!) Mr Huff is lying. To upset me. To provoke some
kind of ... of un ... un ... unguarded reaction?

Mrs Meadows? Mrs *Meadows*? Of Lamb House? Rye?
Where's *she* fit into the wider picture? That stuck-up redhead?
Sage Meadows? The toff? The 'poet'?
Protein?

I suddenly find myself thinking (stupidly, pointlessly) about
the Truth. I know the Truth isn't very popular any more. I'm
only an odd-jobs man, but I have a general sense of how lately
the clever people – the thinkers, the journalists, the writers,
the judges and what-not – don't really set great store by the
Truth. Because there's always a reason why someone could ...
always an excuse. And then *circumstances* may mean that

something might not be entirely right or completely wrong, because of all those … those … blurred lines and … and … different viewpoints … and hidden causes … and plots … and conspiracies. It's like the Truth is a huge block of ice and all these other things are a million, tiny pick-axes. Just chipping away. Chipping away quietly at the Truth. Until … Until what's left? Eh?

Well I never! Just feast your eyes on that! The Truth is actually a giant, ice-sculpture of Benny Hill dressed as Ernie the Milkman!

Amazing! So lifelike!

But what about *my* truth? All *I* can think is: She was *with* him, Mr Huff, and now she's *with* you.

That's the truth.

My truth.

Isn't it?

That's the Actual Truth of this situation?

Mr Huff is speaking. He is saying something about a secret … a secret that Carla has just confided in him and how … how …

And while I hate the man. I hate him. It's like our thoughts are … are in some kind of natural con-con-con- … in some kind of … of strange *sync*.

'She told me the secret,' he's saying, 'about the—'

'Don't bother,' I interrupt, 'I already know. I already know about the affair with Bran Cleary.' Because I won't let him think – not for one … for one *second* – that he's breaking this news to me. A man has his pride, finally.

'I already know what happened between the two of them,' I run on, 'but I forgave her. I *forgave* her. Although that still wasn't quite enough. She won't forgive *herself*, you see.'

Mr Huff looks at me, astonished. I look back at him, equally surprised (she … she had an *affair* with Bran Cleary?! Do I honestly, *actually* think that? Oh of course I bloody do!

Of course I bloody do! I always suspected it. Always. And nothing else really adds up, does it?).

We are currently thirty miles over the National Speed Limit. Then we turn, sharply, at Stream House (quick change down of the gears, slight touch of the brake), turn a second time (*whoooooo!*), then once again into the hairpin bend (Here we are! Right on cue! Big round of applause! Incredible feats of timing from the Author!), I tug hard on the steering wheel, and ...

And the seat belt – his seat belt – snaps open and he flies out. On to a grassy verge – rolling like a barrel – then into a hedge beyond.

But ... but like I said earlier, the seat belt *wasn't* faulty! It was a lie! I *lied*. I even double-checked, remember? That's the God's Honest ...

Or ... or ...?

(Dirty chuckle from Benny Hill.)

Did I ...?

Did she ...?

Did we actually just ...?

BRAKE, RUSTY, YOU DAMN FOOL!

BRAKE, MAN, *BRAKE*!

Oh *God*, what the hell have you ... I ... we ... us ... me ... we ... you ...?

23

Mr Franklin D. Huff

I was trained how to fall by the Vaqueros. This was pre-Tlateloco. Late 1967 or thereabouts. An entire month of riding and falling. All this to pad out a photo-story for the *National Geographic* which ultimately didn't run (kind apologies from the editor – a tiny kill fee). Nothing wrong with the words, but the pictures were disappointing. Kimberly was off her game. Second month of pregnancy. Then the miscarriage. But I learned how to fall from the Vaqueros. And God only knows it came in handy. I've certainly done a fair old bit of it since then.

In fact, the editor who killed the piece was the same man who later put me in touch with Winston Scott (was it merely out of guilt or by design? I now wonder). Scott – former CIA Mexico City Bureau Chief – was writing his memoirs and needed someone 'in the know' to tidy them up a bit. But was that generous *National Geographic* assignment (which landed in Kim's lap, quite out of the blue – a virtual Gift From God) merely part of some coordinated attempt to banjax my bumbling investigations into the pre-1968-Olympic socio-economic meltdown? I'd written several pieces for the English press about President Ordaz's government's brutal suppression of Mexican farmers and the independent labour unions. Now he'd set his sights on those poor students …

There are still no firm statistics on the number of people who died that day. But I saw with my own eyes the bodies piled up high on the pavements. How they just bundled them

– like so much garbage – into the back of their trucks and sped off.

Strange that we should suddenly receive that call – just as things were really starting to hot up in Mexico City – to spend a month getting saddle-sore in the back of beyond. If I recall correctly, it was Kimberly who convinced me to take the commission. We were a *team*. She desperately wanted me with her on that job. I did it for her – against my better judgement. I did it for *us*.

Do I suspect Kim, too?

Yes.

No.

God. Who don't I suspect?

(I barely even trust my devout Catholic housemaid, Juana. I'd do anything for her. She knows that. Anything. But I've still been known to carefully count every teabag left in the tin, just to be sure.)

Once burned, twice shy.

Scott was noxious and paranoid. He and I had history. It was Scott – he later confessed this to me in one of his many late-night drink-fuelled rants – who came up with the spiel about Chinese rifles being used at the Tlateloco massacre. My source had seemed legit. A social worker called Juan Manuel Reyes Vargas whose brother Paulino was in the military. And I ran with it. Oh, how I ran with it! Even though – perhaps even because – everything I had discovered under my own steam (the fruits of my own messy observations), added up to something entirely at odds with this theory.

I guess I just lacked confidence. Or maybe I had an excess of it back then? (What a fool, though! What a gullible fool!)

Just try and imagine (if you can) how that might feel? If the sum total of your role in the grand panoply of human history was that of an idiotic obfuscator? Not a traitor or a plotter (surely there's some measure of glamour in those Judas roles? I mean at least you have the comfort of a dark yet coherent subterranean agenda?), but as someone who persistently – no, *determinedly* – gets things wrong. An incompetent dope. You are presented with the facts (whatever they may be) and then you gamely proceed to cook up a series of the worst possible hypotheses. You conjure a miserable five out of a happy two plus two.

When Scott died, unexpectedly (from a heart attack), while the book was still being edited, I carefully pondered my options and then ran, long-distance (like a skinny barefoot Kenyan) with the information provided. How could I not? I fully understood the risks. But this was huge. The CIA had known – they *knew!* – way in advance, that Lee Harvey Oswald posed a serious threat to American national security. Scott had all the documentation to prove it! Why didn't they admit to this, you wonder? Because it made them look like a bunch of incompetent chumps, that's why. But they knew. They knew.

This was career-making stuff. This was the world's biggest scoop. A coup. This could finally undo the Tlateloco mess. This could set me up for life. Was Scott's death suspicious? Yes. No. Who could say? Were the FBI desperate to stop the book? Uh … does a rabid dog crave water?

Publish and be damned, though! That was my mentality. So I put out my feelers. I cast around for all my best media contacts. I made calls. I wrote letters. I honestly thought they'd be biting my arm off at the wrist! But nobody – *nobody* – seemed eager to take the bait. I was ignored, fobbed off, laughed at, avoided. No one wanted to risk it. But why? *Why?!* My theory (but who can trust my theories?) was that British Intelligence had put the word out on me. Institutional self-protection. Their people knew people who knew people … Everybody was implicated. I suddenly found myself (although it wasn't actually sudden, it was lethally gradual, like frostbite) sitting bang in the middle of yet another 'left-wing cover-up' scenario. There were sly winks and subtle nudges, casual rumours, incriminating documents in circulation which nobody ever read, nobody ever saw – even compromising photos.

What could I do? I booked a flight to England (we were broke, but I needed to confront this many-headed Hydra, head-on) then suddenly there were a whole host of 'visa problems' (if I leave, they tell me, there's no guarantee of ever getting back *in* again). A house burglary. My car's brakes are tampered with. The bank stops my credit. A friend is imprisoned. I can't travel, *can't* travel; so Kimberly takes the flight instead – and ... and, well, she never comes back.

Bye-bye, Kim old girl.

Fine. So it was pretty much over by then anyway. My fault. *My* fault. I had contracted the virus of cynicism. It's a kind of flu of the soul. It fed on me like a cancer. It hollowed me out. It finished me off. Because there was *no agenda*. I was a pragmatist. I wasn't political. I didn't ... I didn't *feel* that stuff (the heart, the gut, the soul) so much as want to ... Let's put it this way: I was a surfer. Just a surfer. I was never the wave.

But now I'd been voided. I was a blank. I'd been silenced. I had no means ... no way of getting the information *out* there. It wasn't even as if I *cared* about the information, as such (no agenda, remember? No great battle between right and wrong, no sense of a profound moral and political injustice having been done), I just cared that I couldn't ... had been ... was straitjacketed, was disgraced. I was helpless. *Helpless.* I just wished there was some way of ... a means to ... some way to reach out and ... and *share* what I knew with the world. Not because I *needed* to ... but just because I ... because I ...

Who knows?

Vaquero is actually a transliteration of cow man. Not cow boy (note). Cow man. I told Mr Pemberton this as I clambered to my feet and brushed myself off.

He seemed astonished that I was unhurt. In truth, *I* was quite astonished. Not so much as a scratch on me! And my suit – apart from a tiny tear on the seam of a pocket – was fine.

I went on to tell Mr Pemberton how the cowman had been rendered obsolete, virtually overnight, by the invention of barbed wire in 1873. I said, 'It was the New Mexican equivalent of enclosure. You know – when the British landed gentry eradicated the right for peasants to graze their livestock on common land?'

'I do know what enclosure is, Mr Huff,' Mr Pemberton assured me. Then he apologized for speeding. Then I apologized for kissing Miss Hahn. I tried to explain, once again, how I wasn't … it wasn't … I'd just been trying to stop her from … from *talking*. He seemed to find this strange. He said, 'I thought you *wanted* Miss Hahn to talk.'

I said I was beginning to suspect that I had developed a series of unconscious phobias in relation to Miss Hahn and the book. That being around Miss Hahn made me feel a deep sense of panic. I also said that the secret she'd told me was about the four digits – the 4.0.0.4 – not about … well … and that I would treat the information that he had shared with me – about her 'relationship' with Bran Cleary – with great sensitivity and discretion.

He responded to this statement in an emphatic manner (arm waving, reddened cheeks etc.) but was rendered inaudible when a nearby bird-scarer started to quick-fire, indiscriminately. He suggested (a series of hand gestures) that we climb back inside the van. I refused. I said – in as polite a way as I possibly could – that I would never knowingly get into a moving vehicle with him again. Not ever. I then added that I didn't intend this to be a criticism of his driving, *per se*. But I think it was obvious that this is exactly what it consisted of. A devastating criticism of his driving. *Per se*.

I hope we parted friends.

I really do think that Mr Pemberton is intensely unstable. I like him, though. And I am absolutely convinced now that it was he who put the shark under my bed in order to cast suspicion on Miss Hahn and make our relationship untenable. Hang on ... Let me put that ... uh ... 'our relationship' (mine and Miss Hahn's) into inverted commas. Yes. Good. That's so much better.

I feel deeply sorry for him. I do. And for Miss Hahn, too. He must've been a thorn in her poor side for many a long year now. He plainly believes that every man she ever has contact with finds her completely irresistible!

Kimberly – poor, dead Kimberly (they were *her* photographs. In circulation. The compromising ones. They were hers) – was perfectly right about our Miss Hahn, though. She's this story's barbed wire. She is the thing that both contains and expels. She is the truth at the heart of it all. But if I see the truth (or the heart) how might I tell? My instincts for such things are notoriously unreliable, after all. And if I do find out the truth (stare it in the face, but don't recognize it) will I find Kimberly (with her white-blonde hair and her beatnik style and her chattering camera) still more compromised? Will I discover that everything was a lie? My whole adult life? That I was just ... That I am just ... what's that phrase again? In the approaches? On the outskirts? But never reaching a destination of any note? Just driving around on life's eternal ring-road – too frightened, too unwitting, too stupid, too compromised to make that sharp turn into the very heart of the matter?

These were my thoughts as I walked home. And when I arrived, I discovered two things. The first was a line of dilapidated caravans (old cars, several horses) blocking the road to Toot Rock. Oh, and a host of disgruntled neighbours raising merry hell about it. The second was a painstakingly typed letter from Father Hugh Tierney (having been placed under considerable pressure by Miss Alys Jane Drury I don't doubt. Ha! I *knew* the old trout would ultimately prove useful!), finally agreeing to meet up.

24

Miss Carla Hahn

Three phone calls – one straight after the other – from furious residents of the Coastguards' Cottages, topped by a flustered Mrs Barrow ringing 'on behalfs of poor Mr Huff', who is 'set about havin' hisself a coronary', and demanding (I can hear him muttering away in the background) that I COME IMMEDIATELY to sort everything out.

Well I don't know what they're expecting me to do, exactly, especially (the thudding realization dawns on me, halfway through my second call – Neil Oakley, from number 12) as it's only two days before Orla's birthday.

Aaaargh!

The birthday! Orla's birthday! How on earth could it have slipped my mind? She'd have been … twenty … twenty-three this year? Twenty-four? And if the visiting party generating all this trouble belongs to Orla's most passionate (and colourful), living advocate, Sorcha Jennett, self-styled 'Pavee Princess' (Mrs Barrow calls her 'Lady Muck' because of her lofty manner and because the knees on her skirts are always so muddy on account of a) her foraging lifestyle and b) her propensity to fall down on them in prayer at the drop of a hat), then I won't have any chance of shifting her (or her vans, or her cohorts, or her kids, or her grandkids, or her horses) before the occasion has been celebrated with due Pavee-style ceremony.

Oh please God, just don't let anybody have told her about the photographs!

I jump on to my bike and pedal hell-for-leather. Even as I approach the turning into Toot Rock, I can see a series of cars spilling out on to the Sea Road. Stranger still, a camera crew up on the sea wall and a dramatically shirted and skirted individual with long, hennaed hair performing what I can only presume to be some obscure Travelling Ritual on the shingle up there.

It's Sorcha! It's got to be! It's definitely Sorcha! Bugger. Bugger. *Bugger.* I throw down my bike and stride out towards her, clambering up the sea wall and waving at her (quite bossily – yup. That's it, Carla. Be strong. Be brave. Or else she'll smell your fear) from what I consider a respectable distance. Sorcha stops what she's doing, exclaims (inaudibly) at the sight of me and then bends down to pick up ... What is that? Is it a ... a video camera? She affixes it to her eye and walks over. I cover my face with my hands (to indicate that I am not *at all* happy to be filmed), but peek at her through my fingers as she draws within shouting range.

Sorcha must be pushing sixty, but she looks much younger. Her skinny, tanned arms are weighted down with bangles, her nails are filthy from ... from, well doing what she does (foraging for herbs, lighting real fires, setting spells, tending to the horses). Her head is crowned with its habitual daisy chain. Her eyes are a smoky grey and keen and hard and searching. She is covered in bells, tiny bells. She jingles and jangles as she moves.

Oh please God, don't let anybody have told her about the photographs!

'No cause to worry yerself, darlin'.' She chuckles as she draws in close (I know her voice is low, but it's always still several tones lower than I actually remember). 'I got me no film in this here damn ting. I'm just doin' it for the TV folks over there ...'

She indicates, airily, over her shoulder. Bells jangle.

I don't drop my hands, just the same.

'Sorcha, your vans are blocking access to the road,' I tell her. 'I thought we had an arrangement ...?'

'Well it's lovely to see you, too, my beautiful girl.' She grins, lowering the camera, then encasing me in a firm hug. 'And we *did* have us an arrangement, yes ...'

One, final, violent squeeze (a lovely blast of sweet musk from her nape) before she releases me (social etiquette compels me to lower my hands at this stage). '... and we *still* got us an arrangement, Carla,' she insists. 'All this galvanization and doodah is only for them TV peoples. They needs a measure of drama, see? They cleaves to certain, well, I suppose you might call it "*stereotypes*" of we Travelling Folk; they expect free behaviour – colour – song – mischief – mayhem, fisticuffs – rumpus – bedlam ... It's just ... just *show*-business, Carla,' she pooh-poohs, 'nothin' else.'

'So what's with the camera?' I ask.

Oh please, please God, don't let anybody have told her about the photographs!

'I got me some funding from the Arts Council,' she explains, 'to make a short fillum for the Pavee about Orla. To show to my people at horse fairs and so on. I been carryin' this damn ting around wid me for the best part of three month already, gettin' testimony an' the like. Well,' she confides, voice lowering, 'mainly it's just bin myself readin' poems and reminiscin'. Aishling and Saoirse an' the smaller girls have bin drawing and painting to add a bit o' colour. Donnie has wrote a song, God bless his soul.'

'So why ...' I gesticulate towards the bigger cameras and the crew.

'Well some bright spark over at Channel 4 got it in their heads to make a television programme about all what I'm set on doing. Like the dumb play in *Macbeth*. You ever read that book, Carla?'

'At school.' I nod.

'A fillum wid'in a fillum, see? And to my way of tinking, if it exposes more people in the world to our Pavee saint, Orla Nor Cleary …' – she crosses herself, reverently – 'the patron saint of all Aboriginal peoples, then that mustn't be any bad ting, eh?'

Okay. Okay. Okay …

I struggle to process the ramifications of this news. They're not good, are they? The ramifications? They *can't* be good, can they? For … for this … for us … for me?

'Fine,' I say (Oh no, *no*, it *isn't* fine! It *isn't* fine! Not at all!), 'but you must know that the cottage is currently occupied, and I can't give you permission to just …' (I mean how could I *possibly* have imagined this? How? *How?* How could I have possibly …?)

'Don't you worry yourself about nottin', Carla,' Sorcha clucks, reaching out a sandy hand and rearranging my fringe with it, then gazing at me (a slight tip of the head) through the camera lens. 'I don't need no permission. The TV peoples will sort all that out for us.'

'But you're blocking access to Toot Rock, Sorcha,' I repeat. *Oh please, please, please don't let anybody have told her about the photographs!*

'No, I'm not actually blocking it, my love,' she insists, 'I'm pretending to block it. For the fillum. But I'm not actually blocking it. I wouldn't do that to you, my poor sweet darling girl.'

'But you *are* actually blocking it,' I maintain, 'nobody can gain access.'

As I speak, a TV sound-woman (well I presume that's who she is) is gesticulating towards us both.

'There's a woman,' I say, 'holding a big grey fluffy thing on a pole, waving her arms at us.'

Sorcha lowers her camera and turns. 'Ah, that there'll be Claudia on sound. My mike must be playin' up.'

'So you're … this is being …? This entire conversation is being recorded?!' I stammer.

'Well it should've been, my love, but if the damn mike's back to its old tricks …' Sorcha fiddles with something tiny, black and mechanical on her shirt. 'We might need to re-stage this, Carla …' She turns and waves the sound-woman over.

'Perhaps start off wid a little bit more of a formal introduction next time around? Like, filter in some useful information as we talk, you know, along the lines of, uh, "As the official custodian of Orla's shrine, it's a joy to welcome you back to Pett Level, Sorcha …" I mean I don't really know what kind of a *role* you'll be wanting to play, there, Carla …'

What kind of a …?

What kind of …?

'Oh and before it slips my mind – would you be so kind as to have a little chat with the uptight stick of a man who's tenantin' that cottage of yours?' she asks. 'What's he go by again? Mr Hunn? Mr Hick?'

'Mr Huff,' I automatically correct her. 'A little chat about what, exactly?'

Oh please, please, please, please don't let anybody have told her about the photographs!

'About gettin' some proper access to the shrine, of course!' she answers, indignant. 'He set a cold hose on the lighting engineer earlier. A shockin' poor show, it was.'

I begin to breathe a quiet sigh of relief.

'An' about gettin' me a quick peek at them old photographs what he got,' she adds, almost nonchalant.

'Sorcha?'

It's the sound-woman, Claudia, who is suddenly hard upon us, grey, fluffy appendage waggling ominously as she walks. 'Sorcha? Bart says the pebble scene might work better if you take your pumps off first. Maybe string them around your neck with the ribbons?'

I promptly turn and flee, hands firmly plastered over my face again.

'Oh come on, Carla!' Sorcha yells after me, outraged. 'Where's your ... your sense of *adventure*, woman?'

Mr Barrow has been stationed by the gate in his new role as Official Guardian of the aforementioned (and offending) hose. 'Did *you* tell Sorcha about the photographs?' I demand, but I've already charged on past before he can compose himself to answer. I find Mr Huff sitting on the back porch bench, feet up on a stool, knitting. There is no physical evidence here of a man on the cusp of some major pulmonary event. He appears perfectly relaxed and at his ease.

'Ah, Miss Hahn!' He smiles. 'At last! And fully dressed, to boot!'

'Somebody told Sorcha Jennett about the photos,' I all but explode.

'Sore ...?'

'Sorcha Jennett. She knows about the photographs! She wants to see them. She probably wants to feature them in the film she's making. Which means that Channel 4 will also want to use them in the documentary they're making about Sorcha's film.'

Short pause.

'Hard cheese.' Mr Huff shrugs.

'It's Orla's birthday in two days,' I run on. 'I'm sorry – I should have thought to warn you – people often like to visit the shrine to pray and pay homage at around this time. Some come from really long distances. A couple of years ago we had a woman all the way from New South Wales. Sorcha will definitely want access. There'll be no getting rid of her for the next three days at the very least.'

Mr Huff just knits.

'There's no point in trying to refuse her access,' I persist.

'Well there *is* a point if you don't actually *want* her to gain access,' Mr Huff avers.

I ponder the awful logic of this statement while over his shoulder (in the middle of the dining-room rug) I see the tiny rabbit, sitting quietly on some old newspaper under the upturned mesh fireguard from the sitting room.

'Either we grant her access or you'll wake up one morning with a flaming mattress on your roof,' I warn him. 'Worse still, she'll take it out on all your neighbours. Her kids will decapitate their prize dahlias or leave steaming piles of horse manure on their doormats.'

'Hmmn. Just a standard Mulberry Cottage-style welcome, then.' Mr Huff smirks.

I find it difficult to respond directly to this snide (but perfectly justified) comment without the threat of an involuntary blush.

'I saw you embracing,' Mr Huff adds, still smirking, 'on the sea wall.'

'Oh,' I say.

'It was very touching,' he continues. 'Did they manage to get it all on camera?'

'Sorcha asked me what kind of a "role" I wanted to play,' I respond, turning towards the beach, irritated (why does he always feel the need to make everything so ... so *difficult?*). In the distance I can see a small group of TV people discussing the possible imminence of rain.

'"Facilitator",' Mr Huff volunteers, then '"Pushover",' then, '"Pimp!"'

'I'm no happier about all this than you are,' I grumble, still facing away from him (pimp? *Pimp?*), 'but I know Sorcha, and there's simply no point in resisting her.'

Mr Huff merely clucks.

'She really ... really *worships* Orla.' I turn, trying to explain. 'She honestly believes that Orla cured her family of a long-running hereditary birth disorder. To Sorcha, Orla is the Pavee's equivalent of the Virgin of Guadalupe.'

I pause for a moment, thoughtfully. 'In fact I'm struggling to understand why you wouldn't want to interview her for the book. Plenty of other people have. She was quite close to Orla in Ireland. Father Hugh brought them together at the cathedral in Monaghan.'

'So you're going to give her permission to access the shrine, then?' Mr Huff blatantly changes the subject. 'Against my professed desire as your legal tenant?'

'I made it perfectly clear in the rental conditions that the garden might occasionally be visited by pilgrims,' I snap.

'I've seen the gypsy children tunnelling through blackthorn bushes.' Mr Huff shudders. 'Tunnelling through them. Like a little pack of rodents.'

'There's always been a strong tradition of blackthorn tunnelling in the area,' I tell him. 'When Jacob Epstein – the sculptor – rented a house here in the early part of the century, the main access to his place was through a thick tunnel of the stuff. Epstein had a very productive few years in Pett Level. That's partly what drew Bran and Kalinda to Mulberry.'

'Now you come to mention it, I think there might be a photo …' Mr Huff suddenly recollects, 'some lunatic emerging victoriously from a clump of blackthorn.'

'Kalinda, probably,' I hazard a guess.

'Was it Kalinda?' he muses, half to himself.

'Well it wouldn't have been Orla. She couldn't crawl. Her arms were too short.'

'I think it might've been you,' Mr Huff avers.

'Me? I don't think so!' I scoff.

'In fact I'm sure that it was you.'

Mr Huff places down his knitting and stands up as if to go and check. Then – just as suddenly – he changes his mind and sits down again. I – by complete contrast – am initially horrified at the idea of seeing the photograph (I just couldn't possibly bear to ...), but then, when he sits down again, I feel strangely disappointed. Almost ... almost *hurt*.

'Well I'm sure it wasn't me, in the photo,' I say (perhaps hoping thereby to provoke him into fetching the damn thing after all).

'No,' Mr Huff concedes. He picks up his knitting. He *knits*. I watch the needles sliding up against each other and then being pulled apart. I see the yarn tying them together and then slipping off and releasing them once more with a typically dispassionate woollen shrug.

What is it with these photographs, anyway? I wonder. How to account for my complete lack of ... of any desire to ...? This feeling ... *What* is it? Not indifference. Almost a ... a *coldness* ... A grim chilliness. An icy resistance. But what exactly am I resisting? Is it the idea of seeing something that can't then be *unseen*? Clues? Evidence? As if by my seeing those photographs – just the act of ... – as if by my *seeing* them – him, her, them, *me* – it might all suddenly become too real again? Might I find myself engulfed again? Becalmed? Overwhelmed? Helpless? *Scorched?* Or – worse still – having to ... to ... reassess ...?

What if I find myself marginalized in those photos? What if I finally have to accept – to realize – that I'm not actually ... That I was always stuck on the outside – in the outskirts – that I was really just ... just incidental, even though I sometimes felt as if this – here, then – was the only time I truly ... The only time I truly worked? Truly *meshed?* What an awful prospect.

To be rendered so ... so unnecessary. And to finally be completely and utterly assured of that fact. To see it. Right there. Once and for all. In black and white.

I stare at the needles again, depressed.

Mr Huff has such graceful hands; lean yet still quite ... quite *manly* hands. And as I watch them work away, mechanically, something odd suddenly dawns on me ... It's like ... It's almost as if ... yes ... as if Orla was the wool. Orla was the wool, the yarn, and Bran and Kalinda were the needles and I was the ... Me. I was the thing that they knitted. I was the thing that they made. Before everything just ... just imploded, exploded, faded. I was the thing that they made. I am what remains – their creation – the little garment they wove ... And maybe ... maybe I'm not the most useful or important or *significant* of garments (a lone baby's mitten, one half of a tank-top) but I'm *their* garment ... And maybe (I stare at Mr Huff), maybe *he* was their garment, too – poor, old Mr Huff, stuck a million miles away in Mexico, wifeless – almost by default.

So if that's the case, then why not just ...?
What?!
Why not ...? No. No. It's too complicated. Too dangerous. Just to ... to *care*. Just to open yourself up again to all that terrible light and savage bliss and deafening reverberation.

I mean the damn things were taken by ... by *her* (the source of all my ... the cause of all my ...). They were *hers*. They were what *she* saw! How to keep in check all those ... those ... those ... urgh ... *feelings*? That powerful sense (even way back then!) of something being ... being stolen ... snapped. *Taken?* Like a photograph! And that desperate need (by contrast) to keep something *un*-recorded, something *real* – something safe – still nestled away deep inside me. My memories, untarnished by ... unspoiled by ... by ... what? The world? The actual facts? The truth?

'How many are there, altogether?' I wonder, still watching the needles.
'How many ...?'
Mr Huff seems lost inside a dream of his own.
'Photos.'
'Oh. Hundreds.'

Hundreds?

'And what will happen to them now?' I ask. 'I mean now that Kimberly is ...?'

'Dead,' he fills in.

'Dead,' I echo (why did she get to survive when Bran died? Why did she get to live when Bran died? What made her so ...? So special? So important? So resilient?).

'They'll be sold, I suppose.' He shrugs.

'But you have copies with you,' I persist, 'duplicates of the originals?'

'Yes,' he concedes, 'of course I do.'

He glances up, irritated. 'I thought you just wanted to forget about the whole thing.' He scowls. 'And anyway, there's a legal ...' – he stumbles – 'an embargo. On all her possessions. The laws of probate. Until the will is read. You can tell that to your gypsy pal if you want. Take some of the heat off.'

'But you showed them to Alys,' I argue.

'I showed a few of them to Alys,' he grudgingly concedes.

'So why can't *I* see them, then?' I demand.

(Why am I asking this? It's utterly counter-productive. I really don't want to see them. No. I really don't.)

'It's out of my hands.' Mr Huff shrugs. 'It's an issue for the lawyers.'

Then something astonishing suddenly strikes me.

'But if you were Kimberly's husband ...?'

'I was,' Mr Huff snaps. 'I *am* Kimberly's husband.'

'Did she leave a will?'

A long silence follows.

'Because if she didn't, then surely ...?'

The full implications of all this finally start to filter through.

'Oh my goodness!' I exclaim. '*You* own the photos! They're yours!'

'Like I said,' he continues, 'it's an issue for the lawyers.'

'So why won't you let me see them?' I demand.

'It's not a question of ...' he begins.

'Let me see them!' I say.

'No,' he answers, calmly enough.

'I'll evict you from Mulberry,' I quietly threaten (and are there …? Are there actual *tears* on my lashes?!).

'All right then,' he responds, 'refuse the gypsy access and I'll show them to you.'

'But I can't possibly deny Sorcha access to the shrine!' I exclaim. 'It would be … it would be cruel. She visits the shrine every year.'

'Then there you have it, Miss Hahn!' Mr Huff smiles, victorious. 'There's your answer!'

I gaze at him, amazed. Why is he doing this? Why would …? What's the …? Is there something I don't …? Is there …? Something Kimberly said, maybe? Does he … did she … does he …?

'What size are your feet?' he asks.

'What?'

'Your feet,' he repeats, 'what size?'

'Six.'

He nods.

'Why?' I demand.

'Because I'm knitting you some socks.'

I continue to gaze at him. I don't mind confessing that I feel some terrible urges towards him. I just want to … to strike him, to scream at him, to scratch his eyes out, to burst into tears.

I turn to leave.

A smoking candle! Just like Alys said. A smoking candle! A weirdo. A sadist. A smoking candle. A truly bad man. Why is he here? This awful man? Why is he here, ruining everything, complicating everything? What can he possibly want with us?

'Enjoy your ride home!' Mr Huff chirrups (he almost sings!).

240

It's all uphill back to Fairlight. With rain imminent. *All* uphill. And he ... he ... he knows it, he *knows* it, damn him!

25

Mr Franklin D. Huff

You know what? I had looked at the photos. Several times. I
had looked at them, but I'd never truly ... I'd never truly
looked at them – digested them, engaged with them, felt them,
understood them – until I took them out after that little spat
with Miss Hahn and sat down at the dining-room table and
properly *scrutinized* ...

I am a journalist by trade. I once credited myself with a
measure of objectivity. Of dispassion. Of analytical skill. But
when I looked at those photos this time around, with these
new eyes, with this fresh perspective brought about by ... by
what? By my sudden need to torture Miss Hahn because Miss
Hahn has this ... this quite maddening way of ... of detaching
herself ... this unreachable quality, this strange composure,
this aloofness, this untouchability?
Glacial!

She talked about those glaciers (didn't she?). In the sauna?
Those huge pieces of ice sliding into each other and then
producing those ghastly noises, almost 'intelligent'-sounding.
Communicating. Is it really any wonder that she felt so drawn
to those arctic soundscapes, when she's all but glacial herself?!
Glacial.

And when you communicate with her – or attempt to – you
also feel yourself suddenly reduced to the level of inanimate
matter. And for some reason this makes me long to ... to
undermine, to prick, to *shatter* ...

Do I *really* want to hurt Miss Hahn?

Miss Hahn, of all people?

The Barbed Wire?

Isn't the barbed wire the thing that keeps in, the thing that keeps out, the thing that snags and tears if you draw too close?

Why would I ...?

More to the point, *how* could I ...?

Eh?

Well, there's the rub.

I suppose this can't be unrelated to the fact that after I got home – I mean *back*, to Mulberry – I suddenly felt this overpowering impulse, this urge to ... to launch a secondary attack. To try and bolster myself. Because I'd felt so vulnerable, so emasculated, so discomposed out there by the bus-stop. Then the drama with Mr Pemberton. My magnificent tumble.

She was an itch I longed to scratch.

Crazy, really.

So I made Mrs Barrow ring her up – on the pretext of being angry about the gypsies ... and ... and then I ... so when she ...

After the kiss. Let me just come out and say it. Okay, fine, I won't pretend that it was the most successful or the most erotic or the most ... most *romantic* of encounters, but still ... Still.

Because it was all about Bran and Kimberly, before. The photos. It was all about trying to see how Kimberly saw Bran. How Bran looked back at my wife, the camera. It was all about trying to work out whether what had happened between them was merely an accident – a feeling, that suddenly developed – or something connected to Kimberly's ... something more calculated and ... and ... and terrible. Were they just the bungling victims of cruel circumstance – Kimberly's line – or the evil perpetrators of something way more dark and insidious? Because if the state didn't think

there was a serious case to answer, then why – *why?!* – did
Bran end up incarcerated? On remand, yes. But refused bail?
Considered a flight risk? Because he was parked in his own
driveway! The incendiary device was hidden inside the boot of
his own car! Did it explode accidentally or (as Kimberly
always insisted) had it been planted there?

Kim was a photographer! Just a photographer!
And he was a muralist. A Republican sympathizer, yes, but
not a terrorist.

Bran and I met at university. He was in the year above.
Dashing. Handsome. Sullen. Charming. Vulgar. Debonair. He
quit his history degree after eighteen months to train to
become a … a *stonemason*, no less! Spent all his time back in
Ireland, dangling off old churches on creaking harnesses,
preserving gargoyles. Designing ornate tombstones. The
painting came later.

But we kept in touch. Kim photographed some of his
earlier work in Belfast as part of a larger post-grad project
she'd undertaken on 'Protest Art'.
Kim's father died when she was twelve. He was raised in
Derry then emigrated to Canada in his mid-twenties. Worked
as a cabbie. Drank himself to death. Kim had no interest in
politics. When talk would turn to politics at dinner parties,
she'd help to clear the table, pull on some Marigolds and get
started on the washing-up.

I suppose this was something else we had in common.
Although I've never been afraid to *engage* with a subject,
intellectually. Throw out a few fresh ideas. Play the devil's
advocate.

Was Kimberly *too* blank? Was it her very blankness that
drew me to her? And our dear Miss Hahn? The 'glacial' Miss
Hahn?

When she did eventually turn up … (the aforementioned
ice-block). Well, I saw her before that. I was standing on the
front porch, waiting for a first sighting of her, you know,

pelting down the Sea Road – as she generally does – on her ancient bike. Awful trousers held in check by a pair of stainless-steel bicycle clips. I've seen her walk around in those things for hours on end. Sometimes just one. The other leg flapping freely. Or wearing them like two bangles on her wrists. Or even like an Egyptian-style ornament on her upper arm. Totally unselfconscious about it. What an extraordinary combination of studied and careless she is! Extraordinary! Who can possibly account for it?

And then there she was (anyway …). And I felt … This awful, violent blasting inside my chest. Several landmines triggered between my ribs prompted merely – it would seem – by her distant outline. The mere suggestion of *her*. This ludicrous vibration (so counter-productive! So unhelpful! So unnecessary!). Like a high-pitched whine which you can't actually register but which is killing your ears, just the same. And the mind knows. The body senses the damage. Not … not a good feeling. Not a welcome feeling. A disastrous feeling, in essence.

I think I may even have gasped! Leaned forward, clutching at myself. The sheer shock of it all! The horror that I might have … that this repellent creature might have … have worked her voodoo on me. And my rational mind screaming all the while: STOP THIS, YOU BLOODY IDIOT! IT'S ALL WRONG! IT'S HOPELESS! RIDICULOUS! LAUGHABLE! THERE IS SOMETHING SO … SO *UNAPPEALING* ABOUT THIS CREATURE, THIS MISS HAHN! TO FEEL THESE … THESE … LUDICROUS THINGS MUST BE THE UNCONSCIOUS EXPRESSION OF SOME KIND OF PROFOUND PSYCHOLOGICAL SELF-LOATHING!

MISS HAHN DOESN'T EVEN CARE! SHE DOESN'T CARE!

Oh, but she said that we had something in common. Remember? And isn't commonality at the root of all romantic feeling?

NO, NO! MISS HAHN DOESN'T CARE! SHE'S ONE OF THOSE ... SHE'S ONE OF THOSE ABSTRACT CREATURES, THOSE HEARTLESS, MONSTROUS, FECKLESS CREATURES. IT'S ALL ... IT'S ALL SO UPTIGHT, SO UPTIGHT THAT IT ACTUALLY *PROJECTS* CARELESSNESS. BUT SHE'S SO BOUND UP, SO ... SO *GUARDED* ... SO ... SO ICY AND CALCULATING!

Exhausting. This is exhausting. I can't keep on thinking in capital letters. Aside from any other consideration it's just way too gauche. Too adolescent.

I watched her in conversation on the sea wall with the gypsy woman. They embraced. Miss Hahn was covering her face. And when they embraced I felt ... now, this is odd. I felt a twisting feeling in my belly of such profound rage and *jealousy*. In fact I ran to get the binoculars. Okay. I already had the binoculars with me. I had gone to fetch the binoculars (a trusty but rather unwieldy pair which live on a nail adjacent to the little notice-board on the kitchen wall) as soon as Mrs Barrow had confirmed that Miss Hahn was on her way over.

I peered at Miss Hahn through the binoculars. Miss Hahn has this funny habit of repeatedly tucking her hair behind her ear. Then it slips out and falls across her cheek again. Then she tucks it away again. I think she must have tucked her hair behind her ear at least twenty times in the course of a two-minute conversation.

Why doesn't she just slide in a hair-grip? *Eh?*

Are her ears pierced? Impossible to tell, but I doubt it, somehow. Miss Hahn eschews all feminine ornamentation. Miss Hahn is a teenage boy with breasts. Two breasts. Right there. Perched on her ribs. Either side of her breast-bone. Like a small pair of softly cooing, creamy-coloured quails. Just ...

Perching.

Yes.

Where exactly was I heading with this?

The photographs ... the suspicion ... the explosion ... the binoculars ... Miss Hahn's arrival on the porch, her cheeks flaming. Some discussion about the gypsy woman. Then that confounded child – Orla. Miss Hahn gets a special look on her face whenever she talks about the child. Sort of stricken. What's behind that look? Confusion? Guilt? Helplessness? Terror?

And then suddenly I recollect a photo of Miss Hahn crawling through some blackthorn wearing exactly that look. In this little beret. Adorable in this little beret – red, I presume. In the foreground is Father Hugh (*né* Pietr) Tierney being crowned by the child, Orla, with a small daisy chain. The child's expression is radiant. Then I recall another, later, photograph in the same set, where all three of them are sitting on the grass, but now they are four. Bran Cleary has joined them. He's wearing a smock covered in paint. I suppose I should say five. Five of them, because Kim is there too, behind the camera. And in this picture another daisy chain is being made. Miss Hahn is making it. I try to remember whether Father Hugh ...?

Miss Hahn is telling me about ... meanwhile ... Miss Hahn is talking about the sculptor, Jacob Epstein, who once lived for a period of time in the local area.

I've already mentioned the tunnelling to her, obviously. Then I refer, elliptically, to the photo. I stand up to go and fetch it, and as I do so, it dawns on me that the photos must have been numbered – collated – in the wrong order. Because in the second photograph, Father Hugh isn't wearing his daisy-chain crown ...

Unless, of course, he's removed it and the child is stringing yet another ...

Or ...

I stand up to go and fetch the photo. I need to see whether ... Is it possible that Miss Hahn wasn't alone in that tunnel? Is it possible that following up close behind her was ... who else? Bran Cleary?! That they had been ... been ... somewhere – beyond the blackthorn – alone, together? Kimberly was always very strict about keeping the photographs in a particular order.

Very strict. Each one numbered on the back: 01, 02, 03 ... 30 ... 134 ...

I suddenly sit down again. I pick up my knitting. Miss Hahn starts to interrogate me about the tunnelling photo. She demands to see it. From an earlier position of apparent indifference, now she's very keen, almost hectoring.

And me? Oh, I am overwhelmed by the desire to give her what she wants because, well, I love Miss Hahn. I am *in* love with her! Yes! Yes! The same way a sentence can be *in*-coherent or a person *in*-fected. With a virus. It's so obvious, isn't it? But how awful, eh?! How maddening! Ever since I first laid ... from the very ... even ...

But I am *equally* overwhelmed by the need to stop her/it – to stop this *in* love – at all costs. This pointless, inappropriate, unreciprocated '*in* love'. I must deny her/it. But to deny Miss Hahn always seems to spark something within her. A special fire starts to burn deep, deep within the glacier. So I deny her. And I suppose, at some level, I have always denied her. Because ... Why is that, exactly? I wonder.

A profound need to deny myself, perhaps?

To deny myself what, though?

Happiness?

Disappointment?

I watch Miss Hahn blazing – her temper darting and licking like the fluttering yellow flame of a lighted candle. Then away she storms. *Poof!*

One, little puff and she is blown out – back into the world again.

After I've waited to watch her cycle away – there she goes, steam coming out of her lovely unadulterated ears! – I run and fetch the photographs. I spread them out on the dining-room table. I start to re-collate the narrative. Throwing them around, sliding them about ... Because there actually *is* a narrative ...

Mr Pemberton was right! How could I have ...? Was it merely hidden away inside the ...? Or do I simply lack even the most basic ability – the insight, the sensitivity to ...? But then why would Kim feel the need ...? Who was she protecting, exactly? Herself? Bran? Kalinda? Orla? Not Miss Hahn, surely?

Was it just a mistake? An accident?

And – still more importantly – if *this* story was hidden, right here, in plain view, then what else might have escaped my attention? Am I just overwrought, overwhelmed, over-thinking, or is it *really* possible to tell a different story in pictures just by sleight of ... just by switching ... just by carefully ...?

I suddenly start removing some of the pictures from the pile. First this one, then that one. There are eight of them, in total, at the heart of this particular little narrative. But eventually ... after much soul-searching and analysis, I reduce them down to just two. The two most infuriating. The two most incriminating. Yes.

Without these two, the Bran Cleary/Carla Hahn story almost loses its meaning. The tunnel photo I opt to leave. That can stay. But the picture of the four of them ...? Look! *Look!* Bran is staring over towards Miss Hahn, his eyes shining, making *no palpable attempt* to disguise his emotions, wearing the kind of half-dazed expression one might habitually relate to a minor head injury, perhaps, or severe and persistent alcohol/narcotic abuse (and who's to say *either* might not be at the root of it?). Miss Hahn is frowning, biting her lip, gazing anxiously towards an all but oblivious Orla. The second photo? Orla is praying her rosary on the beach, kneeling, her back to the camera, wrapped up in a blanket. Miss Hahn is in the surf, some distance off. Although the casual viewer might not readily identify her ... Only the focused eye, the interested eye, the eye that spontaneously dilates at even the most casual of contact with her irresistible (and I don't use that word as a compliment, more in the sense of 'compulsive') outline.

Bran is to the fore, back also to the camera, sketching. Bold strokes, in charcoal. On his pad, on his small easel, on the floor scattered around him, a dozen brutal studies of ... of Miss Hahn, no less! Head, body, ear, shoulder, arm, foot. This photo is also out of sync with a series of others. Because if you measure Miss Hahn's progress along the beach ... Unless of course she retraced her steps, then turned ...?

In this series – as Kim has numbered them – Orla is the main focus. We start with a close-up (just her wan face, etched in tears), then slowly inch further back, then further still ... The Miss Hahn photo comes last in order of number. But in fact – if we study her distant progress along the tideline – it was actually the first.

How extraordinary, I muse, that simply by swapping the order of these images Kim has transformed so completely the mood and the focus ... The original order makes Miss Hahn the centre of it all (Bran Cleary is watching her, painting her, and Orla, quietly ignored – marginalized by her wanton 'nurse' – cries and prays). The new order? Orla is crying, then, as we pull back, she is praying, alone. But after a while, we see the father, standing guard. Orla isolates herself, but she is, at some level, cherished and protected.

And yet ... If Kim was so eager to keep Miss Hahn's significance to a minimum in the narrative (and the question this inevitably begs is: how, if Bran Cleary and Miss Hahn were ... were ... *you* know, did it happen that merely a few weeks later Kim and he were apparently ...? Well, I suppose stranger things have happened. Did Miss Hahn ultimately reject Bran Cleary's advances? Did the affair with Kim happen on the rebound? These two interludes were separated by the tragic death of his daughter, after all; did this damn family ever *do* anything, ever *say* anything, that wasn't riven with drama, with significance? The rest of us live dreary lives in a slightly smudged close type. Their life was handwritten in exquisitely ornate calligraphy. Gold-embossed. With tiny, inked illustrations highlighting the opening letter of every paragraph) ... uh, no, I was saying, why, if Kim was so keen to keep Miss Hahn's narrative significance to a minimum, did she tell me to come to Pett Level in the first place and actively seek her out?

Why undo all her hard work like that in one fell swoop? Why?

Well I suppose if she *didn't* recommend I come here, if she *didn't* mention Miss Hahn like that, just casually, in passing, I might have felt a surreptitious impulse to travel here under my own steam. And then I'd have been way more ... more professional, more inquisitive, more alert. As it was I simply felt ... obliged. Hence the first month of resentment, casual charm and sloth. Followed by two weeks of arguing and doodling (during at least one of these, permanently drunk).

Did Kim honestly understand my little proclivities, my idle faults so well? I find the thought quite ... quite bewildering, no, *no*, almost touching, somehow.
Am I really to be considered such a formidable adversary, then? Or – and this *isn't* such an appealing idea – so ridiculously easy to play, so pathetically biddable, so ludicrously transparent?
Hmmn?

If only I could remove myself – my natural prejudices – from the equation. If only I could step away and ... somehow detach ... be truly clinical, dispassionate ...
How invested am I? Really? Or how cleverly have I been played (perhaps)?

Might it help to analyse Kim's purported opinions on various individuals and then to gradually work my way back?

With regard to ... to the child (for example), or Kalinda, her mother? Father Hugh?

Kalinda 'Lonely' Alloway/Cleary?

Orla Nor Cleary?

Father Hugh/Pietr Tierney?

The first: tough, creative, brilliant, fiercely ambitious, flawed.

That's Kim's view. And my view? Pretty much identical to hers. But throw 'slut' into the mix, will you? Oh, and 'castrator'. To put it baldly, Kalinda 'Lonely' Alloway (we only met twice, and on the second occasion she stuck her tongue into my ear – it was a very, very long tongue – for a bet, apparently) always scared the living daylights out of me.

The second – Orla Nor – a Thalidomide child and a daddy's girl. Utterly captivating, intriguing, tragic. Hysterical. Gentle. Sincere.

That's Kim's view. My view? Honestly? Attention-seeker, hysteric, circus freak.

Well you *asked*, didn't you?

The third: Father Hugh (Eh? Father ... Father *who*?!), a priest totally, *totally* obsessed. Slightly desperate and pathetic. Kind but somewhat weak. In way, *way* out of his depth.

That's Kim's view. My view? The priest was the patsy. Or was he the controlling genius? Might he even – with a little stretch of the imagination – have been *both*?

Because – let's face it – if Kimberly *wasn't* actually an honest witness ... and if I *am* to be found so ... so partial, so ignorant, so easy to manipulate, then what the heck else might be eluding me about this story?

My mind quietly wrestles with these questions as I take the two most 'incriminating' photographs of Carla Hahn to the open fireplace, turn them over and shove them into the grate. I find a match, strike it and, one after the other, in quick succession I ... I burn them. I burn the very *idea* of them. I alter history.

It's only as they flame up that my eye alights on the two numbers, written in Kim's careful hand, at the rear. The first: 40. The second: 04.

Ha! *Ha!* Just a coincidence. Surely? I promptly stand up – knees creaking – somewhat chastened, then issue an involuntary yelp as the telephone commences its strident ring. (Ho-*ho!* Guilty conscience, anybody?)
Hello?

It's Father Hugh/Pietr Tierney. He's cancelling our meeting. Father Hugh has a very soft, lilting, Irish voice, a kind voice. He's ringing from a call box. He sounds a tad furtive. He apologizes and says that he's changed his mind. He's very sorry to have given me the wrong impression, and doubly sorry about my recent loss ...
My recent ...? But how ...?
He will naturally be offering a mass (had offered? Would offer?) for the repose of Kimberly's soul.

No. No. No. *No.* I won't be fobbed off! I'm still coming, Father Hugh, I say, I *must* come (if only to have a chance to meet ... well, *myself.* My double. Him. *Me:* the genius, the dupe). No, he says. There's no point. He won't see me, he ... he *can't* see me. It's impossible.

Nothing is impossible, I say, not if you want it badly enough (this is a terrible cliché and a lie, to boot). Father Hugh shows no sign of buying this, but still I persist with it, I fly with it. I find myself waxing lyrical, emboldened by the Kim scenario (poor Franklin D.! The grieving widower!). I don't have too much success with this approach, however. Father Hugh seems quite stern, quite determined. I cast my mind around ... uh ... uh ... What would Bran do, I wonder, what would that over-stated, under-stated, sneaky bastard Cleary do?

If you won't see me then I'll ... I'll walk to you, I say (yes! Suddenly quite the Irish Lothario!). I'm coming to Douai on foot. Forty-odd miles. Like a pilgrim. I'm leaving now. This

very minute. Would you turn away a man who had *walked* to see you, Father Hugh? Yes. I am coming on foot. I'm going to put down the phone and then I'm walking out of the cottage. No. First I'm gathering up the remaining photographs and placing them into an envelope in order to bring them over to you. I'm writing the monastery's full address into my jotter. I'm grabbing a map, a compass. I'm putting on a coat, feeding two carrots to the rabbit, uh ... a quick note for Mrs Barrow ... is the oven off? And then I'm ... I'm ...
I'm running at high speed towards – or ... or away – from heaven only knows what.

26

Teobaldo

It has been twenty-four long hours since Teobaldo has moved from his fixed position on his perch or made a *single sound*. Teobaldo is transfixed. Teobaldo is transfixed by King. Teobaldo is transfixed by the *sheer evil* of King. And not a little impressed, by it (the sheer evil. The evil *genius* of King).

Teobaldo perceives that the sending of King (the *arrival* of King) into Baldo 'space', Baldo 'home', Baldo 'sun', Baldo 'sitting room', Baldo 'Bitch's affections' is a marker of Baldo's prestige as true owner-occupier of 'space', 'home', 'sun', 'sitting room' and 'Bitch's affections'. Yes. Baldo perceives that King is a great – perhaps one of the all-time great – adversaries. And this is a marker of Teobaldo's *own* greatness.

Because King has been sent simply to meet his match in Baldo, surely? Why else would he have been sent but to engage with his equal, and then be vanquished?

Teobaldo longs to indulge in a pre-emptive WAAAAAAAAAH! of victory. But he cannot. The WAAAAAAAAH! has been temporarily stolen – appropriated – by the master-thief, King. And anyway Teobaldo is transfixed (remember?). Teobaldo is studying his enemy. Teobaldo is deceptively placid (not even a sneeze, no! Not even a brief raising of the crest!). Teobaldo is biding his time. Soon, soon, too soon (but not *too* soon), he will strike.

[*Fast-forward.*]
YARRAHHHH!

But not quite yet.

Teobaldo isn't much given to analysis, in general (in fact, at all), but as he watches King he wonders at how a bird can be so cheerful and yet so profoundly evil. Both impulses operating in perfect unison. The one not apparently contradicting the other. Because, well, Teobaldo is evil, too, on occasion (a parrot *must* be evil, on occasion, it's mandatory – it's genetic) but not nearly *so* evil and not nearly *so* cheerful as King.

It's almost as if the magnitude of the evil *creates* cheer. Or is this cheer perhaps the very *source* of the evil?

Baldo waits until King has turned to take a drink from his water bowl and then he shits, copiously. He longs to scratch his wing-pit, but he resists. King completes his drink and then returns to his perch. He peers at Baldo, cocks his head, quizzically, clears his throat, bows 'ironically', and then:

[*King.*]

'Ring-ring! Ring-ring! Ring-ring! Ring-ring!'

King performs an astonishingly loud and unerringly accurate impersonation of 'phone'.

Baldo listens (no head cock) as Bitch is heard to rush down the 'corridor' from the 'kitchen'. Bitch answers 'phone'. Baldo observes how peerlessly King times the cut-off for 'phone' ring with the moment Bitch picks up the 'receiver'. He doesn't know what any of this really means, but he is profoundly impressed by it, just the same.

[*Bitch speaks.*]

'*****? ** ****? ** **** ...?
****! ****, ****, ****, ****, ****!'

[*'Hello? Mr Huff? Is that …?*
Damn! Damn, damn, damn, damn, damn!']

Bitch slams down the 'receiver'.

King listens intently to Bitch's irate response to his 'phone ring jape' and then expresses his intense delight by shaking himself, violently, from beak to tail. Baldo observes millions of minuscule pieces of old skin and bird dander fly around his 'cage', illuminated by the gorgeous shaft of 'sun' in which King is currently perched. Baldo's own urge to ruffle and shake and scratch himself is very strong – *very* strong – but still, he resists it.

King and Baldo both listen intently as Bitch returns to 'kitchen'.

All is briefly quiet. Baldo inhales slowly and deeply. He knows that it is almost time ('sun' on 'back wall', hitting left-hand edge of 'side table') for Bitch to leave 'kitchen' and go 'outside'. Every day at this time Bitch goes 'outside'. Bitch will be gone for a lengthy spell ('sun' on 'back wall' to 'sun' creeping over towards Baldo's own 'side wall'. Of course if it's a 'cloudy' day, this interlude cannot be measured and is simply calibrated as 'eternal').

Baldo is not much given to calculation, but he calculates that King – fiendishly clever as he is – might still be too new to the household to have fully digested the exact niceties of Bitch's schedule.

Baldo waits. He is still. Very still. Soon Bitch can be heard turning off the 'radio', picking up her 'keys' and putting on her 'coat'. Shortly after Baldo hears her slam out of the 'house'.

King also listens intently (in 'sun', *bastard!*) to these comings and goings. Every so often he glances towards the immobile Baldo. Baldo has been immobile for so long now that King has almost forgotten that Baldo has the inbuilt capacity *for* mobility.

Baldo waits. Five 'minutes' pass, ten 'minutes', fifteen, twenty. Half an 'hour'. King starts to doze in the 'sun' (*bastard!*). Forty 'minutes'. Fifty 'minutes'. 'Sun' is now 'inches' from Baldo's 'side wall'.

Baldo's eyes are fixed on 'side wall'. Yes! Yes! IT IS TIME! Finally!

He sneezes. Baldo sneezes. That's all. But this is more than enough! King's keen, evil, almost *handsome* beetle-black eyes fly open. He glances over towards Baldo. Baldo sneezes again. Then slowly, very deliberately, he raises his crest and pushes out his chest.

King watches, fascinated, as Baldo lowers his head and performs a little half bow, then clears his throat and snaps his beak together in preparation for ...

[*Baldo noise.*]

'Wang! *W-w-w-w-w-ang!* W-w-w-w-wing!'

Baldo shakes himself violently and then tries again.

[*Baldo noise.*]

'Wing-wing! Wing-wing!'

[*Terrible impersonation of phone! Pathetic attempt at phone mimicry!*]

King is astonished at Baldo's pathetic attempt at phone impersonation. He squawks with untrammelled mynah-bird hilarity!

[*King speaks.*]

Wah-ha-ha-ha-*ha*!

'But impersonation is the greatest form of flattery, King, *clever* King, *handsome* King!' This is the message Baldo's cloying, keen-to-please posture seems to exude.

[*Again.*]

'*Wing-wing! Wing-wing! Wing-wing!*'

King watches Baldo, his shiny eyes brimming with scorn. Does Baldo not know that mynahs are the greatest of *all* the bird mimics? Does Baldo – this foolish parrot – not know that to impersonate is the very core, the very *life-blood* of the mynah? Yes, yes, parrots are reputed to be great mimics in their own right, but come *on*, we are talking an entirely different *class* of mimicry, here! A cat might look at a … a … well, a King!

In fact – in fact the sound of Baldo's pathetic phone mimicry (which continues on, laboriously, as King watches, scornfully, feathers gradually inflating with self-regard) slowly begins to grate on the nerves of the talented mynah. It's so very wayward! So ill-conceived! So mortifying! So badly done!

[*King speaks.*]

'Ruko!'

['*Stop!*']

[*Then again.*]

'Ruko!'

['*Stop!*']

But Baldo continues trying – in a kind of avian frenzy – to humiliate and degrade himself.

[*Baldo speaks.*]

'*Wing-wing! Wang-wing! Wong-wang! Wong-wung!*'

King has no hands to place over his monarchical ears, but if he had, he would be firmly affixing them to the spot, right now, to try and alleviate the impact of this horrible cacophony.

No! No! This is impossible! This is … it's degrading! To *all* mimics! To *all* birds. To *all* sounds! I say again, to *all* sounds! It's terrible! Baldo *must* stop! [*Ruko!*] Doesn't he understand …? Can't he …?
What else can King do, under the circumstances, but show Baldo how it *should* be done? Eh?

[*King speaks.*]

'*Ring-ring! Ring-ring!*'

[*Baldo responds, as if energized by King's intercession.*]

'*Wing-wang! Wing-wang!*'

No! King will not countenance the sacred 'ring' performed inadequately! Doesn't this idiot parrot see what a violation this awful display is of all competent mimicry?

[*King rings.*]

'*Ring-ring! Ring-ring! Ring-ring!*'

[*Baldo 'wings' in direct competition with King.*]

'Wing-wing! Wing-wang! Wing-wong!'

King is indignant! He simply has no alternative but to 'ring'
until Baldo is vanquished.

[*King rings.*]

'Ring-ring! Ring-ring! Ring-ring! Ring-ring! Ring-ring! Ring-ring!
Ring-ring! Ring-ring! Ring-ring! Ring-ring! Ring-ring! Ring-ring!
Ring-ring! Ring-ring!'

King grows quite delirious with his ringing! Soon Baldo falls
silent and just watches the 'Ring Master' at his work, in
apparent awe.

[*King rings, delirious, ecstatic, victorious!*]

'Ring-ring! Ring-ring! Ring-ring! Ring-ring! Ring-ring! Ring-ring!
Ring-ring!
'RING-RING! RING-RING! RING-RING! RING-RING!
RING-RING! RING-RING!'

Then, suddenly, he stops.

[*King.*]

'Eh?'

[*Head twizzle.*]

He becomes horribly aware of another presence in the 'sitting
room'.
 Oh dear. It is Bitch, back from 'outside', still in her 'coat',
and she is holding the 'phone receiver' in one hand (the curly

wire stretched straight as it distends from its 'hallway' 'table' position and all the way into the 'sitting room').

[*Bitch.*]

!

[*King.*]

'Oops!'

[*Bitch, incandescent with rage.*]

'*** ** ***, King? *******? *** ** **** ***? ***, King? *** *****?!'

[*'Was it you, King? Ringing? Has it been you? You, King? All along?!'*]

[*Baldo speaks.*]

'WAAAAAAAAAAAAAAAAAAAAAAAAAAAAAAAAAAAA
AAAAAAAAAAAAAAAAAAAAAAAAAAAAAAAAAAAA
AAAAAAAAAAAAAAAAAAAAAAAAAAAAAAAAAAAA
AAAAAAAAAAAAAAAAAAAAAAAAAAAAAAAAAAAA
AAAAAAAAAAAAAAAAAAAAAAAAAAAAAAAAAAAA
AAAAAAAAAAAAAAAAAAAAAAAAAH!'

[*Brief inhale.*]

'WAAAAAAAAAAAAAAAAAAAAAAAAAAAAAAAAAAAA
AAAAAAAAAAAAAAAAAAAAAAAAAAAAAAAAAAAA
AAAAAAAAAAAAAAAAAAAAAAAAAAAAAAAAAAAA
AAAAAAAAAAAAAAAAAAAAAAAAAAAAAAAAAAAA

AAAAAAAAAAAAAAAAAAAAAAAAAAAAAAAAAAAAAAA
AAAAAAAAAAAAAAAAAAAAAAAAAH!'

[*Brief inhale.*]

'*WAAAAAAAAAAAAAAAAAAAAAAAAAAAAAAAAAAAAAA
AAAAAAAAAAAAAAAAAAAAAAAAAAAAAAAAAAAAAAA
AAAAAAAAAAAAAAAAAAAAAAAAAAAAAAAAAAAAAAA
AAAAAAAAAAAAAAAAAAAAAAAAAAAAAAAAAAAAAAA
AAAAAAAAAAAAAAAAAAAAAAAAAAAAAAAAAAAAAAA
AAAAAAAAH!*'

Splat!
Erk!
Thud.

All manner of chaos promptly ensues.

27

Miss Carla Hahn

Two things. They may seem completely insignificant – stupid, even – but I should probably mention them up front. First, the digits. The four digits. Orla's special number: 4.0.0.4.

I double-checked that old stump on my way back out of Mulberry. Remember earlier, when I pulled off all the ivy from the trunk and I thought I saw …? Etched deep into the wood? Just before I was stung by that vile insect and then Mrs Barrow …? It's actually been playing on my mind ever since.

Well (sound the horns!), I *hadn't* just imagined it! Because there they were, large as life: those four digits, cut deep into the bark. Which led me to thinking that maybe it *wasn't* just about Orla, after all (the dream, the whole, strange 'number' fixation). Maybe they'd been there for years and years. Since the war. Since I was a kid. Carved into the trunk by … by an American serviceman, possibly … Although, from what I can recollect (and this wasn't a *big* topic in the family home during my childhood) there were mainly Canadians stationed in these parts during WW2.

I remember something about the Americans writing their dates the other way around, but can't be sure if they put the year before the month (i.e. 1940.04), or the month before the day. Either way, that wouldn't mean the Canadians did it too, and even if this theory *did* hold water, the Yanks only joined the war in 1941.

I mean Orla could always have carved the numbers there herself, I suppose. Which wouldn't really *solve* the problem …

And the second thing? The second little detail? After I arrived back home (soaking wet from a sudden downpour) I was getting changed – grabbing something clean and dry from the old wardrobe in the spare bedroom – when I noticed a small pool of dark sticky *goo* on the old oak planks at the base of the thing. I promptly knelt down to investigate, tentatively prodding my finger into the syrupy mess and giving it a quick sniff only to discover … you guessed it: eucalyptus oil! I clambered to my feet and started searching for the source. Eventually (after climbing on to a chair) I located a tiny, old, brown bottle in a cloth bag on the top shelf which is (and always has been) full of Tilda's stuff: several hand-made felt hats, a moth-eaten Welsh blanket in such an advanced state of disrepair that even *I* wouldn't consider using it, an old family kilt, an ancient mauve-coloured lambswool jumper etc.

The little bottle of oil was in a drawstring cloth bag, but when I took a closer look at the bag's contents (pumice stone, broken sunglasses, shoe horn etc.) I saw – *oh dear* – that the rubber seal on the little bottle had corroded and so the oil had been slowly drip, drip, dripping, first on to the shelf itself, then down on to a few of my clothes below, and finally on to the wardrobe's solid base. How long this had been going on for was anybody's guess.

I stayed standing on the chair for a while ruminating on the various ramifications of this curious discovery …

Hmmn. If the oil had been dripping down on to my clothes, then wasn't it entirely conceivable that I'd been smelling it, just randomly, over the past couple of days (a sudden blast of heat, a gust of wind, a moment of heightened emotion/stress) and then cheerfully *attributing* it to Orla and some kind of mystical/spiritual event?

I was struggling to come to terms with this idea (trying to work out whether what I was feeling was a sense of welcome relief or of crushing disappointment), when Alys Jane Drury (no less) barges into the room (doesn't anybody *knock* in

Fairlight these days?) almost tipping me from my chair (the wardrobe is behind the door).

After wobbling precariously for a few seconds I grab her shoulder (from behind. For support). She duly screams and then freezes to the spot like a small doomed rodent.

'Alys? Good heavens! What on earth are you doing here?' I exclaim, releasing my grip on her shoulder, just as soon as I've regained my balance.

'You'd left the front door wide open!' she squeaks, turning around, traumatized. 'Why are you hiding behind there? Half-naked? On a chair?'

'I'm not hiding. I only just got in myself, soaking wet from the downpour' – I jump off the chair, grab a shirt and pull it on, struggling to explain all the while – 'so I threw my bike on to the front lawn, rushed straight inside, peeled off my wet clothes and then ran in here to find something to ... but then ... well, there was this little, pool of ... of *eucalyptus* oil.' I point. 'So I started to hunt around to see if I could find ...'

'Orla's scent!' Alys automatically crosses herself, sniffing the air.

'... find the source of it and so I stood on the chair and hunted amongst Tilda's old stuff stored up there and found this little bottle of oil in a wash-bag with its seal corroded ...'

'But aren't you allergic to eucalyptus?' Alys demands. 'In fact aren't you allergic to *all* disinfectants?'

'Yes I am.' I nod.

'There's been a disaster with Teobaldo.' Alys promptly changes the subject. 'I drove him to the vet's in Rye. They have a bird specialist there – Martin Dugdale – who Baldo knows well and, more importantly, trusts. Martin's very worried about him. *Extremely* worried. He's keeping him in overnight for observation.'

'Will he be okay?'

I pull on some trousers and then lead her through to the kitchen.

'Tea?'

She nods, gratefully.

'Will he be okay, though?' I repeat, filling the kettle and plonking it down on to the stove.

'I just tried to pay a flying visit on Mr Huff,' she murmurs, slightly dazed, 'but he wasn't at home. Apparently he's gone. He's – would you believe this, Carla? – he's *walking* to Douai!'

'But I only just got back from Mulberry myself ...' I scowl (slightly concerned – even confused – by the powerful sinking sensation in my belly at the conjunction of the words 'Mr Huff' and 'gone').

'It was Mr Barrow who told me,' she continues. 'He was guarding the gate.'

'Douai?' I murmur (Mr Huff *walking* to Douai? Can that be right?).

'It seems he consulted with Mr Barrow about the best route before he left. Mr Barrow said that Mr Huff had been operating under the illusion that Douai was only thirty or forty miles away. Mr Barrow gently informed him that it was well over double that. Closer to ninety, in fact. Ninety miles! Just imagine! On foot!'

'But why on earth would Mr Huff feel the need to ...?' I mutter.

'I'm guessing it's because they had this big meeting all set up,' she explains, 'but then I rang Father Tierney and warned him off. I told him that Mr Huff simply wasn't to be trusted. I was really spooked after the conversation we had earlier. Following your little session in the sauna. When you hinted that he might be working for the CIA.'

'It *wasn't* a "little session",' I almost snap, offended, 'and I *didn't* say he was working for the CIA, Alys.' I add, 'I was just sharing something funny that Mrs Barrow had mentioned to me in passing ...'

'And after all those creepy phone calls!' She shudders (oblivious). 'I was convinced it was him! *Completely* convinced! Oh my goodness' – she covers her face with her hands – 'what a complete and utter *fool* I've been, Carla – in fact we *both* have! *Both* of us! Such a pair of hysterical idiots!'

'So if it wasn't Mr Huff ...?' I start off, after a brief pause, rather tight-lipped (my slight irritation at the CIA slur now compounded by being branded a 'hysterical idiot').

'It was King!' she exclaims.

'King?' I echo.

'It *wasn't* actually a person on the phone! It was just King!' Alys grabs a couple of the mugs from the small group suspended on hooks under the top cupboard. 'Unbelievable as it may sound, it was *him* – King – all along!'

'Sorry?' I'm still confused.

'King!' she repeats. 'The mynah bird I'm taking care of. It was him. He was simulating the sound of the phone!'

'A mynah bird?' I'm bemused.

'Yes! He was pretending to be the phone. For a prank. He had me running up and down that house like an absolute maniac. And whenever I answered, he'd simply hang up.'

'So a mynah bird has been ...' I murmur.

'Yes! And poor, old Baldo ... Well, I can only presume that he was in a complete frenzy about it all. He's incredibly protective of me, Carla. He kept yelling and shouting out in alarm all the time, but I just thought he was being a pest ...'

Alys inspects the inside of the mugs and then changes one of them, before peering, suspiciously, inside its replacement. 'So you think Baldo was wise to King's little prank and was trying to ...?'

'... warn me about it. Yes. Exactly. Does that sound a little too far-fetched?' Alys wonders.

I shrug.

'Well, when he was unmasked – King, I mean – a couple of hours ago, Baldo went absolutely mad. Completely loopy! I think it was probably just an overwhelming sense of ... of *relief* ...'

She places the mugs on to the table. 'He started making this awful, perfectly hair-raising WAAA-WAAA-WAAA noise. And suddenly there was this ...'

She gesticulates, limply.

'What?!'

'This ... this awful *expulsion* ... and he collapsed.'

'An expulsion ...?'

'I gathered it all up into a little polythene bag and then took him – and it – to Rye. I showed it to the vet and he knew instantly what it was. He said it was an *egg*, Carla!'

'An egg?'

'Yes' – she nods – 'but it didn't have a shell. It was only half-formed. The vet said there was a problem with his ovaries, some kind of infection or over-activity ...'

'But I thought Baldo ...' I start off.

'... was a boy,' she completes my sentence. 'I was *told* he was a boy when I first got him, and I never had any particular reason to doubt ...'

'But he's a girl!' I exclaim.

'Yes! Exactly. A girl! Poor Baldo!'

'So you think he – she was in some kind of internal discomfort, and that's why ...?'

'The vet seemed to think so. But he said he – *she* was very stressed. I mean to collapse like that ... It was terrible. Almost like a little fit.'

She shakes her head, mournfully. We stand together in silence for a few seconds as the kettle starts to clatter on the stove.

'So Mr Huff isn't a smoking candle after all,' I mutter, removing it from the gas.

'Sorry?'

'A smoking candle. Mr Huff.'

Alys clucks, forlornly.

'Although simply because it wasn't *him* making the phone calls doesn't necessarily mean that he isn't still ... you know ... evil.'

Alys raises a brow at my somewhat dramatic vocabulary, then walks over to the fridge and removes a pint of milk. 'It doesn't, no. But I still felt I should come over and apologize to the poor man. While I was in the area. I mean, for blackening his name to Father Tierney. It wasn't terribly ...'

She sniffs the milk, winces, then quickly replaces it back into the fridge again. 'D'you have anything herbal?'
I trot over to the cupboard.
'... it wasn't terribly *Christian* of me,' she finishes off.

I look inside the cupboard and locate two boxes of herbal tea: camomile and peppermint. I proffer them both. She opts for the peppermint, grabs the box, checks the date and then grimaces (Alys is, and has always been, insanely fastidious).

'So why not just contact Father Hugh directly and set him straight?' I wonder.
'Now that he's officially a "Brother",' Alys confides, 'Father Hugh – or Father Pietr, as he's currently known – isn't really supposed to receive personal phone calls, especially not from women. But there's a church in Woolhampton Village where he sometimes covers for the local priest, and I'm in contact with Phoebe, the parish secretary, who tries her best to keep the lines of communication open. Oh and sometimes he helps out with the choir and in some of the art classes at the school – he's a trained draughtsman, in actual fact – so I ring the office and ask for him by name, pretending to be a parent. But it's all a little bit hit and miss ...'
She frowns. 'D'you happen to have any fresh mint in the garden?'
'Afraid not.' I shake my head. 'It was completely decimated by all those aphids in June. But I have sage and wild lemon balm out back ...' I indicate.
She peers through the kitchen window, somewhat ominously. 'This used to be a bijou property "close" to the beach,' she sighs, 'soon it'll be a bijou property *on* the beach.'

I place a couple of the camomile bags into the pot.

'Plain hot water's fine for me,' she says, 'just tip it straight into the mug.'

She remains by the window for a short while longer, admiring the view.

'Mr Huff refused to let me see the photographs,' I grumble, pouring.

'Really?' She turns. 'Did he say why, exactly?'

'Because of Kimberly dying. He said it wouldn't be ... I don't know ... appropriate – *legal*. Until the will had been sorted out.'

'Well I suppose he might just have a point.' Alys shrugs, coming over to the table to take possession of her mug.

'But then it dawned on me that the pictures are actually *his* now. Mr Huff owns them, or at least he shall do, soon. Because he was married to Kimberly and I don't think there was a will ...'

Alys seems perplexed by this news. 'Did you ask him about it directly?' she asks.

'Yes' – I nod – 'and he didn't bother denying it.'

Alys frowns.

'He wants me to refuse pilgrims access to Orla's shrine over her birthday,' I add.

'But isn't there a clause in the rental?' she interrupts.

'Yes. He *knows* that. And when I told him it was non-negotiable, he tried to blackmail me. He said he'd only let me see the photographs if I denied all pilgrims access. That's why Mr Barrow was posted on the gate.'

'But I thought that was simply to stop Sorcha Jennett and the TV cameras from rampaging over the ...'

'That was partly it, but not entirely.'

'D'you think he would've denied *me* access?' Alys wonders.

'Who knows?' I shrug. 'But if he's walking to Douai, then at least we have a couple of days' grace, now. In fact I'll head over there first thing tomorrow and have a quick word with

Sorcha and Mr Barrow. Try and figure out some kind of compromise.'

'It's rather funny when you think about it, though ...' Alys muses.

'Funny?' I echo.

'Yes. Funny. *Ironic.* That the one person who's spent the last twelve years running away from anything and everything to do with the Cleary family should now be getting so irate about the behaviour of someone who seems to feel exactly the same way as she does about the whole thing.'

I gaze at Alys, indignant. 'But I've done everything *humanly possible* to maintain the cottage and the shrine since I inherited the place.'

'Apart from being there yourself. Saying *yes*! *Giving* of yourself.'

'I made a prior commitment to Tilda!' I exclaim.

'Of course.' She shrugs.

'And I hardly think it's fair to compare my need for privacy ... to keep something back for myself ... with ... with Mr Huff and his ... his strange vendetta against the Clearys.'

'It's perfectly ridiculous to think that Mr Huff has a vendetta against the Clearys!' Alys snorts. 'Bran Cleary was his best friend, remember?'

'His wife had an *affair* with Bran Cleary, Alys!' I howl.

'There was never any final proof of that,' she snaps.

'Well how else to explain what happened? Either they were having an affair or ...or ...'

I can't finish my sentence. Neither one of us really wants to ponder the alternatives.

Alys returns to the window and takes a sip of her hot water. 'Why wouldn't he let me see the photographs, though?' I persist. 'What possible harm could it have done? And why's he so desperate to stop people from paying their respects at the shrine, come to that? And why didn't he make *any* attempt to try and interview me over the past six weeks –

Orla's nurse, her closest confidante around the time of her death – if he was so eager to tell the full story? The same applies to Sorcha. He's not remotely interested in speaking to her, but Sorcha – for all her many faults – was one of the first to recognize Orla's holy aura, to believe in her and to grasp the nature of her mission with Aboriginal peoples. Sorcha was there at the very beginning, Alys. She knew Orla better than virtually anybody. It's almost like Mr Huff is ... like he's determined to ... like he's going out of his way to ... to *avoid* the truth.'

'And whose truth would that be, exactly?' Alys wonders, dryly.

I am momentarily floored by this question (Whose truth *would* that be, exactly? I wonder).

'Yours?' Alys pushes in her short sabre with an effortless precision.

'You can't have it both ways,' I murmur, wounded. 'You can't accuse me of not doing enough with one breath and then attack me for being too involved with the next.'

Alys pulls a face which says, 'Oh I *can*, Carla, and I just did!'

We are quiet for a while and then she smiles at me, almost tenderly, and says, 'Perhaps if you finally decided for *yourself* what you think about the whole thing, took a leap of faith instead of just ... just constantly evading the issue, you might eventually find some kind of ... well, happy resolution; dare I even say it: *peace*.'

My eyes suddenly fill with tears. 'It's fine for you,' I mutter, 'you were born a Catholic, Alys. It's your culture, a fundamental part of your psychological make-up. But it's all so ... so foreign, so *alien* to me. And it sometimes feels like such a huge ... such a *struggle* ...'

'Then why not just stop struggling?' she suggests (as if it would be as simple as that! As simple as merely *deciding* to stop. To stop struggling. To ... to give up the struggle and admit defeat).

'I *loved* Orla, Alys!' I groan. 'And I still can't accept – I won't, I just *won't* – that what happened to her was *right*, something to be … to be *celebrated*. Her death was a disaster, a tragedy, a failure. That's what Bran thought, and Kalinda. And because I was so weak I …'

My voice starts to shake, uncontrollably. 'I *loved* Orla, Alys,' I repeat.

'I know.' Alys nods. 'And she loved you too, Carla. Better still she *trusted* in you, trusted the final part of her story *with* you, so why can't you trust in *her*? Why this need to always make everything so difficult? What's the earthly good in it? Why not just *embrace* your memory of her? *Love* her. Just *love* her. Accept her. As she was. Exactly as she was.'

I turn away, blinking, frantically.

We are silent for a while.

'Did Orla ever discuss St Faustina with you?' Alys asks, fishing around inside her mug for a moment and removing something from it on the tip of her finger.

'Cat hair,' she murmurs.

'St …? Uh … No.' I'm thrown slightly off kilter. 'I don't actually own a cat.'

'Well, St Faustina was a Polish nun.' Alys wipes her finger on a tea towel, then inspects the tea towel and shudders. 'She was born in 1905 and she died when she was only thirty-three years old. She's one of the greatest saints of this century and had many holy visions throughout her life. Part of her mission was to write extensive diaries about "The Divine Mercy", which is the loving mercy Jesus afforded mankind when he died for us on the cross. For that reason she's sometimes nicknamed "God's Secretary".'

I nod, wearily.

'Well anyway, St Faustina was a "suffering soul", just like Orla was,' Alys continues. 'She offered her life up to Jesus – her Holy Spouse – so that she could suffer for all mankind, just like he had. And she *did* suffer. She was rejected by her superiors and by all the other nuns in her community, her visions were ridiculed, she was constantly humiliated and doubted, she was prone to terrible bouts of ill health ...'

Alys breaks off, momentarily. 'You have that look on your face,' she observes.

'What look?' I try my best to expunge the look, whatever it may be.

'That look of quiet but deep resistance,' she elucidates.

'God's Secretary,' I say, smiling brightly, wiggling my fingers as if poised over a typewriter.

Alys pointedly ignores my attempt to lighten the atmosphere. 'One of the several tasks St Faustina had been instructed to perform by Jesus' – she returns to her story – 'was to commission an artist to produce a painting of his "Divine Mercy", which was essentially a painting of Jesus, as she saw him in her visions, standing in a white robe, one hand slightly raised as if in blessing, the other placed over his heart from which two bright arcs of light emerge, one blue-white, the other red. These arcs of light were to represent his "Divine Mercy" – the blood and water that poured from the wound cut into his side by the Roman soldier, Longinus, to finally establish that he was dead on the cross.'

I nod, keenly, still trying (possibly failing) to hold back 'that look'.

'Well it was very difficult for St Faustina to get the painting commissioned. There was a great deal of suspicion and resentment directed towards her at the nunnery. And at one point – alone and despairing – she almost caved in under the great weight of the combined opposition she faced. Then Jesus appeared to her in a vision and said, and I paraphrase this, obviously; he said, "If you neglect to complete the tasks to promote my Divine Mercy, as I have described them to you, on the Day of Judgement you will have to answer not only for your own soul, but for a whole multitude of other souls which will have been lost for all eternity because of your ..."'

'Stop, Alys!' I explode, almost laughing at the pure indignity of it all.

'What's the problem?' Alys demands.

'Isn't it obvious?!' I throw up my hands, exasperated. 'The very idea that it's considered acceptable for someone to try so hard, give so much, *sacrifice* so much, and then, at their lowest ebb, in their darkest hour, face the sadistic wrath of an apparently heartless God!'

Alys looks shocked by my analysis.

'St Faustina was a "suffering soul",' she patiently explains, 'like Orla. The greatest saints aren't built like the rest of us, Carla. They empathize with Jesus – identify with his pain, and the sorrow of his Holy Mother – at such an intense level that they voluntarily take on the burden of his suffering to save souls. It's their mission. A kind of reparation. It's what they do.'

'I just don't understand how anyone could actively *embrace* suffering like that,' I tell her. 'It seemed – it seems ... crazy – *wrong*. There's enough pointless suffering in the world already. Why this misguided need to conjure up still more?'

'Because they are suffering for *love*, of course!' Alys laughs, quite astonished by my ignorance. 'It's their sacrifice to God, their gift to God.'

'People shouldn't *want* to suffer,' I persist. 'It isn't normal. Life's tough enough as it is. Suffering is something to be avoided – shunned. And I don't care what you say, love is *very* different to suffering. Love is ... is joy and ... and happiness and fulfilment and contentment. It's the very *opposite* of suffering.'

'Has that been your experience of love?' Alys wonders.

I open my mouth to answer and then close it again.

'Love is 90 per cent heartache. If people knew in advance how painful love was, they'd cheerfully run a mile. Although in my experience you can sometimes run away from something so hard that you eventually only end up running straight back into it again.' Alys sighs. 'Either that or you live half a life, crippled by the fear of pain which is almost worse than the pain itself. Because fear is limitless.'

'So your nun was fearless through all her suffering?' I mutter. 'But if she was fearless then she couldn't truly *be* suffering. You can't imply that suffering is the opposite of fear. Suffering and fear are one and the same thing, surely?'

'But what were Orla's actual options?' Alys shrugs, ever the pragmatist. 'She was destined to suffer because of the serious nature of her disability. So she faced the choice of either just suffering, for nothing, or of offering up her suffering for a purpose, to God and for souls. It made a perfect kind of sense to her.'

I consider the inalienable truth of this statement.

Alys smiles, weakly. 'Remember how when she tried to pray, her poor dear hands couldn't quite …?'

My eyes flood with tears again. I remember Orla praying on her calloused little knees, sick and weak, struggling to fit her palms together. But her arms were too short. Just the tips of her middle fingers could touch, but only with considerable effort and not a small amount of discomfort. Yet still she persisted. And the more difficult it was, the more blissful she grew. This was the great paradox. This was the strange mania. This was the deep mystery of Orla Nor Cleary.

I had been employed expressly to stop her from praying, to guard over her, to police her. That had been my allotted role, as 'nurse'. And I thought I had succeeded, too; basic exercise, teaching her to bake cheese scones (her father's favourite, although because of her chronic reflux she herself was fed only in liquids by that stage), reading to her (she'd never read *The Secret Garden* – 'The secret garden is Mary Lennox's soul!' she'd announced, delighted, 'and the more she tends to it, the more beautiful she grows!' – or *The Lion, the Witch and the Wardrobe*, or *Alice in Wonderland*), teaching her rummy, talking inanely about my life, my family ... until I realized that she was calmly taking the considerable agony of being *stopped* from praying for souls and *offering it up* for souls! And so either way – let's face it – I had failed. I had failed.

Alys is speaking, but I hardly hear her, I am so preoccupied by that image of Orla and her little hands; struggling to press those little palms together in prayer.

Why would God design her in such a way that the one thing she longed to do more than any other was physically impossible for her? So that in order to worship him 'properly' she should experience only a sense of pain and failure?

'To purify my heart,' she had answered my question herself, quite effortlessly, 'to purify my heart, Carla! "Blessed are the pure of heart, for they shall see God."'

And then she had smiled. And that smile was glorious. Glorious but completely ... well ... *demented*, surely?

Alys repeats herself.

'Your hands, Carla!' she is saying, putting down her cup and walking around the table towards me. 'Why didn't I notice them before? Look! They're healed – *completely* healed!'

She takes a hold of my hands.

'Why didn't you tell me?'

'Oh, uh ...' I struggle to concentrate. 'Because it only just happened. Last night. I woke up this morning and ...'

'They just healed themselves? Overnight?'

Alys is astonished.

I wait, steeling myself, for Alys to proclaim this 'a miracle'.

'I heard an allergy specialist on the radio the other day,' she muses, scowling, turning my hands over and inspecting them, front and back, 'saying that one proven way of treating an allergy is to familiarize the body with the allergen by subjecting it to tiny, *tiny* amounts of the toxic substance over a long period of time until the body is gradually able to build up its own natural immunity; or, more accurately, stop its natural – but illogical – *over*reaction to the so-called "toxic" element ...'

I decide not to tell her about the dream.

'Didn't you say there was a small pool of eucalyptus oil at the bottom of your cupboard?' she asks.

I nod (No. I will definitely not tell her about the dream).

'Well isn't it possible that it's been slowly dripping down on to your clothes for days, weeks, *months*, even, and you've been wearing them without knowing, perfectly oblivious to the fact that you're building up a gradual immunity?'

I consider this scientific explanation for a moment.

'I suppose that isn't the craziest idea in the world ...' I concede, heartened.

(Should I actually mention the dream after all?)

'A miracle!' she exclaims. 'It's a miracle!'

'But I thought you ...?' I start off, bemused.

'That the bottle should corrode!' she gasps. '*That* bottle, in *that* cupboard! And for your hands to be healed *now*, at *this* time, virtually on the eve of Orla's birthday anniversary!'

Oh dear, oh dear.

Praise be!

Alys sings, applauding ecstatically.

Praise be!

Praise be!

Glory, glory, *glory* Hallelujah!

28

Mr Franklin D. Huff

Mr Barrow very kindly loaned me ten pounds. This was to be my fuel. I spent it on cans of pop (I drank from streams when best I could – spent two hours bent double and vomiting so violently my throat bled, copiously, just due north of Crawley), meat and potato pies and chocolate bars. Energy food.

After thirty miles, my blisters had blisters. My nipples were raw. I had walked all night. Like a chump. It was 8 a.m., precisely. I fell over and then slept in a ditch just outside Uckfield. I was awoken, at ten, by a black Labrador bitch whose owner thought I was a corpse. I *was* a corpse. The gentleman in question took me home for breakfast. Special K and a nice cup of Nescafé with a generous spoonful of lo-calorie creamer (Q. *What the hell's happening to the English working classes these days? A. Please print your responses on a postcard and mail it to* …).

His wife then kindly dressed my feet (Savlon, Germolene). They offered to drive me on to East Grinstead (the wife ran the tearooms at Hever Castle) but I declined. I'm not sure why I declined. But I declined. I suppose it was something to do with my being a pilgrim. Some rubbish of that sort. Ten minutes later, I regretted it, heartily, but I was too exhausted to turn tail by that stage.

I could go into endless detail about my various (mis) adventures. I rescued a sheep from a cut. Pulled her out by her ears. I found a gold locket in a storm drain (stashed it away in my pocket where it got caught up in a crisp packet which I duly tossed into a bin). I was almost hit by three cars, four times. On the third occasion the female driver reversed to pull off and bruised my shin with her mudguard.

I lost half my thumbnail trying to break into a barn and the angry farmer attacked me with a rake (ripped my jacket) and then gave me a bag of apples and a spare oilskin which stank of horse. I spotted a Wild Bee Orchid in a little wood west of Reigate, alarmed a nightjar in Send and inadvertently stepped on a rare, Long-tailed Blue in a car park in Aldershot.

I imagined I might think a great deal during my voyaging – philosophize (as surely pilgrims are wont to do), but in fact all I thought was, Why the hell am I doing this? I hate this! Why the hell am I doing this? How far am I? Is that car going to hit me? Will my knees hold? Why the hell am I doing this? Is it time for a break, yet? A Planter's salted peanut or … or a quick Rolo, perchance?

After approximately sixty-five miles (a mere marathon left) I tried to stand up, following a brief rest, and I realized that my buttocks had sealed.

Yes. Yes, I'm afraid that they had. My buttocks had sealed. There's no polite way of putting it. They had melded. Plasma from the copious blisters on either cheek had (somewhat unwisely: *Q. What kind of pilgrim am I? A. A rank amateur, that's what!*) been given the brief opportunity to dry and so had set into a fierce, crystalline glue. Two buttocks had merged into a single buttock. They had become permanently conjoined.

I ripped them apart (by brute force, with my hands – the pain was excruciating! – so I could walk once more; quite extraordinary how one depends on two buttocks to perambulate!), but after that I knew I couldn't stop again, or they would meld for good and the game would be up entirely.

(Q. Why are you doing this to yourself, Franklin? Eh? Why, you damn fool?! A. Sorry ... Simply have no time to get into all that right now.)

I don't want to be dramatic, but the final five miles I have virtually no memory of. I was a bloodied stump. A husk. My scalp was very itchy. *Very* itchy. And at one stage, when I scratched at it (back left-hand side. *Q. Fleas? A. Most probably*) my fingers discovered a small, mysterious, slightly spiky ridge on the skin. It wasn't ... this wasn't the kind of sensation – the kind of *feeling* – one expects to experience, quite out of the blue, on one's own scalp. It was *un*expected. Alien. I tried to inspect the area in shop windows and car side-mirrors but its difficult positioning (the back of my head) made this nigh on impossible. It was all but invisible to the human eye. Unseeable.

Perhaps I was just tired?

Hallucinating?

In the manner of all great pilgrims (and of all great imbeciles, come to that)?

I developed a theory that if my mouth stopped working (and why it might, I had no idea) then I could just as easily and audibly talk through my nose. One nostril for consonants, the other for vowels. For the most part I was thinking and speaking in pidgin Spanish. *No te pares! Idiota! I no puede! Mis pobres pies! He terminado! Suficiente!*

I was approached by concerned bystanders on several occasions.

Dejame en paz! Se ha ido! Pah!

Yes.

Pah!

(Dramatic hand gesture!)

Pah!

(Slight stagger. Fall to knees.)

Estoy desesperado!

(Noisy tears etc.)

By the time I found myself at the abbey (I didn't have a clue what time it was, possibly early morning) I was no longer in any kind of pain. I was just doing things automatically – a stinking, squelching automaton. I had – to all intents and purposes – reached my destination, but there was no sense of relief. I didn't stop. I'm not sure I knew if I *could* stop. If I had the requisite power (physical, spiritual, emotional) to desist. If I even *wanted* to stop. I had adapted, you see. I had become a creature of perpetual motion.

My nostrils were now at war with each other. The consonant nostril decried the vowel nostril, cruelly and persistently. With every in-breath and out-breath puh-puh-puh! Warred with ow-ow-ow! My septum tried – and failed – to arbitrate. My philtrum latterly got involved, but it was anxious in case the mouth should get wind of it (the mouth being, at this stage, in official retirement). Perhaps I couldn't trust the mouth? Perhaps the mouth was the weak link? Remember how the mouth – the lips – had betrayed me with Miss Hahn? That agonizing kiss?

I was walking in circles on a large expanse of lawn in the monastery grounds when I was approached by two brothers, fully robed. One pushed the other in a wheelchair. There had been rain at some point and the wheelchair's progress across the lawn was rather halting. The brother who was pushing asked the brother in the chair if he might leave him for a moment and walk on alone, but the wheelchair-bound brother said 'no'. Just 'no'. Which I felt was rather mean of him, under the circumstances (not at all the kind of behaviour one might hope to expect from an elderly Benedictine). Finally, they reached me. The 'pushing' brother – a shorn redhead, tall but stooped, with giant, pale hands and deeply melancholic yellow eyes – stepped forward and introduced himself.

'Good morning,' he said, 'I am Brother Linus and this' – he indicated, respectfully, towards the older monk – 'is Brother

Prosper. You currently find yourself in the grounds of Douai Abbey and school. May we be of any assistance to you?'
This monk had a slight accent. Dutch? Flemish?

'I am here to meet up with Brother Hugh ... uh ... Pietr,' I stumbled. 'I have walked here from Pett Level which is close to Hastings, a distance of around ninety miles.'
'May we be of any assistance to you?' the brother repeated.
By now a small group of schoolboys in PE gear were sauntering by. There were a few sniggers and barbed comments, which I suppose were only to be expected under the circumstances.
'Move on, boys!' Brother Prosper bellowed.
The boys moved on, sharpish.

I was still walking in a circle (Brother Linus closely in tow), but had circumscribed my movements to an area of – at best – ten square feet from the still centre of Brother Prosper's chair. Brother Prosper's head spun like an owl's to keep up with my perambulations.

I was probably still speaking in Spanish. I was probably still speaking through my nostrils. Brother Linus had a kindly demeanour. In fact Linus was my favourite *Peanuts* character (among the cast of 'humans'. My actual favourite was naturally Woodstock – with Snoopy a close second). After several more circuits I finally decided to take a risk and confide in him, in English, with my lips.

'I have walked here from Hastings, Brother Linus,' I puffed, 'to see Brother Hugh. A kind of pilgrimage. In fact' – I stopped walking – 'could you just ...'
So many unanswered questions! Where even to begin?

'Here ...' I showed him the strange ridge on the back of my head. 'I recently discovered this strange ... this curious *ridge* on the back of my head; might you possibly do me the great favour of describing it to me?'
Brother Linus quietly inspected the aforementioned area.

'Is it some kind of parasitic infection?' I demanded. 'Some kind of ... I live in Mexico and there's a disease spread by the sand fly, *Leishmaniasis* ... I've seen ... in my time ... terrible ... *horrible*, festering bumps, with strange, ridged edges; a man I once worked with had the infection on his arm ... Or there's River Blindness which can sometimes exhibit itself in its early phases through nasty-looking skin lesions ...'

'There's nothing "infected" to speak of,' Brother Linus finally passed judgement, 'although you do appear to have a small, shaven area around a gash with a couple of stitches at the centre of it.'

A gash?

'Are you certain, Brother?'

'Yes.'

'Stitches?' I repeat. 'Would you just ... could you just double-check that for me?'

Brother Linus double-checked.

'Yes. There seems to be a measure of ... a tightness ... Perhaps the wound is healing and so itching. There is also a small area of inflammation near to one corner. A stitch has come loose. Perhaps you've been scratching ...?'

'Stitches?' I repeat.

'A minor head injury,' Brother Linus confirms.

'There was a sudden landslip,' I say, 'a rockfall ...'

'Ah.' Brother Linus nods. 'I see.'

A landslip? Did I actually just say that? Me? Franklin D.? A landslip?

'Perhaps you should go and fetch Father Pietr?' Brother Prosper suggests (from his chair). 'I can always keep an eye on him if you like.'

As Brother Linus ponders the wisdom of this course of action, something terrible suddenly strikes me: I have stopped walking! I have stopped walking!

'OH GOD I'VE STOPPED WALKING!' I yell, panicked.

'You *have* stopped walking,' Brother Linus confirms, very calmly, touching my arm, very gently. 'Perhaps if you just ... if you just calm yourself down for a minute, Mr ... uh ... I don't believe you've formally introduced yourself to us, Mr ...?'

'Mr Huff!' I pant. 'You don't understand, Brother. I have *walked* from Hastings to see Brother – Father Hugh. I am covered in blisters. And my ...'

I close my eyes, humiliated.

'... my buttocks connived to seal together somewhere along the way. They *stuck* together. With the plasma. So I tore them apart to enable me to continue ...'

Brother Linus flinches.

'Of course I knew then that if I stopped again for any sustained period I would be ... I wouldn't be able to ... at least not without ...'

A brief silence follows in which we all consider our options. Mine, I suspect, are quite limited at this stage. So I inhale deeply and take another small, completely experimental step forward ...

(*One small step for man, one giant leap for a behind ...*)

Quite a modest little step by all accounts. Just the one. That really was all it took.

29

Miss Carla Hahn

I took a leaf from Mr Huff's book and was – by my own standards – quite ruthless about the arrangements. The garden was formally opened for filming between the hours of ten and two. The house was strictly off limits. I told Sorcha that I could only provide access so long as I didn't appear 'on camera' myself (and both parties involved grudgingly accepted this condition).

Sorcha naturally wanted some footage of Orla's tiny box bedroom. In fact we were having an argument about exactly this ('The cottage is being rented, Sorcha. It's full of Mr Huff's private stuff ... Uh ... are the Channel 4 people actually filming this conversation? *This* conversation. *This* one. Right now? No? Are you certain? Because if they aren't then why is that little, red light flashing away on the ...?) when Sage Meadows turned up.

I say again: when Sage Meadows turned up.
Sage Meadows! Pretty as a picture in her immaculate, tastefully low-cut cream-coloured silk shirt (silver Celtic brooch pinned at the shoulder) and plain, but figure-hugging knee-length brown suede skirt. High-heeled open-toed cream sandals. Holding a tureen. Yes. A tureen. Of ... well, *soup* I suppose.

Oh great. *Great!* The crowning glory! The cherry on the cake! Sage Meadows and a tureen! *Exactly* what this situation required!

Mrs Meadows appraised the hectic scene before her with one cool glance, tossed back her red mane (it didn't move by so much as a centimetre), shimmied into the garden and approached a cameraman to politely enquire if Mr Huff was around at all. In the course of this transaction she managed to get somewhat tangled up in one of Sorcha's many Orla-related 'installations'. The Pavee Queen had tied lengths of string between several of the trees and one of the gutters and the children had strung them with tiny, coloured fabric swatches and little teddies and old, brightly painted wooden pegs and small bunches of wild flowers. It was very festive. There had been much dancing and singing and wailing and processing and chanting and praying, meanwhile. And the lighting of many candles. And daisy crowns strung and proudly worn – of course.

At one point, several rabbit skins had been produced and the children had been encouraged to draw (with black felt-tips) on the smooth white side, in tribute to Orla's first, legendary vision of the Holy Virgin, during which she appeared holding a branch of Australian bloodwood in one hand and a sprig of Irish goat-willow in the other, wrapped up – head to toe – in a richly decorated possum-skin coat announcing: 'My Son thirsts dreadfully for the souls of all the Aboriginal peoples, Orla. Please bring them to us, my dear child.'

On another occasion (as Sorcha never tired of telling), the Holy Virgin had appeared to Orla while in Sorcha's presence, and – under close questioning from the sceptical Pavee – had told Orla to tell her, in her own gypsy tongue: *Dhaylon bin bonar, nill stedi nolsk dha tera* (this was an old Romany proverb which roughly translates as 'God is good, but don't stand too near the fire').

Sorcha had promptly burst into tears. What Orla didn't know was that as a small child Sorcha (who was always precocious) had once been entertaining the family as they sat around the campfire by reciting a prayer she'd learned during confirmation class ('Hail Holy Queen, Mother of Mercy ...') when a spark had suddenly set her long densely layered (and chiefly nylon) skirts and petticoats aflame. She'd gone up 'like a firecracker' and the fire – which instantly consumed her – had only finally been quenched by her father hurling her to the ground and rolling her around, violently, in the dirt. Her father's hands and arms had been badly burned during this process, but Sorcha herself had remained miraculously untouched by the flames. 'Even the hairs on my little legs,' (as she never tired of telling) 'was left perfectly unharmed ...' (Cue audible gasps from her awe-filled child audience who – I don't doubt for a second – had heard the anecdote many hundreds of times before.)

Since this formative incident, Sorcha had held the Holy Virgin in especially high esteem, as, indeed, had her whole extended family.

I ran over to de-tangle Mrs Meadows, but Mrs Meadows had already de-tangled herself quite efficiently.

'Can I ...?' I flustered, and then, 'Oh, yes, I see you've already managed to ...'

Mrs Meadows was, it seemed, quite an efficient creature, in general. She smiled at me, appreciatively, nonetheless – head cocked, brown eyes shining brightly and darkly, the way a pretty bird's eyes shine as they appraise a tiny grub.

'I was just asking this gentleman' – she indicated, gracefully, with a little lift of her shoulder – 'if he knew the whereabouts of Mr Huff. He wasn't certain, but he suspected that he might have gone away for a few days. Would you happen to know anything ...?'

'Let me ...' I offered to take the tureen from her.

'It's a chilled trout soup,' she explained, passing it over and then shaking out her arms. 'I've been carrying it around for hours. The road up here is completely blocked by vans. I had to leave my car down by the pub.'

'Trout soup! How delicious!' I responded (quite sincerely). 'Yes, I'm afraid Mr Huff is currently ...' How to explain it? 'He's had to go away for a couple of days. On business.'

'Oh. Well is there any chance I might be able to gain access to the cottage and store this in his refrigerator?' she wondered. 'Or maybe a kind neighbour might ...? I mean it seems such a shame to lug it all the way back home again.'

'I do have a spare set of keys,' I confessed, after a short pause, 'so that should probably be manageable ...'

I smiled and turned – somewhat abruptly – hoping to make my escape, but Mrs Meadows stuck close by me as I started off across the lawn. 'Could I possibly just tag along and scribble down a short note to leave with it so he knows where to return the tureen?' she asked.

'Yes. Yes, of course.' I nodded (grimacing internally) as we picked a route across the garden and around the allotment, then climbed up the porch steps and Mrs Meadows waited, patiently, *fragrantly,* as I handed back the tureen, unlocked the door with my spare keys (no problem whatsoever with the lock mechanism this time around) and we entered.

The house smelled of ... I frowned ... rabbit pee. And fresh straw. And old tweed. And new wool. And ... and creosote? Bacon rind? Of Mr Huff himself in other words.

'Franklin didn't make mention of any filming when we shared breakfast together yesterday,' Mrs Meadows mused. 'Is all this commotion connected to that poor dear girl with the tiny arms by any chance?'

'Orla Cleary, yes.' I nodded.

'My late husband – Dr Meadows – was actually her physician,' Mrs Meadows confided. 'He thought the child was the most awful hysteric.'

I didn't respond to this – at least not verbally – just walked into the kitchen and deftly moved a few dirty cups and plates from the counter into the sink to make room for the tureen.

'I'm Sage, by the way,' Mrs Meadows volunteered, appraising me intently (perhaps sensing a slight frost in the atmosphere). 'Have we met before? Now I come to think of it, you *do* seem quite familiar …'

'Uh, I'm not sure that we have,' I confessed. 'I'm Carla. Carla Hahn – Mr Huff's landlady.'

Mrs Meadows's brown eyes widened with surprise.

'You? *The* Miss Hahn?!' she exclaimed, then burst into ringing peals of laughter. 'But you aren't *at all* as Mr Huff described you to me!'

I was initially uncertain whether to be amused, confused or offended by this violent reaction, or – indeed – whether the laughter itself was rooted in delight or something more akin to irritation.

'How curious, though!' she expanded. 'I thought you'd be an old crone! From the way he described you, I honestly thought you'd be *twice* the age you are!'

As she spoke she rapidly moved forward, and then, 'Good heavens!'

She almost tripped over the fireguard containing the rabbit.

'Ah,' I muttered (struggling to keep the satisfaction from my voice), 'one of Mr Huff's more recent acquisitions.'

'A dwarf rabbit!' Mrs Meadows exclaimed. 'Under a fireguard!'

She started to put the tureen down on to the rickety dining table.

'You should probably …' I started off, just as the flap on to which she'd begun to place it tipped alarmingly. She quickly tightened her grip and whisked it away again, only narrowly averting disaster.

'Perhaps straight into the fridge?' I suggested with an apologetic smile.

Mrs Meadows tripped obligingly into the kitchen.

'So this is *your* house,' she mused, gazing around her. 'Franklin said you kept it as a kind of dilapidated ... well, *museum* I suppose.'

I opened my mouth to respond to this statement, but then closed it again (unable to bring myself to compose an acceptable sentence).

'We do have *that* much in common at least,' she conceded (as if there wasn't – in all probability – anything else). 'I'm an aspirant poet and live in Lamb House, Rye. Former home of ...'

'Henry James.' I nodded.

'You may well have known my late husband, Dr Meadows – Don Meadows?' she expanded, graciously.

'Yes, but not ... not especially well,' I admitted. 'He wasn't my GP. I'm with Dr Sap at the Hastings surgery. Although we met on several occasions in my capacity as ... as Orla's nurse, obviously.'

'All this was *way* before my time,' she sighed, almost petulant, now, 'and Don rarely spoke about it – he was incredibly professional like that.'

I nodded.

'But I always got the impression that he found the whole situation terribly unhealthy and claustrophobic ... Although the father – Bryn?'

'Bran,' I corrected her.

'*Bran*. Bran Cleary. He was an artist of some repute?'

'A muralist. Yes.'

'He had a measure of success internationally, Don said, although I can't pretend,' she confided, in faux-shame, eyes sparkling, one brow coyly arched, 'to have ever seen any examples of his work.'

'I believe he was thought to be very talented,' I murmured.

'Did you say this was a trout soup?'

I lifted the lid and peered into the tureen, eager to change the subject. The soup was bright pink and smelled slightly of aniseed.

'The pink colour comes from beetroot,' she explained.

I replaced the lid and then opened up the fridge. It was empty, apart from three old leeks and a couple of spare carrots for the rabbit.

Mrs Meadows carefully slid the tureen on to a lower shelf and I closed the door. Now a pen and some paper ...

'Franklin – Mr Huff – says you own an extremely ancient cat.' Mrs Meadows smiled, walking over, somewhat mystified, to peer once again at the tiny rabbit.

'Yes.' I nodded. 'He was my mother's originally.'

'Apparently his sister ran over its tail in the hire-car when they first arrived ...' She chuckled.

'Yes. No, not his sister ...' I started off, then quickly stopped myself.

'Pardon?' Mrs Meadows looked up.

'It was unfortunate,' I conceded.

'He said your garden fell into the sea,' she continued, walking over to the wall to inspect a framed sketch of a herring gull.

'Yes. Up in Fairlight.' I nodded, uneasily, tucking my fringe behind my ear. 'It's not actually *my* garden. I'm house-sitting for a—'

'He said you were *constantly* tucking your fringe behind your ears – *just* like that!' she interrupted, grinning. 'He did a little impersonation of it. He said he found it perfectly riveting. He said he honestly couldn't understand why you didn't just pin it back, like any *normal* person would.'

'Oh,' I said, resisting the urge to tuck my fringe behind my ear again.

'Although it's a perfectly lovely fringe,' she added. 'Men understand nothing of these matters, do they?'

'Oh,' I repeated, 'thanks.'

'In fact he talks about you a great deal ...' She moved over to the sideboard and picked up an old tin which had once contained typewriter tape, then another one (from Miss Vaughn's small collection of old tins) that had a picture of the queen on it (although someone had scratched a large, walrus-style moustache on to the top lip). 'He's very funny – very engaged, very witty – whenever he talks about you,' Mrs Meadows maintained, 'which is why I thought you'd be a little bit ... well, *older*, somehow, slightly less attractive.'

'It's possible that you're confusing me with Mrs Barrow,' I suggested, 'his elderly housekeeper. She's considered quite a character.'

'Did Mrs Barrow's garden fall into the sea, too?' Mrs Meadows wondered.

'No,' I conceded, 'Mrs Barrow lives next door ...' Again, I resisted the urge to tuck my hair behind my ear. 'And her garden – so far as I'm aware – is relatively secure.'

Mrs Meadows burst out laughing again. I gazed over at her, confused.

'Sorry, it's just that ... when you *talk* I just ... I just can't help seeing the way Franklin ... His little impersonation. It's so amazingly *accurate*! I mean he really does have you down perfectly.'

I tried not to look offended. I was offended.

'I do hope you're not offended.' Mrs Meadows quickly placed down the tin. 'I mean he's never said anything especially *vindictive* ... he just seems to find you very ...' – she frowned – 'entertaining, I suppose.'

'Well I'm sure I find Mr Huff quite "entertaining" too.' I smiled, grimly.

'Oh you *are* offended!' Mrs Meadows looked crestfallen. 'Please don't be! I was only ...' She frowned again. 'This might sound rather pathetic, but I was only a little bit put out because ... I mean only wondering whether perhaps he might

… whether he might sometimes talk about … well, about *me* in an equally entertaining way to … well, to you.'

How to respond to this? I drew a deep breath and tucked my hair behind my ear.

'If I can be honest with you,' I said, 'Mr Huff and I haven't spoken very much, not about general subjects. Only about – you know – practical things, really.'

Mrs Meadows looked slightly dejected.

'But he did … uh …' I frowned, racking my brains. 'He did mention that you had very lovely borders this year. Over at Lamb House.'

'The garden's opened to the public for several weeks during the summer' – Mrs Meadows nodded – 'as a part of the leasing arrangement. In fact you probably know that already as a long-term local resident …' She sighed. 'Not terribly *entertaining*, though, is it,' she added, 'the borders at Lamb House?'

I gazed at her, blankly, and then:

Oh my goodness! Oh my *goodness*! Mrs Meadows is actually … is actually *in love* with Mr Huff!

(Or – at the very least – she *thinks* that she is.)

Why didn't I …?

Oh my … Oh my goodness!

She's in love with him – with Mr Huff – the foolish thing!

I tucked my hair behind my ear, somewhat at a loss for anything to say, then I tucked it again, a second time, behind the same ear.

'You know, now I actually … in fact now I actually come to *think* of it …' I stuttered, cheeks reddening (why am I blushing? Why?), 'he *did* mention something about … about your being very beautiful – beautifully *groomed*. And a poet. And that you got a … a first-class honours degree in English and Philosophy from Durham University.'

'My degree was actually in Pure Maths and Engineering.' She grimaced. 'I lied.'

'Sorry?'

'I had a kind of a … a crisis of confidence during my Ph.D. and then reinvented myself as a lady poet.'

'Oh.'

'Did he say anything else?' Mrs Meadows persisted, her appetite for compliments plainly not yet quite satisfied.

'Um …' I frowned, momentarily stumped. 'Uh … Oh yes! He was very … very *droll*, as I remember, about a lunch you shared at the Mermaid when he first arrived in the area. He said the food was absolutely terrible – *unforgivably* bad—'

'Really?' Mrs Meadows interrupted, looking slightly put out.

'But that the company was truly excellent. Wonderful. In fact he said how disappointed he was when you were called away to Coventry to help your sister stage-manage the grand opening of her butterfly farm. He said that it was something you both shared … you know, had in common … this … this strong entrepreneurial … uh …'

Mrs Meadows was beaming.

'And a love of nature,' I added, just for good measure.

She was utterly delighted.

'And of words,' I finished off, 'a love of words.'

Had I gone too far? A love of *words*? Had Mr Huff given *any* evidence during our short acquaintance of a 'love of words'?

'Is there something the matter with your lip?' Mrs Meadows enquired, concerned.

'Sorry?'

'You keep touching … putting your hand up to your lip, patting away at it, as you speak.'

'Do I?'

I removed my hand from my lip and used it, instead, to tuck my hair behind my ear.

Why was I touching my …?

Guilt, perhaps?

But *was* it really a kiss, though? In the sauna? An *actual* kiss? Wasn't it more of a …? Something more in the emotional realm of a cough or … or a sneeze? A joke, but without the funny bit? Without the punch-line? Like the … like the scaffolding, but without the actual building inside?

I gazed, in silence, at Sage Meadows as she painstakingly removed a stray red hair which had become tangled around the tiny pearl button on the cuff of her shirt sleeve. Oh how could *any* sensible woman with her wits about her be in love with a bounder like Mr Huff? I wondered. Least of all such a fine example of the sex as she? Such a thoroughly finished and polished female? With her hair and her heels and her lipstick and her utterly impractical dry-clean-only suede skirt? (And please let's not forget her Pure Maths and Engineering degree!)

'I have a terrible weakness,' Mrs Meadows confided (*Why* does she feel the need to confide? And in *me* of all people?), 'for men who aren't likely to want to hang around for any extended period.' She pulled out a chair from the table and sat down on it (it creaked, alarmingly). 'My first college boyfriend signed up for two years with VSO straight after graduating and then promptly fell in love with a beautiful Sudanese woman who was spearheading a campaign in North Africa against involuntary female genital mutilation.'
I winced.
'My next worked on the oil rigs. Then there was Mr Meadows' – she sighed – 'who died. Then a long-haul air pilot. Then a foreign correspondent for the BBC who was posted to Hong Kong …'
'You weren't tempted to go with him?' I enquired.
'I was. But he didn't ask.'
'Oh.'
I tucked my hair behind my ears.
'What kind of men do *you* have a weakness for?' Mrs Meadows wondered, in all good faith (and there we have it!

The worst part of exchanging confidences – the *exchanging* of confidences!).

'I'm not sure that I have a weakness for any particular kind of man,' I say.

'Well how would you go about describing your current partner?' she persisted.

'Uh ...' I frowned, uneasily. 'I suppose I must quite like tall men,' I 'shared', 'because my last serious partner,' (Clifford Bickerton, circa 1972) 'was very ... very *tall*.'

'I see.' Mrs Meadows quietly digested this information. (Gracious! How riveting! How revealing! She likes tall men! Just fancy that!)

'And I suppose I quite like ... well, practical men. And *kind* men. Gentle. Brave. Loyal, with a ... a bit of a social conscience ...'

'You prefer boring men.' Mrs Meadows nodded. 'I don't mean that in a critical way,' she added, 'it's very sensible. You're not attracted to unpredictable, creative men. Or dangerous men.'

'No.' I shook my head. 'Not dangerous men. The very opposite of that.'

'A safe man. Someone reliable.'

'Yes.' I nodded.

'Not a charmer, like Mr Huff.'

'No.' I shook my head again. 'Although I've never actually witnessed Mr Huff's charming side.'

'Haven't you?' Mrs Meadows looked shocked.

'No.'

'How odd.'

Mrs Meadows appraised me, intently, as if expecting to detect some kind of glaring piece of physical evidence about my person as to how I might have developed an immunity to the abundant charms of Mr Huff.

I had found a pencil (in the cutlery drawer, from which I also removed an old toothpaste tube and an ancient stick of celery. Mr Huff really *was* a pig). Now I just needed to find a small scrap of …

'He's so *very* charming, though, and my worry is' – Mrs Meadows grimaced – '… my worry is that I might've been a little bit too … too attentive … too … demonstrative … too eager to please, too …' She struggled to find the right word, then finally settled on, 'too easy.'

Easy?

'Easy?' I repeated, concerned (for whom, I'm not entirely certain).

'Yes. After breakfast yesterday. When he confided in me about his … his *wife* …'

'Kimberly.' I nodded. 'It was terribly sad. But I believe they were separated. They lived on different continents, you know.'

'Are the North and the South Americas different continents?' Mrs Meadows wondered. 'Aren't the Americas one continent?'

'I'm not entirely sure,' I admitted.

Easy?

'I just felt this enormous *rush* of compassion towards him,' Mrs Meadows continued, 'and then afterwards, after I …' – she waved her hand, expressively – 'I mean after we …' – she waved her hand again – 'he started going on about the incredible *intensity* of his grief. He said he was almost … almost *insensible* with grief, how his grief was actually almost … had an almost *"psychedelic"* quality about it … which – I must confess – is definitely a new one on me.'

Psychedelic?

She looked over for any input. I just stared back at her, wide-eyed.

Did this …? Was she …? Had they …? Was Sage Meadows actually saying that there had been – between them – the two of them – that they'd actually had … had *relations*? Mrs Sage Meadows and Mr Franklin D. Huff?

Relations?

Intimacies?

How else to interpret that non-specific yet very specific waving of the hand, *twice*?

I felt quite horrified.

I couldn't pretend otherwise.

I don't really know why.

But I did.

Relations?

After *breakfast?*

Yesterday?

With Mr Franklin D. Huff?

Just before he …? With … with *me* …? In the sauna?

Was the man some kind of … of *beast*?!

'And then he rushed off,' she continued, oblivious. 'And I just thought … Oh, maybe that was a mistake, Sage. Maybe I've … I don't know …'

'Been cruelly manipulated by Mr Huff?' I suggested, huskily.

'No. *No.* Quite the opposite,' Mrs Meadows insisted.

'Ah.' I nodded, unconvinced.

'I mean it can't be any coincidence that I keep on trying to establish relationships with the kind of men who all just seem to want to … who all just seem to want to up and to … to *leave* …'

Silence.

'Well Mr Meadows didn't actually *want* to leave,' I corrected her.

'No. I simply thought because he was older, more stable, had a reliable profession, that he might actually manage to stick around for a while.' Mrs Meadows smiled, wryly.

'He was very dashing,' I said (even though he wasn't, particularly).

'And I suppose it's because I'm always expecting the men I'm attracted to to suddenly charge off,' she idly extemporized, 'that I kind of … I tend to cram everything in as quickly as I possibly can. Just in case they … you know. Especially if I

304

find them attractive. Like Mr Huff. Who's so charming. So clever. So ... so exciting and exotic. I can sometimes tend to be a little bit ... forward. And perhaps this leads them into thinking that I'm pushy or ... or ...'

'Easy,' I filled in, without thinking.

She shot me an accusing look.

'Sorry,' I mumbled, 'I was simply ...'

'But it's only because of this nagging doubt, this *fear* that they'll run off and abandon me before I've even had a chance to ...'

Mrs Meadows is crying!

Oh no! Mrs Meadows is crying over Mr Huff! Or if not over Mr Huff himself exactly, then over all the other men in her life who have used and then abandoned her. *Like* Mr Huff! Although Mr Huff hasn't formally abandoned her. Not as yet.

She started feeling around in her shoulder bag for a tissue. I reached into my pocket, removed a large, cotton handkerchief and carried it over to her.

She took it, gratefully, and blew her nose on it, noisily. In truth, the most I had expected (in terms of wear) was for her to quickly dab away at her tears with it.

'For the record, I don't find Mr Huff *remotely* exotic,' I said, hoping to bolster her with a small serving of the plain old truth. 'It's like the life he's lived hasn't left a single interesting mark on him. He's so stiff and so uptight and ... and so polished, so *finished*. The very idea of him in Montserrat—'

'Monterrey,' she interrupted.

'Yes, Monterrey. It just seems extraordinary to me.'

Mrs Meadows blew her nose, explosively, for a second time.

'And I can't honestly fathom why you'd want to lie about a Pure Maths and Engineering degree, either,' I continued.

'Because men find it such a turn-off.' She shrugs.

'Intimidating. My speciality is Undecidable Problems, specifically the "word problem" in algebra and computer science. These aren't the kinds of things your average person can have a casual conversation about.'

'Well maybe you need to stop having so many casual conversations,' I suggest, 'or, better still, start worrying about problems that *are* decipherable.'

'Decidable,' she corrected.

'Exactly.' I nodded. 'Decide on your problem and then solve it.'

'Easy for you to say.' She smirked (amused, for some reason). 'I bet you weren't educated beyond your O-levels.'

'I trained as a nurse.'

'Exactly.' She shrugged. 'Men love nurses. But they aren't remotely attracted to mathematicians. Life is just so much more *complicated* in the intellectual realm; so full of rivalry and viciousness and confusion and disappointment.'

'Life can be fairly complicated in *all* its realms,' I aver. 'Even the most basic ones.'

'I suppose so,' Mrs Meadows sighed, pushing herself to her feet. I pulled open the little drawer at the other end and hunted inside it for some paper, finally locating an old handbill for a table-sale in the Village Hall at Winchelsea Beach – circa 1968 – with a nice, plain back. Mrs Meadows, meanwhile, has gone for a small, slightly aimless mooch around the living room and then on into the hallway and beyond. I shut the drawer and followed her. I found her in the little box room, sitting on the unmade bed, pressing Mr Huff's grey-striped flannel pyjama bottoms to her chest.

'This is where he sleeps,' she murmured, dreamily. 'It smells of … what is that smell exactly?'

'Eucalyptus.'

'Yes. Eucalyptus … Oh!' She gazed around her, suddenly anxious. 'This wasn't that poor little girl's room, was it?'

I nodded.

She grimaced.

'Were you very close?' she wondered. 'With her, I mean?'

I shrugged. Then I nodded again.

'Is this where she …? In this bed …?'

I nodded.

'This … this *mattress*?' She bounced, gently, on the mattress.

I nodded.

'What a repellent thought!' she murmured. Followed by another small bounce.

'So, Mr Huff's wife was having an affair with Bran Cleary,' she mused.

I tried to nod, but for some reason I couldn't quite.

'And now Mr Huff is writing a book about it all.'

This time it was my turn to grimace.

'His wife was horribly burned in that car explosion …'

I nodded.

'And Mr Cleary? How did he die again?'

'He was involved in a …' my voice started to shake, so I drew a deep breath, 'a tiff. An argument. While he was on remand. Over a Kit Kat. It escalated. Someone hit him on the side of the head with a snooker cue. He seemed fine. No blood was drawn. He didn't even ask to see the doctor. Then twelve hours later, he was dead.'

'Of course it wasn't really *about* the chocolate bar, was it?' she muttered.

I couldn't bring myself to respond. I just wished she'd put Mr Huff's pyjamas down. And get off his damn bed.

'You must be aware of the things people say …' she all but whispered.

'I don't care what people say,' I answered, at normal volume. (No. I *don't* actually care. Not a jot. And if I keep on saying it – firmly, out loud, quietly, in my head – then maybe I'll even start to …?)

'Because as an artist he naturally had *carte blanche* to travel to and fro across the border without attracting that much attention to himself,' she reasoned. 'And he never made any secret of the fact that he was an active supporter of the IRA—'

'I'm not sure that he *was* a supporter,' I interrupted, unable (despite my best efforts) to hold my tongue. 'He was always very vocal in his opposition to the policy of internment without trial in the North. Perhaps that was a mistake. He attracted a lot of negative attention to himself. But I think he thought all topics were fair game in the realm of art. He just wanted to … to broaden the discussion. He said he always felt like everything was so … so *stuck*. So formalized. Into sides. Into teams. And art is fluid. It loves to cross boundaries. It can move people – intellectually, emotionally – in unexpected ways. It stands outside. It provokes questions. So it wasn't really a matter of taking sides – not at all – just another way of expanding the …' What was the word he'd always used? That favourite word of Bran's? '… discourse,' I finished off, somewhat clumsily.

Mrs Meadows didn't respond directly, just lifted Mr Huff's pyjama bottoms to her nose and inhaled, deeply.

'And apparently,' I added (slightly disgusted), 'he and his wife were *constantly* being harassed by the army and the police when they crossed the border. Partly because they were a mixed-race couple, which was quite unusual in Ireland at that time.'

'Surely it can't have been purely a coincidence, though,' Mrs Meadows persisted, 'that the child should suddenly have a spate of strange warning "visions" just prior to a bomb being planted several streets from where her father was at work?'

'It was placed outside a café where he often ate his lunch.' I shrugged. 'Maybe the bomb was *about* his work?'

'But he had Republican sympathies.'

'He was a lapsed Catholic, yes, and a "radical", but not formally a Republican …' I paused, glancing over my shoulder, suspecting that I'd just heard the latch clicking shut

on the door from the back porch. 'I found you a pencil and some paper ...' I held them out. 'Should we ...?'
I indicated towards the front room.

Mrs Meadows took the pencil and paper and placed them down on to the counterpane. 'The child had obviously been party to something,' she muttered, folding up Mr Huff's pyjama bottoms, then shoving them under his pillow, 'and ended up confiding the details to her local priest. Which was the right thing to do, under the circumstances. She saved many lives. But the father was definitely involved.'

'Orla's visions had started a good while before that,' I argued. 'The first one was in the Australian Rangelands. On a trip to visit her maternal grandfather who ran a sheep farm just outside a place called Bourke. She collapsed into what appeared to be a dead faint. She wasn't able to feel any kind of external stimulation. She started talking – prophesying – about an extraordinary contagion, an epidemic, which would infect the entire planet ...'

'A lethal disease?' Mrs Meadows asked, eyes widening. 'Like ... like Aids?'
'Not lethal, no. Almost a ... a good virus, I suppose. She said people would infect themselves. Voluntarily. She said it would change the face of the world – as we then knew it – for all time.'
Mrs Meadows scowled.
'Of course they initially thought she had heatstroke, even Orla herself ...'

'Although prophesying a terrible virus—' Mrs Meadows shrugged, not really buying it.
'People also say that she predicted the Sylmar earthquake,' I interrupted. 'She talked repeatedly during another trance about seismic activity in the San Fernando Valley. But when the quake happened in the February of the year before she died – 1971 – she insisted that the quake she had seen – or

been shown in a vision – was much, much larger and more powerful and that the aftershocks would be felt ...'

While I was speaking there was a crashing sound from the neighbouring room as someone walked into the fireguard and then swore. It was Sorcha, of course (who else?).

'Sorcha?' I turned, scowling.

She appeared at my shoulder, with her camera.

'What type of idiot keeps a rabbit under a fireguard?' she demanded, rubbing furiously at her shin with her spare hand, and then, 'Are you'se two talking about my beautiful little angel Orla by any chance?'

Mrs Meadows nodded.

'Orla *loved* her daddy, so she did.' Sorcha passed me her camera (it was recording) and indicated, brusquely, that I should film her with it. 'As God is my witness, that dear child would never, *never* grass on her own father!'

'What if she confessed something to the priest – in confidence – and then ...' Mrs Meadows persisted, '... I don't know, they cooked up some kind of a scheme between them to try and warn people off?'

Sorcha was looking around the room. She reached out her hands – wearing an expression of great reverence – and touched the bedside table and the lampshade, then sat down on the bed next to Mrs Meadows and put her arm around her shoulder (much to Mrs Meadows's evident dismay), spreading the fingers of her other hand across the counterpane.

'This here was the very bed where my beautiful Orla breathed her last upon this sorry earth ...' She spoke straight to camera, indicating (brusquely, again) that I angle it correctly (I naturally obliged; Sorcha, at the best of times, is difficult to resist).

'I always *feel* my little girl's spirit in this room,' she sighed, squeezing Mrs Meadows. 'It's a holy place, so it is ...' She gazed down at Mrs Meadows's skirt as she spoke. 'Is that a suede skirt you have on you there?'

Mrs Meadows conceded that indeed it was.

'And what a lovely head of red hair you got!' Sorcha observed, adding, 'Although I suppose as you'd call it auburn yourself, eh?'

Mrs Meadows shrugged.

'"When red-headed peoples are above a certain social grade their hair is always auburn!"' Sorcha cackled. 'Mark Twain. He had him a mop of ginger hair, so he did. He wrote as how he thought Adam and Eve was red of hair, even our dear Lord hisself. All Aboriginal peoples, all Celtic peoples – all Orla's people – venerate the red gene. There was a tiny taint of red in Orla's hair was there not, Carla?'

I grudgingly allowed that, yes, yes there had been the smallest of reddish tints.

'"While the rest of the species is descended from apes," Mark Twain once wrote,' Sorcha continued holding forth, '"redheads are descended from cats."' She smiled to camera then turned and made a funny, little cat noise – a kind of '*prrrrup!*' – directly into Mrs Meadows's ear.

Mrs Meadows promptly jumped up (much to Sorcha's evident hilarity), one hand covering the offended lobe, the other brushing off her skirt. 'I should probably ... uh ... yes ... head off,' she said (then did exactly that).

'*Muni got-in to, Mo rud'u!*'

Sorcha called after her, in Shelta ('Goodbye, my sweetheart!' to the rest of us), before delivering a mischievous wink to camera. I promptly lowered the infernal thing and handed it back to her. 'I thought we agreed there was to be no filming in the cottage, Sorcha,' I said.

'You know ...' Sorcha pondered something for a second, 'sometimes when you feel so, so much ...' – she patted her chest – 'such an abundance of *love* for someone, like what you and me did for our gorgeous little angel, words just *can't* contain ... so you end up ...' She shrugged. 'I make a big old song and dance about the whole ting. I'm full of the blarney.

That's how I cope. It's just my nature. And you? No words. Nothing at all. A big silence. A sadness. If a person even so much as dares to mention her darling sweet name, your eyes fills up with tears. But surely there's no harm in it after all, eh? Because that's exactly why we was chose, Carla. To be her Apostles. You to be too damn quiet and me to be too damn loud. She's the saint of the too much and the too little. The saint of sudden infestations and last-minute breakdowns. The saint of picked clean bones and potato peelings. The saint of all the kitchen scraps. That's why she chose us, Carla, because God always shines his brightest through weakness.'

She patted the bed next to her. I hesitated and then I sat down. It was suddenly such a relief to be with someone who … who *knew*. Who felt it too – the craziness, the ridiculousness, the fullness, the emptiness.

'Ah, my heart is so heavy. *Turk l'ag tom leskos* …' she muttered, grabbing my hand and holding it between hers. 'Time forgets too many stories!'

She peered up at the ceiling, rocking, slowly, backwards and forwards, blinking back the tears. 'Pray with me, Carla,' she whispered. 'Pray with me that we'll both do our level best for the darling child. You're my lightning conductor, Carla, so you are. I always feel especially close to our little angel when you're around.'

30

Mr Clifford Bickerton

Shimmy has no idea about the Brighton bombing (poor, old Norman 'on your bike' Tebbit carried from that crumbling seafront hotel in his blue and white flannel jim-jams), which is odd (is this part of some strange sub-plot *she's* hatching?) considering how he's got his radio blaring out, full blast, in the kitchen.

He's called me over because Carla has gone AWOL (something to do with Sorcha and filming (?) Up at Mulberry (?)) and the badgers have been hard at work overnight digging up the giant, rotting corpse of dear old Rogue.

'*Ipish!*' He waves his hand around in front of his face as we gaze down at the mess. 'Look at *mein* poor Rogue! *A shtik fleish mit tzvei eigen,* eh? A piece of meat viz two eyes! *Farfoylt! Farshtuken!* Vat a *shtink!*'
I confess to Shimmy that I can't really smell anything.
'*Ech!*' he exclaims, and gazes heavenward.
I wander off, looking for the shovel, but it isn't where I left it just thirty seconds before (is this *her* again?).

Shimmy is in an especially bad mood because of the pains in his legs (I can't remember the name of his condition offhand, but Carla – the little tart – says it's neurological. The brain sends his feet and his legs the idea that they're cramping. There's some involuntary movement. Sudden spasms. Sometimes a burning sensation. St Anthony's Fire? Is that it?). As Shimmy oversees my activities he kindly keeps up a sarcastic commentary (in case any of the neighbours, or the birds, or the insects aren't yet fully aware of what a dick I am).

'Look at zis fool!' he mutters (with a bitter laugh) as I search for the shovel. 'Vandering around like a fart in a barrel!'

'Did you move the spade?' I demand.

'Of course I moved ze spade, *schmuck!*'

(Dramatic throwing up of hands – I'm hazarding a guess that this is sarcasm.)

'Well if I can't find the spade …' I mutter.

'*Yah, yah*: if I don't come today I come tomorrow, *hah?*' he grumbles.

(I'm guessing that this is some kind of an attack on my levels of enthusiasm … which are low – very low, quite frankly.)

'Are you sure you didn't …?' I repeat.

'*Ech!* Someone else's arse *iz* easier to kick!' he snorts.

As he speaks, I spot the spade leaned up against the fence directly behind him. I grab it (some quiet muttering – on my part) and start piling the dirt back on to Rogue's giant body.

'*Leck, shmech!*' Shimmy grumbles.

(I'm guessing that this is an attempt to tell me that my work is slapdash.) I stop what I'm doing. 'There's about two foot of soil here and then it's all solid rock,' I explain. 'This is as deep as I could dig the original hole.'

Shimmy shrugs. It's a shrug that contains two thousand years of unspoken insults.

'This was the spot *you* chose,' I emphasize.

Another shrug.

'If the corpse wasn't so bloody huge …' I grumble.

Another shrug.

'You said you didn't want to risk disturbing one of the other animal graves further back in the garden, remember?'

(And there are many of them. As Head Undertaker *I* should know.)

Another shrug.

'Well if you think you can find a better spot ...' I mutter, trying (and failing) to disguise my irritation.

Shimmy remains silent. I honestly don't know how Carla copes with the old bastard. Poor Carla (the little tart. With her flirty ways. And her damn sauna). Maybe she doesn't?

'How about I cover him up and then we drag over one of the larger pieces of corrugated iron from behind the sheds,' I suggest, 'lay it across the top for a while until the badgers lose interest?'

Shimmy sighs. 'A pig remains a pig!' he murmurs. '*A chazer bleibt a chazer, eh?*' and then, '*Argh!*' he exclaims, with the very next breath, his face contorting with pain as he bends forward to grab his right leg which suddenly seems to have gone into spasm.

(Good one! A medical emergency! Looks like that loose guttering in Iden isn't getting dealt with any time soon.) I toss down my spade (and it *is* my spade. I'm providing my own equipment today because Shimmy's misplaced the key to the padlock on his main shed) and stride over to support him. I am loaded with insults for my trouble (My pleasure!).

'Did you take your tablets?' I ask.

'I took my tablets, idiot!' he shouts.

'Well at least let me help you get back into the house,' I persist.

After a short (and unsuccessful) attempt at walking himself (a man has his *pride*, after all. Yes, and – like you – I'm pretty sure that there must be a great Yiddish expression to illustrate this point more colourfully than I'm able to, but for once we are to be spared from it), Shimmy accepts my arm and we stagger into the kitchen together. I settle him down into his favourite red vinyl-covered armchair (which lives there, by the old black fireplace), then turn to grab a low stool (he likes to suspend the foot when it's troubling him) and he kicks out his leg 'involuntarily' and delivers me a hefty swipe on the back of the knee with it.

'Bloody hell, Shimmy!' I exclaim, almost collapsing head first into the sink.

'Forgive me, *bubbee*,' he mutters, forlorn, 'forgive a foolish old man who just lost his best friend in all ze vorld! *Mein klein* Rogue, eh? *Mein klein khaver*, eh?'

Next, the waterworks (standard Shimmy), but with the leg constantly kicking out as if it's playing its own happy little game of football, while the rest of him sobs and grizzles way back in the stands.

I busy myself filling a plastic bowl with cold water and then add some ice to it from a couple of trays in the freezer. After a minute or two he finally calms himself down and the leg stops its kicking and merely twitches. I carefully remove his sandals (Shimmy wears sandals summer or winter, rain or shine, to keep the feet cool) and roll up his trouser-leg, then pull the bowl over, gently place his gnarled old foot into it and do my best to hold it still.

'You got no idea what it's like' – Shimmy is still full of self-pity – '*mein fis* not even *mein fis*!'

(I'm guessing '*fis*' might be 'foot'.)

'Call zis a life?!' he adds. 'Nothing ever *mein*?! *Eh*? Not *mein* war! Not *mein* country, not *meine frau*, not *meine* daughter! No!' he repeats, with emphasis. 'Not even *mein bubbellah*! Not even *meine* Carla, eh? *Eh*?!'

I say nothing, just hand him a (slightly dirty) dishcloth to dry his face on.

'Not even *meine* Carla!' he sighs, taking the cloth and patting it over his face, then throwing it back at me. It lands across my shoulder. 'My poor vife *fargvaldikn*. By ze Russians! So vat's *your* excuse, huh? *Huh*?'

He suddenly laughs, wryly (I take comfort from the fact that my pathetic record with his daughter seems to provide him with some slight cheer).

'*A mentsh tracht und Gott lacht!*' he observes. 'Huh? A person plans *und Gott* laughs! He laughs! *Ha ha ha!* He finds

316

it hil-*a*-rious! He finds *us* hil-*a*-rious! You *und* I, eh? Hil-*a*-rious!'

I say nothing.

He nods. 'Yah. Ve're ze same – you *und* I. Like a jelly. Spineless.'

Still, I say nothing.

'You gonna let an old man like me kick you up ze arse, heap you wiz insults *und* still, nothing?! Eh? *Gornisht?*'

'Maybe you don't remember,' I interject, 'but I'm actually in a perfectly happy eight-year relationship with ... with ...' What's her name again?

Oh yes. Alice.

'*Pah!*'

'And Carla's moved on, too,' I continue. 'She's been spending a lot of time with Mr Huff lately by all accounts.'

'If *meine* grandmother had *baitsim* ... uh ... uh ... *testicles*, eh? – she vould be *mein* grandfather!' Shimmy chuckles. (I guess this means he's taking this information with a hefty pinch of incredulity.)

'Okay, fine, go ahead, insult me all you like,' I mutter, scooping handfuls of the iced water over the arch of his foot ('Oi! *A kitsel!* It tickles!' He chuckles), 'but give yourself a break, at least,' I continue. 'You did the decent thing all those years ago with Else and with Carla. It can't have been easy for you after the war.'

'Argh. You sink I vas a *happy* bunny about it?' Shimmy demands. 'My fiancée raped in Berlin? Und she vants to keep ze damn *byyby*? Of course I'm not happy! Not at all! But did I have ze *balls* to walk away? *Nein*. No. You call *zat* bravery? Eh? A pretend life? A pretend family? A pretend happiness? A big *kazab*? A big sham?'

'What choice did you have?' I scowl.

'Choice?!' Shimmy snorts. '*Kein briere iz oich a breire, yah?* Not to have a choice iz *also* a choice. Always remember zis, *bubbee*.'

He leans forward, ruffles my hair and then hugs me.

This tender moment is orchestrated by Giorgio Moroder and Philip Oakey's 'Together in Electric Dreams'. I wince through an especially terrible guitar solo.

'Bravery is sometimes only cowardice, huh?' he mutters. 'I *like* you, *royt-chik*. You're a *langer lucksh*. Too damn *tall*, huh? But still, *still*, I like you.'

The music fades into the news, the moment passes and we are pushed apart (I thank God for small mercies) by the dog, who shoves his giant head into the washing-up bowl to refresh himself.

'*Feh!* Drink your own vater, you big, *k'ry chamoole!*'

Shimmy swipes at the animal and it dutifully shuffles off, then, 'Now go! *Go!*' Shimmy pronounces. 'Go *bagroben mein* Rogue, eh? Cover him up! Zat's my boy!'

Three seconds pass. The dog has waddled from the room leaving a trail of mud and filth in his wake. We both stand up, in silence, turn, and follow. We find him in his favourite place, flat on his side, panting, blocking the front door with his considerable heft.

Shimmy screws up his eyes and stares at the creature, thoughtfully. Another three seconds pass, and then, 'A *bomb?!*' he explodes. 'A *pitzootz* you say?! In *Bgriiighton?!*'

31

Mr Franklin D. Huff

I'm lying flat on my belly, pinned to the bed (a straw mattress
– yes! A *straw* mattress!) by a powerfully starched sheet. My
pillow – if you can call this sorry artefact a pillow – is about
an inch thick. I try to turn over, but my arm – my free arm (I
have a free arm!) seems to be affixed ...

'Please don't try and turn yourself!'

Eh? Who ...? My eyes fly open.

A monk is sitting quietly by the head of the bed, reading a
book. He quickly rises to his feet and places the book, still
open, face down, on the seat of his chair.

'You're in the sanatorium, at Douai Abbey,' he explains
(slight Scottish accent – an Edinburgh man, I'll wager), before
walking to the other side of the bed and fiddling with some
kind of medical contraption. 'You're lying on your stomach
because your buttocks have become extraordinarily inflamed
after your epic walk. You've been delirious for the best part of
five hours. Try and keep still, if you can. We've dosed you up
on antibiotics and there's an intravenous drip in your arm.
You were very dehydrated, and you seem to have suffered
some form of a concussion ...' He pauses. 'I'm Brother
Cosmas. I'm a trained medic.'

As Brother Cosmas speaks I try to focus on the spine of the
book. *The Coll ... The Collected Poems of ... of Jo ... Jo ...
John ... Donne!*

Phew.

I wiggle my toes. *Argh!* My toes feel raw! Skinless! *Wet!* I tense my buttocks.

OH GOD THAT HURTS!

Brother Cosmas watches me closely. 'Your buttocks are extraordinarily inflamed,' he repeats.

'Could we just ...' I start off.

Not talk about my buttocks, please? Pretty please?

'I've never seen anything like it,' Brother Cosmas continues, undeterred. 'I served in the armed forces for seven years. That's where I acquired my nursing qualifications. And trust me, I've seen a whole lot of inflammations in my time – some in places you might find it difficult to imagine could *get* inflamed – but never, *ever* anything quite like this.'

I grunted. I refocused on John Donne.

'Would you like me to read to you for a while?' Brother Cosmas asked.

'Is Brother Hugh—' I started off.

'Father Pietr left for Ormskirk this morning after Matins,' he interrupted.

Ormskirk?

*Orm*skirk?

(!)

Damn. Damn. *Damn.* My spirits sank. How many miles to *Ormskirk*? I quietly wondered.

'It's about two hundred miles away,' Brother Cosmas volunteered, without prompting, then picked up his book and sat down again (casual rearranging of the ebony folds of his robe). 'We have reached Sonnet number 5,' he informed me, then cleared his throat (from this I presumed that he had been reading to me prior to my regaining consciousness, which I found odd but strangely touching).

'*O, my black soul, now thou art summoned,*' he started off, '*By sickness, Death's herald and champion ...*' he continued,

Thou'rt like a pilgrim, which abroad hath done
Treason, and durst not turn to whence he's fled;
Or like a thief, which till death's doom be read,
Wisheth himself deliver'd from prison,

Brother Cosmas paused, portentously.

But Damn'd and haled to execution,
Wisheth that still he might be imprisoned ...

I inspected Brother Cosmas in profile, from below, as he
read. He was a very small, compact, yet intensely sinewy man
– early to mid-thirties? – who exuded an intense kind of
vitality. His boyish demeanour – there were still traces of acne
on his cheeks – stood in stark contrast to his slightly turned-
down mouth and a series of dark rings around his eyes.

Yet grace if thou repent, thou canst not lack;
But who shall give thee that grace to begin?

Almost a kind of *passion* in Brother Cosmas's voice at this
point ...

O, Make thyself with holy mourning black,
And red with blushing as thou art with sin;

First dolorous, then chastising, and finally ...

Or wash thee in Christ's blood, which hath this might,
That being red it dyes red souls to white.

... cheerfully sanctimonious.
I turned and attempted to crush my face into the pillow,
but the pillow lacked sufficient substance to render this a

feasible option. Brother Cosmas completed his Holy Sonnet and sighed again, then quietly turned the page.

'*I am a little world made cunningly* ...' he started off, cheerfully (on what I presumed to be Sonnet 6). I clenched my teeth, almost regretting that I wasn't still *non compos mentis*.

'And how is the patient progressing, Brother?'

My head spun back around (what relief!) at the sound of a familiar voice. It was the lanky, strawberry-blond Brother Linus come by to check up on my progress.

'He can answer for himself, Brother,' Brother Cosmas responded. 'He's awake at last.'

'But for how long, Brother Cosmas' – Brother Linus smiled – 'if you persist in reading him those dreary poems of yours?'

Brother Cosmas looked wounded. It was immediately clear to me that Cosmas suffered from a case of intellectual inferiority, and that Brother Linus (privately schooled? University educated?) enjoyed teasing him on this matter, quite relentlessly.

'Sonnets, Brother,' Brother Cosmas corrected him, tightly.

'Apparently Brother Hugh has gone to ...' I interrupted them (trying – perhaps failing – to keep the desperation from my voice).

'Ormskirk, yes,' Brother Linus confirmed.

'If you have a few, spare minutes, Brother' – Brother Cosmas indicated towards the chair he'd just vacated – 'I promised several hours ago to pick Brother Gabriel a handful of fresh oregano from the kitchen garden and Mrs Thane ...' (Mrs Thane? Perchance the school housekeeper?) '... has been kept busy all afternoon managing the leak in the small reading room.'

'Oh ... Uh ...' Brother Linus hesitated for a second (just to wind Brother Cosmas up, presumably) and then grinned, broadly. 'Of course, Brother. I'd be happy to sit with the patient for a while.'

Brother Cosmas nodded abruptly and left the room. Brother Linus picked up the volume of poetry, closed it, sat down and rested it on his lap.

'Did Father Hugh really leave for Ormskirk?' I asked, just as soon as Brother Cosmas was out of earshot. Brother Linus had struck me – right from the off – as one of life's straight dealers.

'Yes, he did.' Brother Linus nodded.

'Was it only because I turned up?'

Brother Linus glanced towards the door, warily, before he answered. 'Father Pietr is strictly forbidden from talking to strangers who arrive at the monastery and ask for him by his old name,' he confided. 'It's official protocol. I'm afraid your fate was sealed the minute you opened your mouth and uttered the words "Father Hugh", although I believe you might *actually* have called him Brother Hugh, which is also wrong as Father Pietr is ordained priest which means that – unlike myself or Brother Prosper or Brother Cosmas – he can officiate mass.'

'Oh. That was clumsy of me.' I scowled, irritated by my own stupidity.

Brother Linus shrugged, diplomatically.

'Do you know Father Pietr well?' I wondered, still determined to push for more information, nonetheless.

'If you're asking whether Father Pietr ever discussed his life as a parish priest in Ireland with me in any detail' – Brother Linus smiled – 'then my answer is no. Father Pietr has left that part of his chequered history far behind him now.'

'I wish it was quite that easy for the rest of us,' I muttered.

'Mortification and prayer can play a useful role,' Brother Linus suggested.

Mortification?

Prayer?!

'I wish it was quite that easy for the rest of us,' I repeated, drolly (and perhaps even a tad facetiously).

'I didn't say it was easy,' Brother Linus demurred, 'I said they could be useful, that's all.'

'Do many people come to see Father Pietr?' I wondered. 'Father Pietr mentioned, before he left for Ormskirk, that your wife recently passed.' Brother Linus calmly changed the subject. 'That must have been difficult.'

'We were separated,' I confessed, 'for over a decade. But it was certainly a shock, yes.'

'We offered a mass for the repose of her soul,' Brother Linus divulged (again a glance towards the door). 'It was beautiful. And Father Pietr became quite emotional at a couple of points. I imagine they must have been very close.'

'I'm not ...' I started off, and then, 'Yes, yes, perhaps. Possibly even closer than I'd initially ...'

Quite *emotional*? That was odd. I tucked this little piece of information away to ponder on later in greater detail.

Brother Linus opened the book again and flipped through it, idly.

'It's difficult to pinpoint your accent.' I yawned. 'Are you Swiss, Brother?'

'Belgian. But I speak Luxembourgish. It's a very particular and quite obscure west-central-German language ...'

I yawned again, then promptly apologized (due to various physical restraints, it was virtually impossible for me to cover my mouth as I did so).

'Don't worry' – Brother Linus chuckled, dryly – 'people invariably start to yawn when I get into the finer details of my cultural and linguistic identity.'

'Sorry,' I apologized again, 'I'm just ... I suddenly find myself ... just incredibly ...'

Tired.

So *tired.*

Another yawn.

Tired.

'Don't give it a second thought.' Brother Linus smiled. 'Close your eyes. Get some rest.'

While he was speaking he pulled a long dark wooden rosary from a pocket in his habit, which – dropping down and unwinding to its full length – clattered, unexpectedly, against the leg of the chair as the little metal crucifix made temporary contact with it.

I don't know how many hours I'd been asleep for, exactly – five? Six? – but I'd certainly been conscious of the return of Brother Cosmas, and registered the sound of a nice, well-modulated woman's voice at several points (the aforementioned Mrs Thane, perhaps, the 'crisis' in the reading room now in temporary abeyance?), although when I finally regained full consciousness, there was nothing remotely 'nice' or 'well-modulated' about the experience.

It was dark and I was rudely awoken by a sudden heavy weight on the edge of the mattress, followed by a series of guttural exclamations. My eyes flew open and when I lifted my head (alarmed – I don't mind admitting it) I could just about decipher the outline of an elderly male monk – bent over, infirm, heavy cane leaned against the wall – struggling to settle himself on to the chair at the bed's head. It was none other than Brother Prosper who – much as during our earlier brief encounter – exuded the fractious atmosphere (and scent, if I can be perfectly honest) of an injured boar badger.

I suddenly missed Mulberry. Which was odd. Why would the sight of Brother Prosper lowering over me, breathing heavily, in the dark, make me miss Mulberry? (I mean it's hardly as though my personal space ... *integrity* hadn't been significantly violated there as well.) But I missed it, even so. I missed ... What did I miss? I missed the now-familiar individual creaks and groans of the blackened pine floor, the scuff of the rag-rugs and tatty off-cuts of seagrass under my toes, the whine of the old refrigerator. I missed the way the cheap toilet seat clattered down when you least expected it to (a problem with the hinge; well-detailed by myself – you'll be relieved to know – in the 'comments book'). Even the old white crocheted blankets. Yes. And the fraying cane umbrella-stand by the front door which I had – twice, now – snagged my trousers on during quick exits. And that infernal picture of the seagull! The herring gull! Hung on the wall in the kitchen-cum-dining area.

I missed them all.

'Did I awaken you?' Brother Prosper demanded.

'Yes you did,' I answered, frankly.

'I couldn't rest,' Brother Prosper muttered (as if his not resting was sufficient reason for me – a lesser mortal – not to, either). 'My cell was stifling. My nostrils were so full of the damn smell.'

'Smell?' I echoed.

'Disinfectant.'

'Ah.' I nodded.

'Other saints smell of lilies or violets I'm told,' Brother Prosper confided, 'sweet scents. The Holy Virgin is reputed to carry a heavenly aura of roses. But not *her*. Her scent has a … a *bleaching* quality, a sharp, harsh, antiseptic quality …'

He paused, thoughtfully, still breathing heavily.

'What's the difference?' he wondered. 'Between the two?'

'Sorry?' I wasn't quite following.

'Antiseptic and disinfectant. The difference?'

'Well I suppose the one is used to kill germs on the body – has a medical application – while the other is used mainly in the—'

'Not pine …' he mused, interrupting.

'Eucalyptus?' I hazarded a wild guess.

'Exactly.'

'I think it possibly has two types of application,' I persisted (determined to complete my intelligent analysis), 'one medical, the other domestic.'

'Are you mad?' Brother Prosper enquired.

'Pardon?'

I wasn't sure whether Brother Prosper was objecting to my former definition (which I was pretty certain was spot-on) or making further – and unrelated – enquiries as to the overall state of my mental health.

'Am I talking to a madman?' he repeated.

Ah. The latter, it seemed. I paused before responding since I was (I openly confess) somewhat perplexed by this question. I had never really considered myself 'mad' before. Maverick, wilful, tough, free-spirited, certainly. Although …

'Am I talking to a madman?' Brother Prosper enquired for a third time.

… although I could easily imagine how some of my behaviour hitherto could conceivably have been construed as … well, as slightly …

'I paddle my own canoe, Brother,' I said (feeling as though only a thoroughly *sane* person – at root – would have the calm self-assurance to respond in this manner).

'I won't speak candidly to a sane person,' Brother Prosper helpfully followed up.

'I see.'

(Well that was certainly going to cast the cat amongst the pigeons!)

'I took the photographs,' Brother Prosper muttered, 'I stole them from your bag while Linus ran off to get help – earlier, after you collapsed …'

A measure of grunting followed as Brother Prosper pulled the envelope of photographs out from under his robe and pushed them back into my bag which – it appeared – was presently stationed under his chair.

'They'll have checked your bag when you first arrived,' he whispered, 'but I think they'll leave it alone now – now that you're fully conscious.'

'They?' I echoed, slightly panicked.

Brother Prosper didn't respond.

'Did Father Hugh leave this morning of his own free will?' I asked.

'Of course!' Brother Prosper snorted. 'Father Pietr does exactly as the abbot tells him. It's a matter of obedience. It's his choice to always do as he is told.'

'Did he ever mention ...?' I started off (thoroughly perplexed by this curious response).

'No' – Brother Prosper shook his head – 'Father Pietr never discusses his past. It's a closed book to him – to us all. He knows how lucky he was to be accepted into the Order. If it hadn't been for Brother Richard's influence ...'

'Brother ...?'

'Pietr's father was a Benedictine himself. He became a monk when Hugh turned eighteen. They were always a devout family. Pietr never seriously considered any other kind of vocation. Both his sisters became Missionaries of Charity.'

'But I'm sure I read something somewhere about Father Hugh working as a draughtsman in an architect's office ...' I averred.

'No, no,' Brother Prosper clucked, 'that was Brother *Richard*, before he became a monk. He was a draughtsman. He worked for Davin Cleary who was an architect based in Monaghan. Brother Pietr attended the Benedictine school at Glenstal Abbey just outside Limerick. He boarded there. After his mother died. Davin Cleary, Bran Cleary's father – God rest his soul – paid the fees. Maeve Cleary – Bran's mother – was always very fond of the child. She was a passionate Catholic herself. Father Pietr was taught by the Benedictines. He was training to become an architect – sponsored financially by the Cleary family – when he got the call from God to be ordained priest. He was still very … very green when the situation blew up with the … you know. Maeve was instrumental in bringing them together. The parents were often away, working, in the North. The child had gone on a holiday to Australia to visit her maternal grandfather and had suffered from heatstroke. Since then she'd not been right. Emotionally. Maeve was convinced it was connected to the dark arts. To the Dreaming. That she'd been … possessed. So she got Father Pietr involved. A laying on of hands – something of that order. But he knew straight away – as soon as they met – that the child was very special. He said there was a strong sense of awe, and of fear. She was a quiet child. Calm. Very serious. Sincere. Of course, when the parents found out about Pietr's involvement with her they weren't best pleased – although Pietr and Bran had been friends since childhood. They spent most of their school holidays together …'

Brother Prosper shrugged. 'But Pietr's credentials were pretty solid – as far as the Benedictines were concerned. They'd loved him at the school. He was head boy. And of course his father was tight with our abbot at that time.'
'The abbot …?' I echoed (automatically).
'Me,' Brother Prosper admitted, before adding, 'for my sins.'
'Ah.'

'It's not encouraged,' Brother Prosper continued, 'for a parish priest to, you know, change his vocation. It's not encouraged. But he was in a difficult predicament. His situation in Monaghan became impossible after Bran Cleary died. The rumours and speculation.'
'But you weren't …?'
'What?' he growled.
'Suspicious?'
'I could always see the good in him.' Brother Prosper neatly sidestepped my question.
'And the situation with the girl, Orla?' I persisted.

'He was devoted to the child. But she was gone – God rest her soul.' Brother Prosper hastily crossed himself. 'That chapter was closed.'

A brief silence followed.

'So why exactly are you …?' I broke it, somewhat trepidatiously.

'What?' Brother Prosper snapped.

'Here? With me? Now?'

'Because …'

Brother Prosper exhaled, sharply. 'Because she *haunts* me, that's why. She torments me. The child. She reveals herself to me.'

'Oh.' I frowned.

'It's not … it's never been *welcome*,' Brother Prosper continued. 'The first time I saw her she was standing outside Father Pietr's cell. She was waiting for him. Outside the door.'

'How did you know?' I wondered, intrigued. 'That it was her?'

'She was wearing a long coat. A long, fur coat. Lots of little rabbit skins sewn together. Very ornate. And she was dark-skinned. Aboriginal.'

'Had you been subject to …?'

'… supernatural visions before?' Brother Prosper completed my sentence for me.

'Absolutely not. No. Never.'

I nodded.

'But after that – after the first time – I saw her constantly. Outside his door. Waiting. Eventually I had to ask him, you know, if he had seen her there himself.'

'Had he?'

'No. And he became quite …' – Brother Prosper struggled to express himself for a second – '… distressed by my asking him.'

'Why was that, do you think?'

'Perhaps he thought I was testing him. Maybe he felt like he'd let her down. Shut her out. By entering the monastery. I don't know.'

'What did *you* think?' I asked.

'It wasn't my place to think anything!' Brother Prosper snorted.

'And then what happened?' I persisted.

'I was retired. As abbot.'

I gazed at him, in silence.

'Father Pietr expressed certain … misgivings – *concerns*. About my mental stability. To some of the other monks. To the wider community. I lost my authority. In the end I felt obliged to … to step down.'

I was shocked.

'Were you angry?' I wondered.

'Yes! Furious!' Brother Prosper barked. 'But I'd have done exactly the same thing myself under those circumstances.'

'I see.'

We are quiet for a while.

'So did you continue to see her – Orla – after that initial spate of …?'

'No. No, I didn't see her again,' he admitted, 'not until last night, that is. She was outside his door again last night. So I knew something was brewing. And then this morning …'

He cleared his throat, awkwardly. 'She was standing on the lawn.'

'The lawn?' I echoed, blithely.

'With you. She was standing with you. You were talking to her. Arguing.'

The skin on the back of my neck suddenly started to goose-bump.

'I've never … I wasn't … I wasn't talking to her,' I stuttered.

'And then this evening, before dinner. I saw her again. She was standing outside your door. But without her coat. I could tell – for the first time – that her arms were unnaturally short. I hadn't seen that before. Your door was slightly ajar. She beckoned towards me. Then she pointed inside and she smiled.'

'She … she wanted you to speak to me?' I murmured.

'She has the most … most luminous smile!' he whispered. 'Such purity! It brought me to tears. I cried for hours after that. Uncontrollably. I sobbed throughout Compline. The brothers were horrified.'

'So … so let me get this straight …' I frowned. 'You took the photos from my bag not because you thought … but just in order to …?'

'To confirm. That it was actually her. Yes. I'd never seen her photograph before.'

I nodded.

'I think that's why she wanted you to bring them here. Not to see Father Pietr after all. Not to test Pietr. But to show them to me. As proof.'

'I see.' I nodded again (although I didn't see at all).

'Because she needed me to bring you her cloak.'

'Sorry?' I was yet more befuddled. 'Her …?'

'When she was standing outside your door earlier, she was without her special cloak. She wanted me to bring it to you. Father Pietr had given it to me when he entered the Order. For safekeeping. She wanted me to give it to you. I could tell. She told me that you were to be an important part of her story and that I was to confide in you everything that I knew.'

'She actually *spoke* to you this time?' I was incredulous.

'No. But she told me. I could just … just *tell*. Same as with your bag and the photographs.'

I was quiet for a while – almost conscience-stricken.

'I'm just … I'm not sure if I'd be the proper … the correct … *recipient* of such a … an important artefact,' I said. And I meant it, too.

'She told me that you should have it.'

Brother Prosper's mind was clearly quite made up.

'I already have the photos,' I said. 'And if I can be perfectly frank with you, Brother, the photos are quite enough for me to be going on with.'

'She wants you to have it.' Brother Prosper shrugged.

'But what about Father Hugh?' I demanded (indignant for Father Hugh, almost).

'Forget about Father Hugh,' Brother Prosper snorted, 'Father Hugh is in the past. This is all about you, now.'

'Well how can you be sure that I can be trusted?' I demanded.

'She's sure. She trusts you,' he muttered (in such a manner as to imply that if it was down to him things would be proceeding quite differently).

'I don't want the cloak!' I gulped.

'Well it's yours,' he sighed. 'So you can like it or lump it.'

He started the laborious process of standing up.

'Where is it?' I asked, nervously.

'Don't worry about it,' he clucked. 'Don't think about it again. Put it out of your mind. Go back to sleep.'

Brother Prosper grabbed his stick, adjusted his weight, and slowly started to make his way, with some considerable effort, across the room. Every few steps he'd pause, battling to catch his breath.

'Are you all right, there, Brother?' I called out at one point, concerned, when the breathing became especially shallow and rapid.

'Sssssh!' he chastised me, then, a few moments later, 'She likes to exact a price,' he panted, 'I can see that now. And you'll find out yourself soon enough. An extreme, little spirit – stringent. Beautiful but stringent. An outcast. An oddity. Invasive. Like a little ... a little weed ...'

'A daisy, Brother,' I murmured, half to myself, suddenly remembering the photograph.

Then again, once he'd finally reached the door and was leaning against the frame, steeling himself for the corridor, 'Still there?' he whispered, followed by a short pause. 'I did as you asked, didn't I?' followed by, 'He paddles his own canoe, little one. That's what he ... But why are you ...?'

Another pause. '*No!* No more of your smiles, my dear child. It's too painful. I'm much too old – can't you see? – and much too sinful. Please. *Please.* No more. No more. No more of your smiles.'

32

Miss Carla Hahn

Clifford was incredibly hot and bothered – poor thing – from re-burying the dog. Then (a real glutton for punishment) he'd broken into Shimmy's big shed (which has been inaccessible for months) with a giant pair of bolt-cutters and liberated an old rabbit cage. Shimmy was glued to the radio, all the while, switching frantically from channel to channel, listening to every available piece of coverage on the Brighton bombing. I could hear the stentorian tones of a series of newsreaders, intercut with the dazed voices of witnesses, victims and furious pundits from all the way out in the garden.

'So Rogue wasn't actually dead.' I tried to get to the bottom of the situation. 'He was in some kind of a ... a *coma* ... and then he ...?'

'Yes. Either he dug himself out of the hole,' Clifford confirmed, 'or possibly the badgers ...'

His mouth suddenly tightened. 'Or maybe *she* did it,' he muttered, darkly, 'maybe it was just *her*.'

'She?' I echoed.

She? Who did he mean, exactly? *She?* Surely not ...?

Not ...

Not *Orla*?

I scowled.

But Clifford didn't even ...

I mean Clifford wasn't especially ...

I stared down at the newly covered grave again and ... and ... Oh I can't *believe* they had relations! Mr Huff and Mrs

Meadows! In Lamb House! Birthplace of *The Ambassadors*!
(Which I've never actually read.) And straight after breakfast,
or ... did they even *eat* breakfast? Maybe they just ...

'How's the bird?' he asked.

'Sorry?'

I glanced up, but I just couldn't get that awful image of Mr
Huff and Mrs Meadows having ... being ... doing ... out of
my head.

'Sorry? The bird?' I repeated.

Clifford still seemed to be avoiding all eye contact.

'The parrot,' he expanded.

'The parrot?'

'Yes,' he snapped. 'The *parrot*, Carla!'

'Oh, you mean *Baldo*?' I finally made sense of it. 'I don't
honestly know. The last I heard Alys had taken him over to—'

'She just can't resist it!' Clifford interrupted, plainly livid.
'Over-egging the damn pudding!'

'Who ...?' I murmured.

Was Clifford angry with ... with *Alys* now for some reason?
Was he up to speed on the whole ...?

Oh God! Did they *really* have relations? Really and truly? Not
that ... not that I had any particular reason to doubt the
trustworthiness of Mrs Meadows's account of the situation ...

'Forget it.' Clifford grimaced.

'But how did ...?' I started off.

'I should probably just grab a mop and get started on all
the mess inside,' he said.

'I can do that,' I insisted, before adding, 'I just need to try
and ... The dog was dead, you say, but then you were in the
kitchen with Shimmy ...'

'He'd developed cramps,' Clifford reiterated (this was the
second time, now. And still no eye contact), 'Shimmy had. He
was upset. And we were soaking his feet in some icy water
when the dog padded into the kitchen from the garden and
tried to shove his head into the bowl.'

'Just padded into the kitchen!' I echoed.

(Mrs Meadows wouldn't have any reason to lie about … about … *you* know … surely?)

'Shimmy pushed him away – almost without thinking – so he trotted through to the hallway and lay down in front of the door.'

'He wasn't in any kind of … of …?' I stuttered.

'No. No, he seemed fine. But I phoned the vet anyway. He turned up after about twenty minutes, gave Rogue the quick once-over and pronounced him officially dead.'

'It's just all so …'

I shook my head.

Improbable.

Just like Mrs Meadows and Mr Huff!

So silly. So unedifying. So … so *inappropriate.*

'The vet thought he might've been in some kind of diabetic coma the first time around, then slowly revived but the poor sod was already …'

'Buried alive!' I murmured horrified.

'Yes.' He smiled, grimly.

'I can't imagine how …' I slowly shook my head.

'*Can't* you?' Clifford's grim smile turned into a mean smirk. (Yes! He *smirked*! Clifford Bickerton actually … actually *smirked*! A *mean* smirk!) 'Because *I* sure as hell can!'

Then he looked up into the sky. 'Be sure and write that down!' he instructed the clouds. 'It's very profound, very … very metaphorical!'

I frowned over at him. He was still holding the rabbit cage. Gazing up into the sky. Shaking his giant head. Proudly. Quite majestically.

'I would *never* use the word meta-meta-*meta* … *Argh!*' he exploded, frustrated. 'I can't even get the damn thing out of my mouth!'

'Are you all right, Clifford?' I asked, taken aback.

337

'What?' Clifford yelled (still upwards), his neck spasming under his beard. 'No plane crash? Eh? No deafening machinery? No swan attack?!'

He looked down again. This was our first real piece of eye contact since the conversation had started. His eyes were red-rimmed and furious-seeming. As if he hadn't slept. As if he'd been crying. Then he looked back up again. 'Are you *determined* to make them all think I'm completely bloody crackers?' he demanded.

'Are you all right, Clifford?' I repeated, concerned.

'No.' He shook his head. 'No. No I'm not all right. Not at all. I'm dreadful.'

He looked up. 'I would *never* use the word "dreadful"!' he bellowed, and then he paused, apparently stricken. 'I don't even know why I'm looking up,' he whispered, half to himself, 'or ... or shouting. You could be anywhere. You could be *every*where. In this hutch. On the radio. Buzzing around like static electricity inside the mind of a little wasp sitting on the toe of my work boot ...'

We both stared down at his work boot (well *I* did, and Clifford tried to, although the hutch obscured his view somewhat). For the record, there was no wasp sitting on the toe of his work boot.

'Why don't you put that hutch down for a second?' I suggested. 'Come inside and have a glass of something cooling ...'

I stepped forward to take it from him.

'I'm fine,' he insisted, stepping back, as if repulsed by my approach. 'It needs a bit of patching up. I'll do it tonight and run it over to Mulberry in the morrow ...' He suddenly spluttered, mid-sentence, '*Morrow*?! In the *morrow*?! *Bah!*' then he seemed – with some considerable effort – to regain control of himself. 'I have a pile of guttering to sort out right now. In Iden ...' He turned.

'If Iden isn't just a figment of my over-active imagination,' he muttered.

'Well at least let me … this must've … we must reimburse you in some way.' I trotted after him, horrified. 'For all your …'

'Forget about it,' he barked, 'I did this for Shimmy. You *couldn't* reimburse me, Carla Hahn. There's no amount.'

And that was it. He marched off.

'No amount?'

I gazed after him (*Carla Hahn?!*).

'There's no amount?' No amount of what? Was that even a proper sentence?

I made a pathetic half-attempt to follow him, and as he walked around the side of the house and through the gate I could've sworn I heard him yell, 'What kind of a writer *are* you? Your timing's a joke! Mr Huff woke up in darkness! In *darkness*! But now we're back in the early afternoon again! And what *day* is this exactly, eh? It just doesn't add up! It's all totally skew-whiff! And how about the parrot chapter? Eh? That entire segment was a disaster! You broke your first-person rule! You slipped into the third! D'you seriously think you'll get away with that?'

This was followed by a loud 'OW!' as he knocked his funny-bone into the lock on the gate.

'I suppose that was you, too!' he bellowed.

Holy Queen, Most Joyful Mother, we are sinful weeds in your fragrant garden. Please bind us in your gentle hands …

… in your gentle …

… in your …

… and offer us all in a daisy crown of love to your merciful Son, and to God the Father.

She was sending me a message, wasn't she? Orla? Darling, crazy, doggedly persistent Orla? Saint of the Potato Peelings? Through my ... through ... through *these*, my hands? Through my hands and ... and through the landslip? Perhaps? Or was the landslip just ...?

And through that hornet sting on the back of my neck which suddenly, miraculously ... (How I despise that word! If I could just get rid of that word – expunge it from the face of the earth – *zap!* – once and for all – then maybe I might finally be able to ...? Oh I don't know.)

And Clifford? Poor, poor Clifford! Remember? Clifford's strange rantings? His furious conversations with the blue sky and the clouds? Dear Clifford, normally so sane, so calm, so rational, so *reliable*, suddenly – unexpectedly – reduced to ... to ...? To *that*?

And finally (last, but by no means least), the death and then the re-death of stupid, lumpen old Rogue. Who will be mourned (well, a little. Although he was a very ... a terribly inconvenient animal. And too fat. Greedy. Over-indulged. Mr Huff was right. It *was* cruel. But *Tatteh* always seems to feel compelled to ... to overfeed his animals. Ever since *Mame* died, I suppose. He kills with kindness – at least I think it's kindness. I don't honestly know why. I'm constantly telling him not to. And if I did – *know*, I mean – I'm sure I wouldn't like what I ... I'm sure it would probably be completely my ... *you* know ... fault. Same as it always is).

She was sending me a message. Surely? *Orla*. Saint of the Kitchen Scraps (isn't that what Sorcha had called her? What a curious turn of phrase that woman has!). Because if she's the Saint of ... then doesn't that make me – by extension – you know ... just ... just *compost*? A pathetic little leftover? Something cut away – too bruised, too tough, too mouldy to be considered worthy of the main table? Refuse (refuse-d). An off-cut. But still, curiously, somehow, still *cherished* at some level? Part of a little pile? *My* pile. *Our* pile. The rejected. The unwanted. Hers. Her pile. Still here. Still included. By ... by *her*? The Tiny-Armed Saint of God's Compost Heap (okay, I'm not nearly so good at this as Sorcha is. I accept that)? Because there's still life on the heap. Not ... not anything to get too ... *you* know, worked-up about, but still ... yes ... still life. A second-rate kind of life. Life on a shoestring. Cut-price life. No frills. And *tiny*. Microscopic. Infinitesimal. Virtually invisible to the naked eye.

But there's still ... still life. Of a sort. And heat (a tiny glow). And hope.

Orla. Saint of the Kitchen Scraps. Saint on-a-budget. *Our* Saint.

But the message (that message? Her message)? It was the *same* message (surely?) being sent over and over and over (she was hammering her point home. Because that was what Orla did. That was her faith. She'd just keep on and on and on, regardless. In spite of everything. She'd always persist. Always. Until she stopped persisting. Until she stopped existing. Until, well, until she died. And then she was ... then she was dead).

I was hearing it (the message), but not hearing it (I'm doing my best, Orla, but there are eggshells to be negotiated – down here, in the heap – and a dense layer of newspaper, and an unhealthy preponderance of ... of ... *urgh*! tiny flies and ants and earwigs). I was hearing it (Yes! Truly!) but not ... not *hearing* it. Her voice was vague and indistinct. But it was crystal clear. Part of me understood the message (utterly lucid! Completely transparent!) ... but then the other bit (the other part?) ...? Nope. Absolutely nothing. Terrible reception. A pointless roar. Humming static. A sarcastic laugh. The sharp, peremptory clearing of an irritated throat. Then silence. Not even silence. Nothing so ... so sweet, so *pure* as ...

The message was about ... well, about the nature of mortality, I suppose (love, loss, risk). But it was more than that, wasn't it? Wasn't it, though?

Or less? Less than that?

Holy Queen, Most Joyful Mother, we are sinful weeds in
your ...
Sinful weeds in ...

    It was about *Mame*. Surely? The message? It was about my
mother. It was about mine and Orla's secret pact. Our secret
pact to save her. Poor, desperate *Mame*. From her dreadful
fate.
    Can a saint be *sinful*? Or ... or *encourage* sin? Would that
...? Does that ...?
Does that make any sense at all?
I can't think about it!
Answer me, Orla!
No! No, please don't.

... bind us in your ...

I cycled part of the way home from *Tatteh*'s (uphill! Almost
all the way!) and then my front tyre went flat. A slow
puncture. I reinflated it, twice, but the tiny rubber seal
connecting the little metal nozzle to the elasticated hose on my
pump, which had been leaking small amounts of air for quite
some time, suddenly started gushing it out. Which meant
pumping one-handed (bike flat on the ground, body of the
pump supported between my knees) while struggling to keep
the damn thing airtight with the fleshy part of my other hand.
    I was tired and frustrated by the time I reached home. But
I couldn't relax. I prepared myself a small supper, but I
couldn't eat it. I was restless. I turned on the TV and I saw
bodies being carried out of a collapsed hotel on the Brighton
seafront. I walked to the window and I saw the garden
crashing down to the sea in crazy terraces. Everything
suddenly so ... so fragile. So temporary. So random-seeming.

And me, standing in the middle of it all, tightly shuttered, locked up, emptied, like an old, out-of-season beach hut. Scared of feeling anything. Bright paint peeling in the damp. A light sprinkling of sand across the partly rotted top step. An old collection of shells tucked under the dripping eaves. A special pebble with a hole in it. A dried starfish. A single broken flip-flop.

What was the word Alys had used? That formal, old-fashioned word ...? Rep ...rep ... reparation? To make amends? To pay back? Is that what I was doing? Almost without knowing (but still ... still *knowing*, deep inside)? Staring the problem straight in the face – incapable of looking away, of blinking, of re-focusing – so that all I could *really* see (finally) was a horrible blur of ... of everything (*everything!*) and absolutely nothing in the self-same instant?

If Mr Huff was a smoking candle (but was he? *Was* he, though?), then somewhere along the way I'd become that abandoned beach hut. A little shack. Uninhabited. Shuttered up. Quite empty inside.
And why?
Guilt.
That's why.
Guilt.
Guilt and ... and fear.
Guilt and fear and ... and more guilt.

Clifford was right. It wasn't just me. I'd buried us all alive. We were all up to our necks in fine blond sand (Goodness gracious! Is that the tide on the turn?!). And *I* had the spade. It was only a little spade. Not a proper tool. Just a children's toy. Red. Plastic. But I'd done an impressive job with it.

'It is time, *meine* Carla!'

Time for what, Orla? To dig us all out again? But it's been way too long! The spade's been carried off – way off – and is

lying on the high water line! My arms are pinned to my sides!
I can't ... I can hardly ...!

'Please bind us in your gentle hands
And offer us all ...'

Yes. *Yes.* I needed to start digging (But what about God and
sin and guilt and hell and ... and ...?).

I needed to dig us all out again (But what about ... about
...?).

I needed to reoccupy the hut. Yes! Tear down the shutters.
Yes! Break open the padlock. *Yargh!* Step back inside. Blink.
Blink. Breathe. Look around.

It's what Orla wanted (isn't it? Wasn't it?). In ... in
reparation? A new kind of payback? Like ... Like God's
Secretary? Remember? Who gave everything she had and then
God said he didn't like the quality of the paper she'd been
using ('But it isn't Basildon Bond, my dear!') so could she just
... would she mind ... could she possibly just re-re-re ...?

And how best to achieve that? Reparation? *How?* Why,
total degradation, of course! Complete humiliation!
Confession. *Confession.* Give Mr Huff (my hunter, my
tormentor, my opposite, my nemesis) a searchlight to shine
into my heart. Open myself up to him. Reveal myself. Expose
myself. *Squirm.* Tell him the truth. Finally. Even if he didn't/
doesn't – as I strongly suspect/ed – actually want/need to hear
it. Especially if he did/doesn't. Yes. Yes! *Exactly!* Especially
then.

This was to be my punishment. Then I could offer it up.
As a gift. Just like ... well, just like *she* did.

It was time. She was right.

It *was* time.

Meine Carla.

33

Mr Clifford Bickerton

I made a silent pact with God as I screamed her name down into the black, surging abyss. (This is ridiculous – sorry to spoil the moment – but I'd never 'make a pact' with a God I don't even believe in. I'm agnostic! I mean an atheist. No. Agnostic (she can't even get *that* right! Me neither, come to think of it); sorry, *sorry*, double bracket. And I'd never say 'surging abyss'. Even though it *was* surging – the tide was high – *and* an abyss i.e. a sheer drop.) (Quick re-cap for those who need it: *I made a silent pact with blah blah as I screamed her name down into the blah* … etc.) that I'd never mention the Author again if he just let her live. Carla. Not the Author. If he just. If he – if the writer – she – he – if they just let her live. I'd never presume to (I'd never say 'presume'! Never!) comment on/argue with/question her again. I'd just accept whatever crap she doled out (and I know we've been here before, but this time I mean it. Last time I was just trying it on for size. As an idea. This time I'm completely sincere). Even if – whatever she does; the so-called 'plot' *ha!* – it involves stuff that is very cruel and very ignorant and very irritating. I'd just … just buckle under and get on with it.

I'd even … I'd even abandon all … all contact with Carla. I'd leave her completely alone. I'd cut all ties. Stop all the pining and the hankering. Stop all the accidental meetings and the funny business. Just so long as she was …

The surveyor arrived after half an hour. He said he'd issued Carla with an eviction order three days ago. There was a huge crack, he said, running right across the middle of the back lawn. 'It was so deep, it quite literally gave me the heebie-jeebies,' he said (I thought his use of the word 'heebie-jeebies' was clumsy. Inappropriate. Under these difficult circumstances. But then I told myself that it was probably just the Author being a thoughtless cow – or, who knows, maybe she has plans to expand the role of this dickhead surveyor person later on in the story and is going to make him constantly say inappropriate things at difficult moments? Oh brilliant! Inspired! Great idea! Although ... well that's *my* role now, isn't it? The nutter? The sayer of inappropriate things? Just out of the blue? That's my character now).

We were standing in what remained of the living room and the TV was still on, and a small side light. The fire brigade were running around trying to sort out the electrics. I knew they thought the TV being on was a bad sign. I kept saying, 'Her bike isn't on the lawn', but I knew that she often stored it in the garage when there was rain. But the garage was gone now, too.

I wish I was more ... you know ... more talented with words because then I could describe this scene to you in all its ... its incredible ... its incredible majesty. The bungalow literally cut in half. The inside of the bungalow – all Carla's ... her things, her *stuff* ... just as before ... still all neat and quiet and ... and innocent and ... and *her* ... Then this crazy drop. The churning sea. The fractured brickwork. Like a giant fist had suddenly ... or a big fish had jumped straight out of the waves and taken a huge bite ...

I was on the phone – the phone was working! – holding her address book in the half-dark and the spitting rain, making call after call asking if anyone had – Alys, Mallydams, Shimmy: 'Have you seen Carla, Shimmy? I'm up in Fairlight. I'm afraid there's been another landslip. I got a call from the coastguard. Yes. Yes I am. Well it's ... I'm afraid it's pretty serious this time. The whole back section of the bungalow ...

No. That'll be the fire services ... No. That'll be the TV. Yes. Still on. No. No. Nothing. A couple of hours ago? Did she happen to mention ...? Straight home? But her bike isn't on the ... Okay. Well I ... I ... I ... I'll keep on searching. I promise. No, no please don't ... they ... please don't cry, Shimmy. I'll come down and ... when ... You won't be ... I'll come and ... I'll look after you, I promise. I will. I promise. You'll be okay. She'll turn up. She'll be ... Yes. Yes. It *is* too much. Both of them in one day. Yes. Well I'd better get back to ... From the bungalow. It is. Yes. I'm just standing in the living room staring down into the ... into the surging abyss. Yes. Okay. Well I'd better ... Uh ... Right. *Right.* Well if the shops are open by the time I manage to ... then I'll ... Full fat. Okay. One pint, same as ... I'll try and ... okay. Before breakfast. Yes, I will. As soon as I ... Yes. Okay. Goodbye. I will. Goodbye, Shimmy ... Yes, very bad luck. Yes. Goodbye, Shimmy. 'Bye. 'Bye. Goodbye.'

They'd called out the Land, Sea and Air Rescue (They? *They?!*). The police were cordoning everything off. Someone had contacted a priest. He was from Our Lady Star of the Sea, Hastings. A priest. Who said a short prayer.

I put that down to the Author. I can't think an actual priest would turn up and start praying and sprinkling Holy Water everywhere at ... 2 a.m. No. She set it all up. Definitely. I mean to have him standing there, muttering. All in black. And the helicopter flying overhead, making his robes flap like a raven's wings (did that sound as clumsy when you just read it as when I just thought it? It did? Sorry. How embarrassing). And the searchlights picking out random household items in the cascading wall of mud and rubble. Like the climax of a bad disaster movie. You know, it just doesn't strike me as ... as credible. It seems false. Staged.

Okay. I was torn. I was trying my best to step outside myself and see this from the Author's point of view. It was certainly a grand send-off. It was huge. Dramatic. A huge send-off for such a quiet and basically … I don't really mean 'quiet', and I kind of want to say 'blank', but I don't really mean that, either. Just … well, private. Will that do? Private and … and … the opposite of an extrovert. The opposite of an attention-seeker. Modest. And natural. The Author keeps trying to feed me 'unassuming'. And the Author is right. It's a good word. It describes Carla to a T. But I'm not going to … Okay. Okay. Unassuming. Such a gentle and unassuming character as Carla.

Happy now?

I mean to finish her off like this. In such a … you know … dramatic …

I actually think I'm feeling … I'm almost feeling *grateful*. Grateful that I didn't have to sit around and watch the two of them together – her and Huff. Instead she's just (the Author) … she's just, you know, *torn* everything away. Just like that. So it's almost … I mean there's no drip, drip, drip, it's just CRASH! WAAAAH! It's *removed* the problem for me. KA-POW! Over. Done.

I'm not actually thinking this. No. *No.* I'm far too traumatized to be thinking crap like this. Not here. Not now. In the middle of all this chaos and … and uncertainty. With the helicopters and the priest (although the priest has gone to one of the neighbours' houses for a cup of tea). I'm not actually thinking this stuff, because I wouldn't – couldn't – under the circumstances. I just couldn't. But a tiny part of me, hidden away, is being … is being investigated, I mean … Like in an operation when the layers are drawn back by the surgeon's scalpel and far, far below all the good, honest, open feelings there are these other less … appealing … but equally honest, at some level …

I'm tying myself in knots now. Is there a bit of … of gladness? Relief? That the Author didn't kill me after all? Because I honestly thought she was setting things up to make *me* the human sacrifice. I've had this … this axe … hanging over me for what feels like … But then … then … *this? Carla? Gone?*

I broke down. I was on my knees in the mud and the rubble, blubbering. And after a while, my mother turned up and begged me to come home with her. Then my dad, who was acting up a storm in front of the policeman, but I could tell he was livid that he'd been dragged out of bed three hours before milking. I wouldn't leave, though. I had it in my mind that I should stay until daylight at the very least. It sounds calculated, I know, but I just wanted to be there when the sun came up. I could imagine how great it would look in the book if I stayed. The first, fragile rays of the sun would rise over this scene of total devastation and there I would be, midst the ruins, caked in mud, hairy, howling, like some prehistoric being. The Author keeps suggesting the word 'primal', 'a "primal" scene'. Yes. I can see that. The end of something, the beginning of something.
Primal.

I had already made my silent pact with God by this point. All that 'screaming into the abyss' etc. was hours ago now. The tears. The slamming from room to room calling her name, over and over. Punching my fist through a wall (a thin wall). The fight with a police officer who didn't think I should be there … An argument with the fireman because I couldn't bear for them to turn the TV off. In case she came home and … I don't know why. 'I think she might be videotaping *Coronation Street*!' 'But she doesn't own a video recorder, sir.'

I don't really know why that happened. Looking back it all seems a bit … pathetic. 'Please don't turn off the light! Please, no! Not the light!' Pathetic. Especially for someone who has worked so long in the Lifeboat Service.

A hell of a lot of stuff happened. Mum called Alice who arrived (hair arranged into dozens of tiny plaits – she was frizzing it. Don't ask me why) at around 4 a.m. A difficult exchange took place in which I told her that Carla was the only woman I had or could ever love, and that it was over between me and her. The engagement was off. She said a lot of nasty stuff about Carla always being in love with Bran Cleary. Everybody knew it. I said I knew it too but I didn't care.

I didn't care.

Lots of stuff happened, but at the same time, hardly anything happened. Because there was nothing we could actually do but stand around and … and … 'emote' (*her* word). The Author is sniggering. I don't think she … I mean I don't think she is actually *capable* of …

Eventually the sun came up. It was just as I had imagined it would be. And that made me feel a bit hollow and phony because it was like I was setting a stage for my own little drama, but it wasn't really … appropriate. I was just a whining gnat perching on the back of Napoleon's collar. I wasn't significant enough for all *this*. So I walked away from it. I backed off. I wanted it to be all about her. Carla. I wanted *her* to be in the middle of it. Her absence to be in the middle of it. All the bigness. The grandeur. The cruel devastation. I wanted it to speak of her life, not mine. Her dilemmas, not mine. To represent … to underline … to illustrate …

Was she always one of them? And I just never … I never quite realized? Was she always one of those strangely hypnotic, cut-off, brightly coloured people? One of the stars? The main characters? The *real* characters? Is that why it's ended like this? So dramatically? To make her a necessary part of *their* story? At last? Where she always truly belonged?

As I turned to leave, my eye spotted something sitting, half-concealed under a pile of muddy rubble. Could that … is that …? I reached down and pulled a tiny, wooden minaret from beneath all the mess. Russian. Hand-carved. Hand-painted. Humble. Functional. 'Unostentatious' (The Author keeps prompting me; oh yes, just like our love was – I suppose that's what she's trying to get across in her own typically patronizing and cack-handed way). Just lying there, it was. Quietly. Unobtrusively. A tiny, Russian minaret. Still perfectly intact.

34

Miss Carla Hahn

It was all about the extremity of the gesture. He had walked to Douai. Or he'd claimed that he was going to (how trustworthy is Mr Huff, though? Very? Not remotely? Well, if not remotely then all the better for me. All the better for me and my crazy, wilful act of self-sacrifice. I needed something spectacular to offer up, didn't I? To tip the balance ... to ... to ...?).

Ninety-odd miles! Incredible, really. So I was sitting here, on his front porch, waiting patiently for his return. I had resolved to sit there and wait for as long as was necessary. Right there. In the dark. Fighting off the midges and the mosquitos. Watching the badgers scuttle past like low side tables enveloped in old rugs to forage for slugs in the borders.

Sitting it out. On his porch. Well, my porch. But eventually I got cold. So I went inside. I had a conversation with the rabbit under its fireguard, drank a glass of water. Then I went to bed. In *her* room. In *his* room. In *their* room. Furtively. Like Goldilocks.

My dreams were turbulent (how could it be otherwise?). The phone rang and rang and rang. I was surrounded by strange lights and curious vibrations. Complete psychic chaos. If that makes any sense.

It was morning when I woke up. I was embracing Mr Huff's pyjamas. Which was ... *urgh* (remember Mrs Meadows? Hugging and sniffing? Urgh. *Urgh*. No. I tossed them away from me – to the far end of the bed – disgusted). I had no idea what time it was, but there was a measure of activity in the sitting room – someone crashing around while emitting a strange, otherworldly wailing sound (human? Animal? Spectral? Wind-based? Mechanical?). I adjusted my clothes and plodded into the kitchen, my face marked by the pillow, my hair a crow's nest (doesn't matter how bad I look. Nope. Not a jot. Because I can offer it all up) half-expecting to see Mr Huff, returned from his voyaging, or Mrs Barrow setting about some arcane cleaning task, or even Sorcha Jennett performing a terrifyingly pagan-seeming pseudo-Catholic Pavee ritual. But it was none of the above. It was Clifford. It was Clifford Bickerton, his clothes, hands and beard covered in mud, his face soaked by tears, crashing around the sitting room like a partially felled tree.

'Clifford?'

He froze to the spot. He didn't move for a few moments. And then very slowly, very cautiously, he turned his head to stare at me.

'Clifford?' I repeated.

'You were here?' he whispered, hoarsely. '*Here?* All along?!'

(Angry? Was he? Disappointed? Hard to tell.)

'Here?' I echoed.

'Mrs Barrow came over to search the cottage ...' He gestured, clumsily. 'Last night. Late. How did you ...?'

'Uh ... I don't know.' I shrugged. 'I was sitting on the front porch. Maybe she came in through the front door and I didn't actually ...'

'I rang a dozen times. You didn't hear the phone ringing?'

'The phone?'

'You didn't hear it ringing? All night? All through the night?'

Perhaps he was angry. And disappointed.

'I heard it ringing,' I conceded, 'but I didn't think it would be ...'

Clifford covered his face with his hands. He was quiet for a few moments. Then finally he said, 'I brought over the rabbit cage. It's outside.'

'Oh. Thank you.' I nodded.

'And I took Shimmy a pint of milk. But they only had skimmed left at the shop.'

'Oh. Okay.' I nodded again.

'You may need to sit down.'

He motioned towards a nearby chair.

'Why?'

I didn't move.

'Your bungalow fell into the sea. Last night.'

'It fell into ...?' I echoed.

'We all thought you were lost. Gone. Dead. All of us. They even called a priest to say a prayer over the drop. The Land, Sea and Air Rescue have been conducting a search. But you were just ...'

He drew a deep breath. 'YOU WERE JUST HERE, ALL ALONG!' he yelled. 'SITTING ON THE BLOODY PORCH!'

I flinched.

'YOU IDIOTIC BLOODY COW!' he bellowed.

I went and sat down.

'That's *it*,' he muttered, half to himself, 'that's just ... that's *it*.'

Then he suddenly started to sneeze, very hard, very quickly, as if he was experiencing a severe allergic reaction to ... well, to *me* I suppose. To my non-death.

'I'm done!' he wheezed, eyes streaming, followed by yet more frenzied sneezing.

I stood up and went into the bathroom to get him some toilet tissue (Mrs Meadows had absconded with my hanky, remember?). I returned and handed it over to him. His nose seemed to be ...

I started to question whether I was actually awake – sentient. Was this all just a ...? I blinked.

'Is he here?' Clifford demanded (between sneezes).

'Who?'

'Eric Morecambe! Richard bloody Burton!' he yelled. 'Who the hell d'you *think* I mean?'

'Mr Huff?' I hazarded a guess.

'Mr Huff!' He sneezed. And a series of ... I can only describe them as ...

'No!' I exclaimed, horrified. 'He's in Berkshire, at Douai. The abbey. At the monastery.'

Then I watched – we both watched – in complete amazement, as line after line of ... This will seem perfectly demented, I know, but line after line of thin, black typescript started to run out of his nose. In sentences. Properly punctuated. It flooded out of his nose. And when he sneezed, whole paragraphs came spraying out of his throat. Some words and letters stuck briefly to his hands and to the walls and the furniture. Some floated in the air and then simply evaporated. I couldn't read most of them but I was sure I saw ...

'I mean I can't speak for you, obviously, but I know I'm totally insignificant – just a minor character ...'

'I'm far too tall to be hanging myself for one thing. It'd be too difficult to arrange ...'

'He was married to the photographer! Why didn't I know that? I mean if I knew about the parrot ...?'

'But like I said earlier, the seat belt wasn't faulty! It was a lie! I lied!'

'I made a silent pact with God as I screamed her name into the black, surging abyss ...'

'Carla! Carla! Carla! Carla!'

Clifford caught a couple of the 'Carlas' in his hand (like moths), crushed them and then wiped his palm on the front of his jumper. After a couple of minutes the words trickled out more slowly, in half-sentences and exclamations. A few seconds and then ... then they dried up completely and were gone. Clifford was just ... just Clifford again, wiping his nose with the toilet paper.

'Would you like a cup of tea?' I asked (what else could I possibly say?).

'Uh ... No. I should probably get on the phone and tell everybody that you're not ... that you're still ...'

He stepped forward and then staggered slightly. I sprang over to support him, held on to his arm and guided him down on to the chair.

'I feel drained,' he murmured, rubbing his forehead, 'but weirdly ...' He frowned, slightly dazed, struggling to find the right word ... 'In ... inart ... inartic ... inart ...'

But the word wouldn't come. Nothing came. So he just shrugged, reached into his pocket, withdrew the little Russian minaret from inside it, placed it down on to the arm of the chair, then gazed at it, half smiling, every once in a while slowly shaking his giant head, resignedly.

35

Mr Franklin D. Huff

I don't think I could be accused of over-dramatizing my situation when I say that the circumstances of my return to Mulberry Cottage, Pett Level, were not only bizarre, perilous and profoundly uncomfortable, but also humiliating in the extreme. The monks had taken it upon themselves (while I was still incapable of coherent speech/movement/thought) to go through my notebook and contact Alys Jane Drury (of all people?!) to ask for her assistance in transporting me back home again (a sudden outbreak of mumps at the school had raised questions over my ongoing presence in the sanatorium). But obviously I couldn't yet move or even sit up, so Alys (in her turn) called upon the considerable goodwill of her son-in-law, Fergal Kemp (the proud owner of a small window-cleaning business in Deal), to ask if she might possibly borrow his van for this purpose.

So it was that I found myself being puffingly deposited (they puffed, *I* puffed), flat on my belly, like a ... an animal carcass being casually transported from a poorly managed abattoir – or a great alligator, the giant quarry of an illegal Rhodesian game hunt – or (still more aptly) a partially folded old ladder – into the back of this somewhat dilapidated vehicle. I suppose I should just be grateful that they didn't tie me to the roof.

I was laid out on two sleeping bags. But I was slightly too long to fit. There was discussion (I kid you not) of roping together the back doors (perhaps this was only a joke), but in the end they pushed forward the front passenger seat and I was slid (slud? Slidded?) in on the diagonal, my head resting, uncomfortably, on an old blue sheet rolled up in a large plastic Woolworth's carrier bag which was crammed into the resulting gap and exuded the heady aroma of cheap detergent, bad taxidermy and lactating cats. I then waited a full fifteen or twenty minutes for Miss Alys Jane Drury to reappear and take charge of her steed. According to Brother Linus she had 'gone to pray in the abbey'.

Well, that's great! That's terrific! Why don't I just lie here (in unseasonal heat) crammed (diagonally), into the back of your son-in-law's window-cleaning van on a couple of filthy sleeping bags for an indefinite period while you saunter off to commune in – I don't doubt – a suitably heartfelt manner with the Lord Almighty?

That's absolutely fine and dandy! That's great! Please don't hurry yourself on *my* account! Only when you're *completely* fit and ready, Miss Drury!

Eh?

Resentful, you say?

Resentful?!

Me?

Then (can I start a new paragraph with then? Why ever not? This is meant to be a chapter about change and insecurity and … and 'transition', after all), once she did finally turn up, Miss Drury seemed to be behaving in a manner that could only be described as 'capricious', 'vacillating', 'dithery'. To start off with she called me 'Mr Puff', which I found disquieting. Then she confessed that she hadn't really 'got to grips' with the van's antiquated gearbox. Then she slammed her seat belt in her door (Brother Linus was running up the gravel path behind us gesticulating wildly – this I only imagined, since I was unable to see anything from my obscure angle in the back). Then, once the seat belt had been properly retrieved and applied ('Thank you,

Brother!' she bleated, and, 'I'm so very sorry, Brother!'
Brother Linus, meanwhile, could be heard opining dryly that,
'The metal tip was sparking against the pebbles on the
driveway – I thought the whole van might suddenly ignite!'),
Miss Drury slammed the car into first gear and applied the
accelerator (with some considerable force), only to discover
(as we shot off the driveway and up on to the grass verge,
knocking over a temporary fence which had been constructed
by the monks to protect an area of newly laid turf) that she
had accidentally placed it into reverse.

Brother Linus was very understanding. Many kindly
platitudes were murmured (although I think he would've
happily said anything – literally *anything* – just to get us the
hell off the abbey grounds at this juncture).

I don't drive. I never learned. I just never really felt the
urge. But I am an expert at being driven (usually – I readily
admit – while inhabiting the vertical plane) and the experience
of being driven by Miss Drury was not a remotely relaxing or
a pleasurable one. In some ways I'm just grateful that I
couldn't actually see the road (ignorance is bliss!). Another
source of gratitude (while we're on the subject of gratitude)
was that I hadn't seen Brother Prosper (or that dratted child's
dratted fur coat) on the morning of my departure, either
(which, for those of you interested in such ephemera, was the
morning after the night before. Same as it generally is, I
suppose).

Ms Drury maintained what I can only really describe as a
constant trickling effluvium of chit-chat throughout the first
segment of our drive. She seemed ... I don't know ... *anxious*.
But it was difficult for me to concentrate on her feelings
because I was very much preoccupied by my own feelings at
this stage. My own feelings just seemed more ... more
important. Yes. Much more important. Than hers.

I was monosyllabic. I didn't really feel much inclined to
talk. And I knew that if I did (feel so inclined) I may well

have been obliged to discuss the fact that my buttocks remained, if not stuck together (I fear the doctor may have put paid to that with a sterilized scalpel while I was still out cold), then hugely swollen. No. I had no desire whatsoever to talk about the intensive Vaselining sessions (a quietly whistling Brother Anselm in a latex glove), the salt soaps, the mortifying 'wash downs', the strict no-solids diet. I had no desire to talk about those.

I was monosyllabic. Like I said.

Ms Drury made up for it, though. I was given a potted version of pretty much her entire life story, for starters. Born in Cork, strict Catholic upbringing, dreamed of one day becoming a veterinarian (her marks were good enough!) but got 'with child' at seventeen to her girlhood sweetheart, a boy with the curiously evocative name of Gabe Highly (highly what? I wonder. Disappointed? Sexed?). Her parents sent her to a special home for pregnant girls (with the intention of getting the child adopted once it arrived), but a couple of weeks before her due date, she absconded from the home and fled to England. Well, Wales. I forget the exact details of her epic journey (I was thinking about Miss Hahn at this stage. Miss Hahn's distinctively aristocratic nose). But blah blah ... she ended up in blah ... then blah ... and it really blah ... but she never blahed ... until she ... and then it was actually in her capacity as blah ... that she eventually met ... and Orla, Orla just *knew* ... (This is old territory. She told me about Orla just 'knowing' during our formal interview. But she didn't specify exactly what it was that Orla *knew* at that stage, only that Orla looked at her and she just ... just 'knew'.) Orla then told her that the Holy Virgin loved her 'most especially' because she too had suffered the indignity of a pregnancy out of wedlock (although – I say again – she didn't furnish me with these precise details during our interview). Ms Drury was naturally 'quite overwhelmed' by this demonstration of such immense wisdom and insight from so young a girl. Terribly disabled! But never complained! Just offered it all up! And she suddenly found herself, after many, many – too many! – years of self-hatred and guilt and consuming *shame*, somehow just miraculously … just *lifted*. Restored. *Healed.* There and then. In one instant. And experiencing a sudden urge, an eagerness to … to *love in return* the Merciful God whose Beloved Only Son's Most Holy and Sacred Heart had burned so keenly, so constantly, so relentlessly *for her*. Phew.

I think I got that all down.

Oh yes, and … blah blah … Orla had this astonishing … I can only call it a … a *gift* … a *genius* for drawing even the most forlorn and the most miserable, the most despised and the most utterly, *utterly* abandoned back into the loving arms of Mother Church. Yup. God apparently hosts a small party in heaven (sparkling wine, finger food) when the Most Lost and the Most Wretched return to him. Here follow lengthy quotations from the parable of the Prodigal Son etc.

I mean it feels unnecessarily cruel to call what Miss Drury was doing 'pointless wittering'. But it was. Kind of. Pointless. Wittering.

Next I had the full saga of the sick parrot. Baldo. Turns out the parrot was a *girl*! A *girl*! I didn't mention this (monosyllabic, remember?) but – believe it or not – I actually already knew. I have possessed the unusual ability to sex birds ever since I was a boy. My father kept a small aviary and I was never wrong about the gender of his newborns. In fact, I could often tell before hatching, simply by inspecting the egg. I suppose – if all else fails, and the import/export business finally goes belly-up – I could always fall back on a not-so-distinguished career in the battery hen farming industry. Hey-ho.

Finally (I mean we're talking a good hour and a quarter into an already perfectly interminable journey, and she has prattled on – *blethered* on – virtually non-stop throughout this entire interlude … okay, with one failed attempt to tune in the radio for the news), she started muttering about the fact that while she was praying for Carla in the abbey, she had been approached by an old monk in a wheelchair who was being pushed around by an equally old monk (I have no idea as to the identity of this second old monk, but someone called Brother Symeon aka Brother 'Hard of Hearing' [*sic*] was referred to, sidelong, several times in my presence during my short stay in the sanatorium) who told her that she needed to: 'Trust him, my dear. Even though your *every natural instinct* fights against it. *Trust* him. The child told me most particularly to tell you that.' Then he tapped his nose, apparently.

What?!

Even though your *every natural instinct* ...?!

Followed, three seconds later, by:

'Sorry ... I ... sorry but when you were ... you just said that when you were *praying* for ... when you were *praying* for ... for Carla? For Miss Hahn? Isn't that what you ...?'

Silence.

'Miss Drury?'

Silence.

'Miss Drury?'

Miss Drury suddenly pulled the van off the road, rested her forehead on the steering wheel and burst into noisy tears. I was unable to comfort her due to lying on the diagonal (I really was jammed like a peg into that tiny space). So I just said, 'Please don't cry like that, Miss Drury!' (Quite tenderly at first.) Then (a couple of minutes later) I said, 'If you could just find some *other* way of expressing your emotion that was slightly more constructive and fractionally less irritating ...' Okay. I didn't. Okay. I did. But I said it with a smile in my voice. Honestly.

Eventually Miss Drury calmed herself down and after blowing her nose on some clean rags kept in the storage pocket of her door, she half turned.

'I've been trying to keep a lid on it, Mr Huff. I knew that if I
... if I referred to what's been going on back in Pett Level, I
probably wouldn't be able to ... to negotiate the road.'
'A lid?' I echoed.
'Carla ... Miss Hahn is currently missing, presumed dead.
Half of her bungalow fell into the sea. Late last night. I
received a call from Rusty – Clifford – at about half past one
this morning. Then another call at five. In between times I
hardly slept a wink. He said Air, Land and Sea Rescue had
been at the site for hours but there was still no sign of her ...'

   'And he was absolutely certain that Miss Hahn was at home
when this occurred?' I snapped.
'The TV had been left on. He rang Shimmy – Carla's dad –
and Shimmy said she'd definitely headed home a couple of
hours earlier. But he also said – Rusty, I mean – that her bike
wasn't on the lawn where she usually leaves it. But the garage
was gone. And sometimes, if it's raining, she puts her bike
into the garage.'
'Was it raining?' I asked.
Silence.
'WAS IT RAINING, MISS DRURY?!!' I bellowed.
'It was pouring down in Hythe,' she sniffed.

   I rested my cheek on the blue sheet in the Woolworth's bag
for a second to try and process this sudden, overwhelming
glut of information.
I had no sense, in myself, in my ... in my *soul* that Miss Hahn
was dead. Gone. None. In fact I had been conducting a
curiously convivial little conversation with Miss Hahn over the
past several days. My mind would tentatively reach out ...
Miss Hahn? And then I would receive a tart response. She
would say things like, 'You look utterly ridiculous, Mr Huff!'
or 'Perhaps you should be slightly more grateful for that!' or 'I
would be frightened too, if I were you. But not quite as
much.'

And then I would feel better. Or worse. Depending on what she had said.

In fact she had called Brother Prosper, 'A big lumbering old moose!' And then she had tucked her hair behind her ear and had commented ruminatively on the full moon. She knows a lot about the stars. More than most girls generally do.

'You think she's dead?' I lifted my head again.

OF *COURSE* SHE ISN'T DEAD, FRANKLIN!

'I don't know.' Miss Drury's voice broke.

'Just answer me – quickly, instinctively,' I persisted. 'Do you think she's dead?'

OF *COURSE* SHE ISN'T DEAD, FRANKLIN!

'They called a priest,' she sniffed. 'He said the last rites over the—'

'That's not what I'm asking, Miss Drury!' I hissed.

Miss Drury was silent for a second, and then, 'Yes. I think I do.'

'Well I don't,' I growled.

Miss Drury half turned to look at me. 'You don't?'

'No.'

OF *COURSE* SHE ISN'T!

It may be helpful to add at this point that the more emphatically I stated that Miss Hahn wasn't dead the less certain I became (deep within) that she had survived. Which I suppose says something moderately interesting about the connection between language and the emotions. Although I'm damned if I have the time or the inclination to think about all that right now/possibly ever.

We sat together in silence for several more minutes while Miss Drury struggled to regain her equilibrium. I was signally incapable of regaining mine.

OF *COURSE* SHE ISN'T DEAD!

Get a grip on yourself, Mr Huff! Miss Hahn chastised me.

Because while at one level I knew that the death of Miss Hahn might make forgetting her easier ('Out of sight, out of mind' etc.) ... (Miss Hahn said nothing at this, merely rolled her eyes, drolly) ... on another, I worried that it might actually make it *harder*, dammit (that dangerous capacity we foolish men have to idealize the fairer sex etc.)!

We hit the road again. Miss Drury was very quiet.

OF *COURSE* SHE ISN'T DEAD!

I – for my part – felt an indescribable need, a compulsion, to speak about Miss Hahn. Even to just ... to just ... to say her name out loud. That was all. Just to say her name. As if uttering her name might almost be enough to make her corporeal, give her ghostly self a little extra substance, temporarily ...

Substance?! Miss Hahn chuckled, wryly. *But I never had any substance in the first place, Mr Huff!*

'Carla Hahn, Carla Hahn, Carla Hahn,' I found myself murmuring.

OF *COURSE* SHE ISN'T DEAD!

Oh dear, Miss Hahn sighed.

'When Clifford first told me I just ... I felt like my legs would give way,' Miss Drury suddenly started up again (as if she too might be suffering from the same compulsion), 'like it simply didn't make any ... it wasn't *possible*. Then I suddenly found myself thinking, But it's so terribly fitting, Alys! It's so terribly ... so terribly *fitting!*' She shook her head, horrified, plainly consumed by guilt at harbouring such ideas.

OF *COURSE* SHE ISN'T!

'Because of the Clearys?' I asked, slightly bemused.

Oh, here we go again! Miss Hahn snorted.

'I mean I was constantly trying to undermine her sense of ... of connection with the Cleary family,' Miss Drury confided. 'I just didn't think it was healthy. Either she needed to embrace it fully, you know, *embrace* it – fully – spiritually – and celebrate it, openly, or ... or just forget about it and move on. But instead she insisted on living in this ... in a kind of ... I

suppose you could call it a kind of "emotional purgatory".
She just didn't seem capable of—'
OF *COURSE* SHE ISN'T!

'Perhaps if you drove me straight to the airport ...' I
interrupted.
You don't have any money for a ticket, Mr Huff! Miss Hahn
chuckled. *You returned the stupid envelope, remember?*

Yes. *Yes.* The airport. If those idiotic executors of
Kimberly's estate would just ... just pull their damn fingers
out and make that deposit into my bank account so that I
could ... So that I could just ... just jump on to the next
available flight and ... and *leave*. Run off. Cut all connections.
Move on. Never know for sure that she was ... that she might
not ... Eliminate all certainty and thereby eliminate any need
to ... to suffer ... to mourn ... to ...
IS SHE REALLY DEAD?!
Make a ridiculous amount of fuss! Miss Hahn chastised.

'Sorry?' Miss Drury was confused.
'To lose the two of them in a single week?!' I garbled. 'It
makes no sense! I mean statistically. It makes no sense at all!'
IS SHE REALLY DEAD?!
Do you understand statistics, Mr Huff? Miss Hahn wondered.
*Because I always thought strange improbabilities were pretty much
par for the course ...*

Oh why oh why did I burn those stupid photographs? I
pushed my nose into the Woolworth's bag and slowly ground
my teeth.
That's quite the most horrible habit, Mr Huff! Miss Hahn
clucked reprovingly.
IS SHE? REALLY? REALLY *DEAD*?!
Was it ... was this all *my* fault? Did *I* do this? By spitefully
trying to eliminate her 'truth' from the narrative ...?
The truth is the truth, Mr Huff! Miss Hahn snapped. *It can't be
falsified. It's like a ...* her voice softened slightly, *a shining light.*

An eternal verity. The truth is ... well it's ... it's God, I suppose. If you choose to believe in such ephemera.

No. *No!* Stop self-dramatizing, Franklin! I agonized. So you burned a couple of photographs? Big deal! You've still got the negatives back in Canada, haven't you? They're *yours* now, you idiot!

'She once told me that the first time she ever met Orla, Orla took a hold of her hand, looked deep into her eyes and whispered ...'

'*Orla!*' I all but choked on the name, then smacked my forehead, repeatedly, into the Woolworth's bag.

Not sodding *Orla* again!

CARLA HAHN IS DEAD! SHE'S DEAD! SHE'S DEAD!

'... "There's a bruise,"' Miss Drury persisted. 'She said, "I see a terrible bruise – a bleeding – hidden, deep under the skin, held in, which has spread throughout the whole of your life. It started in Germany. It started with your mother and it has continued to throb and to sting and to darken and to consume your whole family ..."'

'An eleven-year-old girl said *that*?!' I snorted.

DEAD!

Out of the mouths of babes! Miss Hahn sighed.

'Yes.' Miss Drury nodded. 'But then Orla understood Carla, instinctively. "I understand how you feel," she said, "right here, in my heart. Because my family is marked by exactly the same stain."'

DEAD! DEAD! DEAD!

'Pardon?'

I lifted my head, mystified.

Oh, do try and keep up, Mr Huff! Miss Hahn grumbled.

'I don't suppose they even called it "rape" back then,' Miss Drury mused. 'The native women on those huge, isolated farmsteads had no real choice in the matter. I suppose they were just expected to tolerate it. To accept it and even be grateful – *honoured*. He was her boss. And he was already

369

married. That's why, after Kalinda was born, they nicknamed
her "Lonely", because none of the natives would speak to her.
And none of the whites, either. None of the other farm kids
would ever play with her. It made her very ... very defiant.
Angry. Self-reliant. The virtual opposite of darling Carla.'
DEAD! DEAD! DEAD! DEAD! DEAD! DEAD! *DEAD!*
I lowered my head again and rested my cheek on the
Woolworth's bag. My throbbing mind turned to Brother
Prosper.
That poor, dear, grumpy old Moose! Carla murmured.
    'I mean people gossip about Carla and Bran,' Miss Drury
tutted. 'Behind her back. I know they do. They always have.
About this so-called "great attraction" between the two of
them. And I know she sometimes ... she posed for him. As a
favour. But the real connection wasn't with Bran at *all*. It was
with his wife. It was with Kalinda. Because they had so much
in common. They were both cultural exiles. And Orla could
see that. She brought them together, purposely. To console
each other.'
AND NOW IT'S FINALLY ALL OVER! BECAUSE SHE'S
DEAD! SHE'S DEAD! SHE'S DEAD! DEAD! DEAD!
DEAD!
    I lifted my head again.
'Miss Drury, does this Woolworth's bag belong to your
son-in-law?' I asked.
Of course it doesn't! Miss Hahn clucked.
'Sorry?' Miss Drury quickly glanced back.
DEAD! *YES!* DEAD!
'This Woolworth's bag. Was it here – in the van – when you
first ...?'
'Oh. Uh ... No. No, I don't remember seeing it there before
...' she confessed.
I lowered my head again and jinked it sideways to try and
push open the bag a little with my chin.

'Are you all right there, Mr Huff?' Miss Drury asked, a minute or so later, concerned at the sound of teeth tearing furiously on plastic.

Good question! Carla snorted.

I paused for a moment to draw breath.

SHE'S DEAD!

'So did Carla grow up always knowing that she was the product of ... of ... *you* know?' I asked, before returning to my former task.

Spit it out! Miss Hahn scoffed.

'Oh. Uh, I'm not really sure.' Miss Drury scowled. 'Yes. Probably. I mean I didn't know her as a girl. And it isn't something she ever talks about in any detail. But I do think she always sensed she wasn't ... she didn't fit comfortably into ... well anywhere, really. And of course the family were already slightly ostracized socially because of it being just after the war and Shimmy and Else being German originally. I get the impression that there was a bit of a ... a *bunker* mentality at home. And then Else's job with the Planning Office ... The beach and the marshes were completely covered in illegal holiday shacks back then. But the council was determined to get rid of the squatters. Else became quite a local hate figure as a consequence. Loathed by some, a heroine to others ... I suppose your heart has to go out to her with everything she went through. Although I saw her treat Shimmy and poor Carla with such ... such incredible contempt sometimes. She could be brutal. And Shimmy himself isn't immune from ... He can be very selfish, Mr Huff, and insensitive. Carla probably internalized it all over the years. Possibly even felt a measure of ...'

Oh do shut up, Alys! Carla snapped. Then she quickly apologized: *Sorry, Alys!*

POOR, DEAR MISS HAHN IS ... IS *DEAD*!

I – meanwhile – had torn open the bag and pulled the blue sheet (actually more of a tea towel) partially aside with my nose and my teeth. Yes. Oh yes. I had managed to do that quite successfully.

Well done, Mr Huff! Miss Hahn kindly congratulated me.

SHE'S DEAD!

Hmmn. I don't suppose I need to describe in *too* much detail what I found balled up inside, eh? Hidden beneath?

'Drat!' I exclaimed.

Gracious me! Miss Hahn gasped, then burst into peals of delighted laughter.

'Mr Huff?' Miss Drury half turned, frowning.

'Drat! Drat!' I repeated.

The coat! Miss Hahn cheered.

'Mr Huff? Are you sure you're all right back there?'

Yes! The coat! Orla's coat! Orla's sodding ... the sodding *coat*.

The coat! Miss Hahn repeated.

AAARGH! JUST GIVE IT A *REST*, MISS HAHN, WILL YOU? YOU'RE DEAD, YOU INFERNAL CREATURE! DEAD! DEAD! *DEAD!*

REMEMBER?

36

Miss Carla Hahn

I suppose my abiding impression of being dead, and (like Rogue – or other still more lofty antecedents) suddenly returning back to life again, is that there's quite a lot of apologizing to be done afterwards. It would be foolish (intensely foolish – naive even) to think the aftermath was all untrammelled joy and popping champagne corks. The standard response (in my experience) is generally one of inarticulate rage. Pique. Irritation.

And some people are deeply suspicious. They think you might even have set the whole thing up *on purpose*. To get attention (Oh yes, yes, I engineered a massive landslip and then ran away and just ... just *hid*. Out of ... out of pure *spite*. Or an unbridled sense of mischief! Or simply as an experiment. To see if I'd be missed. Which – so far as I can tell – I wasn't. Miss-ing, yes, but ... but missed? *Missed?* Um. No.).

Shimmy was incandescent! He even went so far as to refuse me access to the house. 'So selfish, *bubbellah!*' he screeched through the letterbox. '*Oi! Ze stress! Und* zat *golem* brings me ze skim *melk! Skim!* Is he *crayzee*?! How's a *mensch* to drink hiz *cafe*, *bubbellah!* Wiz zis skim *melk?* Wiz no *creeem*, *bubbellah!* Eh? *Eh?!*'

I actually got the distinct impression that some people (zat *golem*, Clifford Bickerton, for one) might even have preferred it if I'd remained ...

What was I? What had I been? Submerged? Crushed? Swept away? Or simply …

Just … just lost.

Lost.

Which is funny.

Because I've never really been 'found' so far as I can tell. I've *never* been 'found'! I've never felt 'found'. I've always been strangely absent. Or present but not … not entirely adequate. The wrong fit. Part of a faulty batch. Except, perhaps …

'Offer it up,' a little voice whispered.

And I was just starting to think about doing exactly that (If I 'offer it up' will I be able to … I don't know … to pass it on? And so finally stop …?) when Mrs Barrow stormed into the kitchen (clutching a large box of sea salt, several old newspapers and an industrial-sized container of a generic, petroleum-based baby emollient), in the most revolting temper.

'I'll never get over it so long as I lives!' she exclaimed. 'Not nor Mr Barrow neither, come to that! Pretendin' as if you was dead an' gone, Carla Hahn! Sending all them poor folk foolish enough to give a hoot about you quite doolally!'

'I wasn't *pretending* anything, Mrs Barrow,' (I commenced a pathetic attempt to defend myself) 'I was just sitting outside on the balcony, waiting to have a word with Mr Huff …' I pointed, poignantly. 'And I honestly had no idea – *none* – that the bungalow in Fairlight …'

'I came straight over an' searched this place myself!' Mrs Barrow insisted. 'I even gave that there poor rabbit a carrot.' She pointed – with a folded-up newspaper – at the rabbit who (Oh dear. First blood to the Prosecutor!) was still in cheerful possession of a good half of said vegetable, then tossed the paper towards me, contemptuously (intending that I replace the old used stuff, I suppose).

'I was *here*, Mrs Barrow,' I insisted (kneeling down to do her bidding).

Mrs Barrow just scowled.

'Although ...' I grimaced, trying to piece it all together as I lifted the fireguard off the rabbit and quickly grabbed it, 'my bike had a slow puncture, so I came down from Fairlight mostly on foot. Maybe I hadn't even made it to the cottage by the time you ...?'

'The whole sky awash with searchlights!' Mrs Barrow exclaimed. 'We've not seen nothing like it around these parts since the war! An' poor Rusty blubbin' his heart out on the phone at all hours. Your poor dad in hysterics I shouldn't wonder! Mr Barrow up at dawn trawlin' the beaches searching for your battered corpse. Shame on you, Carla Hahn!'

'I really am very sorry, Mrs Barrow,' I sighed, kissing a rabbit ear (trying to dispel the curious image of my corpse preserved – for all eternity – in a lightly fried cornflour coating).

'Well that's as been a most *scandalous* waste of time and energy!' Mrs Barrow persisted. 'A *scandalous* waste!'

'I'm very sorry, Mrs Barrow,' I repeated (mushy peas, giant portion of chips. A vinegar bottle the size of a carthorse to the side ...).

'Can you imagine what all that dreadful commotion will've cost the local taxpayer?' Mrs Barrow wondered. 'An' what if some *other* poor soul in mortal danger had been in want of them *same* human resources, but they was all took up by searching for such as the likes of *you*, Carla Hahn?!'

'That would've been a terrible tragedy,' I conceded, standing up and plopping the rabbit into a large mixing bowl.

'Some *real* emergency. Like a fire in a care-home. Or a gas explosion on a maternity ward. Or a boat full of disadvantaged little 'uns on a sightseeing trip suddenly capsizes!'

'An awful thought.' I nodded, preparing to replace the paper on the floor and then thinking better of it (Clifford had gone to the trouble of bringing the new hutch over, after all).

'Imagine as those little kiddies paddling around in them crashing waves, barely able to stay afloat, an' all the searchlights is off looking for you! Or else all the necessary funds is dried up so's they can't *affords* them to mount a proper search when the disaster finally strikes!'

'Perhaps the national government might consider stepping in and offering support ...' I suggested, moving the carrot and the little water bowl out of harm's way.

'Imagine them poor mothers weeping their eyes out all the ways along the sea wall.' Mrs Barrow walked to the window, picturing the scene. 'Our local sailing boats settin' out in bad weather, determined to play their part. But it's pitch dark out there, Carla. An' those disadvantaged kiddies will only last a few minutes in them icy waves, at most.'

'Horrible,' I confirmed, starting to roll up the dirty paper.

Mrs Barrow slowly shook her head, struggling to digest the full ramifications of this (let's be honest) perfectly demented scenario.

'I even as saw Sorcha Jennett lighting up some special mourning pyre right in the middle of the blackthorn earlier!' Mrs Barrow scoffed. 'In *your* honour! Surrounded by cameras, she was. Mrs Brightling was furious about it – even allowing for your only recently having passed, Carla! A terrible fire hazard she said it was! And all that infernal singing and dancing! An' those feral kids of hers jumping about banging their little drums and the smoke going all over her clean washing!'

'Oh dear.' I cringed, carrying the scrunched-up newspaper over to the kitchen bin and gently lifting the lid with the tips of my fingers.

'I went up to her myself as it happens an' I says, "Sorcha," I says, "I wouldn't be troubling yourself overmuch about Carla

Hahn, given as that she's only been hiding up at Mulberry, happy as Larry, while all the rest of us fools has gone mad with upset at the thought of her bungalow falling off a cliff!'"

'The bungalow did still fall off a cliff,' I murmured, shoving the paper into the bin, but the bin – alas – was almost full to capacity and so it wouldn't quite fit.

'It wasn't as even *your* bungalow, Carla!' Mrs Barrow was suitably indignant. 'Imagine as what terrible pranks you could of pulled on us all if it *had* been!'

'So how ... how did Sorcha Jennett react to the news?' I wondered (refusing to engage with this harrowing new example of Mrs Barrow's extraordinarily round-about logic) while trying to force the paper down with a shove which merely – in turn – dislodged the bin-lid.

'Well she as laughed her head off!' Mrs Barrow harrumphed. 'Then sang a hymn of thanksgiving, an' then give them filthy kiddies a pound to go get 'em some marshmallows to toast on the fire. A right little pow-wow it ended up! I'm surprised as you didn't hear it. It's been drivin' everyone in the Coastguards' round the twist for the past nigh-on two hour!'

I nodded (quietly satisfied that the children, at least, had benefited positively from my unexpected return to the Land of the Living), then crouched down and removed the paper, adjusted the lid and tried to shove it back in again. At this moment the doorbell rang (which struck me as curious, given that the doorbell never rang because of a fault with the wiring).

'A person might almost think as the whole thing had been set up for the benefit of them pesky cameras!' Mrs Barrow muttered, going off to answer it.

'I don't think even Sorcha's generous filming budget would stretch to the demolition of a small bungalow,' I called after her, trying to flatten the paper slightly so that the flip-top lid might still flip. It was then, as I smoothed the paper, that I happened upon …

'A telegram for Mr Huff!' Mrs Barrow returned. 'Ought we to open it in case it be somethin' urgent?'

I scowled and stood up. The tiny rabbit made several heroic attempts to jump out of the mixing bowl, but the surface was too shiny for its little paws to grip.

'It might be private,' I said, heading out on to the porch where the hutch now sat, a clean bag of straw leaning up against it. I gazed at the straw. What an immensely kind person Clifford was. To provide the straw like that. Without even being asked. So thoughtful. So considerate. Even after … even when … even considering …

Mrs Barrow followed me out on to the balcony. 'I suppose as your dear friend Miss Drury will've been worrying herself into a thin paste all day on your account,' she grumbled, 'drivin' her son-in-law's old window-cleaner's van halfway across the country to collect Mr Huff from that monastery.'

'Sorry?'

I turned.

'She took her son-in-law's van so's Mr Huff could lie his'self in the back,' Mrs Barrow expanded.

'But why would Mr Huff need Alys Drury to …?'

'On account of his buttocks sealing up of course!' Mrs Barrow exclaimed.

'His …?'

'Buttocks! The monks told Miss Drury as they'd sealed right up. With all of the blisters. After his long walk. They had to cut 'em apart. And now he can't so much as move.'

I knelt down, opened the hutch, spread out some of the clean newspaper and then covered it over with a couple of handfuls of the straw.

'Poor Mr Huff!' I finally managed, through tight lips (after approximately a minute of frenzied activity).

I could feel Mrs Barrow's disapproving eyes fixed upon me from the rear. My shoulders were so stiff and so high that my head nestled between them like a boiled egg in a plastic eggcup.

'Mrs Drury said as Mr Huff had fainted clean away and was out cold for five, straight hours,' she said.

I sprang to my feet and dashed past Mrs Barrow (face turned to the wall so she couldn't see my cheeks streaming with hysterical tears), heading back into the cottage to fetch the rabbit.

'All's he can do is eat soup and lie flat on his belly!' Mrs Barrow called after me.

My nose (on account of my lips being so firmly sealed) emitted a fearful snort.

'STOP LAUGHING, CARLA!' Mrs Barrow boomed. 'THERE'S NOTHING FUNNY ABOUT A POOR MAN'S BUTTOCKS SEALING!'

It was at this moment – of course it was, yes, yes of *course* it was – that I apprehended a scowling, ghostly pale Mr Huff (strung between a panting Mr Barrow and an exhausted-seeming darling Alys), being half carried, half dragged up the hallway to his bed.

'Carla! Thank God!' Alys exclaimed (embarrassed *and* astonished). 'Mr Barrow was just telling us ...'

'Yes. Alive.' I nodded, wiping the mirthful tears from my cheeks with my flattened palms (but not my deranged grin, alas), then, 'You have a telegram, Mr Huff,' then, 'Sorry,' I added (as an afterthought), 'for any, you know, distress caused.' I shoved my hair behind my ears. 'I always laugh when I'm terribly upset,' I explained. 'It's just a ... a nervous reaction, that's all.'

'I recently read how scientists believe the *cockroach* to be the only living creature capable of surviving the ravages of a nuclear holocaust,' Mr Huff murmured, eyes blazing.

'Yes. I read that too.' I nodded. Then I grabbed the ball of rabbit paper from the bin, pushed past Mrs Barrow for a second time, and made as rapid an exit as I possibly could – still grinning, madly – through the back porch.

37

Mr Franklin D. Huff

What really worried me was the way that the voice in my head didn't match with the real voice of Carla Hahn. They didn't match because the voice in my head continued to tell me things even when the actual Carla Hahn was telling me something entirely at odds with them.

Okay, that wasn't what really worried me. What really worried me was how incredibly *hurt* ... how incredibly *wounded* ... how incredibly *emasculated* I'd felt on finally entering my home – my *home*, yes? My *retreat*, my *refuge*! – after an incredibly fruitless and exhausting and confusing and disorientating and ... and ... *traumatic* interlude, only to hear Mrs Barrow yelling out ... you know ... and then to see her, *her*, Carla Hahn, just ... just grinning hysterically like some big, ugly, red-cheeked blonde monkey. So undignified. So cruel. So utterly ...

And she wasn't even dead! Carla Hahn *wasn't* dead. It was all just a vindictive lie! And I'd barely even had a chance to reconcile myself to the fact that ...

You knew I wasn't dead! Carla Hahn snorted. *I told you I wasn't dead, didn't I?*

Short pause.

And I'm very sorry that I laughed at you. But it is quite funny. In the abstract. For a person's buttocks to seal. It really is quite funny. You know, just ... just in the abstract.

'Indestructible!' I muttered. 'She's indestructible! Like a cockroach!'

'Pardon me, Mr Huff?' Mrs Barrow straightened up, one giant rubber-gloved hand slick and shiny with a thick coating of glossy emollient.

Okay, yes, *yes*, funny, perhaps, but only in the sense of a strictly vulgar, bawdy, lowest-common-denominator kind of …

Miss Hahn was like one of those dreadfully unamusing Shakespearean knockabout characters – a fool or a tradesman or a rustic – whose jokes are all obscene puns which nobody really understands but which the 'modern thesp' tries to articulate by dint of a series of desperately lewd thrusts and grunts and gurning gestures.

'An' I'll as say it ag'in, Mr Huff,' Mrs Barrow grumbled, 'these sheets is not what I'd call hygienic. And your pyjamas have got a red stain on the elastic which if I didn't as know better I would say was like lipstick.'

An especially noxious shade, too, Miss Hahn observed.

'Don't be ridiculous!' I snorted.

Mrs Barrow handed the bottoms over with her spare un-gloved, un-unguent-ed hand, then marched off to the bathroom.

I inspected the bottoms. Oh. Yes. How odd. That did look like lipstick. And the shade *was* rather noxious.

Ha! Miss Hahn *ha!*-ed.

'Will you be wanting a bowl of the soup?' Mrs Barrow called through. 'I reckon as it should be warm by now.'

'I don't really think I could manage anything, Mrs Barrow,' I responded, somewhat plaintively.

Mrs Barrow (never a woman to take no for an answer) brought the soup through in a small bowl.

'Shall I as spoon it in for you?' she asked.

'If you balance it carefully on the bedside table I should probably be able to cope,' I sighed.

She balanced it on the table then took the precaution of placing a tea towel over my pillow.

'I'm not a child, Mrs Barrow!' I grumbled, then took the spoon, lifted it out of the bowl, and promptly spilled soup over the cloth.

Congratulations! Miss Hahn trilled.

It was simply a problem with the angles.

I took another spoonful, cursing, and promptly spilled that over the cloth, too.

Third time lucky! Miss Hahn chortled.

'Well I'll as leave you to it, Mr Huff,' Mrs Barrow purred, smiling grimly (I don't think I've ever *seen* Mrs Barrow smile before), 'I can see as how you've got everything under control.'

Then off she waddled.

As soon as she was out of the room, I applied my lips to the dropped soup. It was a curious pink colour. And fishy. I sucked and then winced. I wasn't entirely sure it was ... that it should ... that it hadn't ... hadn't 'turned'. Was that ... (I sucked my teeth, thoughtfully) oh dear ... beetroot?! Aniseed?!

'I as forgot to bring you your telegram, Mr Huff!' Mrs Barrow had silently re-materialized in the room, meanwhile, damn her. She was holding out a telegram.

Oooh. A telegram! Miss Hahn exclaimed. *How exciting!*

'Could you possibly ...' I rotated my hand. She tore off the end of the envelope, removed the contents and passed them over.

Thank you, Mrs Barrow! Miss Hahn cordially thanked Mrs Barrow.

I took the small sheet of paper and inspected it. The executors of Kimberly's estate had finally made the necessary financial transfer! And this was the confirmation! What a relief!

Thank you, Mrs Barrow! Miss Hahn repeated, tartly.

Mrs Barrow had temporarily left the room (She's left the room! I told Miss Hahn, crossly) but then she suddenly reappeared in the doorway again holding out the Woolworth's bag.

Thank you, Mrs Barrow! Miss Hahn sang.

'What will you as have me do with this old bag?' Mrs Barrow asked, wincing fastidiously. 'It was left over by the bin. Is it meant for the rubbish, Mr Huff?'
'N ...' I started off, and then, 'Thank you, Mrs Barrow!' I sang (incredibly heartfelt). 'Thank you *very much*, Mrs Barrow,' I repeated (just in case she hadn't heard me the first time around).

Mrs Barrow grunted and exited (she isn't in this for the thanks. D'you *hear* that, Miss Hahn? Eh? She isn't *in* this for the thanks. Nope. And I knew that. I *knew* that. Mrs Barrow and I really have established quite a bond).

Miss Hahn emitted a sound which I can only really describe as a combination of a squeak and a growl.
I blithely ignored it and picked up my spoon again to try for another mouthful of the disgusting soup. This time, though, instead of just tipping it on to the pillow I somehow managed to ... to knock my elbow into the bedside table so that the spoonful of soup flew ... It flew. Quite literally. Straight into my face.
Gloop!

The inside of your head is so gloomy ... Miss Hahn quietly mused, *like a filthy old storeroom in a disused museum. Full of strange objects covered in brown paper and cracked display cases and ancient dust-cloths ... It really does need a good ...*

I suddenly felt an unbearable tickling sensation in my sinuses.
'Thank you very much, Mrs Barrow!' I bellowed. Really, really loudly. Purely out of spite, I suppose.
Then I sneezed.
Then I smelled an incredibly strong blast of eucalyptus.
Then I ... *hic*! I ... *hic*! Then I ... *hic*! ... I *hic*! ... I *hic*! ... Then I *hic*! ... I ... *hic*! ... Oh you ... *hic*! ... know ... *hic*! ... what I ... *hic*! ... don't ... *hic*! ... don't ... *hic*! ... don't you?

38

Miss Carla Hahn

I walked into Rye. I didn't have any money for the bus (my purse was in Fairlight. In the bungalow. Or not in the bungalow). I didn't have anything, in fact. Only the piece of old newspaper, a nagging hunch and that inane grin which was still plastered right across my face. But it wasn't a happy grin. Or even a cruel grin. It was a kind of a ... a safety valve. A necessary release. It was the only thing holding all this ... all this *stuff* in. Holding me together (that crazy tension – each side of my mouth). I suppose if (like, say, Mr Huff), you were given to bouts of chronic over-self-dramatization you might even call it a 'deadly' grin.

Because when I saw that piece of old newspaper (how old was it – a week?), I suddenly realized that it had all happened – all of it, every, little bit of it, even the *rabbit* – for a reason. Everything was interconnected. We were all chosen. We. *Us.* You know – the dregs. The pointless. The flawed. The unconvinced. The least worthy in many respects. Just like Sorcha had said. We were all chosen. Because majesty shines most brightly through ... through frailty, I suppose. Through failure. Through weakness.

But I still found it perplexing – almost *perverse.* To choose a group of the least good, least functional, least hopeful, least ... least reverential individuals to fulfil a mission so ... so unknowable, so ... so ...

So it had all happened for a reason. Hadn't it? But even worse than that (far, far worse than that), I had finally realized (didn't I *always* know? Yes? No? Didn't I?) that I was stupidly, *excruciatingly* in love with Mr Franklin D. Huff. That awful man! That skinny, sneaky, arrogant, strange, slightly unstable and patently unreliable aspirant Lothario ...

Or *was* it actually love? How to describe the feeling, exactly? Hard to pin it down ... A kind of squint-eyed keenness. An infuriated interest. A passionate irritation. A midge-bite on my heart which I just longed to scratch and itch and pick away at until it finally got infected and then ... then *hurt. Stung.* Most dreadfully.

If that is love. If that qualifies as love (and I'm hardly much of an expert in these matters) then yes, *yes*, I was in it, right up to my chin, and the one thing I was certain of (before I'd even got to grips with it, before I'd even ... I don't know ... so much as teased away at it with an idle nail), the one thing I truly *knew* (a feeling of indescribably hollow dread deep down in my gut) was that I was going to be asked to give him up. To offer him up. To hand him over to Mrs Sage Meadows, no less. For Orla. For my sins.

'Good heavens!' Sage Meadows exclaimed, answering the door at Lamb House after my third extended ring on the bell. 'I thought you were ... Didn't your bungalow just ...?'
I handed her the piece of newspaper.
'Would you mind explaining this to me, Mrs Meadows?' I asked, pointing to the four digits. 'In a little more detail, perhaps?'

'I heard about it on the local news!' She grabbed my arm (as if to check that I was real). 'It was all the talk on the Wednesday market! Was it terrible? I could hardly believe it. I was all a-tingle! I kept thinking, But I was only with her a few hours ago ...!'

'I wasn't home when it happened,' I said. 'I actually stayed in Pett Level overnight.'
'With your father?' she asked, sharply, quickly releasing her grip on my arm.

'Uh ... My father's dog had died,' I quickly sidestepped the issue.

'Oh. Well that was lucky.'

She frowned. 'I mean unfortunate, but, you know ...'

'Yes. He was very fat. Rogue. The dog. He slipped into a diabetic coma.'

'Oh. I see. I'm very sorry to hear that.'

'Yes.' I nodded.

She continued to gaze at me, perplexed.

'We had to dig him a very big ... a very big hole,' I aimlessly expanded.

'What an eventful twenty-four hours you've had!' she exclaimed, almost satisfied, inviting me inside, pouring me a glass of water and then leading me out into the garden where the air was redolent with the scent of ... of ...

'Do you smell that?' I asked, spooked.

'It's wintergreen' – she nodded – 'and thyme and eucalyptus. The gardener's been burning them. Smoking them. He thought there might be early signs of a Varroa mite infestation in the hive.'

She pointed to a small, old, white WBC hive in the far corner of the garden.

Mrs Meadows (I noted, with a small twinge of irritation) currently looked quite lovely – a good ten years younger than she usually did, because she wasn't yet (I quote her guilty admission) 'in full make-up'.

We sat down on a bench and she inspected the piece of paper again, frowning.

The borders were charming. They were buzzing. And there was a little hole in Mrs Meadows's tights over her big toe. A slightly chipped painted nail poked out through it – on her right foot – which was only visible when she slid it from her leather clog and employed it to scratch her opposite calf. She was wearing glasses, too: large, heavy, tortoiseshell glasses.

What a strange, pointlessly feminine and formal creature she was, I mused, but yet underneath it – the uptightness, the hairspray, the polished veneer – something half-formed and musky, something organic and interesting, quietly throbbing and pulsing, like a delicate little mollusc – a freshwater bivalve – tucked quietly away inside its shell.

Hmmn. Was there actually more to Mrs Meadows than I had initially reckoned on? Was this to be *all* about Mrs Meadows from here on in? Mrs Meadows? Who two days ago had seemed – well, insignificant? Excess to requirements. A mere frill?

'4.0.0.4?' I prompted, clearing my throat, irritated, at myself – by my changing perceptions, I suppose (was I starting to try and see my way towards ... towards *loving* Mrs Meadows now, like Mr Huff eventually would?).

'It's a central processing unit chip,' she explained, 'or a microprocessor, which is part of a family of four chips called the MCS.4. The MCS.4 basically consists of the "four thousand four" – as it's generally known – alongside a supporting read-only memory chip – which we call a ROM – for custom applications, a random access memory chip – which we call a RAM – for processing data, then finally a shift register chip for the IO port ...' Her eyes kept on scanning the borders, worriedly, as she spoke, then returning to the beehive a short distance off.

Of course I didn't have the first clue what she was talking about.

'A chip,' I said.

'Yes. Intel originally designed the four thousand four for the Nippon Calculating Machine Corporation in the late sixties,' she expanded, 'they manufactured calculators, of course. But then they quickly realized – Intel, I mean – the chip's amazing potential for universal applications, so they bought it back again and relaunched it in 1971, and that's when it became the first general-purpose programmable processor on the market. A simple building block for engineers ...'

'But what does the 4.0.0.4 actually *do*?' I wondered.
'Well a memory chip is sort of like the computer's brain. It's very tiny – the size of your smallest fingernail – but incredibly powerful. You'll find one at the heart of everything and anything digital: super-computers, data-centres, communications products ...'

She suddenly smiled. 'You know I was actually very ... very *struck* by something that you said to me the other day, Miss Hahn.'

'Something *I* said?' I echoed, slightly bemused.
'Yes. When I mentioned my half-finished Ph.D. in Undecidable Problems. And you said, "But why don't you simply concentrate on the problems that you *can* make a decision about?"'

'I said that?'
'Yes. And at the time I just thought, What an idiot – she doesn't even grasp what an Undecidable Problem *is*, but then later ...' – she grinned – 'when I was under the misguided impression that you'd toppled into the sea, and I was dissecting the conversation we'd had previously in much greater detail – imbuing it with so much more significance on account of your being ... you know ... dead, I thought, She's right. Why always focus on the things that *can't* be decided? That's always been my problem – my Achilles heel. Emotionally, intellectually. Focusing on the undecidable – love, chemistry, loss, attraction – when in fact there are all these ... these eminently *decidable* problems out there. Problems that *need* solving. Questions that can and should be answered. By me.'

'Well I'm delighted if the thought of my untimely death spurred you into ...' I shrugged.

'Art is undecidable,' she sighed, 'and that's why I'm a useless
poet, Miss Hahn. I lack conviction. In fact that's why *all*
poetry is useless. Because there's no certainty.'
'All poetry?' I echoed, slightly worried now.
'Yes. Yes, I think so.'

She handed me back the piece of newspaper.
'I hope I managed to clarify things for you.' She smiled.
'You did. Thank you.' I nodded.
'Why exactly are you so concerned about it?' she wondered.
'A twelve-year-old computer chip? On the day after your
bungalow fell into the sea?'
'Because Orla – *Orla* – Orla Nor Cleary the ... you know ...'
She nodded.
'Orla was always scribbling those four digits down after
praying, or muttering them in her sleep, or scratching them
into the sand on the beach with a stick, or—'

'4004 BC is when Ussher claimed the world was born,' Mrs
Meadows interrupted.
'Ussher?'
'He was the Archbishop of Ireland in the seventeenth century.
Of course the date was biblically sourced. And nobody takes it
seriously any more.'

'The birth of the world,' I mused, pushing my hair behind
my ear.
'And I suppose with the Intel 4004 another kind of world was
born,' Mrs Meadows expanded, 'a new world. A digital world
... Here. Hold on a second ...'
She suddenly reached up to her hair, felt around blindly for a
moment, withdrew a small, eminently tasteful, antiqued brass
and pearl filigree hair-clip, leaned forward and deftly pinned
my fringe back with it. She then paused for a moment to
inspect her handiwork, grimaced, removed the clip and
quickly readjusted the positioning slightly.

'There!' she exclaimed.
'Thank you,' I murmured, somewhat daunted.

'I have an old college friend who was working for Apple a while ago,' she idly volunteered, slipping her clog back on, getting up and going to tear off the bent and browning flowerhead of a white, scented phlox in a nearby flower bed. 'The computer people?'

I stared down at the newspaper article.

'Yes. She was the sister of my first serious boyfriend. The one who ran off with the Sudanese, remember? The one who broke my heart. She introduced us to each other, in fact. We were the only two girls taking engineering at our university. She was a couple of years older. We've stayed in touch over the years. She lives and works just south of San Francisco in a place they call Silicon Valley. Her husband helped to get ARPANET up and operational ... Have you heard of ARPANET, Miss Hahn?'

I shook my head.

'They were one of the world's first packet-switching networks ...'

I looked blank.

'Packet-switching is the dominant basis for all modern data communications, worldwide. In fact I was just thinking about him earlier when you rang the bell. Watching the bees moving out from the hive, into the garden and then back again ... Thinking about the mites – the re-infection ... Her husband actually worked on the team that helped crack the so-called "Creeper" virus ...'

She fell silent, still watching the bees.

   'Mr Huff is back from his pilgrimage,' I said.

'Really?' Her focus rapidly shifted. 'Have you seen him?'

'Yes.' I nodded. 'And he seems to have sustained a small injury on his travels ...'

'Oh.' She frowned. 'Nothing too serious, I hope?'

'His ... his ...' I felt a now all-too-familiar tightening at both corners of my mouth, 'his *buttocks* sealed together.'

'Really?'

She looked horrified.

'Yes. I'm afraid so.'

I watched closely for any signs of levity on Mrs Meadows's part. But there was nothing. *Nothing*. Not a trace. Not so much as even the tiniest, little glimmer of anything.

39

Mr Clifford Bickerton

I was driving the van along the Sea Road, not really ... you know ... when there was suddenly some kind of a ... a problem with the clutch ... it just ... it just stopped *catching* ... and so I ... I pulled in ... I pulled in to the side of the road and I climbed out of the van and I slammed ... and I slammed ... and I walked around to the front of ... and I opened up the bonnet to ...

... had turned into quite a fine day, overall, with a soft, warm breeze-*eeze-eeze* ... (eh?!) ... breeze-*eeze-eeze* ... (what the ...?!) ... and ... and I heard the hap ... hap ... sounds of laughter and ... and singing ...? Music? On the beach? So I glanced over, towards the sea wall, and I found that I could see the top of what looked like ... like ... like *ban* ... *ban* ... *banners* flying and my ... (what's that word?) ... curi ... my inquisiti ... it ... it got the better of me. So I ...

... so I left the van and I ... I looked right and then I looked left and then I ... I crossed the road-*oad-oad* (eh?!) and I clambered up the sea wall and when I got to the top the breeze was stronger, a fresh ... a fresh ... and the rich, mina ... mini ... mineral ... fresh smell of the ocean and I ... I saw a large group of people standing together in a hud ... in a hud ... on the peb ... on the peb ... the pebble of the ... the ...

... there was a picnic table covered in food-*ood-ood* (eh?!) and a brightly coloured awning-*ing-ing-ing-ing* (?!) which had the flags – the pen ... the pen-*dance* ... pen-*dance* (?) ... the pen ... fluttering around it in a sort of ... a ... a med ... medi

... medi-evil ... medi-eval ... like in my favourite ... the best
... my favourite children's books as a ... as a ...

... and when I looked-*ooked-ooked* (?) at the people I had a
strange-*ange* feeling of fam ... of ... fami ... that I had met
them all before ... that ... that we were ... that we had ... but
I ... I ... I'd be hard-pressed to ... to ... to say when or how
or ... or ... or ...

... there were several monks-*unks-unks*! In robes-*obes-obes-
obes*! One sat in a wheel ... a wheel ... a wheelchair! And they
were ... ah! ... sing-*ing-ing-ing* or chant ... chant-*ing-ing-ing*
something or ... or at least the air was full of a lovely ... a
sound ... a music ... a sound which had a hum ... a hum ... a
humming quality-*tee-tee* like a kind of ... as if it was ... as if it
had an echo-*ho-ho* which moved forwards and backwards
through ... through time because ... I don't have the words to
express how everything-*ing-ing* was, but it was in the ... in the
future and in the ... the past because it was all playing-*ing-
ing-ing* for ever ... together ... and that made me feel so ... so
... I don't have the words to ... to ...

... and like I said they all seemed to ... to know that ... to
expect that I would ... that it was me ... that I was Clifford
Bicker-*icker-icker* ... and that I was coming and several of
them smiled and beck ... they ... beck ... they waved to me
... at me ... And we spoke with each other, we com ... com
... com ... but it wasn't speaking so much as sending pictures
and words and ideas to each other and every picture and
word and idea moved so very ... so very fa ... so fa ... so
quickly and it was hard to catch-*atch-atch* them, but when you
did they stayed-*ayed-ayed* with you and then you ... like a
strange game of ... of ...

... Look! There's that nice woman who works at the café in
Rye, and another woman from the bank-*ank-ank*, and look!
Mrs Barrow-*arrow-arrow* is serving tea from a giant urn, and
Mr Barrow-*arrow-arrow* is deep in conver ... conversat ... is
talking ... is talk ... with a tiny, golden angel ...!

... Look! A beaut ... a beaut ... a little, golden angel ...!
With her ... with ...

... And I ... I real-*eel-eel-eel* ... I real-*eel-eel*-ized without
even ... even ... realizing-*zing-zing-ing* that it was Orla Nor
Cleary who had come so very far to get here and to be here
on this day and ... and over by the water was Bran Cleary
hide ... hide ... standing behind an easel painting-*ting-ting* the
scene and he was unrecog ... unrec ... so badly burned – not
his skin, but inside ... *inside!* – but that was then and now he
was fine but still-*ill-ill* and how to ...?

... there were other people there who I ... who had been a
part of ... like Alys Jane ... like ... like ... holding a little bird
cage which was a ... a little screen ... of ... of feelings ... and
there was a parrot ... a ... a *bird* ... inside it who when you
pressed something softly-*lee-lee* he began to sing ... to caw ...
to tweet-*eat-eat* and just ... he took to the wing and then he ...
I can't really ...

... and everyone was talking and laughing-*ing-ing* and the
echo-*ho-ho* and the reverba ... reverbaray-*ray-ray-ray-ray* ... it
was so ... so ... like something solid and yet liquid which ...
which ...

... but we were only really ... were only really ... all eyes
were upon-*on-on-on* ... just watching-*ing-ing* the little angel
who was holding-*ing-ing* out her arms which were tiny arms
but long arms because it was ... so ... so warm ... and for
ever and ... and always-*zays-zays* and ... and ... and her arms
were full of white flowers and people would come forward,
one by one, and bury their faces into the flowers because ...
the scent was so ... so ... so beautiful and clean and when
they lifted their heads-*eds-eds-eds* again they would be laughing
and crying too, and some of them ... well, they just melted
clean away with the joy-*oy-oy* of it all ...

... and Sorcha stood close by ... by the angel-*gel-gel* ... sur
... sur ... surrounded-*ed-ed* by little lambs-*ambs-ambs* with a
... a big ... a big eye-*ay-ay-ay* in the mid ... the mid ... in the

centre of her hand-*and-and* which would ... which was rec ... rec ... recording-*ding-ding* everything that the angel did and said and every ... everything-*ing-ing* that happened, and once she had recorded it she would send it ... post it ... mail it ... around the world and then it returned before it was even gone-*on-on-on* full of light-*ight-ight* because the more-*ore-ore* it trav ... jour ... trav ... moved ... flew, then the faster and the brighter and the clearer-*rer-rer-rer* it came back ... but ...

... but there were dark forces here, too-*oo-oo*, shadows hiding-*ing-ing* in the smo ... smo ... smoke from the barbecue-*you-you-you* and they were beyond the smoke and in the ... and in the ... and sometimes they would catch the messages ... the love ... and the message ... the love ... would get heav ... would get heav ... and the light would get darker, but I didn't want to ... to look at them I didn't want to ... to focus on them because the ...

... because the party was so wonder-*der-der*-ful and at the heart of it this great brightness and great movement and ... and speed-*eed-eed-eed* ... which turned galaxies of stars into streams of ... and it's so hard to explain with the words-*urds-urds* of this mouth and this ... this lang ... langu ... langu ... place because there are other ways of talking which we can't even begin to ... to dream about and I ... oh I didn't even really care-*air-air* about the child when she arrived and I suppose there was some-*um-um* confu ... confuse ... confusion and some resent-*ent-ent*-ment but when I saw her, so tiny and so bright on the pebbles with the armfuls of flowers I just ... I understood that it had to be-*ee-ee-ee* exact ... just this way, exact ... just as it is and I ...

... I wondered where Carla was and I ... I looked around for her ... and I became confused-*used-used* because she was on the other side of the smoke-*oak-oak-oak* with the ... the ... in the heat-*eat-eat-eat* ... in the ... but she was ... of course she was ... wasn't too close, she was ... she was ... she was very dis ... very dis ... far away on the hor ... hor ... horizon walking with two other people who I couldn't quite-*ite-ite* disting ... disting ... tell ... but one was a man who was a word – a pen-*en-en-en* – and the other was a woman who was a thought-*ought-ought-ought* and ... and the woman drew the messages towards her and then sent them out again like a kind of ... of magnet, a magnetic-*ic-ic-hic-hic-hic* thing I can't quite describe and she seemed ... she seemed powerful-*ul-ul-ul* but Carla-*la-la-lah* like a song-*ong-ong* was ... was in the middle ... and she was drawn to the light-*ight-ight-ight* like a ... like a butter ... a butter ... a moth ... like a moth which flew into the ... flew into the ... caught the light on her ... on her wings-*ings-ings* and it came from her and surroun-*ound-ound-*ded her because I could tell that it was her ... confuse ... her need ... her refuse-*use-use*-ing-*ging-ging* ... that made it ... made her ... made it so ... so ...

... like almost a ... a ... gulf ... a giant ... a crack-*ack-ack* which zig ... zig ... zig ... a can ... a can ... a canyon-*on-on-on* which opened up behind ... which I thought could ... might ... might engulf them or ... or ... or *us*! ... engulf *us*! ... and then it would all be ... all forgot ... all waste ... all ... and I ...

... so confused ... so confusing-*ing-ing-ing* and yet I could see the sense in it and the truth of it and we had all been a part of it and we were laughing-*ing-ing-ing* and so grate-*ate-ate*-ful-*ull-ull-ull* and we wanted the crowd to get bigger ... we longed for-*or-or-or* the happiness to expand-*dand-dand-dand-dand* so that it might ... so that everyone might-*ight-ight* join-*oin-oin-oin* the great light-*ight-ight-ight* ...

... then my thoughts turned into symbols-*ols-ols* and there isn't the ... there isn't the ... the means-*eans-eans-eans* ... the way of ... to place it all ... all down here-*ear-ear*.

If I could then I would ... I would ... I would show you-*woo-woo-woo*.
But I don't have the ...
I can't ...

Not like the others ... with the ... at least I ... the big gulf-*ulf-*
ulf-ulf ... Not like them ...

    I don't ... I must turn now, and-*dand-dand* ...
Head back to the van.
I must turn now, and-*dand-dand* ...
I must turn now, and-*dand-dand-dand* ...
Move past this great ... this giant and strange and for ever
echo-*ho-ho-ho* ...

    I must turn now, and-*dand-dand-dand* ...
I must turn now, and-*dand-dand-dand* ...
Head back to the ...
I must turn now, and-*dand-dand-dand-dand* ...
... *and-dand-dand-dand* ...
... *and-dand-dand-dand-dand* ...
God help me –
God *help* me –
go.

40

Miss Carla Hahn

It took the best part of an entire afternoon to salvage what I could from the bungalow, which in the broad light of day looked as if some cruel deity had just laid into it, willy-nilly, with a huge jackhammer. Or a monstrous shark had leapt from the sea's depths and bitten a big chunk away. Or a passing giant had paused for a brief interlude during a beachside stroll, rested his elbow – unthinkingly – on the roof, gazed out to sea and debated whether or not to risk the short wade across to France.

There seemed no rhyme or reason to what was lost and what still remained: an untouched supper of sardines on toast, resting (knife and fork casually crossed across the plate) on half a kitchen counter, my copy of *Andromeda* lying open on the bedroom floor at the very page I left off reading it, but my bed – in which I happily lay to do so – and the wall the bed generally leaned up against, now mysteriously evaporated.

If I gazed down at the new rows of jagged mud and rubble terraces, I could see rugs and torn posters and incidental tables and the spare Baby Belling and the old lawnmower and my best bedspread (the old blue one with the rose pattern) poking out from the murky scree. There was the horrible avocado-coloured china bath and its matching hand-basin lying far below on the beach, the toilet (which completed the suite) and the ugly hammered-copper chimney-breast cover (from the living room) hovering twenty foot above. There was a door – still vertical and in its frame – repeatedly opening and closing in the wind, as if a series of ghostly inhabitants were appraising the suitability of this strangely airy new residence before retreating, unconvinced.

I packed up what I could. It almost seemed a kind of … a sort of betrayal not to clamber down the slope and retrieve what lay just beyond reach (my best teapot, a bottle of good shampoo, a collection of tape cassettes …) and then another kind (if not of betrayal, then a small defeat) to carefully pack up an egg timer that had never worked, a painting of Camber Castle that I had been given by an old neighbour and had always secretly loathed, a rusty frying pan – the trusty little Le Creuset I inherited from my mother now apparently gone for good.

Ross and Marian Seaton and their grown-up son Jeremy – from around the corner – helped me pile up their old Land-Rover and we drove three full loads over to Shimmy's. Marian had kindly prepared a flask of tea and a round of ham and egg sandwiches which we ate on what remained of the front lawn. She asked if she might take some of the plants from the garden. There was an old honeysuckle she had always admired and a small jasmine and a wonderfully florid pink English tea rose.

Some of the stuff went into Shimmy's front parlour, some into a shed, but we were obliged to take the final load (mainly Tilda's stuff) over to Mulberry and store it, temporarily, in the air-raid shelter. This wasn't an easy task: access to Mulberry isn't generally good, and there were still quite a number of vans parked illegally on the lane, oh … and a succession of overexcited children running about, several of whom were baiting poor Joyce – Mrs Seelinger's spaniel – (they'd dressed him up in an old yellow cardigan and had tied a blue hydrangea flower to his tail; heaven only knows whose garden they'd acquired it from) and so they had to be quickly apprehended (Mrs Seaton – a former tree surgeon, who can be quite terrifying on her day – undertook this mission) and then strictly reprimanded.

It was heavy work, and a warm afternoon, and Mr Seaton, Jeremy and I were just in the midst of working out the appropriate angles at which to manoeuvre an especially large and unwieldy dresser through the two tiny doorways when our calculations were disrupted by a series of strange creaks and thuds (interspersed with a succession of loud and quite dreadful hiccups).

It was Mr Huff, of course – who else? – struggling manfully down the garden path, barefoot, on a pair of (actually rather fine, if not entirely functional) old brown-leather-padded wooden crutches. He was wearing his pyjamas. His glasses were on askew and his hair was all lopsided.

'Miss Hahn! *Hic!* What *is* this? *Hic!*' he demanded, lifting an irate crutch to gesticulate.

The Mr Seatons promptly put down the dresser. On my foot.

'It's a dresser, Mr Huff, from the bungalow ...' I tried – and failed – to remove my foot. 'It belongs to ...' I paused. 'I'm sorry, Mr Seaton, but you've placed the dresser down on to my ...'

The two Mr Seatons quickly lifted the dresser again and I slid the bruised digit out from beneath it. Mr Huff watched on, impassively, still hiccuping.

'Have you tried taking a deep breath?' Ross Seaton wondered.

'Sorry?' Mr Huff glared at him.

'A deep breath. Have you tried holding your breath? Carbon dioxide kept for any kind of extended duration inside your lungs automatically releases your diaphragm.'

(Mr Seaton was once a science teacher.)

'Of course I've *hic!* tried holding my *hic!* breath!' Mr Huff snorted.

'How long have you been hiccuping?' Jeremy Seaton enquired.

'Six or *hic!* seven hours *hic!*' Mr Huff answered, scowling.

'My grandmother once hiccuped for twelve days.' Jeremy shrugged.

Mr Huff looked impressed, in spite of himself.

'Then she dropped dead,' Jeremy added.

'Exhaustion.' Ross nodded. 'But she was eighty-five and suffered from severe angina.'

'Shimmy often gets hiccups,' I volunteered, 'and I generally get him to sip on a glass of water.'

'Eight or nine quick little gulps in a row,' Ross concurred, 'so the rhythmic contractions of the oesophagus override the spasms in the diaphragm.'

'That was *hic!* the first *hic!* thing I tried *hic!*' Mr Huff confessed.

At this point, Mrs Seaton arrived (Joyce in tow). She instantly assessed the situation.

'Have you tried pushing your right thumb into your left palm and then pressing the palm really hard?' she wondered.

Mr *hic!* Huff *hic!* instantly *hic!* attempted to *hic!* follow *hic!* her instructions.

'No, not ...' Mrs Seaton (dissatisfied with his technique) strode over to him, grabbed his hand and showed him exactly what to do.

'Now press *really* hard for about ten seconds.'

Mr Huff tried his best to oblige her. He looked ashen, painfully thin and seemed quite unsteady on his feet. My heart – in spite of itself – went out to him.

Alas, Mrs Seaton's *hic!* technique *hic!* didn't quite work on Mr Huff. *Hic!* Mrs Seaton *hic!* was nonplussed. 'That always gets rid of mine.' She shrugged, then, after a pause: 'Did you know you've got some kind of pinky-orange liquid splashed all across your cheek?'

Mr Huff scowled and put up his hand to feel his face.

'No. Over there ...'

Mrs Seaton indicated with her finger. Mr Huff tried, once again, to *hic!* locate it, but failed. Mrs Seaton quickly lost patience with him, pushed her hand into her trouser pocket, withdrew a tissue, spat on it and applied it to Mr Huff's *hic!* cheek.

I tried to repress a smile. This wasn't lost on Mr Huff.

'I'm glad you *hic!* seem to find *hic!* such evident *hic!* delight in my *hic!* various misfor – *hic!* – tunes Miss *hic!* Hahn!' he hissed.

'Stick your fingers in your ears for twenty seconds,' I suggested.

'Why? *hic!*' Mr Huff demanded, paranoid. 'So you *hic!* can all *hic!* make *hic!* fun of me *hic!* on the *hic!* sly?!'

'Better still, apply steady pressure to the soft areas *behind* your earlobes,' Ross Seaton added, 'just below the base of the skull; that'll send a powerful relax signal via the vagus nerve to the diaphragm.'

As Mr Huff (quite obligingly, I felt) started to lift his hands to his ears, one of his crutches became dislodged from beneath his armpit and clattered down on to the path. I ran over to retrieve it.

'I would strongly advocate *combining* pressing your ears with sipping water rhythmically through a straw,' Mrs Seaton suggested, 'which naturally doubles your chances of success.'

The two Seaton men – after a brief discussion – lifted up the dresser again and recommenced their attempt to gain access to the bomb shelter. Mrs Seaton quickly trotted off to oversee this process.

I passed Mr Huff his crutch. We stared at each other, and I felt a sudden, overwhelming feeling of self-consciousness. Then Mr Huff hiccuped.

'My mother always used to get me to stick out my tongue,' I said.

'Sorry? *Hic!*' Mr Huff muttered. He looked a little flushed.

403

'To get rid of hiccups. My mother always used to ...'
'I know, *hic!*' Mr Huff nodded. 'You already *hic!* told me that.'
'Sorry?' I frowned.
'Forget *hic!* it!' Mr Huff growled.

Out of the corner of my eye, I could see Joyce devouring a
couple of rotten windfalls from the old apple tree.
'Joyce!' I yelled, clapping my hands violently to attract his
attention. 'Away from there! Go on! Home! *Home!*'
Hic!

Mr Huff inspected my hands, grimacing, apparently deeply
offended by the cacophony they'd just produced.
'It can sometimes be of help if you gently cup your fingers
over your nose and mouth but continue to breathe normally,'
I added.
'It's gone *hic!* way beyond that *hic!* I'm afraid, *hic!* Miss
Hahn,' Mr Huff groaned.
'Or ... or people often say that a sudden, you know, a sudden
shock ...'

'Carla?' Mrs Seaton called over. 'I think we may need to
take off the handles from the front. Will that be okay with
you?'
Hic!
'... to just ... you know, to jolt the mind out of ...'
'Carla?'
Oh God. *Oh God.* I *have* to, don't I? Tell Mr Huff?
Don't I, though?
'Carla?'

'It was me, Mr Huff,' I murmured (because desperate
situations require desperate measures, I suppose).
'Pardon? *Hic!*' Mr Huff leaned forward slightly, struggling to
hear.
'Carla?' Mrs Seaton repeated. 'The handles!'
I turned, waved my acquiescence, and then, 'Joyce!' I yelled.
'Away from the bins! Joyce! *Joyce! Away!* Away from the bins!'

'What did *hic!* you just *hic!* say?' Mr Huff persisted, his manner suddenly quite urgent, taking a hold of my wrist and pulling me still closer.

'Oh. Um. Uh ...'

Hic!

I gazed down at his hand. On my wrist.

'Uh ...'

Hic!

Oh well. Caution be damned. Here goes.

41

Mr Franklin D. Huff

It was her! It was *her*! *She* put the shark under my bed! Miss
Hahn! *She* put the shark under my bed! My own landlady!
Miss Hahn! *She* put the shark under my bed! The instant she
told me, my hiccups stopped. For about a minute. From the
shock. And I ...

Oh dear! Why'd I have to go and say that? Miss Hahn
grumbled.

The tangible Miss Hahn – the one who stood before me –
the *actual* Miss Hahn who had just leaned over and pressed
her lips against my ear to whisper ...

Why on earth am I wearing that awful hair-clip? Miss Hahn
wondered.

Aaargh! I can't help it! I just can't help it! Whenever I lay
eyes upon the actual Miss Hahn I just feel all these terrible
impulses ... these overwhelming urges of ... of impotent rage.
Because I am *in love* with Miss Hahn – *Aaaargh!* – and I
couldn't be more unhappy about it! And worse still, Miss
Hahn, with her strange, grey-green eyes and her over-large
nose and her strong jaw and her wide, unpainted mouth
patently despises me! Palpably so! *Heartily!* Yes! Despises me
sufficiently to place a rotting shark – *a rotting shark!* What
kind of a person even ... even *thinks* like that (aside from
some high-status members of the Neapolitan Camorra crime
syndicate, of course)? – under my bed *on the very day* that I
discovered my first wife—

Your only wife, Miss Hahn corrected me.

—had died!

Although I didn't know that she had died, Miss Hahn
excused herself, *and you had just cruelly insulted my father's dog
on the beach. Although I accept that it's hardly an adequate
defence …*

That's hardly an adequate defence! I yelled back.

I just said that, Miss Hahn sighed. *Oh, and you made me cry,*
she mused, *and I never cry. Never! But I was blubbing like a
baby. Now about that coat …*

With the mention of the coat my hiccups promptly started
up again. And there was a powerful whiff of …

Need I even say?

The actual Miss Hahn, meanwhile, was trying – and failing
– to explain herself.

You … you really *cried*? I murmured, mortified. On the
beach? After I … I really made you *cry* that day, Miss Hahn?

Now about that coat … Miss Hahn repeated.

Hic!

The actual Miss Hahn was now staring at me, very
concerned. 'Mr Huff?' she was saying. 'Won't you at least *say*
something? Please? Anything?'

Why am I conducting this strange conversation with you in
my head, Miss Hahn? I asked the imaginary Miss Hahn.
When the actual Miss Hahn is standing right in front of me? I
scowled. Did I invent you, perhaps, simply to avoid engaging
emotionally with the actual Miss Hahn? As a … as a conduit
for my real feelings which I can't actually … which I'm
signally incapable of …? Or just because I'm so … so lonely
and so … so desperate to … to be close to you that I literally
…? Or are you actually the *real* Miss Hahn, Miss Hahn, and
this curiously coarse and scruffy creature which stands before
me is simply a …?

Hello? *Hello?* Miss Hahn?

The Miss Hahn inside my head had gone unusually quiet. I
really had no idea what she was getting up to in there.

Miss Hahn? I repeated.

Oh, uh, sorry! the imaginary Miss Hahn juddered back into consciousness. *Could you possibly … uh … repeat all that for me? I'm afraid I must've nodded off after 'engaging emotionally' …*

The actual Miss Hahn, meanwhile was … she was … she looked …

'Mr Huff? *Please?!* Won't you just …?'

'It's *hic!* fine,' I said, harshly, 'don't *hic!* give it *hic!* a second *hic!* thought. *Hic!* I already *hic!* knew.'

The actual Miss Hahn looked stunned.

'You … you *knew?*'

Oh excellent! A double bluff! The imaginary Miss Hahn chuckled.

'Yes. It was *hic!* obvious! I'd already *hic!* guessed myself, *hic!* but then your friend *hic!* Mr Pemberton *hic!* kindly confirmed my *hic!* suspicions for me. *Hic!*'

'Clifford told you?'

Miss Hahn seemed taken aback. I was both delighted – and pained – by her patent shock at Pemberton's betrayal.

'Yes! *Hic!* Days ago, now! *Hic!*'

'And you … you didn't think to … to *mention*—'

Miss Hahn looked hurt and slightly tearful. (Miss Hahn? *Hurt?* Making *me* feel guilty? After what *she'd* done?!)

'To mention it *hic!* to you?! *Hic!*' I interrupted, roughly. 'No. *Hic!* Why should I? *Hic!* Why should I *hic!* mention it? Hic! I'm the *hic!* wronged party here, *hic!* Miss Hahn! *Hic!* I thought it *hic!* was up to *hic!* you to *hic!* mention it. *Hic!* Not me. *Hic!*'

I do wish you could see what happens to your brain when you lie, Mr Huff! Miss Hahn chuckled, plainly highly entertained. *There's a huge amount of activity in your medial inferior and pre-central areas. And your hippocampus is pulsing quite extraordinarily!*

Who made you such an expert on brain physiology, Miss Hahn? I demanded, slightly suspicious.

The old nursing qualification, Mr Huff, remember?

Oh. Yes. I grudgingly conceded, of course.

'I really did feel terrible about it, Mr Huff,' the actual Miss Hahn confessed, plainly traumatized, 'and I fully intended to come around that afternoon and apologize, but then there was that first landslip – in Fairlight – and I just got caught up in all the ... the administration, you know ... and the moment just seemed to ... to pass.'

As Miss Hahn speaks, I inspect the strange contours of her lips. I still have a tight hold of her wrist. I suppose I should really have released her wrist several minutes ago. In fact I'm surprised I didn't let go of it as I recoiled in shock when she first confided her terrible secret. That would certainly have been a more ... well ... more appropriate response. Because now, after all this time, in conversation, it's almost as if we are ... I don't know ... involved in some kind of intimate ...

Hmmn. I really don't understand why she's pinned her hair back with that ridiculous clip. It doesn't suit her *at all.* Although she's acting as if the fringe is still there! Her free hand has already been lifted four ... five times to this now de-activated hair curtain during our brief, two-minute exchange. There it goes again! Dutifully miming its habitual, little tucks on those invisible, blonde swags ...

And the eye – which is normally obscured by the aforementioned fringe – exudes a slightly vulnerable quality, as though it's generally hidden because of a dangerous excess of ... of, well, *sincerity.* That eye must be concealed! It *must* be! If only for its own (and Miss Hahn's) personal safety! Because of a natural frankness ... this wonderfully artless ... unadorned ... uncontrived ...

Oh dear! the imaginary Miss Hahn murmurs (some way off), *that naughty dog appears to be ...*

Blah blah blah.

In fact her eyes truly are the most exquisite grey-green colour ... like a ... a quiet sea held at the exact point of tide-turn under a lowering sky ... the most feathery-gentle, dove grey ... calm yet curiously animated – *arresting* ...

Good gracious! the imaginary Miss Hahn sniped, *your descriptive powers certainly aren't improved by an excess of woolly sentiment, Mr Huff!*

Because here I stand, I thought (ignoring the senseless carping of the imaginary Miss Hahn), holding the actual Miss Hahn's arm, her wrist, in my hand, touching her ... feeling her ... (Have I ever touched or felt Miss Hahn's arm before? Might this actually be a first?) so ... so why don't I just ... well, *indulge* myself for a moment and ...

Mr Huff? The imaginary Miss Hahn cleared her throat, noisily, *you should probably* ...

... and focus my mind on the extraordinary sensation of her skin under my fingers. It feels so very ... so very warm and ... and ...

Mr Huff! the imaginary Miss Hahn snapped. *Do try and keep your wits about you!*

... and so very, very soft. And if I subtly loosen the pressure of my ... and then slowly slide my thumb up the inside of her ...

MR HUFF!

I suddenly came back to myself and saw ... Oh no! *No!* It's that damn dog! It's that damn spaniel with the stupid name! Janice or ... or ...

Joyce

... or Susan or ...

Joyce

or ... or Wilde or Shaw or Hemingway or Fitzgerald or ...

Joyce

... or Joyce. Exactly! Or Joyce.

'... then even when I came round with the pork pie,' the actual Miss Hahn yammers blithely on, 'I fully intended to ...

you know, but it simply didn't pan out. You just seemed so incredibly …'

Okay … okay … I started to try and lead Miss Hahn, very gently, very unobtrusively, back towards the house, but I wasn't especially mobile, alas, and Miss Hahn was far too engrossed in what she was saying to respond as promptly as I would have …

'… incredibly *vulnerable*, you know,' she said, 'because of … of Kim … and even though I was tormented by guilt – this awful … awful *weight* of guilt – I sincerely felt that it might do more harm than good if I …'

She's going to look down, Mr Huff! Miss Hahn trilled.

Shut up! Shut *up*! No she isn't! No she *isn't*!

'… if I casually reintroduced such a painful subject at an inappropriate moment …'

As she spoke, Miss Hahn started glancing down, frowning, because that damn dog …

Joyce

Exactly. That stupid spaniel was muttering to itself – a kind of … an excited yiffling-whiffling growl – and dragging …

'But I need you to understand that I really *did* feel terrible, Mr Huff.'

Pause.

Hic!

'What on earth are you doing, there, Joyce?' Miss Hahn scowled. 'Why all this silly fuss and commotion, eh …?'

Hic!

'Joyce? *Joyce!* What in heaven's name have you …?'

Then the penny dropped.

Ka-ching!

42

Miss Carla Hahn

At first I thought it was ... I don't know ... It took several
seconds to process the whole thing. What did I think it was?
Something ... something still alive or recently dead or ... or
slightly subterranean – or even ... even *occult*. I thought it
was ...

What did I think it was? All of the above, I suppose. But
then it wasn't ... Or ... or at least, well, it *was* ...

It was the coat! Orla's special coat! And the damn dog (or
the blessed dog – the jury's still out) had this most precious of
artefacts, this most ... how can I explain it? This most rich
and sacred and intimate and ... and *rare* and talismanic of
jewels caught between its jaws and it was dragging it through
the dust ... A dog ... the dog had ...

No! No! No! *No!* It took literally a split second for me to
realize – for me to put two and two together and realize – that
Mr Huff had ... He must have ... He must have been
throwing Orla's beautiful, hand-made, exquisitely decorated
coat out *with the rubbish*! With the *rubbish*! And in that same
instant it dawned on me that he had been subtly trying to lead
me towards the house. He'd been holding me by the wrist and
gently moving us both backwards, but I'd been so engrossed
in my apology that I hadn't ...

I snatched my arm away from him with a gasp, as though
burned by his touch, and then swooped down, with a cry, and
grabbed that astonishing little coat, that astonishing little fur
coat which I hadn't laid eyes on since ...

I scooped it up and I held it in my arms and as I held it ...
I just ... I was suddenly racked with a series of terrific sobs ...
I was so ... so *hurt*, so deeply offended that anyone could be
so ... so ignorant, so heartless ... such an ... an unthinking
vandal as to ...

Mr Huff (for his part) looked somewhat taken aback. Then
he lifted his hand to his chest. 'My hiccups ...' he muttered.
His hiccups had stopped.

'How *could* you, Mr Huff?!' I groaned. 'Orla's little coat.
Her *coat*. How *could* you, Mr Huff?'
'I didn't ...' Mr Huff started off, then, 'Mrs Barrow must
have ... when I came back from the monastery. It was shoved
inside an old Woolworth's bag. Mrs Barrow must have
inadvertently ...'

I buried my face in the coat and continued to sob. It was
simply ...
To have lost so much! In one day! To have lost so much! And
I hadn't really even *felt* anything until now. I'd been so ... so
preoccupied, so muffled by the overriding need to ... and the
terrible fury of Clifford ... and the strange newspaper article
... and the thudding realization that I was in love – in *love*!
How utterly ridiculous! – with the kind of person who would
be capable of ...

A worm! A backsliding, conniving *worm*! I growled my rage
into the coat. I roared into the coat. I gripped on to the coat
until both sets of knuckles turned white. I almost bit into the
coat – gnashed away at it – the way I longed to gnash away at
Mr Huff himself. Although I didn't (of course I didn't!)
because this was Orla's coat. Because this was Orla. This was
my darling, little Orla. Here, in my arms. So I hugged her and
I kissed her and I told her how much I loved her and after a
minute or two the fury just melted clean away – it was offered
up – because that was Orla's special gift, wasn't it: to give by
taking? That was her power.

Mr Huff was speaking, meanwhile. He had been speaking for some time but I couldn't pretend to have heard a thing he'd been saying.

'... extremely painful and testing,' he grumbled, 'and I hadn't really bargained on becoming the unwitting repository of the entire Cleary legacy, because I'm just ... I'm too *close*, Miss Hahn. I'm too close. And they might trust me, even though their "every natural instinct fights against it"' – he snorted, derisively – 'they might trust me, Miss Hahn, but *more fool them*! Because I'm *not* to be trusted! No! Not *remotely* to be trusted! And I resent being trusted when I'm not ... I'm *deeply* frustrated by this, Miss Hahn, deeply, *profoundly* frustrated by this ...'

I lifted my face from the fur. 'Where did you get it from?' I demanded.

'Sorry?' He was halted mid-flow.

'The coat. Where did you get it from?'

'I was given it.'

'Who? Who gave it to you?' I croaked.

'A demented old monk at Douai called Brother Prosper.'

'And how did *he* come across it?'

'Father Hugh had given it to him for safekeeping, apparently. Years ago. And he, I was told, had been given it by Kalinda.'

'But what on earth possessed him to give it to you?' I exclaimed, astonished.

'Because ...' – he rolled his eyes, irritated – 'because the damn child *wanted* me to have it I suppose.'

'You suppose?' I echoed.

He turned and started to make faltering progress back towards the cottage.

'You suppose?!' I repeated, somewhat incensed at his sudden withdrawal.

'Not you, too, Miss Hahn!' he exclaimed, throwing up his hands, despairing. 'I can't bear it!'

'Mr Huff?' I was indignant.

'*Please!* Not another giant serving of completely hysterical pseudo-mystical mumbo-jumbo, Miss Hahn!' he called over his shoulder, then, 'I just can't bear it!' he repeated.

'This coat is a priceless heirloom, Mr Huff!' I called back.

'Am I fated to be *entirely* surrounded by religious maniacs?' he groaned.

'And *very* old!' I added.

Mr Huff didn't react. So I followed after him, haranguing him. 'It was a gift to Orla from her maternal grandmother, Mr Huff. It had actually belonged to *her* grandmother as a child. It's ancient. *Ancient.* Each little skin is sewn together with kangaroo sinew. Every individual patch decorated with ancient Aboriginal symbols. See? It's decorated with the Ngemba clan insignia ...'

I began to unfold it. 'Have you even had a chance to take a proper look at it, Mr Huff?'

'Leave me alone, Miss Hahn!' Mr Huff panted over his shoulder.

'But I thought you had a great *interest* in native antiquities, Mr Huff!' I chided.

Mr Huff entered the house and laboriously made his way through to the living room. When he reached the living room he swung around on his crutches, frowning. 'Yes,' he admitted, 'yes. I suppose I do have an interest in native antiquities.'

He was sweating heavily, and out of breath. One of his hands was trembling.

The hunter, hunted, I thought.

'The hunter, hunted,' he said.

'I was just ...' I started, then stopped.

'What do you want from me, Miss Hahn?' he asked.

'I don't know,' I said.

'What do you want from me, Miss Hahn?' he repeated, this time almost ... almost tenderly.

'This was *her* coat, Mr Huff,' I said. 'This was Orla's coat.'

416

I continued to unfold it as he watched.

'Just look,' I said, 'see how beautiful it is ...'

I held it out to him, pointing to all the patches, every one embedded with its own, special and sacred ancient imagery; an exquisitely dense miasma of ochre and black dots, squiggles and dashes, some abstract, some more literal ...

'A bee' – I smiled – 'and the eucalyptus leaf ... and—'

'A bush plum,' he interrupted.

'And that looks like ...' – I scowled – 'a rabbit print?'

'Possum.'

I continued looking, growing ever more fascinated. 'And four wavy strokes followed by an endless circle, and another endless circle, then four more strokes ... four thousand and—'

'That's actually a river,' Mr Huff interrupted, pointing to the four strokes, 'or sometimes it means a very old story ... and the concentric circles represent a waterhole. The waterhole is a sacred place ... or sometimes the camping place of a totemic heroine ... see here ... an old woman's breast ...'

He turned the coat over in his hand. 'The little circle is a child ... and that's a great star ... and this is a journey with the important sites marked out ... that's a fire but it's being obliterated by smoke ...'

As Mr Huff worked his way around the coat I gazed over at him.

He continued searching, frowning, intrigued ... interpreting things, explaining things. We were only a foot or so apart. My eyes followed the irresistible line of his jaw. A tiny shaving cut on his cheek. I was fascinated by his ear. And the way his hair curled. And the tiny scratches on the surface of his glasses. And when he lifted the coat I gazed at his hands and his fingers which were so lean and so incredibly delicate and sensitive ...

'You keep tucking your hair behind your ear, Miss Hahn,' Mr Huff observed, dryly.

'Sorry?' I jerked back to attention.

'Your hair, Miss Hahn. You keep tucking it behind your ...'
He impersonated the gesture. '... but there's no hair there,
Miss Hahn.'
'Oh,' I said, embarrassed. Was he ... was he actually moving
closer? Leaning in closer?

He lifted up a hand towards the side of my face. And as he
did so the crutch under his armpit was dislodged and began
to fall. I flinched. I just flinched, automatically, as it clattered
to the floor. Mr Huff frowned.
'I don't know why you keep ...' he muttered, irritated, his
hand still lifted, still suspended. 'Why do you keep ...?'

'It's just a silly habit,' I muttered.
He started. For some, strange reason he started. Then he
dropped his hand and shifted back slightly.
'What a terrible hair-clip!' he snapped. 'What on earth
possessed you to put that ridiculous thing in your hair, Miss
Hahn?'

'What business is it of yours what I put in my hair?' I
responded, bending down to retrieve the fallen crutch.
Mr Huff started again. He started. For a second time.
'Because you look ridiculous!' he muttered. 'It's all wrong! It
just isn't *you*, Miss Hahn. It's too... It's too feminine. It's too
fussy. Pearls and silver filigree! It's ridiculous ... it's like ...' –
he pondered for a moment – 'like applying lipstick to a giant
sea cow or ...' – he frowned, struggling to find a suitable
example – 'sticking a big, pink bow on a ... a giraffe! It's all
wrong, Miss Hahn. It's ridiculous. You look so much better
with ... without ...'

'Hello? Hello? Is anybody ...?'
Someone was calling.
Neither of us moved.

'Sorry.' He frowned. 'What I meant to say was that it's like
...'
'Hello?'
It was Mrs Sage Meadows. Of course.

'... like ... like gilding the lily ... I didn't ...'

His voice dropped to a conspiratorial hum. 'I didn't intend for it to sound so ...'

'I heard about your awful mishap, Mr Huff' – Mrs Meadows swanned into the room – 'and I brought you a home-made ... Oh!'

She froze in her tracks. Mr Huff and I sprang guiltily apart. I turned.

A cake.

Well just look at that!

A cake.

She'd brought him a home-made cake.

Lucky old Mr Huff.

I'd hazard a wild guess at ... at chocolate. Or mocha. Or coffee and walnut.

43

Mr Franklin D. Huff

I *had* been trying to provoke her. I won't even bother to
pretend otherwise. I had been trying to ... I don't know ... to
get under her skin. Out of pique. Out of pure spite. Out of a
feeling of immense ... frustration – irritation – powerlessness.
And I'm not remotely ashamed to admit this (in fact I'm
happy to admit it – too happy, perhaps).

But when she picked up that child's coat and cradled it in
her arms, and her face ...

It crumpled. Like a paper bag. It just crumpled. As if I'd ...
like I'd crushed the very ... destroyed the very ... scooped out
her very *soul* with my two bare hands. And then her entire
body was racked by these gigantic sobs. The most awful,
desperate, heart-wrenching sobs.

Ah! Such terrible distress! Such unspeakable anguish! Like
a wounded beast, trapped, fatally injured, insensible with pain
(and its young, meanwhile, all back at the den – just waiting,
patiently waiting – still expecting to be fed).

Even the imaginary Miss Hahn – generally difficult to
knock off her perch – was reduced to silence by this most
distressing of spectacles.

What have I done? I asked, tentatively. Very tentatively. In my
head. Looking for reassurance.

You've gone too far, Mr Huff, the imaginary Miss Hahn
whispered, *that's what you've done!*

But ... but she hid the dead shark under my bed, Miss Hahn!
I wheedled.

421

'How *could* you, Mr Huff?!' The actual Miss Hahn lifted
her face from the coat with an agonizing groan. 'Orla's little
coat. Her *coat*. How *could* you, Mr Huff?'
Oh dear. And how might I adequately respond? What could I
conceivably come up with to try and right such a dreadful
'perceived' wrong?

I think I ... I probably just cobbled together some pathetic
excuse straight off the cuff. Said Mrs Barrow had made a silly
mistake. Tried to palm it off on her as best I could.

Miss Hahn shoved her distraught face back into the dense
folds of the coat again.
She's furious! Miss Hahn cautioned me. *Incandescent! Listen to
that!*
I didn't want to listen. It was unbearable! Miss Hahn was
muttering and groaning and clenching her fists. She was in an
ecstasy of rage. An *ecstasy*. And then – just as suddenly – it
stopped. She stopped. Her fists unclenched. Her shoulders
relaxed. Her breathing regulated. And she was ... she was
embracing and kissing and consoling the damn thing,
muttering sweetly into it, nuzzling it, reassuring it.

It was very strange. I (meanwhile) was busy telling Miss
Hahn (the *actual* Miss Hahn) – who I knew wasn't listening –
of my frustrations over suddenly, mysteriously, being
designated the Clearys' chief representative on earth. I mean I
had taken on this role semi-voluntarily at first, although my
motivations, at root, weren't entirely honourable (I can't – or
won't – be a hypocrite about it). But I hadn't intended to
become ... I hadn't wanted to become caught up ... hog-tied
... because I simply ... I simply wasn't equipped *emotionally*
to ... to cope.

Same as Miss Hahn herself, I suppose. And if I think back
I recall Miss Hahn confessing as much in the sauna that day.
Drawing a comparison between us both. But at the time I
hadn't ... I was just too caught up in ... in I'm not sure what.

In proving myself to be above it all. Maintaining a measure of professional distance.

It was at this point, anyhow, that Miss Hahn lifted her face from the coat and demanded to know who it was that had entrusted the damn thing to me. Her tone was disparaging, almost aggressive. I was slightly taken aback. I'd been happily spilling out my guts to this incorrigible female – this veritable banshee – and now here I was being cross-examined on every conceivable detail pertaining to its bizarre acquisition. Either way, shoving aside my (considerable, and utterly valid) misgivings, I set about trying to explain (in plain English, although this language didn't entirely seem to *suit* my explanations) how it had all come about. And as I explained it I became – perhaps it was her combative style of questioning that injured my feelings, or the cynical mutterings of the imaginary Miss Hahn in my head – but as I explained it I became increasingly infuriated. Just the look of contempt in her eyes. And of betrayal (I didn't *ask* Miss Hahn to have any confidence in me, did I? Quite the opposite, in fact!). But it was mainly the hurt – the crushing sense of disappointment. They rankled with me. They *stung*.

So I headed into the house. I fled. Well, I staggered. With Miss Hahn still in hot pursuit, haranguing me about the coat, explaining its history and its significance and its endless virtues in considerable (nay, interminable) detail.

By the time I'd reached the living room I was spent (physically, emotionally). I turned to face her again, panting, exhausted, perfectly willing to concede defeat.

The hunter, hunted! The imaginary Miss Hahn chuckled. And she was right. The imaginary Miss Hahn had put her imaginary finger on it. Yet again.

'What do you want from me, Miss Hahn?' I asked the real Miss Hahn. It was a kind of ... a kind of ... a tortured appeal. Because I didn't know what I could conceivably give. And if Miss Hahn would only ... just *tell* me, then we might be able to negotiate some basic parameters. We might even be able to ... to bring about some kind of ... of a *rapprochement* between us.

'What do you want from me, Miss Hahn?'

'I don't know,' she answered.

But I wasn't sure if I entirely believed her. I think she did know. I think there *was* something. Something she wanted. But she wouldn't allow herself to confess to it. And then she just ... she just started talking about the damn coat again and pointing out all these tiny 'messages' embedded into the skin of it.

'This is a four and a nought and a ... this is a leaf ... this is a rabbit ...' *etc. etc.*

At which point my natural ... shall I call it arrogance? No. Curiosity? Yes. I think I'll call it curiosity. My natural curiosity got the better of me. I'm not sure if that's grammatical (even logical). But anyway. I began looking at the coat somewhat more attentively, and I won't pretend that I wasn't quite ... quite fascinated by the little narrative that quickly unfolded on the surface of those old skins.

It was certainly very ancient. Older than I had originally conceived of. I suppose you might call me something of an expert in the curing and preservation of skins. Miss Hahn had chided me (slightly earlier) about my having 'an interest in native antiquities'. And she was right. I did/do have one. Quite an active interest, in fact. And this coat was immensely old and exquisitely ornate. I really was quite taken with it. I started setting Miss Hahn straight on a few of the details ... the ancient story, the watering holes, the stream, the journey, the great star ...

As I talked I could feel – perhaps I'm getting ahead of myself here – I could feel Miss Hahn leaning in. She was leaning in. And her eyes – once affixed to the coat – were now ... not affixed to the coat any longer. But to me. She tucked her hair behind her ear. It's a nervous gesture. A tic, of sorts.

She tucked her hair behind her ear. And I felt the movement and I looked up and I stared into her grey-green eyes and I said, 'You keep tucking your hair behind your ear, Miss Hahn.'

This wasn't an especially interesting or profound thing for me to have said (I accept this). It was simply an observation. An intimate observation. Then I lifted my ... I raised my hand to ... to ... In fact I'm not entirely sure (on deeper reflection) what I planned to do with that hand. Did I plan to touch her cheek? Or the hair itself? I don't know. Either way, I lifted my hand and Miss Hahn (in her turn) just ... she automatically jerked back. In sheer horror! As if I was intending to ... to *strike* her. Then my crutch clattered to the floor. And I was ... I was ... I felt ... Just to be ... to be so repeatedly, *instinctively* rejected by Miss Hahn. Or if not ... I don't know. So I lashed out. Which is typical of me, when I find myself in a corner. I lashed out and said something cutting about Miss Hahn's ridiculous hair-clip. And then Miss Hahn said something sharp back. As well she might. But the funny thing was that as she said it, as she *said* it – and I don't remember her precise words right now – as she said it the imaginary Miss Hahn uttered the *exact same sentence*! Then she (the real Miss Hahn) said something else, and the imaginary Miss Hahn also ... etc. ... and then I realized that the two Miss Hahns were now miraculously conjoined and that ... well, that *both* were rejecting me! Together! In unison! And I felt very hurt. And bereft. And angry. And I made some ill-considered comment about a sea cow, or a giraffe. Then I had a sudden change of heart and began trying to apologize, but the damage was done. The damage was well and truly done.

At which point ... I'm sorry to just clumsily regurgitate the whole thing like this without any ... without any particular style or finesse, but I'm actually re-telling this sorry tale to ... to *myself* if you must know. To try and make some kind of sense out of it. Because – like so many other stories in my life thus far – it doesn't really add up. Which I suppose *is* the story of my life – my destiny (if you want to get all deep and meaningful about it) – it simply doesn't add up. My life is an incorrect sum. A bad piece of algebra. And that is who I am. My story will always have a big, red cross stuck in the margin at the side of it. Mr Huff, you are wrong, it proclaims. Mr Huff, you are simply *wrong*.

But anyhow … I was just trying to … to backtrack, to apologize to Miss Hahn for my terrible blunder when who should turn up but Mrs Sage Meadows – a Florence Nightingale in heels! – bearing a bloody *cake*. And Miss Hahn closed down. She shut down. Whatever there was between us – before – was gone. In an instant.

It was difficult. Mrs Meadows – for some reason – seemed confused and irritated that Miss Hahn was … and I was confused and irritated that Mrs Meadows was …

Either way, Mrs Meadows put the cake down on to the kitchen counter and then started making a big fuss about … This was odd. Mrs Meadows was just trying to pass off a difficult social situation as best she could, and then suddenly (that part is a bit of a blur, if I'm honest) she was looking at the coat – at the child's coat – which Miss Hahn had just hung over the back of a chair before preparing to dash off (she had that look – that look Miss Hahn always gets when she longs to escape. Which is a look I am all too familiar with, alas). Anyway, Mrs Meadows started cooing over it (as Mrs Meadows is wont to do – coo over things) and then out of the blue she started inspecting it with a real intensity … her eyes lit up.

'How extraordinary!' she exclaimed, reaching into her handbag, removing a rather large and ungainly pair of heavy, tortoiseshell glasses and applying them to her nose. 'What exactly *is* this thing?'

'It's Orla's coat,' Miss Hahn informed her (moving from foot to foot, eye on the door), 'Orla's possum-skin coat. It was a family heirloom, passed down through several generations on the Aboriginal side of the family. The first time Orla saw the Virgin Mary, in a vision, after an attack of heatstroke, Mary was wearing a possum-skin coat just like this one. It's actually very old.'

Mrs Sage Meadows scratched her head. 'But how … how *odd*,' she said.

'Odd?' Miss Hahn echoed.

'Yes. Odd … Strange.'

Mrs Meadows drew in closer to the coat and pointed. 'That's Ludwig Boltzmann's famous diagram of a molecule showing atomic "sensitive region" overlap … and' – she moved her finger – 'that's a Boltzmann Machine … look, the three hidden units and the four visible units.' She slowly shook her head, bemused. 'And over here … that's a Hopfield network … see the four nodes? And that's … that's the Crab Nebula, surely …?'

Of course I was utterly confounded by all this. Sensitive region overlap?! Boltzmann Machine?!

Miss Hahn (with typical acuity) observed my befuddlement. 'Mrs Meadows has a half-completed *Ph.D.* in Pure Maths and Engineering,' she explained.

'Oh!' I said.

Mrs Meadows had a … a *what* …?

'That's a diagram of Heinrich Hurtz's photoelectric effect,' she gushed. 'And surely this is Niels Bohr's quantum model of the atom? See the three circles and the two dots in the middle and the squiggly line over on the right-hand side?'

'I believe in Aboriginal parlance,' I quickly interrupted, 'that would "read" as an old woman's nipple next to a sun with a …'

'The Feynman diagram of gluon radiation!' Mrs Meadows all but shouted, jumping up and down, clapping her hands together. 'I've got to … I really must photograph this! Or at least … at least jot some things down. Because there's an entire … it's like an entire …'

'Map,' Miss Hahn helpfully filled in.

'Yes. Exactly. It's like a kind of … of Rosetta Stone of modern physics; a *key*. A *key* to … Or if not, then … I mean there are things here I haven't ever seen before. But there are people … there are definitely people who could interpret it way better than I can. Remember that friend in San Francisco, Miss Hahn? In Silicon Valley? Her husband? It's just a matter of … a question of getting him to …'

She paused for a second.

'Is this a dream?' she demanded, glancing around her. 'Have I gone utterly mad?'

'Did you see the bee?' Miss Hahn asked, pointing.

'Good heavens, yes! A bee! And the swarm is … Oh my God! That's a stable Dyson's swarm! A swarm! Next to the bee!'

She turned to Miss Hahn, astonished. 'After we were talking this morning, Miss Hahn, and I was thinking about the hive, and I was … something was coming together in my mind but I couldn't quite … a kind of … of *inspiration*. But there was something missing. Something … *undecidable*. It was *this*. Good heavens! I have this extraordinary feeling! In my stomach! A fluttering. A sense of … of *rightness*! Do you understand me, Miss Hahn? Mr … Mr Huff?'

I nodded, amazed. Miss Hahn nodded. She covered her mouth with her hand and blinked several times. She was very pale. Then, 'This is what it was all *for*,' she whispered, 'what it was all *about* – the suffering. Twelve, thirteen years of confusion. So that you would come here, *be* here, at this moment, and you would see this, with me, with …' – she pointed to me – 'with *us*. I feel it too! The fluttering! This is what Orla always wanted, Mrs Meadows. This – *you* – are to take her message forward, take her … her story … her … her *legacy* … her …'

Mrs Meadows looked slightly taken aback by this sudden, emotional outpouring from Miss Hahn, but she nodded at her, gamely, and smiled, somewhat condescendingly. I quickly stepped in (Damage limitation! Miss Hahn didn't want to scare the poor woman off, now, did she?).

'I have a couple of good friends in Silicon Valley,' I said. 'A man called Dr Clark Kipps. I don't know if you've ever …?'

'Dr Kipps did an amazing lecture at my university when I was a second-year student!' Mrs Meadows exclaimed. 'We occasionally correspond. He's working between California and CERN in Switzerland alongside a man called Tim Berners-Lee who invented ENQUIRE. Are you aware of the sorts of things he's been dabbling in at all?'

'Information sharing.' I nodded.

Mrs Meadows then went off on a long tangent about Dr Kipps and how her former husband, Dr Meadows, had diagnosed a particular kind of neurological disorder in him called – I think – 'Dystonia' simply from reading Dr Kipps's occasional letter (apparently the handwriting becomes very scruffy after approximately three lines, due to a cramping sensation in the hand. Dr Kipps also blinked excessively which was very typical of the condition, I'm told. Both of these characteristics were familiar to me as a long-term – although somewhat distant – acquaintance of said gentleman).

It transpired that Dr Kipps had contracted this rare disorder after suffering from carbon monoxide poisoning as a child. Dr Meadows – who I must admit was starting to sound like some kind of inspired medical genius – had always encouraged Mrs Meadows in her interest in the sciences. They'd met at a small 'Science Club' in Rye which Dr Meadows had established in the mid-1960s. Mrs Meadows's parents (late of Dublin; Mrs Meadows was a lapsed Catholic and had attended convent school) had been living in Rye at that time and she had fled there following a rather messy break-up with … I can't recall. It might have been an airline pilot.

After Dr Meadows's sudden death, Mrs Meadows had abandoned all her former interest in science and engineering. The deep passion he'd reignited suddenly dwindled … It was simply too painful for her. It reminded her of Dr Meadows and the 'great enthusiasms' they'd shared …

But … but then what an extraordinary coincidence – she gasped – that it was *my* coming to see her, *my* searching her out over Orla and Dr Meadows's diaries that had led to … this sudden, strange discovery. This revelation! How very extraordinary!

Yes! And after she'd been standing in the garden this morning, watching the bees, thinking about … about … and then to make this … this *connection* … with the stable Dyson's swarm … she pointed … And what on earth is *this*? she added, her eyes shining, here, right next to it? I … I honestly don't know what that means! she panted. 'What on earth does that …? How perplexing! I need to go home and get a camera or if I could just …if I could just get a piece of paper and copy this all down … Is that a Hopf Bundle? There? Is that …?'

I turned to say something to Miss Hahn at this point. I think I had been intending to ask her if she might help me search for a jotter in the bedroom; my suitcase was pushed under the bed and I couldn't bend over to … and if Mrs Meadows could put on the kettle and cut into that delicious-seeming … this was all complete hokum. I just wanted to get Miss Hahn on her own so that I might apologize for my former – my previous – but Miss Hahn was gone. Miss Hahn had vanished. Miss Hahn had left the room – the cottage. Without my even …

And I … this feeling of complete devastation! This shattered feeling. As if I had been blown into a thousand, tiny pieces and those pieces were floating about the room and getting lost under heavy furniture and … and only Miss Hahn had the adhesive. Only Miss Hahn had the glue.

I simply couldn't leave things as they were. I grabbed Mrs Meadows by the hand and said, 'Miss Hahn has gone! But you must run after her with … with …' I quickly improvised: 'with some cake! Miss Hahn adores cake … Or … or …' My eyes looked frantically around the room … some kind of … some kind of *gesture* … some kind of … of *keepsake* … just by way of an … to apologize. To apologize. As a small sign. Of my great … my esteem. My great, my enduring esteem. For her. For the woman who had single-handedly borne … For Miss Hahn. Who had … who had brought us all together and then had quietly slipped away again. Without so much as a … without seemingly even … without …

44

Miss Carla Hahn

I was standing on the roof of the old Look Out. I was standing there because it was completely exposed. You could see for miles around, and you could be seen from miles around. It was a place where you might simply become a part of the landscape. Like the flickering needle on a huge, earthly compass. I was offering myself up, for Orla, finding significance through insignificance. And I was determined not to cry again. If I stood here for long enough, then the urge to weep would eventually pass. The urge to mourn, too. And the urge to feel. I might even bundle them all together, somehow (these pointless emotions) – like a stack of firewood – and offer them up, *en masse* (where's the lighter? Out of fuel? That's just fine. A match'll do).

So this is where I was (yielding to precisely these kinds of ludicrously self-pitying thoughts) when Mrs Meadows found me (well, I was quite hard to miss, I suppose). Mrs Meadows was somewhat out of breath. Her footwear (a cream court shoe) wasn't entirely appropriate for the rough, rubble-strewn terrain, and utterly *un*suitable for scrabbling across the temporary plank-and-corrugated-iron bridge which currently divided us. So she stopped at the other side, called out and waved.

'Miss Hahn? Hello? *Hello?* Miss Hahn?'
She was clutching a slice of cake (deposited – by Mr Huff, no doubt – inside the torn-off lid of an old egg box). I gritted my teeth for a second (staring out to sea with hooded eyes), then

turned and returned her jolly wave (transforming that
benighted clench into a beaming smile) before carefully
slipping and sliding my way back down on to firm land again.

Mrs Meadows proffered me the cake. I took it from her.
'That looks delicious,' I said, sniffing it, slightly suspicious.
'It's a swede cake,' she said.
'Oh. How lovely!' I said. 'And is that a touch of ... of
cinnamon?'
'The original recipe calls for cinnamon,' Mrs Meadows
confided, 'but I used nutmeg. And the plain, butter icing has
been enlivened by a dollop of molasses.'
'That sounds terribly wholesome,' I murmured. 'And also
quite ... quite regulating.'
She nodded.
'It was very kind of you to bring me a slice,' I added (wryly
imagining an infinitely unfurling future in which a traumatized
Mr Huff was compelled – for his manifold sins – to feast on a
multitude of earthy yet exotic combinations from the warped
culinary hand of Mrs Meadows).

'Did I ...' Mrs Meadows frowned. 'I hope I didn't *barge in*
on anything important when I turned up at the cottage
earlier?'

My hand shot up to my head. 'I really must return your
hair-clip,' I exclaimed, removing it.
'But it was a gift!' Mrs Meadows insisted.
'And that was very kind of you' – I nodded – 'but I think its
work is now done.'
'Its work?' Mrs Meadows echoed.
'I'm just not sure if it's entirely my ... uh ... my *style*,' I
confessed, passing it over. Mrs Meadows shrugged, took the
clip, then slipped it, neatly, back into her own hair again.

'And you didn't interrupt a thing!' I added, tucking my
fringe behind my ear. 'Not a thing!'
'I thought you might have been arguing ...' Mrs Meadows still
persisted.

'A frank discussion,' I maintained, 'over nothing of any significance ...' I shrugged. 'The bill for the utilities ... you know ... the faulty cistern ... the ... the badgers.'

'Oh I wish I were a little more like you, Miss Hahn!' Mrs Meadows sighed. 'Aloof and tough and ... and *boyish* and independent. I do have a very practical – I suppose one might best call it a "rational/scientific" – side, but then on the other hand there's always been this powerful need to ...' – she frowned – 'to nestle myself *into* a man, for support and ... and *comfort*. To snuggle in. The way a ... a little duckling feels driven to retreat from the world under its mother's wing.'

My heart sank. I stared at Mrs Meadows, forlornly, wondering how on earth it had finally come about that this patently quite intelligent yet (at root, let's face it) deeply idiotic woman was about to be entrusted to carry Orla's precious legacy forward.

Then something suddenly struck me, and my heart instantly lifted. That was the whole *point*, surely? Orla had always been drawn to the least capable ... the most chaotic and unfocused and ... and *stuck* and undecided ... *That* was her genius. *That* was her message. We were *all* to be a part of it. We were *all* equally significant in Orla's eyes.

It wasn't ever just about the big draws – the main players – it was always about the bit parts. The character roles. Even the extras. The kitchen scraps, I mused. Ah yes, the kitchen scraps. Especially those.

And in Mrs Meadows's case (to give her her fair due) these scraps were all culled from the highest quality of ingredients: the scented skin of an exotic mango ... a feather-light sprinkling of salmon scales ... a barely used lapsang souchong teabag ...

I imagined Orla's message as a tiny, newly hatched quail's egg being transported across the globe by a galumphing horde of panhandle-fingered clowns. Its very fragility (the egg's) and the chaotic nature of that journey (the blocked exits, the open trapdoors, the questionable escape-routes) were an essential part of what might eventually make it so powerful – so explosive. Yes. I needed to believe that. And by this same crazy logic, the sillier Mrs Meadows was, the more luminous Orla's message might become under her careless tutelage.

'Oh, I almost forgot,' Mrs Meadows exclaimed, 'Mr Huff wanted you to have this ...'
She passed over a large envelope.
'What is it?'
I took it from her, somewhat unnerved.
'I don't know. He just told me to bring it to you. He said I shouldn't return to the cottage until you were standing right in front of me, holding it in your hands.'
'The sheer arrogance of the man!' I snorted.
'Yes, *wonderful*, isn't it?' Mrs Meadows nodded (no perceptible sense of irony), then she squeezed my shoulder (a sympathetic squeeze, almost) and off she flitted.

I inspected the envelope. In small, neat lettering on the back, tightly squeezed into the bottom, far-right-hand corner (I imagine the placement of this message was of deep psychological significance), Mr Huff had printed 'Please keep these, Miss Hahn,' in pencil. The please underlined, for emphasis. I stared at his handwriting. My eye delighted (unhealthily) in its various idiosyncrasies.

I then clambered up on to the Look Out again, sat down with a sigh, rested the envelope across my lap, picked up Mrs Meadows's slice of cake and gamely took a bite. I chewed and swallowed. The texture was perfectly light and airy, but the cake itself tasted of ... I grimaced ... of soap and walnuts ... and ... and (worst of all) *innovation*. Urgh! I tossed the remainder to the gulls who devoured it, squawking, then flew away (incognizant) like a little host of tiny guided, swede-and-nutmeg-laden missiles.

The envelope, when I opened it, was full of photographs. What else could it have been full of? *Love?*

But I couldn't look at them. I didn't ... I wasn't ... I just ...
So I re-sealed it, leaned back on to my elbows, and sat quietly
for an hour watching the sun sinking into the Channel (like a
giant melting blob of raspberry sorbet), briefly relieved of all
my burdens (aside from the gnats, obviously), feeling that
special, empty brand of happiness only true melancholy
brings.

45

Mr Franklin D. Huff

I interrogated Mrs Meadows closely when she returned to the cottage.

'Miss Hahn seemed in … in good spirits, when you finally met up with her, then, did she?' I enquired (nonchalantly straightening the rucked-up corner of a seagrass rug with the end of my crutch).

'Yes, excellent spirits!' Mrs Meadows confirmed.

'No sign of … uh …?' I persisted.

'Mildew?' Mrs Meadows rejoined tartly, following it up with a mischievous giggle.

(This referred back to a bad joke I had once made to Mrs Meadows at Miss Hahn's expense; something along the lines of: 'I'm not sure if she perspires so much as exudes a slight mildew.')

'Oh yes. Ha ha. Very funny,' I muttered, 'very witty …'

I gamely steeled myself for the requisite coruscating aside from the imaginary Miss Hahn, but of course none was forthcoming. Instead a child's voice sighed, *I always thought her so very beautiful, Mr Huff. A bright light in her that shone out of her chest through a tiny hole. Because there was this little chink, Mr Huff, chiselled between her ribs by the cruel forces of the world through which the Holy Spirit came and went. Like her heart was a dovecote, Mr Huff! And sometimes I would call him out and he would fly to my hand or land on my head and perch there a while. The Spirit was so strong in her, Mr Huff! But she never knew. And Our Lady told me not to tell her. So I always kept it a secret, Mr Huff, exactly as Our Lady had asked me to ...*

The voice of the imaginary Miss Hahn had generally been possessed of a quiet and unobtrusive quality, but this voice, this child's voice (with its suggestion of a gentle Irish lilt) was like the sound of a wood pigeon suddenly taking off. It had the strangest ... almost an echo. But it wasn't a voice, so much as something whirring or something being dropped. Or dry leaves being sucked up into a mini-tornado. Impossible to explain. And when it spoke I saw ... how to describe it? A kind of golden dust, a tiny shower of glitter, but very golden and very fine, flitting rapidly around the room, like a shooting star or ... or ... a brilliantly camouflaged moth with traces of gold beneath its wings. It would land and then mark the spot and then move off, and the gold dust would remain for a moment before evaporating with a sound like an orchestral wind-chime, but not nearly so ... so strident ... as if ... as though the wind chime was crafted from ancient bamboo, almost.

'... or three?' Mrs Meadows wondered.
'*What?* Uh ... Sorry?' I chittered, staggering slightly.
Mrs Meadows was in the kitchen, preparing a pot of tea.
'Two bags or three?' she repeated.
'I don't care,' I murmured. 'Three.'
'But there are only four left.'
'*What?*' I scowled.
'There are only four bags left.'
'Oh.'

I continued to follow this flittering presence around the room with my eyes.

Shall I offer myself up for you, Mr Huff? the child wondered, with a gentle laugh, drawing closer, leaving a light residue of the glitter on my arms and then withdrawing again.

Offer yourself ...? I asked, jerking my arm away. The sensation of the dust was strangely painful. An exquisite, non-existent pain. I remembered once being stung by a jellyfish while swimming in the ocean off Acapulco. I came out of the sea and there was a bright mark on my lower leg, circling my calf like a whiplash. But I was completely unaware of it until someone kindly pointed it out to me. Then there was this curious interlude – an in-between time – during which my body knew that it had been attacked but my brain couldn't quite process the fact. Like that odd pause after a toddler falls over, when he processes the fall, grades its significance, then inhales, sharply, to bawl out his furious response. Exactly like that.

'Pardon, Mr Huff?' Mrs Meadows glanced up from the tea caddy.

'Nothing,' I said, 'three bags,' I said.

The child had briefly withdrawn, but then that soft sound returned: the broken ... antique ... broken bamboo chimes ... although that hardly describes it ... and I saw the dust in the furthest reaches of the room, settling on the heads of literally dozens of people ... a dense sea of people ... the dust making their presence manifest ... all these ghostly shapes ... holding out their hands to the dust, that they might be made ... whole ... real ... for even the briefest of interludes. A terrible groan of conjoined yearning and love and pain and desire echoed around the room. I even saw a dog – a *dog*, a small shadow terrier, jumping up on to its hind legs. It was with a woman who reached out to restrain it, whispering a muttered expletive ... The entire room was ... like it was exposed by a golden searchlight ... and all these ... should I call them spirits ... souls? Reaching out their arms with this mournful sigh ... then the laugh of the child ... *So many of you!* she tinkled, *the debt is so huge ... but we will pay it off, we will pray for you all ... we will offer everything up ... if we can only just ... if we can only ...*

Then a sudden, terrible roar of interference – a babble of voices, but all shouting together, hysterically – like the start of the day's trading at the London Stock Exchange.

The souls sighed again, a hoarse, whispering *Ahhhhhhhh!* and what struck me was how these two sounds were both completely separate, independent and all-consuming, yet they were both perfectly clear and fully audible, in that same instant, when normally ... the only way I could understand it was that these two things – or three things, even – were all happening together but at *completely different times*. I was very struck by this feeling. Very struck by it. Almost ... almost unnerved by it.

Then – *click!* – everything promptly returned to normal. Almost. I blinked. I blinked again. I suddenly felt very tired. I wanted to throw myself straight down on to the sofa, but this same sofa – only moments before – had been packed full of people. And I still couldn't sit down anyway, physically ... it wasn't possible ... my injuries ... so I adjusted my crutches (in fact these were Mr Barrow's crutches, which I'd temporarily been loaned. Mr Barrow was prone to breaking the tiny bones in his feet – he'd done so twice: hairline fractures, stress fractures, and these were his crutches which Mrs Barrow had kindly ...) ... Where was I? Just ... yes ... so *tired* again. I began making my way, clumsily, across the room. I had a strange and unyielding ... what was it? Like a paper-thin lens across the surface of my eye which was sensitive to shadow – hyper-sensitive to shadow – as if the light from that golden dust – the unearthly brightness – had inexplicably burned ... I was somewhat ... uh ... yes ... *spooked*. Exactly. Ridiculous! Probably just a weird side effect of the huge quantity of painkillers ... I just wanted to ...

'Mr Huff?'

It was Mrs Meadows, standing in the doorway. I was stretched out, face down, on the bed. It was as if I had been asleep and had just woken up.

'Mrs Meadows?' I asked, disorientated.

'Don't you want your tea, Mr Huff?'

'Did I ...?' I frowned, confused.

'Should I ... Should I perhaps go, Mr Huff?'

Mrs Meadows looked slightly put out. I suddenly felt very ... very sensitive to how Mrs Meadows was feeling. My heart thudded, anxiously, at the awful prospect of having somehow inadvertently offended ... And as I gazed towards her, this strange lens on my eyelid picked out an iridescent nimbus ... like a halo, but then I realized that it hadn't been concern (that anxious feeling) but fear. And the halo didn't belong to Mrs Meadows, but it was the light of many golden-tinged shapes – these ravenous figures, hungry figures – crowding in behind her. Yet nothing ahead of her. Everything clear ahead of her. As if it were the force of her sheer presence alone that was keeping them back.

'Oh God, no!' I said, suddenly fearful. 'You couldn't possibly leave. You couldn't possibly do that. You must ... you must stay with me, Mrs Meadows. Until I ... Until ...'

How long, I wondered, how long might this ...? How long might I conceivably be expected to ... to ...?

46

Miss Alys Jane Drury
(*and* Baldo!)

'No it isn't too late, Carla, it's fine. I was actually just ...'

'*WAAAAAAAAAAAAAAAAH!*'

'Hello? Are you still ...? Sorry. That was ...'

....

'Yes he is. I mean she is. She *is* home. I've got her perched on
an old mug tree on the kitchen table while I ...'

'WAAAAAAH!'

....

'Yes! While I clear out the bottom of her ...'

'BALDO! BALDO! BALDO! BALDO! BALDO! BALDO!
WAH!'

'Sorry. Her cage.'

'*WAAAAAAAH!*'

....

'She certainly has! And the vet said she needed to be kept quiet for a few days, but she does seem to be quite … yes. Exactly. Quite revived.'

………

'It is. I'm just so relieved …'

………

'No, no, no. He's long gone, now. I actually got shot of him the day after I …'

………

'I haven't. I *did* think long and hard about it, Carla, and I chatted to the vet about it, too, and we decided that it might be quite confusing for him – *her* – if I made any dramatic changes before she was …'

………

'Exactly! And apart from anything else it would render a good half of everything she actually *says* completely incompre—'

'BALDO! BALDO! BALDO! BALDO! BALDO! BALDO! *WAAAAK!*'

………

'Ha! Oh yes. Yes, that's definitely new. Could you hear the difference over the …?'

………

'Yes. She's been doing that since the vet's. Apparently there was an injured baby jackdaw awaiting collection by an animal refuge in a nearby ...'

....

'They do. Yes. A kind of "waaak" noise.'

'*WAAAAAK!*'

'Exactly. Thanks very much, Baldo.'

....

'Me too! Oh absolutely delighted! Although I suspect you didn't ring me up to spend hours talking about ...'

....

'Really? When was this, exactly?'

....

'Are you still with your dad, then?'

....

'Oh yes, I know how antsy he gets about his phone bill!'

'BALDO! BALDO! BALDO! BALDO!'

....

'Early to bed, early to rise – I think the saying ...'

....

'Exactly!'

'*WAAAAK!*'

....

'So how long did it take you to …?

....

'And you've just been stewing on it ever since?'

....

'Well they were bound to upset you, weren't they?'

....

'I was exactly the same, Carla. Exactly the same. Because there's the stock selection of images which they always tend to use in the press and a person gets … well, *inured*, but it's entirely different to …'

....

'Absolutely. That's *exactly* how I felt. To a T.'

....

'She *did* look well in them. But then looks can often be …'

....

'Poor you!'

[*Shrill, high-pitched whistle.*]

'Baldo! Enough! *Enough!*'

....

'Yes. Yes it *was* a little ... a little confusing just ... just trying to slot yourself back into that whole original ...'

....

'*I* said that?'

....

'Oh. Yes. *Yes.* In fact ...yes ...'

....

[*High-pitched whistle.*]

'Enough, Baldo! Uh, yes, yes I did. I remember now. You were in your little red ...'

....

'Oh ... Well I don't exactly remember them being in any strict kind of order, as such ...'

....

'No. In fact you're right, Carla. Yes. You're perfectly correct. They were. They were numbered, on the back.'

....

'Oh. Well it was probably quite early on in the ...'

....

'04?'

....

'And number 40?'

....

'40.04?'

....

'I do have a vague recollection of that, yes. Very vague. But then there were lots of things that Orla said and ... and did ...'

....

'Hmmn. Perhaps you're over-thinking this just a little?'

'*WAAAAAAK!*'

....

'Yes, I do, though. I do remember it.'

....

'A computer ...?'

....

'Sorry, who? Mrs ...? You mean Dr Meadows's old ... ?'

....

'No. I don't think I've ever actually met ...'

....

'Together? *Really?!* In what sense, "together"?'

....

'You mean since he got home from Douai ...?'

....

'Which coat?'

....

'In fact there *was* something in a carrier bag ... I imagine Mr
Barrow must've brought it into the cottage under Mr Huff's
instruction because I *certainly* had no inkling that it might
have been ... I would most *definitely* have ...'

....

[*Shrill high-pitched whistle.*]

'Are you being *serious?!*'

....

'Gracious me! I actually think you showed enviable restraint under the circumstances!'

………

'BALDO! BALDO! BALDO! BALDO! BALDO! BALDO!'

'I only saw her in it once, Carla. But remember it was the summer when they visited, so it wasn't really appropriate weather for …'

'WAAAH!'

………

'No. Father Hugh never made any mention of it to me.'

………

'Well I suppose it was entirely up to Kalinda who she …'

………

'But why would you want to tell him that, Carla? I mean it's just speculation, surely? And especially after he tried to …?'

………

'Perhaps you should give it a little more …?'

'*WAAAAAAAAAAAAAAAK!*'

'Sorry. He – *she* – gets a bit testy when I spend too long nattering on the …'

......

'Yes. An old monk. In a wheelchair. When I was praying in the abbey. He told me I should trust Mr Huff. I quote: "even though your every instinct fights against it".'

[*Shrill, high-pitched whistle.*]

......

'Orla. He said Orla had told him.'

......

'I'm beyond knowing that, darling. I mean what *is* there in this life to be entirely confident in, apart from God of course? And taxes?'

......

'Okay, death. And God. And taxes. I stand corrected.'

......

'WAAAH!'

'Who told you that?'

......

'Well, I suppose Mrs Barrow would be in a good position to know ...'

......

'*Really?!* The two of them? Travelling together? When, exactly?'

………

[*Shrill, high-pitched whistle.*]

'Enough, Baldo! *Enough* now! Uh … well if they have acquaintances in common then I suppose …'

………

'It *is* quite extraordinary when you actually come to think about it. That he should suddenly be in sole charge of virtually everything to do with …'

………

'No, Carla. Not *everything*. It was just an idle turn of … Sorcha's still a perfectly free agent. And so are you, and so am I … And you've got the cottage. You've got Mulberry. So it's not a *complete* monopoly. Thank God!'

………

[*Shrill, high-pitched whistle.*]

'I don't know, Carla. I mean if you're upset about those two missing …'

………

'I can't really. Not properly. I just … I don't feel entirely qualified to advise you about that. Maybe a priest might be better …?'

454

....

'Like a kind of ... yes ... after ... yes, to offer it all up. I see what you mean ...'

....

'I'm honestly not the greatest of experts on the matter – it's just more of an ... an *instinct*, I suppose. A journey of the heart. And only you can know if it'll make you feel more positive about ...'

'WAH!'

....

'Yes. The missing photos are one reason why you might not feel as if you can entirely ...'

....

'WAH!'

'Well, it's not really down to us to stand in judgement, is it?'

....

'But it's not simply a question of tit-for-tat, though, Carla, because if it were ...'

'WAH!'

....

'Exactly. The dead shark.'

....

'WAH!'

'Oh Carla! I just wish I could be of a little more ...'

'OW! *OW!* YOU EVIL, LITTLE BUGGER! GET YOUR
...! STOP THAT! *STOP* THAT!'

(?!)

'Good heavens! Carla! Did you just ...?'

....

'Baldo! I swear! He just said ...'

....

'Yes! Clear as a bell! An entire sentence!'

....

'I know! But *what* a sentence, Carla!'

'WAH!'

....

'They must've! Yes! Oh my goodness! Baldo! *Baldo!* You
can't just go around yelling out dreadful things like that in
polite society without so much as a ...!'

'WAH!'

....

'He's preening himself, Carla, proud as punch! I mean *she* ... *her*self.'

....

'She is! Well let's pray to God that it was simply a one-off!'

....

'Yes I do! A *very* good mind to tell them! I just forked out for a £250 vet's bill, Carla! And this is how they go about ... ?!'

[*Shrill, high-pitched whistle.*]

....

'Baldo! What were you thinking, eh?'

'BALDO! BALDO! BALDO! BALDO! BALDO! BALDO! *WAAAH!*'

'He's all ...'

....

'Yes. Sorry. I probably better had, Carla.'

'WAAAAH!'

'He is!'

WAAAAAAAAAH!'

'I mean *sh—*'

'*WAAAAAAAAAAAAAAAAAAAAAAAAAAAAAAA ...*'

....

'*... AAAAAAAAAAAAAAAAAAAAAAAAAAAAA ...*'

'Okay. Yes. Okay ...'

'*... AAAAAAAAAAAAAAAAAAAAAAAAAAAAA ...*'

....

'*... AAAAAAAAAAAAAAAAAAAAAAAAAAAAA ...*'

'Goodbye then, darling!'

'*AAAAAAAAAAAAAAAAAAAAAAAAAAAAAA ...*'

'And the very best of British ... uh ...!'

'*AAAAAAAAAAAAAAAAAAAAAAAAAAAAAAAAAAAAAAAA
AAAAAAAAAAAAAAAAAAAAAAAAAAAAAAAAAAAAAAAA
AAK!!*'

47

Mr Franklin D. Huff

I'd been in dreadful pain. *Dreadful* pain. But things (you know, *ahem*, 'things') improved dramatically when I cut down on the analgesics (those awful *sounds* – roaring, keening, strangely individuated – slowly abated). So it was almost worth it. And the pain itself was a distraction. A sharpener. A kind of … of *motivator* of sorts.

Although there was still a strong suggestion of … *you* know … if I moved my head too quickly … a subtle, golden dusting of … a … an ominous *feeling* … this dreadful … this wretched … this terrible, all-pervasive atmosphere of yearning, aching *need* … all these endless legions of … suddenly emerging. That dreadful atmosphere of crushing loneliness!

But it was manageable. Perfectly manageable. With the odd careful adjustment. So long as I kept Mrs Meadows hanging around the place. Which was actually a kind of torment in itself. A kind of punishment in itself. Her slavish adoration. Almost as bad as being loathed by Miss Hahn (I'd even been cruelly abandoned by her voice! Her *voice*! Even her *voice* was gone! Which I suppose, if I'm honest about it, was really *my* voice in the guise of Miss Hahn's voice. Don't they sometimes say that loving someone else is actually only another means of loving the self? Don't they say that?).

Luckily (for me), Mrs Meadows had now acquired a series of notebooks which (when she wasn't plumping up my pillows and making inedible snacks) she spent every spare moment writing in and poring over. She had developed a theory about the coat. It related to the history of what she called 'Cyberspace', which, when I interrogated her about it, she said 'didn't really mean anything – at least not in fact, only in fiction' (she cited William Gibson's *Neuromancer*). She said that the coat was like a 'giant circuit board' of modern communications theory, that it was at once a coherent whole and a series of completely separate narratives. She said it all depended on how close you were, or how far away. She said it sent out different messages from varying perspectives. On two occasions she called it 'the ultimate undecidable problem!' and then laughed, hysterically.

I can't pretend I really got the joke.

Mrs Meadows planned (with my express permission) to take the coat on a visit to see her friend in San Francisco, to show it to her friend's husband, who, so far as I could tell, worked for the government. I had agreed to fly with her. Was it only because I feared that unless I kept her close the golden dust would ... would envelop me? For good? Or perhaps because I was in a state of 'deep denial' about my actual feelings for her (same as I had been with Miss Hahn, remember?)? Or simply because I wouldn't – *couldn't* – in all good conscience, be parted from that infernal coat again.

It was just something I felt I ... I *needed* to do. For Miss Hahn. To try and make it up to her. To undo the casual wrong ... to ... to care for the stupid coat as I secretly longed to care for ... Even if Miss Hahn didn't know – *never* knew – I would protect it for her. Guard it for her. For *her*. Just for her. Not for any of the others. Not for Bran or Kalinda or Brother Prosper or the child. Just for her. Exclusively. Just for Miss Hahn.

It was time for me to move on. My lease of the cottage was almost at an end. And Mrs Barrow had informed me (in no uncertain terms – Mrs Barrow was incapable of uncertainty) that I would need to vacate the place promptly. Miss Hahn had other tenants booked in. A couple that visited the area every year and viewed the cottage as a kind of 'second home'..

So Mrs Meadows and I (well, Mrs Meadows) booked our flights. And she helped me to pack. And she cooked a strange ham and turkey strudel which tasted of stale spaghetti and deep misgivings.

As for Miss Hahn ... Ah. Let's just say that a natural decency (decency being a virtue that has never come all that naturally to me) had compelled me to keep my distance. I had reached out. I had made my grand gesture of reconciliation. I had given her the photos. That was the thing she'd always wanted – longed for, *craved*. Not the photos themselves, of course, but the past. Hermetically sealed. Beautifully preserved. Immaculately maintained. In a series of manageable stills.

Sometimes I lay in bed and thought about how she had cried that day. Holding the coat. Embracing the coat. And then I'd ponder on (Oh God, what had possessed me?!) how cruel I'd been about her hair! The hair-clip, which later (I realized (and I won't bore you with all the interminable details) had been a stupid gift from Mrs Meadows!

A hair-clip! A silly hair-clip! That everything should finally have hung on the fall (or lack!) of Miss Hahn's fringe! The wearing or not wearing of ...! Ridiculous! That something so slight should have ...? Petty! So very petty!

Hadn't it always been this signal lack of feminine guile – of calculation – that had drawn me to Miss Hahn in the first instance? Or drawn me to mock her, more like? To satirize her mercilessly? Because I was such an ignorant fool? So proud? So haughty? So terrified of ... of ...? Of *here*? Of *here*? Of being *here*, feeling *this*, this miserable love?

Or was it actually quite insignificant, this tiny 'slight'? Not important at all? (Although isn't every parlous scenario in this miserable world – war, genocide, famine – merely a gradual accumulation of tiny slip-ups?)

Was it even about the hair-clip, anyway? Wasn't it actually about my curious inability to … to *accept* … to detach … which is also a lethal kind of detachment in itself (from responsibility? From true attachment? From *life*?)?

Hmmn. Which was it to be, ultimately? Eh? Caring too much so you don't care at all? Or not caring at all so you care way too much?

Was I being punished? This is something else I found myself dwelling upon. And was Miss Hahn being punished too (by … by herself? By her past? By the child? By … by *me*?)? Were we all just a tiny part of a much greater scheme? And was the only way to really survive it – pride still marginally intact – simply to *give in*? As Miss Hahn now seemed so inclined to do?

My health slowly improved, and I was finally (the joy! The inexpressible *joy*!) able to graduate to sitting in my favourite spot on the broken bench on the back porch. Perched upon a rubber ring (Mrs Meadows's idea). I would wait for Miss Hahn to appear. On her bike. On the road. On the beach. But she never did. So I would watch the badgers, at dawn, at dusk, crashing around in the borders. Grunting. Instigating a series of pointless – but explosive – arguments between themselves. And sometimes I would sense the child playing on the lawn. Perched among them. Laughing. Or engaged in quiet prayer. But I had no idea why she prayed. Or what she prayed for. Only that (and this I *was* quite certain of) she prayed for me.

48

Miss Carla Hahn

It's always the things we don't have that we crave the most. And in my case it was those two photographs. Those missing photographs: 04 and 40. I tried to tell myself that it didn't really matter – the photos had never particularly interested me anyway (they were Mr Huff's 'trump card', remember? Kimberly Couzens's own patented worldview?). And if I *had* wanted to (to look at them, I mean), then it was only because Mr Huff had tried to deny me that most basic right. Which was almost like being denied permission to … to stare at my own face (examine my own reflection). Which was something (in general) that I preferred not to do.

I tied myself up in knots over it. And it was almost as if the tying of knots and the urge to untangle them was a secret way of … a secret way to … to avoid making my confession. The way I'd previously planned to, that night of the landslip.

Sometimes I told myself that my urge to confess (to unburden or to excoriate?) was the very thing that had 'saved' me. That the original impulse had only really been about the actual journey. Not the journey towards (redemption? Humiliation?), but the physical journey away (from, well, danger). Yet still it gnawed at me. And in quiet moments – which were few and far between over those next few days (those *last* few days) – or when I dreamed in my bed at night, I would find myself frenziedly rehearsing (composing and summarizing, reciting and readjusting). Perfecting my confession.

But no matter how hard I tried (or didn't try), the chance to deliver it never came.

On one early occasion, I was marching up Toot Rock (fists clenched, chest out, resolve duly hardened) and happened upon Sorcha collecting wild herbs (through Andy Melbourne's fence). She promptly invited me to her van for a farewell 'brew' (sage tea, she insisted, to give us 'strength for the journey'). She was packing up to leave Toot Rock (her destination? A studio in Leeds for a spot of 'over-dubbing'). So I naturally obliged her. But then somewhere along the line, during this most laborious and time-consuming of transactions (I didn't realize we'd have to *find* the sage, then pick it, then collect some water, then set the fire), we were crouched on low stools, watching her big, cast-iron kettle bubbling cheerfully on the flames, when a ball was kicked and a child ran past and suddenly the kettle was upended and some gorse started to burn, and … and then, in the midst of all this rumpus (I was stamping out the flames and beating them with my jumper) we realized that the baby had been scalded. He'd been sleeping in his cot. His little dress and blanket were all soaking wet. So we scooped him up and took him to the closest cottage (Mr Presley's), where he ran a cold bath and we dumped the baby in it and he fetched ice from the freezer – and the gorse was still smouldering – and after approximately half an hour, the poor soul chattering with the cold, with confusion, with sheer distress (Sorcha kneeling and praying), we decided that we should take him to the Conquest Hospital, just in case … Which we did.

Mrs Goulder kindly drove us. But the poor baby was perfectly fine, thank God, and the doctor gave Sorcha a tube of special ointment (from under the counter, bless him) and then, as I was leaving the hospital, I saw Clifford. In the car park. In his van. With his mother. And it turned out that his father had suffered a serious heart attack (during milking, the day after the landslip), and his condition was critical. And

Clifford was blaming himself, and his mother was blaming Clifford, and then Alice turned up, and it was all so dreadfully tense and awkward (I'm not entirely sure why), and I promised to come back and visit him the following day. We had always been very fond of each other. Me. Clifford's dad.

The next day we discovered an infestation of rats. At Shimmy's. There was one in the garden and then one in the kitchen and then two in the garden shed. And a huge nest in the compost heap. And then a neighbour complained and demanded that we put down poison, but Shimmy refused to, so they called in the council and the man who turned up kindly informed us that the shed was made from asbestos. Then he called in a friend who happened to be a surveyor with a special interest in asbestos and he turned out to be the same man who had visited me in Fairlight (but of course I had ignored his advice because – well, because I didn't like it and because I thought I knew better and because I didn't actually ... didn't actually *care* what he told me). So he began wandering around the house finding sheets of asbestos everywhere. In the ceiling. In the walls. Shimmy became utterly hysterical and rather abusive. The surveyor was offended. I tried my best to mollify him – the surveyor – by asking him if he might look in on Mulberry to assess the potential damage there (both properties were of a similar age). And he said he would be more than happy to pop by, if – or when – he could find a spare moment.

Then the next day (after visiting Clifford's dad – unsuccessfully; he'd been rushed into surgery), I staggered up to Mulberry and I was almost through the gate when I saw an injured robin, just sitting on the path. And I hurried past it, but then I hurried back again and I picked it up and I took it home and then I tried my best to feed it but it wouldn't take anything and it died overnight and we buried it, at sea, floated it out to sea, Shimmy and me – in an extra-large matchbox – and then I returned to Mulberry and I was about to knock on the door – I was all the way up the path this time – when Mrs Meadows came bustling out and she told me – in no uncertain terms – that Mr Huff was resting and that he should not be disturbed under any circumstances, so I headed home and I sat down and I started to think that maybe it wasn't fated (remember before? When I dropped the cheque off? Remember that?) and I telephoned Alys and I didn't tell her what had happened, I didn't tell her anything, not really, I just … I talked about the photographs and then after – after our conversation – or during our conversation I decided to simply … to just offer all it up. This urge to confess. To just offer it up. Which I did. Please take it, God, I said. Please take it. And I offered it. With all my heart. I offered it. All of it. Every, little bit of it. I offered and I offered until nothing was left. Or at least, so I thought.

49

Mr Franklin D. Huff

Believe it or not I had somehow contrived to forget my knitting! On the porch! We were halfway to Hastings in the cab and I suddenly remembered. So I asked if we could turn back. There was an entire sock – an entire, grey sock! – which I had been making for Miss Hahn. I had grown very fond of it. I had invested a lot in it. In this sock. For Miss Hahn.

Mrs Meadows was none too pleased at the prospect of a U-turn, but after a few furtive clucks and grumbles she resigned herself to it. When we arrived at Toot Rock, though, the road was blocked (ah, t'was ever thus!) by Sorcha Jennett's van. One of the ponies had become distressed after a speeding motorbike on the Sea Road had sounded its horn at exactly the moment they were turning out on to it. The poor creature had reared up in its harness and the Pavee Queen was now carefully assessing the damage which (from what I could tell) was significant but not excessive.

Mrs Meadows had planned to jump out and fetch the knitting, but she had a terror of horses so I was obliged to do so myself. I hobbled up there. And I did quite well. But I was naturally fearful. Of being on my own, *sans* Mrs Meadows, and left at the mercy of the gold dust people.

It was a curious sensation, to suddenly return, having only just left. I felt as if I might catch the cottage unawares, doing something untoward (facing in the wrong direction, slamming all its windows and its doors), but everything was just as we had left it. The sad creak of the gate. The old apple tree bent down with blighted fruit. A slight aroma of badger excrement. The child's shrine bedecked with sodden teddies (it had rained heavily that morning), the long grass flattened with over-exertion, the allotment flecked by dandelion clocks ...

I tried to re-imagine my first arriving. I tried to see the cottage with the eyes I'd once had. And I was suddenly tearful. Yes. *Me.* Franklin D. Huff! Tearful! Just remembering my old self. Just mourning my old self. Poking him in the ribs with my elbow. Chucking him on the chin. Had he been less of a man than the one who now lamented him? Or more of a man? Impossible to tell.

A wood pigeon suddenly took off from a nearby chimney. I spun my head, alarmed, and it was with this movement – this sharp movement – that the dust was released. A bumper consignment of the damn stuff! And in a blink that once empty garden was now heaving with people. Writhing and crawling. Touching each other, blindly, seeking some kind of ... of recognition. And all these dreadful waves of loneliness! This piercing sense of isolation! I took a quick step back – I was fearful – trying to keep my head straight. Because if I kept it straight (and very stiff and still) then the luminescence was less refined (just glancing) and the shadows weren't nearly so deep or so acute. It was simply movement – *life,* only *life* – that made everything so ... so unretractable ...

It was then – here, now – that I saw Miss Hahn. Miss Hahn! She was emerging with a strange man from the air-raid shelter. She was describing something with her hands. A shaggy tree, perhaps. Or a fire. And she was laughing. At herself, very possibly (as she is generally wont to do). I tried to focus in on her (it was no effort, none at all) hoping thereby to dispel the golden horde, but instead of moving back, or away, or behind, in awe (as they liked to do with Mrs Meadows), they seemed especially drawn to her. An audible sigh was raised and they began crawling towards her *en masse.*

How to describe my response? Relief? Horror? The urge to simply flee? The still stronger urge to protect her? But then how, exactly, to go about that? How might an unarmed mortal – a mere man, like myself – set about vanquishing the Lost and the Lonely and the Horribly Abandoned throughout All of Eternity (or thereabouts)?

In that instant she saw me. And her hands dropped. Her eyes widened.

'Mr Huff!' she exclaimed (her companion now quite forgotten). 'But I thought you'd already ...'

Yes. Gone.

'I had,' I confirmed, 'I was.' Then I pointed towards the cottage. 'I think I may have left my knitting. On the back porch.'

'Oh.' Miss Hahn didn't move for a second, and then, perhaps sensing my exhaustion (or my signal inability to shift myself from the spot). 'I'll quickly run and fetch it for you, shall I?' She turned to her companion. 'I'll be back with you before you know it, Mr Tyler.'

Then off she strode. Through the heaving masses.

Mr Tyler and I appraised each other, warily.

'Ryan Tyler.' Mr Tyler walked forward and held out his hand.

'Franklin Huff.'

We shook.

'Carla was just giving me a guided tour of the air-raid shelter.' He smiled.

'Why?' I asked (somewhat aggressively, I suppose. But I was irritated by the intimacy of his address).

'Because I asked her to.' Mr Tyler shrugged. 'I'm a surveyor. I have a great affection for WW2 memorabilia.'

'Well, I can only hope that your interest has been assuaged,' I murmured, 'because I'm afraid the tour is now over. Miss Hahn and I have some important business to attend to.'

'I have an appointment booked,' Mr Tyler maintained.

'Then you'd better scuttle off to keep it.' I waved him on, airily.

'Here,' he finished off.

'What for?'

'An asbestos search.'

'There isn't any,' I informed him, just as Miss Hahn returned, clutching the knitting.

'There isn't any asbestos in the cottage,' I repeated, this time for Miss Hahn's benefit.

'Really?' Miss Hahn handed me the sock. The golden people – many crawling or dragging themselves along on their knees – rippled around her like tentacles surrounding the mouth of a sea anemone (Miss Hahn was the mouth. Obviously. The crux. The centre. Although with anemones it's always worth bearing in mind that the mouth also generally serves as the anus. Which isn't nearly such a pretty idea).

'Yes. My grandfather was in asbestos,' I continued. 'He manufactured the stuff into fire-retardant coatings and bricks during the early years of the century in a factory just north of Cardiff. My grandmother was from Quebec. Her father owned a mine there. That was how they met. Then in 1929 he lost his youngest child to bronchitis. Two years later my grandmother succumbed to chronic fibrosis and died. My grandfather committed suicide within the year.'

I paused.

'There is no asbestos in the cottage, Miss Hahn – Mr Tyler. An asbestos check is the first thing I undertake when I arrive in a property. I always travel with a small but very powerful magnifying glass, a viscous gel, a scalpel and a petri dish.'

'Don't you have a car waiting, Mr Huff?' Miss Hahn wondered (the golden people rippling seismically around her).

'Not a problem,' I said.

Mr Tyler did not look happy. His interest in Miss Hahn was plainly more than just professional. The very idea of this 'interest' quite literally made my blood boil.

'The word asbestos hails from the ancient Greek,' I said, 'and it literally translates as "unquenchable" or "inextinguishable". A *heat* word,' I hissed, 'a *passion* word.' I shot him a significant look.

Mr Tyler seemed confused.

'I once read that Charlemagne, the first Holy Roman Emperor, had a tablecloth fashioned from asbestos,' Miss Hahn piped up. 'He liked to amaze people by throwing it into the fire. It would go in filthy and come out spotless.'

'Hadn't you better be heading off to your appointment, Mr Tyler?' I demanded.

'Yes ... uh ... I suppose if ...' Miss Hahn glanced between the two of us, uneasily, then shoved her hair behind her ear, gnawing, anxiously, on her lower lip.

I took a couple of halting steps towards the outer wall of the air-raid shelter (casually blocking Mr Tyler with the overwhelming force of my sheer physical presence). I leaned my weight against it (the wall. On a straight arm, a spread hand), thereby taking some of the worst of the pressure off my legs (the golden people were everywhere – seething, writhing, *everywhere*). I then commenced a blatantly private/intimate conversation with Miss Hahn to indicate that his continuing presence was now very much 'surplus to requirements'.

'Did you receive the photos I sent you, Miss Hahn?' I murmured.

'I did, yes.' She nodded. 'Thank you.'

I winced. Not too much *movement*, Miss Hahn! I thought.

'You're very welcome to them,' I insisted. 'I can easily print off another, full set from the negatives – if ever I have the need of one.'

Miss Hahn's expression was somewhat quizzical. 'A *full* set, Mr Huff?' she asked.

I frowned.

'It's just that ...' she started off, then she seemed to change her mind and quickly bent over to dust away a spider's web from her trouser-leg instead.

Not too much sudden *movement*, Miss Hahn! I almost gasped.

'So there may've been a couple missing ...' I openly acknowledged (no point in beating about the bush!).

'Don't worry. It doesn't matter – not *remotely*.' Miss Hahn shrugged (and I'm not sure if it actually *did*, either). 'I offered it all up.' She sighed.

'You ...' I frowned (Wasn't that the phrase the child had used? 'Can I offer it up for you, Mr Huff?' Followed by her tinkling laugh?). Eventually I settled on (the somewhat enigmatic), 'It's much more complicated than you think, Miss Hahn.'

'No.' Miss Hahn smiled (a sad smile). 'It's much more complicated than *you* think, Mr Huff.'

I grimaced, irritated (*Why?* Why was everything always such a *struggle* with this infernal female?).

'The truth is that Kimberly – Kimberly herself – had changed around the original order of the photos at some stage,' I explained, 'then carefully re-numbered them, to alter the narrative feel – the ... the *flow* ...' I illustrated these words with an inadvertent hand gesture, then winced, 'possibly in order to ... to *disguise* the fact that you were conducting a secret affair with Bran Cleary, Miss Hahn. And it was these two photos – 04, 40, that were ...'

'Sorry?' Miss Hahn looked confused.

'It's quite difficult to get to the bottom of her motivation,' I continued. 'Perhaps she needed to establish that her union with Bran – later on, in Ireland – was romantic, not political. If the photos seemed to tell a different story ...'

'But I *wasn't* having an affair with Bran Cleary, Mr Huff!' Miss Hahn exclaimed, looking perfectly mortified.

'Steady, Miss Hahn!' I reached out my other hand. The golden people had plainly been traumatized by her slightly raised voice (in fact some were quite incensed by it). They started muttering, belligerently.

'And anyway the photos were *gone*, Mr Huff, not simply swapped around,' Miss Hahn persisted, 'one where Orla's crowning Father Hugh with ...'

'... Another on the beach.' I nodded. 'You were walking down by the tideline and he was sketching you. Bran Cleary. *Sketching* you. Obsessing over you. *Objectifying* you. Dozens of drawings, Miss Hahn. Literally *dozens* of them!'

(That feeling of rage which had formerly assailed me at the thought of Bran Cleary's charming and acquisitive eye, casually affixed upon our dear Miss Hahn, had possessed me once again. And even more powerfully this time.)

'But I wasn't ...' Miss Hahn murmured, perplexed, and then, 'But why would Kimberly ...?'

'*I* destroyed them, Miss Hahn,' I confessed, 'to preserve your reputation.'

'My ...?' Miss Hahn echoed, astonished. 'But I already *told* you, Mr Huff ...'

'And because ...' I drew a deep breath. 'Because – like a damn fool, a *damn* fool – I am *in love* with you, Miss Hahn,' I hissed (still quite furious), 'and they simply ... they infuriated me.'

Silence.

'We don't have time for this,' Miss Hahn eventually muttered, plainly disturbed (even hostile). 'Your car is waiting. *Mrs Meadows* is waiting.'

'I don't care, Miss Hahn,' I said.

'In fact, I think I just heard a horn sounding,' Mr Tyler added.

What?! *What?!* That utter buffoon, Mr Tyler, still standing there?! Behind me? Still standing there, shamelessly earwigging?

'HOW MANY TIMES DO I HAVE TO TELL YOU?!' I
spun around, incensed. 'THERE'S NO ASBESTOS IN THE
COTTAGE, MR TYLER! NOT A TRACE OF IT! *NONE!*'

The golden people all covered their ears and screamed, *en
masse*. This scream (a kind of primordial howl) was like the
whistle of a steam train, or the tortured keening of the north
wind. I gasped, staggering, clutching frantically at my own
ears, nearly losing my balance ...

'Get a grip on yourself, Mr Huff!' Miss Hahn snapped.
'Here ...' She grabbed the knitting, shoved it into the pocket
of her cardigan, slid her arm around my waist, then asked Mr
Tyler to kindly help her support me over to the back balcony
(which he did), where I was gently rested, with due ceremony,
perched atop two cushions, on the bench.

'Would you mind taking a message to the car for us, Mr
Tyler?' Miss Hahn then asked, very politely. 'Just ...' – she
frowned – 'just say that Mr Huff has been temporarily caught
up in something, but it's nothing important ...' (she stressed),
'and he'll be back down with them shortly.'
Mr Tyler nodded (was that a suggestion of a smirk?!) and
headed off.

'I have a confession to make, Mr Huff ...' Miss Hahn sat
down beside me on the bench. We then stared out to sea
together for what felt like a long while, in complete – almost
blissful – silence. This is good, I thought. Silence suits us.
Miss Hahn and I should *always* make a concerted effort to be
quiet while in each other's company.

A further added (although not completely unforeseen)
bonus was that if I sat still – *very* still, in silence – then I could
almost eradicate ... almost, *almost* ... but not ... not quite ...
No. Not entirely ...

'It was me,' Miss Hahn suddenly murmured, 'I killed Orla
Nor Cleary, Mr Huff. My beautiful, darling Orla. Sweet light
of the world. *I* killed her.'

474

Then she tapped an accusing finger against her guilty chest as the golden shadows – springing, once again, into sharper focus – slowly began to prowl around us.

50

Miss Carla Hahn

Such a relief to finally have it out there. Even though I had already offered it up. Such a relief to finally get it off my chest. To make a clean breast of it, at last – at long last – and confess.

I slowly pulled myself to my feet, stepped forward and then turned to face Mr Huff. I needed to look him in the eyes. Only then, I sensed, would reparation truly be made. Because this wasn't about God's forgiveness (I already had that. In abundance. God *always* forgave if you asked him to; wasn't he the All-Merciful, the All-Compassionate?). No, this wasn't about forgiveness. This was about pain. *Pain*. About tearing down the shutters. Letting in the light. Because the more something was pricked and teased, the more violently it baulked and convulsed, the more pitifully it … it writhed and shuddered, the more richly, fully and intensely it *lived*.

The sea was at my back – a giant canvas – roaring – suddenly roaring, and I drew my strength from it, from its implacable grey magnitude, from its infinitely animated deathliness. I clenched my hands until the nails cut into the soft flesh of my palms, then I opened my mouth and started to speak.

'My mother had been very ill, for months, with pneumonia—'

'Hang on a second …' Mr Huff interrupted, then winced, then slowly lifted his hand to silence me. 'What if I don't actually *want* you to justify yourself, Miss Hahn?'

'Sorry?' I blinked, taken aback.

'I don't want you to,' Mr Huff repeated, 'justify yourself.'

'Why ever not?' I demanded, irritated.

'Because ... because I'm in *love* with you, Miss Hahn, and when a person loves someone – as I love you ...'

'Yes, yes, you already *said* that,' I snapped.

'When a person is *loved* by someone,' he reiterated (much to my evident dismay), 'they shouldn't ever feel the need to justify themselves.'

'But I *do* feel the need, Mr Huff!' I scowled.

'But what about *me*, Miss Hahn?' he asked.

'*You?!*'

'Yes. Me. What if I don't *want* any of my questions answered? What if it's all about my simply accepting everything? Everything as it is. And you. Accepting you. Exactly as you are. Flawed as you are. *Faulty* as you are. Warts and all.'

'Warts and all?' I echoed.

'Precisely.'

I pondered this for a while.

'You're being very unhelpful, Mr Huff,' I said, finally.

'This is love, Miss Hahn.' Mr Huff shrugged, airily. 'Love is rarely predicated on things like ...like ...' – he rolled his eyes – 'like "helpfulness".'

'Now you're just being ridiculous!' I exclaimed, throwing up my hands, infuriated.

'Don't throw up your hands like that!' Mr Huff cringed.

'How *can* it be love,' I continued (ignoring him), 'when there isn't any ... any connection or ... or exchange, or *understanding?*'

'But surely they say love is "beyond understanding", Miss Hahn!' Mr Huff smugly quoted. 'Which is precisely my point.'

'Love is entirely *about* understanding, Mr Huff!' I all but shouted. 'You idiot!'

'Why always so ... so *coarse*, so *loud*, Miss Hahn?' Mr Huff covered his face with his hands. He was quiet for a while and then, 'There's something so deeply ...' – he pondered for a second – 'so deeply *unedifying* about a person's need to unburden. It's the modern *disease*, Miss Hahn. And in fact your determination *not* to – not to – unburden hitherto has been an essential part of what I've always found so ... so deeply attractive about you. Your independence. Your self-reliance. Your ... your enigmatic *silence*.'

'Well an essential part of what I've always found so attractive about *you*, Mr Huff,' I tartly responded, 'has been how strangely irresistible you seem to find your own utterly fatuous opinions!'
(Yes! And this was actually true!)
Pause.
'You find *me* attractive, Miss Hahn?' Mr Huff slowly dropped his hands. He looked surprised. 'Is that what you just said? That you find my ... my confidence attractive?'
'No! Yes! I mean I ... I didn't ...' I muttered, glancing off sideways.
'You *do* find me attractive, Miss Hahn!' Mr Huff exclaimed, astonished. 'Just *look* at that! A *double* hair-tuck! You *do* find me irresistible, Miss Hahn!'
Mr Huff gazed at me, intently, bemusedly, his mouth stricken by a perfectly ghastly smile.

'You're quite determined to make this as difficult for me as you possibly can!' I smiled back, equally tortured (equally ghastly). 'And that's precisely why I'm standing here, Mr Huff. It's just what I expected. And it's exactly what I want – better still, deserve.'
Silence.
Mr Huff drew a deep breath. He straightened his glasses on his nose. He knitted his hands together and then slotted them, neatly, between his knees. He closed his eyes.
Then, finally, one word. Just one.

How?

'I wasn't really ... not really Orla's *nurse* as such,' I started off, haltingly (although instantly connecting – in my mind – to all the material I'd been rehearsing, secretly, privately, for so many interminable days now), 'or even her nanny. I was more of a ... I was actually just her jailer, her guard. Because she kept on ... she wouldn't – couldn't – stop praying, Mr Huff. For sinners—'

'I know all this,' Mr Huff interrupted.

'And her health was already so fragile,' I continued, undaunted. 'The Thalidomide had affected her upper torso – her arms – but it had also affected her intestines. She would bleed, internally, when she grew too exhausted. She would haemorrhage ...'

'That's apparently not terribly unusual,' Mr Huff concurred, 'in people with her condition.'

'Nothing her parents tried would make her stop.' I shrugged. 'She really was obsessed. It was a compulsion, a glorious compulsion. She would mutter the Jesus Prayer – repeatedly, constantly – whenever she possibly could: "*Lord Jesus Christ, Son of God, have mercy on me, a sinner.*"' I quickly reeled it off. 'Or she would whisper the Rosary. Or she had this little saying, "*Oh my Jesus, forgive us our sins, save us from the fires of hell and lead all souls to heaven, especially those most in need of Thy mercy.*"'

'A popular Catholic incantation,' Mr Huff sniffed, apparently unimpressed. 'I thought this was meant to be a confession, not a conversion, Miss Hahn!'

'Can't it be a bit of both?' I asked, stung.

He slowly shook his head.

'Are you frightened of believing?' I wondered.

'I'm frightened of everything,' he muttered, 'aside from myself.'

'I'm frightened of nothing *but* myself.' I shrugged.

'So what *do* you believe in, Miss Hahn?' he demanded, eyes slitting.

'Believed,' I corrected him, 'I believed in Orla.'

Mr Huff grimaced.

'And I … I literally had to watch her like a hawk,' I continued. 'If her eyes started to de-focus or if her lips began to shape the words, then I had to stop her. At all costs. That was my job. To police her. To distract her – if simply for her own … her own *good*.'

'It may have escaped your notice, Miss Hahn, but my plane leaves in approximately three and a half hours,' Mr Huff grumbled, inspecting his watch.

'Everything was always so … so *painful* to her, Mr Huff.' I struggled to try and condense it all. 'Because her arms were so short. She longed to press them together, in prayer, but she couldn't. And people were always drawn to her. They would approach her – out on walks, in the car, over the garden fence – and ask for her blessing. She never complained or resisted. She always gave it to them – happily, willingly. Always. But every time she did, something painful was exacted … extracted … a toll …'

'People can be so incredibly selfish!' Mr Huff expostulated, with a tut.

'On several occasions when I was with her she suddenly fell into a state of deep ecstasy,' I battled on. 'She'd be talking or walking or laughing or eating and then in the next instant, she'd keel over. One time she collapsed, face down, into a bowl of hot porridge. It was all up her nostrils, it was matted into her hair …'

'Have you ever heard of a condition called narcolepsy, Miss Hahn?' Mr Huff wondered. I shook my head. I hadn't.

'It's a neurological condition in which …'

'Kalinda seemed to find this especially terrifying,' I calmly talked over him. 'She'd get completely hysterical. She'd pinch Orla, slap her, scream at her. Then Bran would yell at poor

Lonely. But none of it made any difference. Nothing would revive her. Sometimes she'd be gone for just a matter of minutes, other times for many hours. On one occasion she lay unconscious for the best part of a day. So we'd generally call in the doctor ...'

'Dr Meadows.'

'Exactly. Dr Meadows. But he couldn't do anything for her. Aside from recommending that we kept her liquids up, and delivering the odd quiet aside to Bran about the positive benefits of psychoanalysis ...'

'He thought she was a hysteric?'

'I suppose she was.' I shrugged. 'But aren't *all* saints, at some level?'

Mr Huff didn't respond. He seemed momentarily distracted – although by what exactly I couldn't tell.

'When she *did* eventually revive' – I smiled (fondly remembering those revivals, both the timely *and* the untimely ones) – 'she was often incredibly weak, although ... although blissfully happy. This intense atmosphere of joy would emanate from her, but also a feeling of deadly absence. As if on each occasion she left us, it grew more and more difficult to drag herself back ...'

Mr Huff's slightly paranoid eyes continued to scan the garden. 'What about Father Hugh?' he wondered (almost in spite of himself).

'Uh ... Father Hugh visited several times over that summer,' I recalled. 'Orla absolutely adored him. And he and Bran were old friends – almost like brothers. Orla called him her "spiritual father". But Lonely despised him. She loathed him. I think she pretty much blamed him for everything. And she hated the Catholic Church. With a passion. She was naturally suspicious of all big institutions. But she reserved her special hatred for poor, long-suffering Father Hugh ...'

'Do you recall Orla ever mentioning anything about' – Mr Huff slitted his eyes – 'about gold … About a strange, golden dust? About golden … golden *souls*?'

'No.' I shook my head.

'Ah.' Mr Huff nodded, sagely.

'Never,' I added.

'Fine.' Mr Huff waved his hand for me to continue, then winced.

'Part of the problem between Father Hugh and Kalinda was that whenever he visited the Clearys he would often bring people along with him to see Orla. Sometimes from Ireland, on little pilgrimages. Sometimes just needy individuals from the local parish. And they would ask for her blessing, or for special favours in the name of "Our Lady", as she called her. And Orla would ask them to make daisy chains and she would hang them over an old picture frame she had with an image of the *Pieta* glued inside it – Virgin Mary, embracing Jesus, taken down from the cross – which her grandmother had given her; Bran's mother.'

Mr Huff had closed his eyes. He had leaned the back of his head against the wall.

'In fact when Bran's mother visited I had to be especially vigilant,' I persisted, 'because she always had a little list which she would present to Orla when no one else was around. Of various people and their problems. Orla had become especially renowned among the Irish Travelling community after curing Sorcha's sister, then Sorcha's aunt, then Sorcha herself of a hereditary genetic disorder which meant that most of their babies were all born with, and quickly died from, severe congenital defects. Orla had a special love of what she called "Aboriginal Peoples …"'

I paused to draw breath. Mr Huff had opened his eyes again and was now staring, fixedly, at my chest. I looked down. Was there something …? Uh … No. I quickly looked up again.

'Did they argue?' he wondered, frowning, distractedly.
'Bran and Kalinda I mean?'
'Dreadfully.' I nodded. 'Constantly. Over Orla, mainly.
Lonely was an atheist and Bran – I'm not really sure.
Sometimes they would have actual, physical fights. She would
attack him, really *attack* him, in a kind of … a blind rage, and
he would throw her – she was tiny, absolutely tiny, and stick
thin – against the wall or across the bed or on to a sofa. She
was always angry with him.'
'Why was that?' Mr Huff wondered, almost half to himself,
shifting on his cushion, then wincing.
'Because he was a Catholic. Not practising. But that whole
side of things came from him. Although … strangely …'
I frowned.

   'Strangely?' he echoed.
'She wasn't interested in the Catholic faith but she was
completely obsessed by Catholic politics. Which always
seemed like a strange kind of … well, contradiction, I suppose
… But then …' I frowned again. 'I always felt as if what
everything was *really* all about with Lonely – underneath that
prickly surface – was acceptance. It was like the British state
represented something … a kind of patriarchal authority – if
that makes any sense – and there was this profound need in
her – rooted in her femininity, her culture, her race – to
automatically rebel.'

   'And Bran?'
'Bran?' I grimaced. 'He was an artist. But it always felt like
Lonely was the … the trigger … the catalyst. His muse. His
inspiration. It was like she was the source of all the anger in
his work. Like he didn't quite have it in himself to … It was
her energy. He got it all from her.'

   'Did you like Kalinda?' Mr Huff wondered.
'Not at first,' I admitted. 'She was a very strange, very
charismatic woman. Masculine. Rough. Incredibly strong, but
also quite destructive. And there was this difficult dynamic

between the two of them. A constant need to … to *hurt* one another, to lash out. A competition. It was quite hard to be around that. Especially for Orla. I think sometimes it threatened to overwhelm her …'

'She didn't like you?'

'Who?' I scowled.

'Kalinda.'

'No. Not to begin with. At first she was downright hostile. But I didn't ever really rise to it, so eventually she grew bored and just tended to ignore me. Then one day we were out on the beach together, with Orla, and we bumped into Shimmy. There was some problem at home with Mum, who – as I said – was suffering from severe pneumonia … And she watched us together – me and Shimmy, just discussing arrangements etc. – for a few minutes, then afterwards she gazed up at me, very keenly – intently – and she said, "He isn't your father, is he?" Just like that!'

'She was very clever,' Mr Huff muttered, thickly, his eyes ranging around the garden again.

'I ended up telling her all about the circumstances of my birth. How my mother had stayed behind in Berlin during the war and had been …'

I strung my hands together, pained. Mr Huff didn't make eye contact. He merely nodded, grimly. But very slowly.

'Then she told me about the circumstances of her own birth, which were strangely similar. And I suppose a bond was formed. Between us. Because after that she was like a completely different character. Incredibly warm and … and tactile and loving. Almost to … well, almost to the opposite extreme.'

I winced.

'It was Kalinda, then?' Mr Huff murmured. 'Kalinda who was in love with you, not Bran?'

'I admired her enormously,' I struggled to explain, 'but not with the same … the same intensity. It wasn't … I didn't …'

'Did Bran know? Did he object?'

Mr Huff's hands were clinging, tightly, on to the edge of the bench.

I nodded. 'Kalinda was an incorrigible flirt. She rarely formed attachments, though, and if she did ... she found it difficult to give them up. She hated to feel rejected ...'

'Which of us doesn't?' Mr Huff shuddered.

'She was often away. And when she was home she would drink. And she had all this surplus energy. A negative energy, I suppose. Bran was usually working, and her relationship with Orla was difficult at the best of times. Not long after she arrived here she'd made connections with a local farming family. She'd grown up on a sheep farm in the Rangelands. She'd worked for many years as a shepherdess. She had a natural touch with livestock. And at one point she began helping out with a crew of local shearers. They were a pretty disreputable bunch, but Lonely could hold her end up with the best of them ...'

I broke off for a moment. 'Are you all right, Mr Huff?' Tiny beads of sweat were forming on Mr Huff's upper lip. He was ashen. And still the hands clinging to the bench ...

'Fine,' he creaked.

'Clifford told me that she was having an affair with one of them. Then with another. Two brothers. And it all got quite ... quite complicated.'

'Did Bran have any inkling?'

'Oh yes. Bran knew.'

'How did he react?'

'It hurt him. But he was resigned to it. Because Orla was so ill. He saw it as a kind of ... a way for Lonely to control that situation, to manage that situation at home which she couldn't seem to ... to ...'

'He confided in you?'

I nodded.

'Did you like him?'

486

'Very much. Everybody liked Bran. He was charming. Creative. But very quiet and shy. Almost grumpy. So when he confided in you, it felt like ...' I shrugged. 'A great honour, I suppose.'

'He relied on you,' Mr Huff muttered.

'He wanted me to be a real part of the family.'

Mr Huff scowled.

'That day,' I began, anxiously, 'in the blackthorn ...'

'Did he lead the way? Into the tunnel?'

I nodded.

'You followed him?'

I nodded again.

'What did he want?'

'We came to a small clearing. We talked there. In private. He wanted me to ...us to ...'

'What?'

'He wanted the three of us – me, him and Kalinda – to ...'

'A *ménage à trois*?'

I shook my head, then I nodded, pained.

'And you said ...?'

'I said no. For Orla's sake.'

'And he said ...?'

'That it was *for* Orla, because she loved us all.'

'You weren't tempted?'

'I was tempted.'

'You liked Bran.'

'Yes. But he loved Kalinda. He was just ...'

'Using you. As bait. For his wife.'

I winced.

'And then Kimberly ...'

I nodded.

'She'd started to document ...'

'My mother was very ill with pneumonia.'

Mr Huff frowned.

'I'd always had a difficult relationship with her. There was all this … this awful *guilt*.'

Mr Huff was staring at my chest again.

'And one day Orla asked me if she might pray for her.'

'Your mother?'

I nodded.

'She understood, you see. Because she'd endured that guilt herself at some level. Over her own health – even her faith. How her faith was slowly destroying everything. How it consumed everything. How her fore-knowledge about that bomb had cast a dark shadow of guilt over them both.'

'*Weren't* they guilty, though?'

'It was almost as if she was a kind of … like the control board in a telephone exchange. Everything came through her and was then sent back again. It's difficult to explain. Or like … like Mrs Meadows's bees. With that disease. It didn't matter how many times the bees flew out to gather honey if when they returned to the hive …'

'What did you say?' Mr Huff asked.

'Sorry?'

'Your mother.'

'I didn't say anything. I stood up and I left the room. But she knew.'

'She knew …?'

'That in my heart I didn't want her to pray for her. I was harbouring this deep hostility. But in my head I *did* want her to. Just to try and make up for … to give her something back after … after I'd taken so much from her. Almost to be … to be better than her … more generous. Than she had ever been. My whole, miserable life. To me. Her only daughter. Orla saw all that.'

'So she prayed.'

I nodded.

'And you didn't try and stop her?'

'I saw her lips moving. I didn't do anything. That same day Kimberly told Lonely that she suspected I was having an affair with her husband.'

'Who? With *me*?!' Mr Huff started.

'With Bran.'

'Oh. Of course ...' Mr Huff shook his head. 'But you weren't, were you?'

'Wasn't I?'

I shrugged. 'There was a connection – an intimacy ... I was at the centre of everything. Suddenly. In the middle of everything. For the first time in my entire ... Instead of being just ...'

'Stuck in the Approaches,' Mr Huff murmured.

'And I didn't really know who this new person was. I wasn't sure she was really *qualified* to ... It was as if everything started to melt away inside me. To burn with this new energy. And the limits, the standards, that I had always lived by, that I had set myself previously, or been set by ... by ... I don't know ... Nothing felt absolute. For Orla everything was always absolute. But I didn't have that. And I still don't. And it's a kind of ...' – I threw out my arm – 'incredible torment. Not to be clean inside. Not to be good enough. Not to be better than I am. Because—'

'I must interrupt you, Miss Hahn,' Mr Huff suddenly murmured, 'because there's a bright crack of light – a chink of light – shining from the middle of your ... your ...'

He pointed at my chest.

'Sorry?'

I looked down. Mr Huff was blinking, trying to turn away now, covering his eyes with his arm.

'It's *blinding* me, Miss Hahn!' he gasped.

I put my hands up to my chest, terrified.

'What is it?' I asked, swinging around. 'Stop that! Stop frightening me, Mr Huff!'

'It feels horribly like … like *love*,' he said, writhing, in agony. 'It's love, Miss Hahn. The most terrible … most burning … most … most devastating *love*. And it's coming from you, Miss Hahn. It's flooding from … it's flooding out of …'

And I don't know why, but I had a sudden, powerful image of myself – in that moment – as the stylus on a record player, swinging around, over the record – over the album – and the needle crashing, scratching, into the vinyl. Playing tiny fragments of voice and music, then lifting up, jumping, crashing down again. Scratching the vinyl, playing the vinyl. Such a curious image. Such a strange and haunting and inconclusive …

As if the story was done. An awful feeling. As if it didn't … As if it could never – no, not *ever* – be conclusively told.

51

Mr Franklin D. Huff

I am intensely fond of Miss Hahn. *Intensely* fond. Insofar as I am capable of … you know, anything approaching sincere human feeling. I am 'in love' with Miss Hahn (that much must be abundantly clear by now). But the last chapter – 50 – was sheer torture for me. Because the description of events Miss Hahn kindly provided was so *woefully inadequate*! (I commend you simply for getting through it, relatively intact.) I mean all that pointless, interior *gumph*! All that endless self-examination! All that ludicrous self-excoriation when the action – the real *action* – outside her, on this porch, in this place, at this moment …

52

Miss Carla Hahn

But there's still so much I need to say! For the story to … to
hold together! For it to possess any kind of … of deeper
meaning. About my mother, Else, how she recovered from the
pneumonia and lived for a further eight years. But after a few
months we realized that she had early-stage dementia. So she
was saved but it was almost as though the saving of her was a
kind of … almost a punishment. As if the secrets of my soul –
my *soul* – the confusion – had played out in Orla's prayers.
Does that make any sense?

Other things, too. Why did Mr Huff interrupt me like that?
Scare me like that? Other things … Yes. About poor Kalinda.
How she mysteriously disappeared after Orla's death. How
Orla died three days after I asked – or didn't ask – for her
prayers. Three days after I left. Because I hadn't been able to
decide who I was or what I wanted. Because I couldn't be on
the inside. Standing on the main stage. I was never … I was
always … that phrase Mr Huff …

And so was she. So was Kalinda. Which is why, after Orla
died, she turned on herself (first), then afterwards turned
traitor. She entered Witness Protection. Alone. Without Bran.
Bran wouldn't … Bran hadn't … Or had he?

Which means that maybe the nay-sayers were right, all
along, about Orla overhearing, and then confiding in Father
Hugh. We can never be entirely sure, can we? There can
never be true certainty. I suppose the only thing that's truly
certain – right here, right now, on this strange earth – is love.

The way it flames. The way it burns. Almost senselessly. Until everything is devoured. Everything is consumed. And then it dies and is gone. Just the ashes remaining. A pointless little pile of exquisite, feather-light flakes of depleted carbon.

Can I offer it up, though?

Can I offer up the ash?

Can I?

Yes?

Can I?

Even that?

53

Mr Franklin D. Huff

She was surrounded by this giant ocean of souls. That's how I'm seeing them. That's how I'm describing them. I simply can't *articulate* … And then as she reached the closing stages of her confession, descended into a state of moral confusion, this chink of light – that's the only way to … this chink of light began to break through her cardigan (terrible old cardigan, for the record. With evidence of some kind of smoke damage on the shoulder. Revolting old thing. Muddy brown colour. Quite awful. But lovely, I suppose, because she was in it).

I had seen evidence of it (the chink) throughout our conversation. Vague glimmers of it. As if someone was shining a small torch on to her chest. It had been dancing around her chest. Yes. The way a magnifying glass (remember the magnifying glass from a little earlier? A complete lie, I'm afraid) … the way a magnifying glass refracts the light of the sun and then burns a small hole. On a little patch of dry grass. On a leaf. On the back of some poor boy's neck in class, sitting at the desk in front …
Ow! Ow! What was that?
(*Bursts into gales of noisy tears.*)

But to begin with the hand that held this glass (and who knows whose hand that was?) shook slightly. It took a while to steady. To steady itself and then focus. Intently. On the centre of her chest.

The strange thing was (and there are many strange things, I accept that – I openly accept that – but this is the main one, I suppose, from my perspective, at least) was that her words were inconsequential. The story was insignificant. Did Kalinda really plant that bomb? Was Bran innocent? Did Orla know? It was all simply irrelevant. Because, and I've described this before but, at the risk of being repetitive (like Miss Hahn was – in Chapter 50 – and I'm sure she won't resent my saying this, because I say it out of love, principally) ... at the risk of being repetitive, I'll do so again (mention that thing again): time – 'time' – became like ... as if strands of time were like pieces of ... of *wool* (say), in different colours, all running together. Being knitted, into a giant for ever sock (or sweater – no. Better a sock. This tubular shape which turns ... changes direction, flowers, and then feeds into itself again). And the echo. Let's not forget the echo. That extraordinary echo, informing it all. Darting in and out of the weave, drawing together, conjoining ...

It didn't matter (the story. Sorry about that). Or if it did, then it mattered a-great-deal-of-not-at-all.

Either way, the light began to shine more and still more brightly. Miss Hahn seemed oblivious. With Miss Hahn it's all about the story – the pain of revealing, of re-telling – but to the rest of us (me, the souls, Mrs Meadows, who had arrived at the bottom of the porch moments earlier) it was all about the light. How it scorched. How it swung about, dangerously, as she moved (still yammering on, I'm afraid; still justifying, still doubting, still torturing herself – and for *what*? For nothing! Absolutely *nothing*!). Yet for us (like I said) it was all about the light. And I needed to avoid it. This savage love. And Mrs Meadows ducked when Miss Hahn – might I call her Carla? Darling Carla? – half turned towards her. But the souls? So many of them! A sea of them! A wall of them! They swooned towards it. And as it touched them it melted them. Back into a golden dust. And the dust was drawn towards the light and the light was strengthened by it. And soon all the souls were magnetized by the few that had been drawn, and then, with a huge sigh of relief – of ecstasy – they entered the heart of Miss Hahn and they were finally assuaged. They found their rest there.

And it was all over, then. Very quickly. So quickly that it was almost (I'll be honest with you) a slight anticlimax.

Miss Hahn was saying something about … Oh I don't know. Because she had been terrified ('Stop it, Mr Huff! You're frightening me!' Something of that order) but then the story started telling itself (because it *would* be told – it had its own momentum – irrelevant as it was) about how the life of Orla Nor Cleary was so much more beautiful and complicated and lovely and fragrant than she could ever give words to. Because words were just tiny lies. And she was a kitchen scrap. Just a kitchen scrap. But for once, just that once, in the presence of Orla, she had become … I don't know. Fill this in as best you can.

Because I am exhausted. And I don't really know how this will all turn out. And Miss Hahn is banging away at the window – the window of this story – asking to be let in again. And I *shall* let her in, soon enough. But first at least let me … let me relish this moment. At the start and the end of something. Let me take my time to decide what kind of carriage – car – receptacle I am inhabiting, and then push the door open – to welcome her. My dear Miss Hahn.

Perhaps I am simply inside my own heart, and I am steering this conversation from within. And the banging of Miss Hahn's fist is the beating of that heart. I can't say. All I can really be sure of, right now, is that she's standing there. God bless her. (And so are you – God bless you, too.) Pounding and pounding and pounding and pounding.